NORDKRAFT

NORDKRAFT

A NOVEL

Jakob Ejersbo

McArthur & Company
Toronto

This first English translation published in Canada in 2004 by
McArthur & Company
322 King Street West, Suite 402
Toronto, Ontario
M5V 1J2
www.mcarthur-co.com

First published in Danish in 2002 by Gyldendal

Library and Archives Canada Cataloguing in Publication

Ejersbo, Jakob, 1968-
Nordkraft / Jakob Ejersbo.

Translated from the original Danish by Don Bartlet © 2004.

ISBN 1-55278-461-4

I. Title.

PT8176.15.J47N6713 2004 839.81'38 C2004-904218-1

Cover Image by Jens Morten
Design & Composition by Michael Callaghan
Printed in Canada by Webcom

10 9 8 7 6 5 4 3 2 1

To

Teri Hot′ Shott

(1967–1985)

I think of you, I think of you.
I had this friend who told me that
coincidence cannot articulate the best
events. She said she'd rather think of
everything as accident, after all, it's
all heaven-sent. She said I don't think
good but I know how to wait as if when
you wait it is not hours but some forgotten
sense of time. It's very kind of all those
powers to feature love without design.
Letters arrive, spelling out the wish so
clear, making a language of desire and fear.
You said it's not that way . . . God is not the
name of God . . . you'll send a drawing of the heart
I don't draw well but I know how to wait as if . . .
I think of you listening to your fathers voice . . .
Those endless speeches on 'The Gift of Choice'.
Love's not a story I could ever read or write . . .
I guess you'd say I'm not so bright. Show me
how you wait . . . as if . . .
I am so fond of you, so fond of you.
These difficult questions tell me a joke.

—TOM VERLAINE: *Flash Light*

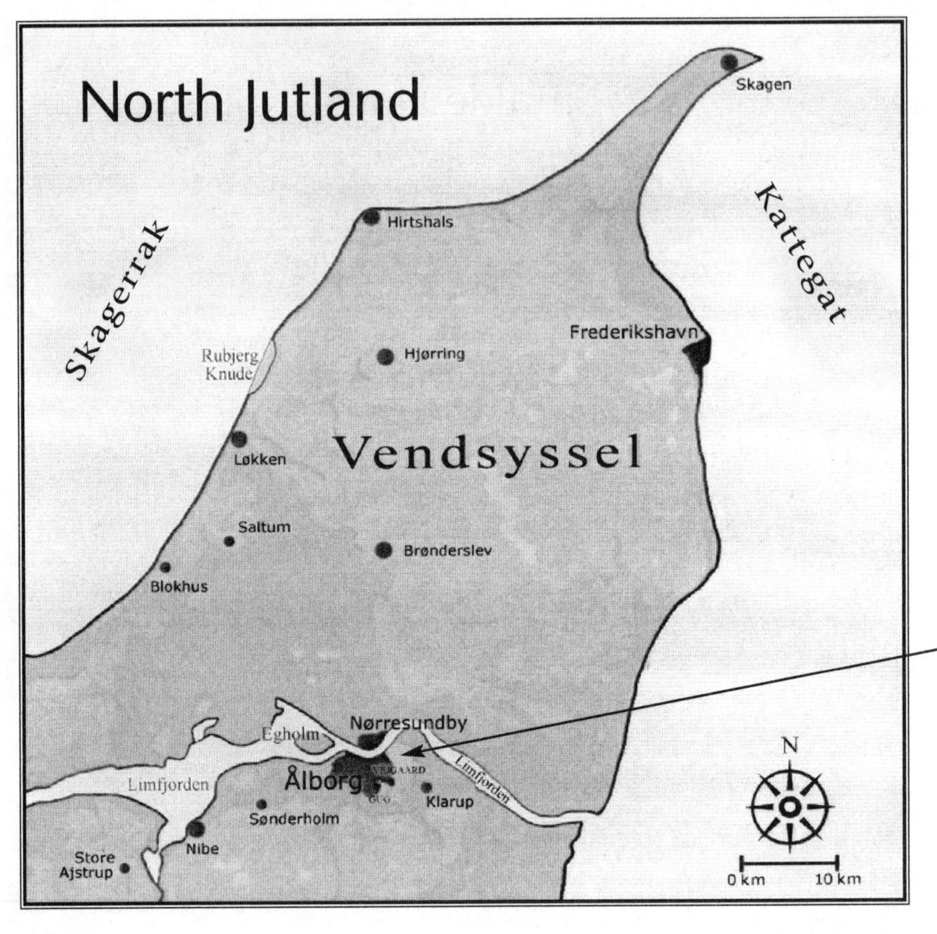
North Jutland
Skagen
Kattegat
Hirtshals
Skagerrak
Frederikshavn
Rubjerg
Knude
Hjørring
Vendsyssel
Løkken
Saltum
Brønderslev
Blokhus
Nørresundby
Egholm
Limfjorden
Ålborg
Klarup
Limfjorden
Sønderholm
Nibe
Store
Ajstrup
N
0 km
10 km

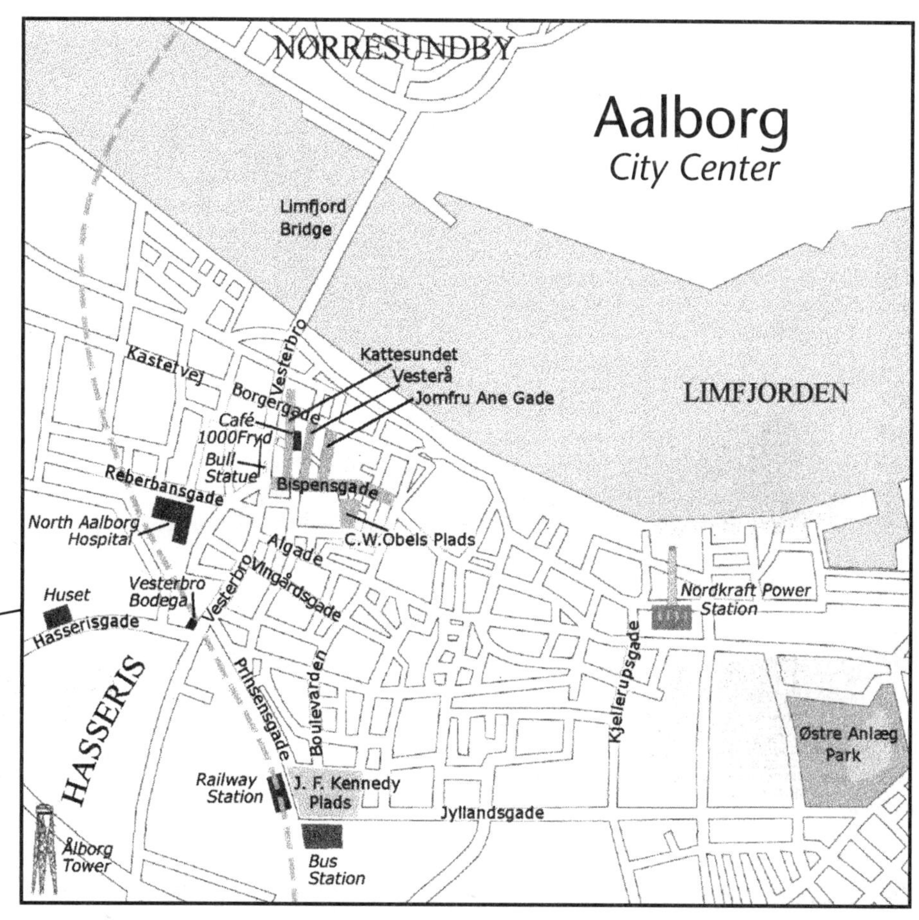
NØRRESUNDBY
Aalborg
City Center
Limfjord
Bridge
Vesterbro
Kattesundet
Vesterå
Jomfru Ane Gade
LIMFJORDEN
Kastelvej
Borgergade
Café
1000Fryd
Bull
Statue
Reberbansgade
Bispensgade
North Aalborg
Hospital
C.W.Obels Plads
Algade
Vingårdsgade
Nordkraft Power
Station
Huset
Vesterbro
Bodega
Vesterbro
Hasserisgade
HASSERIS
Prinsensgade
Boulevarden
Kjellerupsgade
Østre Anlæg
Park
Railway
Station
J. F. Kennedy
Plads
Jyllandsgade
Ålborg
Tower
Bus
Station

NORDKRAFT

JUNKIE DOGS

1990

Coldsweat: i close the door, shouldn't burn yet, the wires get hotter palms are glowing this is hot meat metallic blood this is open sweat. show you with my fingers draw with the eye with your own breath i tear your lungs out this side of the blackest meadows i make my winter dwelling and crush my bones. i'll sail out the window i'll walk down the hedge i will not finish 'till i'm fully satisfied.

–THE SUGARCUBES: *life's too good*

Bitch

The dog snarls. Its canine teeth gleam with saliva and the snapping of its jaws sends a wave of air towards my nether parts. I am standing with 300 grams of hash taped to my stomach, from just beneath my breasts down to my pubic hair. The smell drives the Alsatian wild and its open jaws are only a hand's width from my crotch. The animal stands up on its rear legs, the lead held taut by the policeman; its collar bites into its coat. Hot breath from the dog's mouth billows out into the frosty evening air.

My back rubs against the wall and my boots crunch as they stumble over the filthy snow on the pavement a few metres from the main entrance to Christiania, Copenhagen, where twenty policemen dressed in riot gear and accompanied by dogs have jumped out of nowhere. I try to edge my way along the wall at the back of *Loppen;* the posters advertising gigs at the club scrape against my back and make a rasping noise. Can't move in any direction; on my left there are two potheads staring lifelessly at the dog which is holding all three of us in check.

"Take it easy, man," one of them drawls in a broad Copenhagen accent.

"Don't move," snarls the man behind the visor. To me. I notice his bared front teeth, his piercing eyes.

"I haven't done anything," I say, breaking into a sob. The Alsatian is still pulling at the lead. One man has been knocked down onto the pavement and a second dog has his ankle in its jaws. There are about fifteen police officers standing on the pavement and in the road, some distance from us; they are talking anxiously against the crackle of their walkie-talkies in the background.

"Have you been in buying, junkie whore?" the cop says in what sounds like an Aarhus accent. "Out with the lump or do I have to look for it myself?" He gives me a sweaty grin. The adrenaline is steaming off his body.

I dig down into my pocket and sling a four gram lump of hash down on the pavement in front of me. "Can I go now?" I ask defiantly.

"Nielsen," the dog handler shouts over to a Black Maria that has just pulled up.

And Asger had promised me there wasn't any police activity in and around Christiania at the moment. Said he had checked.

Nielsen, who is now walking towards us from the Black Maria, is of female gender. Probably something to do with using women cops to frisk female suspects. And now she will run her hands up and down my body and the 300 grams is too bulky for her to miss. At the same time I feel like shit because it is that time of the month. I am shaking. I feel cold under my skin.

The dog handler takes a step forward, the Alsatian rears up and lodges its paws on my shoulders, the dog's jaws snap at my neck. Someone screams. It is me. He pulls the dog away – his eyes gleam with a sick sense of superiority. Nielsen approaches. With a hysterical scream I rip open my jeans. I catch a glimpse of her wide-open eyes as I thrust my hands down into my underpants. I grab hold; pull out the blood-soaked sanitary pad and hurl it at the dog, which catches it in the air and starts chewing at it.

Two paces away from me, Nielsen sinks to her knees. A large cobble stone hits the tarmac; she slumps down hugging one leg to her chest. A bottle smashes against the wall above my head. Through a shower of glass splinters I see the cop kicking the dog with my sanitary pad sticking out on either side of its mouth and I think: it can't be a sniffer dog, it is an Alsatian. I look over to the left towards the entrance to Christiania where a group of young men appear, throw stones and bottles. Then ten officers in riot gear run towards them with shields, tear gas pistols and raised truncheons. Nielsen limps back to the Black Maria.

"I haven't done a sodding thing," I yell, hugging my chest. I hear the muffled crack of the tear gas pistols and out of the corner of my eye I can see the tear gas forming clouds and rolling towards the entrance to Christiania. The Alsatian begins to tear at the lead to get into the fray.

"Stay there," the cop barks as he pulls out his truncheon and follows the dog. I run off down Prinsessegade, my legs trembling. Turn left down Bådsmandsstræde; half running and half sobbing and clinging tightly onto the slabs of hash. The edges cut into my breasts and the tape pulling at my skin is uncomfortable.

Have to stop because my trousers – still undone – are beginning to slip off. Snot drips from my nose as I look down. Police sirens, screaming tires, a white minibus with more police in riot gear approaches. Fiddle with my zip, my fingers frozen stiff. They roar past – I imagine I see one officer mouthing a word from behind a visor: *bitch.* Your mother, you, and your various fathers, I think.

Pull out a cigarette as I stagger on. Light up frantically, take a deep drag – could do with a joint. Snot runs down from my nose and wets the cigarette. Throw it away. Taxi to the main station. Into the toilet. I have squeezed the slabs of hash so tightly that two of them have cracked. There is some blood in my underpants, but I have an extra pad in my inside pocket. I think of the time I was in Morocco with my parents. We all got rampant mouse typhus and on the way home in the plane we all wore one of my mother's sanitary pads; none of us had any control over our bowels. It was just seeping out of us. Start giggling. Sounds horribly shrill. Eventually drag myself onto a train to Aalborg so worn out that I immediately fall asleep.

The Heroine

"You're my little heroine," Asger says, holding me tight and kissing my forehead, my hair, my wet eyes. I have started howling again out of relief and I thump him on the chest because . . . just because. Asger's two Rottweilers,

Twister and Tripper, crowd around our legs – they have probably never seen anyone blubbering before and they totally psyche me out.

"There, there," he says and I feel like saying he should be ashamed of himself sending me over to Copenhagen when there were police around, but I suppose he could not have known and I sob and feel like a drama queen because it was actually me who offered . . . because it is me who knows the wholesale distributor, and also because I want to contribute something to our partnership. Well, I don't just want to be a pretty face. After all, Asger pays the rent for the house where we live and he let me move in so that I would not have to crawl back to my mother. He is the one who brings in most of the money as well.

I am still having trouble catching my breath.

"Couldn't you let the dogs into the run? I simply can't . . . ." I say.

"Yes, of course, sweetheart."

I sit down in the living room and roll a joint. It is three o'clock in the morning and I wish I could crawl under a bell jar and shut the world out. I could have ended up in prison. What was I thinking of?

Light a joint. Nice.

Slowly I begin to feel empty inside. Feelings drifting away. Gone. Then it becomes chilly, my breath is so icy it makes the back of my teeth hurt, crack, they are about to explode.

I have never done anything right.

Never.

Nothing.

Feel absolutely dreadful. Never experienced this before. Have been stoned out of my mind, pleasantly stoned – but never frightened. Sitting at the dining table. It must be the joint intensifying everything – I know that but I feel like shit. Am I beginning to get hash psychosis? I have never heard about anybody feeling so rotten from smoking a joint; when you have a bummer, it is more likely to be from mushrooms or LSD.

"I don't feel too good," I say to Asger.

"Just lie down for a while," he says.

"Okay." I stagger into the bedroom and lie down on the bed. Leave the light on and the door ajar. So I can hear Asger in the living room. Feel sticky between my legs. Can see blood on my underpants. Soaked right through. Feel too weak to get off the bed. Raise my backside to take off my underpants.

Suddenly go blind. Fall into the void. Unending. A voice booms out in my hollow body: *Look for the answers where they are to be found. At the bottom of a bottomless pit.* I have heard it before. Don't remember where. Rush downwards turning and tumbling – the air whistles by.

A sudden jerk. My body jerks and I hang there motionless, seven centimetres above the mattress. I can see again. Look at the clock. Eight minutes past four. Keep looking at it. The second hand does not move, but I can hear the sound: clunk . . . clunk . . . clunk. Have no idea how long something like this lasts, whether it is five minutes or twelve hours or . . . for ever? Everything around the base of my nose feels like green swamp. As I try to find a way out of my skull there is swamp everywhere. Try to hold on to the notion that I am me, but I don't have a clue what that means. I only know that I have never done anything right.

Time stands still – and it makes a noise. I send out expeditions far into the swamp – searching. The little bits of me that I find – I fight my way back with them, drag them back home through the boggy mire and plunge them down under the swamp – hide them behind the uvula, frightened all the while that I am going to swallow them. Rumbling noises penetrate my consciousness. Twist my head and see Asger by my side. Snoring. Edge away from him. The clock says 08:12. He must not know how I feel. It is so embarrassing. Feeble.

I wish my mother were here. I miss her. But we are not on speaking terms. She does not even know where I live.

Shell Shock

"We have agreement. You show me people. Introduction." The voice comes from the living room but it is muffled by the bedroom door. Foreign accent. Turk? What's going on? I feel empty inside. The duvet feels heavy and clammy. No underpants on, only an undershirt.

"Yes, but . . . ," Asger starts to say. He is interrupted.

"So I can help you also . . . always. We will be friends. But you not want help me. You pay hard way – right now." Force myself to get out from under the duvet. Everything feels unconnected in my head as if someone has removed the wiring and all the components lie idle, out of order.

"Okay, okay. I'll see what I can do, man. But it is not free." Asger does not sound very sure of himself. Almost fall over as I step out of bed. The freezing chill of floor penetrates the soles of my feet. I wobble over to the cupboard.

"I said it was free? I pay already. Right now. All the time. It cost you nothing." The voice is threatening.

Pull my underpants on, open the door to the corridor, walk over and lean against the door frame into the living room.

There is a tall, dark man standing in the middle of the floor with a gigantic black slug moustache over his upper lip, which makes him look like Saddam Hussein. The fresh perfume of after-shave hangs in the air, but the man has already a dark shadow of stubble over the lower side of his face. Asger sits slumped over the table with a despairing expression on his face, but he is also nervous.

"Who's he?" I ask and that is when Asger notices me. He half lifts himself up from the chair.

"Maria," he replies hesitantly, "Could you just go in? I'll come in a minute." I can feel the man's eyes on me.

"But what does he want here?" I ask, my eyes fixed on Asger. I stand rubbing my feet against each other. Then I stop – I don't want to appear nervous.

"It's just business," Asger says. "I'll soon be finished."

I turn towards the dark-skinned man. "But why are you threatening us?"

He takes two steps towards me and stretches his hand out to me in a way that ensures that he does not come too close.

"*Salaam aleikum,*" he says. "I'm Hossein."

I keep my hands where they are – squeezing the door frame. He once beat up a guy called Bertrand for absolutely no reason and broke his nose. That is what I had heard around town. And that he was a soldier in Iraq's special forces . . . or Iran's, I can never remember which is which.

"What've we done to you?"

"Maria, please . . . ," Asger says.

"What is problem?" the man called Hossein says, casting a fleeting glance at Asger.

"You're threatening us," I say.

"Hossein never threaten," he says, with an offended expression. "What must do – Hossein do it." My legs seem to be frozen. I would most like to go to the bedroom, but I don't want him standing in my home in this way.

Asger stands up and comes towards me.

A sob forces its way up through my throat. I am totally unprepared for it. "I really feel terrible," I say because I think that Asger could . . . well, sort of be there for me instead of sitting and talking with . . . him over there.

"Your woman sick?" Hossein asks.

"Sweetheart, I have to finish talking to Hossein, then I'll come in to see you."

The snot begins to stream out of my nose. "But everything is . . . cold," I say – the tears thicken and spread in my throat.

"Woman has a shell shock," Hossein says and looks anxious. Asger places his hand on my hip and turns me round, pushing me gently in the direction of the bedroom door.

"I'll call Ulla," he whispers. "Shall I do that?"

"But I hardly know her."

"Come on," he says, pressing me gently onto the bed, raising my legs and tucking the duvet in around me.

"Can't you stay for a while?" I ask.

"This business with Hossein's important. I'll call Ulla."

"But what does he *want*?" I ask. In a way . . . looking at myself from the outside I notice that my pathetic tone doesn't even embarrass me and that is strange.

"I owe him a favour," Asger says, getting up from the edge of the bed.

"But how come?"

"Because he helped me with something."

"With *what*?"

"Now don't ask me so many damn questions," Asger says as he goes out of the door, annoyed. "I'll call Ulla." He closes the door to the corridor. He also closes the living room door so that all I can hear is their voices as a distant mumble.

Why can't he just tell me? We are together. I have just risked my . . . my *freedom* smuggling hash so that he can do some dealing and then he won't even . . . tell me what is going on. And as for Ulla . . . I hardly know her. I have only met her because she is the girlfriend of Asger's good friend, Niels. They call him Butcher Niels. She is a couple of years older than me – twenty-three perhaps. I have lost contact with the girlfriends I had at high school – they all think I have become a junkie.

The Consoler

I can hear Hossein leaving and customers arriving at the same time. A long time passes as I lie on my side hugging my knees into my chest. Finally, Asger sticks his head inside the door. "Ulla's here," he says gently, but then the door is thrust wide open by Ulla who puts a hand on Asger's shoulder and shoves him aside as she enters the bedroom.

"Okay, you can buzz off now," she says and closes the door in Asger's face. She turns round, slants her head, looks at me as she kicks off both of her boots and shakes her jacket off her shoulders so that it falls on the floor behind her. Without saying a word she lies down on the bed – under the duvet – and puts her arms round me. "The-e-ere," she whispers and gives me a long, lingering look. I begin to cry again, almost immediately. Tell her all about the green swamp and that I have never done anything right. I can't stop myself.

"Hash can do that to you if you're unlucky. It'll pass – don't worry."

The telephone rings in the living room. I hear Asger say: "No, she took the CDs home with her." Then there is a pause before Asger continues: "Yes, I heard what you said, that lots of people lost theirs." "CDs" is the code word for hash when you talk on the phone. Or else people call and say: "Umm, would it be okay if I dropped by today?" and if you haven't got any hash, you simply answer: "No, it's probably better tomorrow."

"Doesn't he think about anything else?" Ulla declares dryly.

"He's generally very nice," I tell her. But is that right? He never tells me anything that is going on – with that Hossein, for example.

Ulla goes into the kitchen, makes tea and sandwiches, and we sit under the duvet with our arms around each other and watch some indifferent TV while interlacing toes and it is really cosy.

A little later Asger comes and hangs from the door frame. "Hey, what are you doing with my girlfriend?" he jokes.

Ulla turns her head towards him. "She's sad, Asger. And apparently you didn't want to comfort her – that's why you bloody rang me."

"It's Saturday evening," Asger drawled. "What do you want me to do – customers are pouring in."

"You don't have to deal with bloody customers when Maria is like this, do you."

"The coffers are almost empty. I have to earn some dough."

"Yes. If it hadn't been for her you wouldn't have had *any*thing to sell," Ulla tells him.

"Just . . . you know, keep your underpants on." Asger closes the door after him.

"He's simply got no sense of shame," Ulla mumbles. She is fantastic.

The Mother Animal

It is Tuesday before I gradually begin to feel like some kind of human being. I decide to take a trip to town and perhaps buy some new clothes. There are still piles of filthy snow at the edges of the pavement, but the sun shines through the long, drawn out clouds hanging in the sky like frayed white satin.

It happens while I am strolling down the pedestrian street on my way towards Salling, the big department store.

"Hi, Maria." My mother appears in my field of vision with a larger than life smile on her face and pastel coloured ceramic jewellery dangling from her ears and neck.

"Hi, mum," I stutter. She gives me a hug and I can feel her swollen earth mother body pressing up against me.

"I'm *so* glad you've moved away from Gorm," she says.

"Um, how do you know that?" I ask, quite taken aback. Gorm is my ex-boyfriend – he was a drug dealer too, but I didn't think she knew. And she can't know that I have moved in with Asger because I first moved into a small house in West Aalborg and I haven't changed my mailing address yet.

"Well, I went out to Gorm's with some of the things you left," she says. Poor excuse. "And one of my friends said that she'd seen you serving upstairs in Café Rendez-vous. It's wonderful that you've found a job," she says all too effusively.

"I haven't got it any more, the job," I say. She puts her hand on my arm.

"Oh dear, what happened?"

"I've got some problems with my neck," I answered evasively. "I'm off work." I can feel myself getting a lump in my throat. I wish she would remove her hand.

"You do look a bit off colour."

We have not spoken for nine months and I think it is just a little too much to try and brush this under the carpet with a smile and chit-chat. After all, there is a reason for not having spoken. On the other hand, I have no real desire to talk about it – not today, not the way I feel. She gives me a searching look.

"Really? I'm just a bit tired," I say.

"Are you sure you're getting enough to eat?" she says, looking me up and down. I plunge my hand down in my pocket and pull out my packet of smokes – to get her hand off my arm as well. She screws up her nose at my cigarettes, but manages to stop herself. I am glad I don't eat as much as she does.

"Yes," I say. "I'm getting more than enough to eat."

"Why don't we sit down somewhere for a cup of tea?" she suggests.

"I'm meeting someone in a little while," I say.

"Or a quick cup of cocoa," she says, pointing to Underground with a smile.

"Well . . . all right," I say, dropping myself right in it. We go in and my mother orders.

"Is it a nice place you're living in now?" she asks as she sits down opposite me.

"It's a bit cold," I say. The house I moved into before getting together with Asger was in fact freezing cold and I have no desire to tell her that I am now living with Asger – it is none of her business. She continues to send searching looks up and down the pedestrian street.

"But you could always move back home," she says and her eyes wander before she delivers her offer: "Well, if you wanted to spend a little time improving your school grades, you could live upstairs with us and that would make it a bit easier for you." When she says "with us" she means with her and Hans-Jørgen who in my opinion is the type of person you should shit on and flush.

"*If* I wanted to spend my life improving my school grades?" My forehead feels moist and I break out into a cold sweat over the top half of my body. I always rise to what she says.

"I only want to help you, Maria," she says with a worried expression on her face.

"Look, let's just get this straight. I have no interest in wasting any more time on bloody school grades," I say, already knowing what she will answer.

"But what *do* you want?" she says.

"I don't know," I say doggedly, trying to keep the pitch of my voice at a normal level.

"But Maria . . . what is the matter? I've tried to do everything in my power to help you to. . . ." My mother leaves her martyr's speech hanging in mid-air while continuing to scrutinize the pedestrian street. I ask what she is looking for.

"Umm, I was supposed to meet Hans-Jørgen here." She sends me a nervous smile. "And so it was a real slice of luck that I bumped into you." At that moment the waitress arrives and puts tea, cocoa and a blackberry tart in front of us. Hans-Jørgen. I let out a deep sigh, look down at the table and suddenly feel more weary than ever before. I really can't face him today. My mother starts stroking my cheek. I know it is a mistake, but I let her do it. "You look quite . . . out of sorts, dear."

All the pathetic moves she tries on me as if I were some kind of witless baby that has to be prodded, enticed, cajoled and wheedled into doing what she wants. It is a bloody insult.

"I was a bit under the weather the other day after smoking a spliff," I say, looking her straight in the eye.

"A . . . what?" she bursts out before realising.

"A spliff, mum. As in hash, grass, chillum, pot, joint, weed. Ring a bell, does it?" I ask because she is an old hippy, so the terms are not alien to her. Not alien in any way. It is only in the last four years that she has been living on steaks and wine.

She breaks the eye contact and gazes vacantly into the air. A piece of cartilage near her cheekbone pulsates.

"Do you want to end up like your father?" she asks in a thick voice.

"Yes, if that means I don't have to be smug and hypocritical like you." The skin in her face goes taut. I push back my chair, stand up, turn and go to the door; I can feel the other customers staring at me.

"Maria . . . ?" my mother says behind me and then I am out of the door and on my way down the street without looking back. I just catch sight of that idiotic fool Hans-Jørgen approaching in the distance before I turn down Nygade so that I can wipe my forehead and the corners of my eyes – there's something or other there – with the sleeve of my jacket.

Actually I had been on my way to Matas as Ulla told me she worked there, but now I have lost interest. Instead I walk to the main library to read cartoons. I can't concentrate though, so I go home to bed. Asger doesn't say a word.

Commercial Holism

"They keep you in balance," my mother said quite seriously as she was explaining to me the philosophy behind the ceramic jewellery she creates in some kind of cryptic colour coding. She sells it to middle-class women dolphin enthusiasts, forty-three-year-olds in the middle of their seventeenth personality change.

I could put up with that and I could even put up with moving in with Hans-Jørgen, but there came a time when she began to talk down to me:

"Maria, I would prefer it if you . . . did not talk about your father when Hans-Jørgen was here."

"Don't fucking tell me what to do, you pseudo-holistic cow," I said, and moved in with Gorm.

It is true that my father is totally burnt out, but he is still my father.

My hippy parents lived together until I was twelve in a cottage by Halkær Broad. My father worked as a roadie round Europe with all sorts of semi-known bands, but he only worked when the stars were in the right constellation.

"But we really need the money," my mother said to him in the vegetable garden at two o'clock in the morning between the rows of beetroot and mangetout peas. My father was on his knees weeding.

"I can't go away now. The moon is in the perfect position," he said. The vegetable garden was weeded in strict accordance with Steiner's theories about the phases of the moon. And we had a dog, Mr. Brown, who refused to eat meat – he was a diehard vegetarian. If we gave him white rice instead of natural brown rice, he grumbled.

Hans-Jørgen is, of course, the head stage designer at Aalborg Theatre. He only drinks the most expensive red wines and is well into finer French cuisine. And my mother is a full-time hypocrite.

Country Pillocks

On Thursday Ulla comes by in the evening and asks me if I want to go out for a beer. I do, very much. It has begun to snow again. We go down to the fjord and follow it inland to the town. Ulla goes over to a parked car and starts scraping the freshly fallen snow into a ball on the car hood.

"No, no," I say but she throws the snowball anyway and then we go absolutely wild, bombarding each other from a distance of three metres. I am bending down picking up snow from the road when Ulla comes over and grabs me from behind and rubs snow in my face. Some of the snow goes into my eye. "Ow, ow" I shout, holding my hand up to my face.

"Sorry. Let me see." Gingerly, Ulla takes my hand away. "There, there," she says, removing the snow from my face. She kisses my eye. My heart beats faster. She licks it with her tongue. What is she up to? She puts her hand on my hip. Looks deep into my eyes and the tip of her nose touches mine. It feels as if my pulse is about to burst out of my temple. Then she kisses me gently. I part my lips and let her enter. Both tongues are warm in my mouth. It is absolutely wonderful. Then she withdraws. I smile tentatively but dare not look her in the eye.

"Easy now, Maria," she says with a sweet smile and pats my bottom. "It's just for fun, isn't it."

"Okay," I say shyly.

"I really like you," Ulla says, taking my hand, and we begin to walk, "but I'm living with Niels, even though he's an idiot, too." We giggle and at the same time I think of the two lesbian girls who come to Café 1000Fryd. And I think that almost all the other girls have been in the clutches of lesbies at some point or other and have experienced . . . 'rubbing' as Asger calls it."

We take a seat at Tempo. I haven't had a smoke since the green swamp and even after a beer I feel that the void inside me is just lying in wait for an opportunity. After several run-ups I ask Ulla if she knows what Hossein actually lives off. She has only heard rumours: "Some say that he sells opium to all the foreigners in Northern Jutland."

Corner, on the corner of Jomfru Ane Gade, is the next stop and on our way we meet Loser – without doubt Asger's poorest customer. I ask him if he wants to join us. He seems desperate.

"I'll buy you a beer," I say.

"No, it's really . . . because of Jomfru Ane Gade where we . . . well, me and Steso were almost beaten up by a bunch of country bumpkins there last week." Steso-Thomas is a downright provocative little junkie who runs around town with these ferrety eyes of his. Steso once told me that his all-time favourite dope was Stesolid, hence the name. *"But now I'm a lot more versatile,"* he added.

"Well, what happened there then?" Ulla asks on our way to the pub with Loser between us.

"We'd been to Rock Café, and we were going up towards Bispensgade when all of a sudden we were surrounded by these huge country clods who started pushing us about and calling us junkies and dope fiends and all sorts of shit. And Steso-Thomas . . . shot off his mouth of course and they really started laying into us."

"Then what? Did the police come?" I ask because there is usually a patrol car near Jomfru Ane Gade.

"Christ, no. When you finally need the bastards they're . . . but then Hossein appeared. Do you know Hossein?"

"Uh-huh." I say as Ulla opens the door into Corner.

"Wait a sec – I'll just get the beer," she says.

"What happened then?" I ask, following Loser to a table.

"Let's just wait for Ulla, shall we?" he says self-importantly.

"Well, okay," I can see Ulla queuing by the bar, so I ask Loser if it is right that Hossein broke the nose of a guy called Bertrand.

"Yes," Loser says and almost looks happy.

"For no reason?"

"No . . . fuck, no."

"But what did he do . . . Bertrand?"

"Well, he was bothering Tilly, Steso's girlfriend."

"How?" I asked. Tilly is a bit of a fruitcake, always going round in yellow clothes. She's got an alcohol problem, but I don't really know the people Steso hangs out with.

"How should I know? Bertrand is a . . . loser," Loser says with a grin. "He's sure to have deserved it. Got a smoke?" I give one to him and Ulla appears with the beer.

"And . . . ?" she says.

Loser resumes his story: "So Hossein is standing five metres away with a beer bottle in each hand shouting: *You stupid asshole bumpkins. Why you don't fight with man?*" Loser says with a perfect imitation of Hossein's accent.

"And?" we asked in unison. Loser smiles at us and takes a swig of beer.

"Then he smashes the end of the bottle . . . well, on the flagstones, and calls them queers and all sorts of things. And they sort of look at each other." Loser moves his head from side to side as if he is just having a confab with the other bumpkins. "And then they all rush at Hossein together," Loser says, pulling slowly on his cigarette.

"But what happened then?" I ask.

"He ran away."

"What do you mean?" Ulla asks.

"Just as they got close to him he turned around and began to run, shouting: *You queers, you can't catch Hossein.*"

"Did they turn on you then?" I ask.

"No, for fuck's sake – they ran after him. He ran ahead of them and taunted them. Down Bispensgade, up Gravensgade, down Algade and into Vesterbro." Loser takes a large swig of his beer.

"But how many of them were there?" Ulla asks.

"Five," Loser says.

"Well, that's quite a few," she says.

"Yes, but I think he could probably beat up five bumpkins," Loser says, "but he dragged them all round the centre of the town until they were pooped. The man's in peak condition."

"It's strange that he didn't just beat one of them up," I say.

"Yes, that's what I thought, too. But then we met him later down at the Limfjordskro and Steso kept saying that Hossein should have smashed them up." Loser drinks his beer, takes the bottle out of his mouth and pretends to look surprised at the empty bottle.

"All right, all right, I'll get the beer afterwards," I say.

"What? What are you talking about?" Now he plays the injured party. I push my packet of cigarettes over towards him.

"Just talk," Ulla says. Loser smiles and puts a new cigarette between his teeth.

"Well, okay. Then Hossein leans forward towards Steso and says: *How you think it look in the* Aalborg Stiftstidende? *An Iranian put bottle into five*

Danish idiots – bottle stick out of neck till big artery just pump blood on street? The crazy dago, war veteran, reported from Iranian embassy: wanted for desertion, murder everything. It look bad for dagos in Denmark."

Ferries

"Hmmm," I say as I stand up to fetch some more beer. Now I don't exactly know what I think about Hossein. Of course there are other Iranians in town. There was a group of four of them who sat drinking coffee for hours down at 1000Fryd. Then it turned out that they were sitting and dealing and of course they were put away and they found that difficult to accept. "*You fucking Danish racist,*" they stood shouting at the court official when he pronounced the sentence.

And then there was another guy, Bilal, I think his name was. He was long-term unemployed and often at 1000Fryd. Nice guy, but a bit weird, because he had two bullets stuck in his cranium. He was running round with an X-ray in his pocket which he showed to anyone who didn't believe him. One day the manager asked him to paint the toilet up by the stairs facing the office. When the manager came out to see how work was progressing Bilal stood there with a big smile on his face. The toilet was painted; the ceiling, the walls, the floor, the basin, the taps and the toilet bowl right down to water level – all painted in white emulsion.

After Corner Loser goes with Ulla and me to 1000Fryd to have a last beer before the bar closes at two o'clock. I have to go home soon because I don't want to risk falling victim to the green swamp again.

As we walk up Kattesundet we see Hossein pacing up and down outside the entrance to 1000Fryd.

"Hossein. What's the matter?" Loser says and rushes over to him. I can smell that Hossein is puffing away at a joint. Ulla and I stop by the entrance.

"I'm not understanding it," Hossein says.

"But what's happened?" Loser asks.

"Two ferries – they fucking."

"What?" Loser says.

"I come from Kebab House through alley," Hossein said, shaking his head and pointing to the parking lot on the opposite side of Kattesundet which leads to Vesterbro via an alleyway. "I tell you there were two ferries and they just fucking – just over there."

"Are you not feeling well?" Loser asks nervously.

"No – it's filthy disgusting."

"Two ferries?" Loser asks. Hossein seems to be totally out of it – perhaps he is hallucinating. Loser looks worried. "That can't be right, Hossein."

"It is," Hossein says. "They ask me if I want join in."

"Ahh, you mean two *fairies*, Hossein," Lars says.

"Yes, that what I say. Two ferries." Hossein shakes his head and spits on the road. "Now I need the vodka."

Pipe Dreams

After a few days a letter arrives from my mother. It is addressed to the house where I lived after I moved from Gorm's, and the Post Office has sent it on to my address care of Asger. I catch the postman on the garden path and ask him what you do with a letter you don't want to receive.

"You take it to the Post Office," he says over his shoulder. "Then you stick a label on it saying *Return to sender* and post it."

"Can't I just write that on the envelope?" I ask as he starts pushing his bike down the pavement. He stops and gives me a tired look.

"You can do what the hell you like," he says.

Okay.

I cover my address with a piece of masking tape and write: *No-one at this address with this name. Return to sender.* Then I sling the crap in the mail box. She should just stay well away from me.

That same day the first step is taken along the road to shit creek. And in fact it is all very innocent and not at all bloody. Sales are slow and Frank, Asger's best friend, drops in to buy a couple of grams.

"I'm fed up sitting here selling," Asger says with a sigh.

"Well, there are lots of other things you can do," Frank says. "What about the dogs? Any progress there?"

"No, I don't know what the fuck's up with them," Asger says. When I met him he had just bought Twister and Tripper, two Rottweiler pups with pedigrees as long as your arm. He wanted to breed them and sell the offspring for 3,500 Danish kroner apiece. But even though the dogs have been sexually mature for ages they don't screw and, if they do, there certainly has not been anything to show for it.

"You could start smuggling from Amsterdam," Frank says.

"That's not really me," Asger says. True enough. Asger is too paranoid to travel to Copenhagen himself and collect the packets from Christiania. It is me who does that because I know Axel, the wholesale pusher. Before I came into the picture Asger only sold standard hash which he bought off the local bikers.

"It's easy enough," Frank says. "You just take the packs of hash into the toilet on the train before it crosses the border and stick them on the underside of the toilet bowl or inside the garbage can with duct tape." Duct tape is a kind of silver coloured super tape that musicians use to repair their amplifiers or secure cables to the stage; punks use it to repair their military boots, jackets, trousers, whatever. "The only risk involved is that you might lose your merchandise," Frank adds. "Or we could do what we talked about – find a few wealthy customers and start home deliveries, you and me?" They have talked about this for several months and Asger has begun to make ready-made joints for a gang of seventeen- to nineteen-year-old hip-hoppers and skateboarders who have started buying from us. But generally he hasn't done much about it, or else I have filched the ones he has rolled.

"No, that's too . . . I'd like to do something proper," Asger says. "Instead of sitting here waiting for customers who always try to take stuff or unload their stolen goods on us."

True enough. It is sick. We are offered at least one car radio a week and we don't even have a car. Asger spends most of his time sitting doodling little figures on a pad and drinking coffee while waiting for customers. When there are customers he sits smoking with them because that is part of customer care. And that certainly doesn't make him any better company, for Christ's sake. I have also started smoking a bit too much.

"You could also do some tattooing," Frank says.

I am lying on the sofa reading a tabloid, *Ekstra Bladet*, but when he says that I sit bolt upright. Asger looks up from the pad he is scribbling on; he has been quiet for much too long.

"Shit, yes," he says slowly, taken by surprise. Frank warms to his own suggestion and begins to elaborate:

"You're always sitting there drawing and you know a few of the guys in Klarup – I'm sure they would think it was alright."

Asger and Frank grew up in Klarup and the "guys in Klarup" are bikers. Along with the others in Vejgaard they have tried to take control of the drug market in Aalborg because Bullshit have lost their grip and have been slowly disintegrating since their president, the Mackerel, was shot by Hell's Angels. There is a kind of vacuum at the moment in which independent dealers are able to establish themselves on the town's dope scene if they have a few contacts and are intimidating enough to earn respect.

Before, all the pushers were puppets – forced to buy wholesale from the bikers – and it was impossible to buy anything except run-of-the-mill, dry, standard hash for which customers paid fifty kroner a gram. Then fierce reprisals were taken against freelance pushers: gangs of bullyboys and, in extreme cases, mutilation. But now the situation – and the hash – has improved; the quality coming to town is better though the supply is irregular. And it costs. Seventy kroner for anything decent. One hundred and twenty kroner a gram for top quality stuff going under the name of *Goodbye family and friends.* The bikers are gradually regaining their power; they are also about to set themselves up in the tattooing business and without their approval you can't be in open competition.

"Shit, yes," Asger repeats, getting up slowly to go out for a pee. He always has to pee when he is thinking; he does not pee very often.

"Wouldn't that be groovy, Maria?" Frank says to me.

"The question is whether it's realistic," I say.

"Yes, but we're only talking about it," Frank says. I nod in the direction of the toilet and look at him:

"Yes, but you're putting ideas into his head and it's me who has to live with them."

"Take it easy, Maria."

"Don't you tell me to take it easy."

Scrapings

It is the second time I have had a pusher as a boyfriend. The first one was called Gorm. He invested twenty thousand kroner in an enormous pile of freshly harvested pot, but he couldn't manage to work out how to dry it and it went mouldy. So there were toxic chemical reactions when you smoked it. I was happy about the disaster – the smoke from pot stinks like a bonfire of garden refuse. We had already reached the point where I stood shouting: *"You don't have to bloody sit and smoke with ALL your customers."*

"I smoke in self-defence," Gorm said – semi-anorexic and wasted. His breakfast consisted of coffee brewed with skim chocolate milk instead of water.

One day Gorm's creditors came to collect his stereo, which had cost him forty three thousand kroner. He was bankrupt. They also took his store of hash. He rolled down the blinds, turned off all the lights and switched on the TV – a signal to his customers that his hallowed private life was not to be disturbed. He smoked scrapings. Everything was used: joint ends, the cake build-up on the inside of his chillum and pipes and gunk from the pipe stems. He sat with a little bit of tobacco between his fingers and dried the inside of the hookah where there was always a rim of oil from the hash and tobacco dottle.

I went out into the kitchen to brew myself a cup of coffee, but he had already poured water from the hookah through the coffee filter. You squeeze the paper coffee filter thoroughly, scrape the grunge off and heat it with a lighter to remove the last remaining moisture.

Well, okay, I have also smoked scrapings and you can in fact get a pretty strong rush from it, but it is exactly the opposite effect to getting high. You just get smashed.

"Why do you want to smoke that?" I asked him. "You'll just get totally wasted."

"That's fine, too," Gorm said. "It's all about getting strung out." So there he sat, absolutely lifeless, gawking at a TV program show about growing orchids in a hothouse.

For the next three days he scarffed magic mushrooms while sharpening a large sheath knife on a whetstone and spitting on it. I had to turn customers away. The foot sat testing the edge of the knife by cutting coffee filters into thin strips. I simply couldn't be bothered to ask. I had everyone I knew actively looking for an apartment for me.

Then one of Gorm's friends dropped by. He wasn't aware that the party was over and the guy asked Gorm what he was up to.

"I want to cut the tenderloin out of a cow."

"Which cow?"

"There are some cows out by the sewage works," Gorm answered. I packed my bags and called a taxi.

Pop-Up Popsicle

I had fallen out with my mother – even then – and I didn't want to go to my father's because he lives right out by Halkær Broad, near Store Ajstrup.

At first I stayed in a youth hostel on the other side of the trotting circuit, but after a couple of weeks I found an apartment on the first floor of a freezing cold building in Valdemarsgade. The toilet was under the stairs on the ground floor and the pothead I took over the tenancy from had been using the sink in the kitchen as a urinal. It was simply disgusting and I can remember standing there with plastic gloves and disinfectant praying to the Almighty to throw me a joint.

There was a knock at the door and Asger passed a multi-coloured Popsicle through the doorway to me.

"It's for you," he said. I had often flirted with him when we were in town.

"Ooohhh, thank you," I said. "Shall I lick it until it gets all sticky?"

"Well, alternatively you could just put it by the window and watch it melt," he said.

"I don't think I will," I said. "That would be a waste."

"I think so, too," he said, and then I invited him in and sat sucking the Popsicle. He rolled himself a big joint while I admired his muscular forearms tattooed with dragons, skulls and crossbones, knives, flames, hearts and roses. Then we smoked the joint and, shit, how I needed it! I was flat broke, so I told him I didn't have a job. I didn't have anything to smoke, either. Well, I was nineteen years old and I had always been well provided for by

Gorm, so I had no idea where to buy. I didn't know anything, but I didn't tell Asger that. He got up to go to the toilet.

"I may be able to find you a job," he said on his return. And he did – working at the bar in Café Rendez-Vous in Jomfru Ane Gade. It was a pretty far-fetched story. The owner of the cafe was good friends with a man who owed some bikers forty thousand kroner for drugs. The bikers demanded a gesture of appeasement not only to extend the man's period of grace but also to drop the beating he had deserved. Asger was apparently involved in the affair and the bikers owed him a favour. The agreement was that the café owner would employ a girl of the bikers' choice – and that was me even though I didn't know any of them.

So I went along and served; actually, it was deadly as the other employees hated me. Both they and the owner thought the bikers' plan was for me to sell coke to the guests. On top of that, several of the bar staff were serving short measures, so they could sell beer and shorts without going through the cash register, and line their own pockets without the owner noticing when he cashed up.

And then the other waitresses didn't like my clothes. Well, before we went into the café we changed into a kind of pathetic shirt cum blouse, but I arrived wearing my own clothes and then I was given *the look*. And I wear a fifteen to twenty centimetre long silver snake wound around my right forearm; my mother had got a silversmith to make it for me before we fell out. They couldn't cope with the snake at all – especially as many of the guys think it is interesting, and that I am interesting. I was there for three months.

The Butcher's Dog

I began to see a lot of Asger. He picked me up when I finished work. The short sleeves of his T-shirt were strained to bursting point over his well-developed biceps and he always had a packet of King's shoved up his left sleeve. I could smell the tobacco when he held me close. I liked that.

He gave up his job as a bouncer and started dealing in drugs, but the neighbours on his stairway complained about all the people going up and down the stairs until late at night. And of course he had Twister and Tripper as well, so he rented a little house in Schleppegrellsgade and hired a carpenter he knew to build a kennel run for the dogs in the back yard. And then I moved in.

We took the dogs, which were ten months old at the time, for a walk every day. Asger bought them cheap off a friend whose girlfriend turned out to be allergic. The friend had taken them with him on a dog training course, so they understood the usual commands such as 'no', 'here', 'down' and 'sit'. They had also learnt not to bite things, not to jump up people and how to walk nicely on a leash, so that was handy.

"And if they turn out to be attractive dogs, I can enter them for shows," Asger said and rattled on about police dog training, the police dog course, and having the dogs' pedigree approved by the Danish Kennel Club for breeding purposes.

"Do you know how many puppies a bitch like this can have?" he asked and proceeded to answer his own question. "On average, around ten survive. I'll be able to sell them at 3,500 kroner apiece. That's 35,000 kroner!"

I read some of the papers about Rottweilers Asger had lying around. There was something about them being descendants of the Smooth-Haired Herding Dog which the Roman armies kept for looking after the cattle they brought with their armies up through Europe for food. Emperor Nero used them as dogs of war and had them in his palace for protection. Then in the German trading centre of Rottweil butchers and cattle traders used the dogs as guard dogs. They refined the breed further and used them to guard and to herd cattle and pigs. They were also used as draught dogs. *Rottweiler Metzgerhund* or *Butcher's Dog* is their full name.

The description given is that they are powerfully built black dogs with clearly defined rich tan markings; *a dog that despite its powerful presence does not lack nobility and is highly suitable as a companion, a watch dog and a working dog.*

It sounds like an exact description of the boyfriend I have always wanted.

Friendly and placid by nature, it loves children, is devoted and obedient. It is biddable and eager to work. The Rottweiler is bursting with energy and by temperament it is self-assured, bold and fearless. It is particularly alert to everything going on around it.

The travelling cattle traders tied their valuables around the dog's collar to keep them safe.

The pedigrees of the two dogs sound all very grand: Twister is descended from Ulan von Filstalstrand, while Tripper is descended from Cita von Rütliweg who was the daughter of Arco von Arbon and Ola von Limmatblick, which according to Asger is the "finest blood."

The Travel Agency

On one of the first days together we were in the front garden because we had just taken the dogs for a walk and had dropped in at the Kebab House to get some lamb chops, hummus and roast potatoes. Loser and Steso-Thomas wandered in off the pavement. Loser, thin and grey with blurred features, stands shivering in the autumn cold; Steso hops almost frenetically from one foot to the other, his piercing eyes shining out from his hollow-cheeked, bony face. And as always he has a crumpled paperback sticking out of his back pocket. Steso devours books and pills with almost equal avidity.

Then the neighbour peers over the hedge.

"Who are all these people visiting you?" he asks. Asger tells Steso and Loser to go right in and we will join them in a while.

"I run a travel agency," Asger says. "Climbing tours in Algeria."

"You don't look like people who do much travelling," the neighbour says as I make my way towards the house – because Steso can track down anything worth stealing in under three minutes.

"You look as if you could do with a trip yourself," Asger says. "You're much too pale."

Loser is standing inside the living room with his greasy 50 kroner note in his hand and only wants a single gram of standard hash. Steso paces the room with his hands thrust deep into his pockets looking at the household contents. We don't have much worth stealing.

"For Christ's sake, Loser, *one* gram," Asger says, after sitting down at the table and breaking off a little piece of hash so that he can weigh one gram on the pusher's scales. Steso goes over to the table and picks up the slab of hash.

"Hey," Asger warns. It is not good manners to play with the pusher's hash. Steso doesn't care. He rubs the slab with two fingers to assess the oil content and puts the slab up to his nose to sniff the quality. Then he puts it back on the table.

"Haven't you got anything better than CARDBOARD?" he asks with a malicious sneer. It is standard stuff, you won't get wasted smoking it – the quality is too poor even to get high.

"There's nothing else in town at the moment," Asger says, passing Loser his purchase. Asger gives him a little bit extra.

"Lars has got better shit than this," Steso says. Lars is better known as Pusher Lars. He is one of Asger's competitors in West Aalborg, but I think Lars's clientele is more punks and wackos while Asger's customers are rough types – at any rate that is how they view themselves.

"Yep," Asger says. "But I've heard that your credit rating with Lars is zero – and the hospitality is not that great, either."

"Uh-huh, so that's what you've heard," Steso says, completely unmoved. The rumour going round is that Steso once stole a couple of hundred mushrooms from Lars.

Loser is sitting in an armchair rolling himself a little joint with about a third of a gram. Twister and Tripper trot in from the kitchen where they have been drinking from their water bowl. Loser lights up, takes his first drag and starts stroking the pups which have gone over to him. I thought they were vicious dogs, but they are not particularly aggressive. Both Twister and Tripper roll on to their backs and lie with their legs in the air while Loser scratches their stomachs and smokes his joint. I am not sure that it does the dogs any good to have hash smoke blown into their faces – after all they are still only big pups.

Steso gives Asger a crumpled hundred kroner note and turns round to look at the dogs.

"What did you say they were called?" Steso asks innocently. Now you have to be on your guard – he is about to be vicious.

"Twister and Tripper," Asger says. "Tripper is the bitch."

"After a twist of marijuana and acid trips?" Steso asks.

"Yes, exactly that."

"Very . . . INGENIOUS," Steso says.

"Aw, shut up," Asger says.

Steso continues to stare at the dogs and modulates the pitch of his voice.

"It's strange that people like you always tend to have dangerous dogs," he says.

"What the fuck do you mean by that?" Asger asks.

"No-one loves you; so you buy yourself a couple of puppy dogs which are deeply dependent on you and give you unconditional love. And they respect you because you can hit them. And at the same time other people are frightened of you when you strut down the street with your beasts."

"They're for bloody breeding," Asger says. "They've got pedigrees."

Sunglasses

Everyday life with Asger was the same as with Gorm. It was just much nicer being with Asger. He was more fun, he loved me more and he was better at making love.

But now that is all over – it is just like it was before. We are at home, people come to buy and I am responsible for shopping and cooking. The only time the dogs get out is into their run and I keep having to remind Asger to feed them and give them fresh water. Asger almost never goes out. But when I have my period he has to go out and do the shopping because sometimes it hurts so much that I can hardly move. I huddle under the duvet watching TV.

"I can remember, for Christ's sake," he says angrily because I want to write him a shopping list. I write it anyway. There are only five separate items we want from the local supermarket, but his short-term memory is absolutely shot to pieces. Asger puts on his jacket and places his sunglasses on his head even though the weather outside is grey. He shifts the piles of papers and old copies of a tabloid around on the table.

"Where the fuck are they?" he mumbles.

"What've you lost?" I ask.

"My sunglasses," he says. "Have you seen my bloody sunglasses anywhere?"

"There's a pair over by the window," I say. He goes over, finds them and puts them on.

"Right," he says contentedly. "Now I'm ready to go out." He looks a putz with one pair of sunglasses on his nose and an identical pair shoved back on his head. I have to bite my tongue not to laugh, but it is not that difficult since whenever I laugh I have long knives churning round in my tummy.

Asger is very pissed off on his return, wearing only one pair of sunglasses. Steso had gone over to him in the street and told him how fantastically cool it was to wear two pairs of sunglasses: "Sunglasses are cool, Asger. But two pairs of sunglasses, man, that's TWICE as cool."

"I couldn't bring myself to tell you, sweetheart. I just thought it was so funny."

"I can't hear anyone laughing," he says with bitterness, and I suddenly realize that I called him 'sweetheart'. That is what I have started calling him: 'sweetheart'.

Sweetheart – as if he were my spouse, institutionalised. It is so pathetic. And he smokes so much that it has destroyed his sense of humour. And he can't screw properly any more, either. It is amazing how different men can be – some can keep their rods up even when they're absolutely pissed and stoned; others can't even make it out of the blocks. At any rate, Asger can't handle all the spliffs he smokes.

When he doesn't want sex, he always says it is because he can't do it with a condom on – it kills the passion. "No-one sucks cream caramels with the paper on, do they," he says. Brain-dead comment – I don't suck his cream caramel with a condom on, do I. And he wants me to go on the pill, but I don't want to because that is what I did when I moved in with Gorm. At the time I thought: *Right, now I've got a boyfriend I'd better get myself on the pill.* Five weeks later my tits were twice the size and my bum – Oouuuff. My face, too – I got little piggy eyes. There has to be something up with the chemistry if just a little pill can do so much damage. So I chucked the pills away and lost all the weight in no time at all. I refuse to take that shit – it is wrong. But I don't want his fucking seed in me, either. My eggs are fertile and he is not going to father my offspring. He is simply not good enough for that.

Pork Roast

At eleven o'clock I hear someone knocking at the door, but we don't usually get up before twelve. There is a note and a card on the floor. The one from my mother and the other from the Post Office for Asger about a packet. I put my mother's in my underpants before going into Asger, who is still in bed, and give him the card. Then I go to the bathroom and unfold my mother's note.

Dear Maria,

I am very sorry for what I said about your father. Sorry, sorry, sorry, darling. Won't you call me? Then perhaps we could arrange a meal together? I hate it when we fall out.

Lots of love,
your mother.

When we . . . *fall out.* We fell out bloody years ago. The cow runs my father down and then she thinks it can be sorted out with three sorry's and a kilo of warmed up frozen food? It is not that easy. I wish I knew how she had got hold of Asger's address.

I tear her note into tiny little pieces and flush them down the toilet, then I open the door so that I can keep an eye on what Asger is doing.

"What's the packet?" I ask while shaving my legs in the bathroom.

"We-ell," he says, walking round with a smile on his face.

"Come on, what is it?"

"Just wait and see." Then he tries to lure me into picking it up from the Post Office. "There might be some business to do here, sweetheart."

"Then they'll get a cup of coffee while they're waiting," I answer. "Take the dogs with you."

"Couldn't you just pop them into the run?" he asks.

"They have to have a bit of exercise once in a while – they're big dogs," I say. "And you may as well do the shopping while you're down there."

"Oh heck, can't you do that?"

"I've got to go to school," I say with sudden inspiration.

"You don't usually."

"Well, I have to today," I say and tell him what he has to buy. I am going on a course for the unemployed, but I am on a sickie, not that there is anything wrong with me. I just don't feel like going in and I have been diagnosed as having a neck injury. When he arrives back of course he has 'forgotten' to do the shopping – he has also forgotten that I was actually on my way to school.

"The dogs were behaving really weirdly," he says with surprise in his voice as he stands there with a very important expression on his face, opening a parcel on the table. That is blatantly obvious as he never takes them out. At the beginning he trained them, but now they have forgotten what they learnt. The parcel contains a tattooing kit for four thousand kroner. Asger ordered it through an American mail order company he saw advertised in a motorbike magazine. Next time I see Frank I'll cut his balls off.

"Yes. Yes. Yes." Asger says, turning the equipment and accessories over in his hands. There is a power supply with foot pedal, ink, tape, needles, spray bottle, tattooing machine, soap, instructions for use, elastic bands, latex gloves, sticking plaster, disposable razor, stencils for standard tattoos, tracing paper, copying pencils, a watchmaker's glass and needle tubes. But there is no sterilisation kit. Have these people never heard of AIDS?

"Maria, couldn't you nip down and do the shopping?" he asks. "We're going to have roast pork."

"I'm going to school," I repeat, even though it is a quarter to two in the afternoon. He starts phoning round to get hold of Loser. Asger finds him in Café 1000Fryd. "Go down to the local supermarket and buy the biggest joint they've got," he says. I put on my jacket and sail out. That is so fucking irritating. He will never be any bloody tattooist – the longest he can concentrate for at a stretch is twenty minutes. I am twenty years old and he is five years older than me. I don't know . . . I had still expected some sort of cerebral activity.

I go out to do the shopping. On my way I pass a telephone box. All right. I go in and call my mother at her ceramics workshop.

"Where did you get my address from?" I ask.

"Maria . . . can't we just . . . ?" she begins.

"No. Where?"

She tells me that she went to the National Registration Office and gave them my old address with Gorm and that was how she found the present one. For fifty kroner.

What kind of fucking country is it where any idiot can go in and get someone else's address? We have no bloody say about anything.

"Would you like to come for a meal on Thursday?" my mother asks.

"Yes, okay," I say. It is not because . . . she won't be forgiven just like that, but . . . I also need to know what my options are.

Walking home, I think about Ulla. Perhaps I should try . . . well, when I think about it I get a warm feeling inside and, come to think about it, being together with Asger is not so arousing, so I might be . . . ? Well, who knows?

The moment I come in the door Loser arrives with a joint of pork weighing 1.824 kilograms.

"OH, SHIT," Asger shouts because, of course, the rind has been cut into strips to make crackling. "I can't do any bloody tattooing on that if it's been sliced up." Loser stands there looking frightened and miserable. His mind is on the money he has shelled out and the few grams of cardboard hash he was undoubtedly promised to run the errand. Then Asger looks at Loser with a pensive expression on his face. Loser holds up his hands in defence and starts edging backwards towards the door.

"Just a little one?" Asger says. "For four grams of black?" Loser drops his hands, looks non-plussed, and casts a rapid look over to me and then back to the tattooing kit. "Black" is the best hash Asger has in stock – the going rate is 75 kroner a gram and only good customers are entitled to buy it.

"Asger," I reprove.

"You could also practise on bananas," Loser grovels. "If they're not too ripe."

"Bananas," Asger sneers, turning to the window and sighing. "Bloody Loser," he mumbles.

I send Loser an affectionate look and nod down at the tools on the table before sitting down and rolling a joint in a bamboo pipe that I carved and sanded down myself when I was visiting my father in the autumn.

"Err . . . couldn't we . . . umm smoke a bong?" Loser whispers to me so as not to distract Asger.

"No," I say. We have a bong, but smoking a bong head makes me incredibly dizzy, almost nauseous. Well, a bong is basically a hookah, except that there are no holes for the water to pass through. Instead the hole to the bong head functions as a water channel. You suck until the pipe-fill is burnt and then you pull the bong head out of the bong and inhale a lungful in one go. Asger's bong is made of leather and it is unusually disgusting, exceptionally even.

I smoke the joint together with Loser and give him the money for the pork – it is not his fault that Asger is incapable of giving clear instructions.

As soon as this has been sorted out, Loser sneaks off as quickly as possible. I usually love to have a spliff in the afternoon and then chill out watching a video or chatting to people who drop by, but now it is as if the void inside me is lying in wait. I shiver.

Shortly afterwards Asger destroys the five bananas I have just bought. "But you can eat them afterwards," he says. "I doubt if the ink will go through the skin." He writes *I love Maria* on one of them, but I don't want to eat it. I don't think he loves me.

He tries to persuade me to roast the pork in the oven so that it doesn't go to waste, but I am not having any dead pig in my oven. So instead he cuts it into strips and throws it out to Twister and Tripper in the yard, despite my warnings. Naturally enough, they have the shits for two days afterwards because they are not used to raw meat and a pork joint from a bloody supermarket is absolutely crammed full with bacteria. For the next two weeks the tattooing machine lies untouched and I begin to rejoice that this project at least has died in the water, but I rejoice too soon, all too soon.

Flesh and Blood

I tell Asger that I am going to the cinema and walk towards the enormous flat where my mother and Hans-Jørgen live on Boulevarden. What is the point really, I ask myself. I don't want to live with her and Hans-Jørgen. Why should I? The last time it was dire. And I have no intention of improving my school grades, which is the only thing my mother can think about. *Education is important, Maria*: that's her mantra even though she has none herself.

The first course is salmon and then Hans-Jørgen has made a vegetable quiche with lettuce and garlic bread. This really is a step up. They used to sit there with the blood oozing out of their meat while I was left to eat lettuce and potatoes.

"Mmmm," my mother says, chewing her first mouthful of salmon. "My goodness, how delicious this is. Don't you think it's delicious, Maria?"

"It's okay," I answer, as I have always hated it when they talk about food over the meal. Comparisons with something they were served in a restaurant in Provence in 1987. "And there was a *fantastic* view. Do you remember, Maria?" Yes, well, trees, fields, buildings, sky – chill out, will you, woman.

"What does . . . Asger . . . do?" my mother asks.

"Ummm, he's a bouncer," I say because that is what he was when I met him. "And sometimes he works behind the bar." Those are lies, too.

"Oh yes, where's that?" My mother asks, already a trifle concerned.

"Various places," I answer evasively. I certainly won't tell her that Asger is a drug dealer – I don't want her to have that over me. Well, I am perfectly aware that my mother would eat her words if she knew, give up all her attempts to get me back home. But . . . .

So far she has managed to keep off the subject of my school exams, but Hans-Jørgen is keen to re-erect the old scenario.

"And you're about to prepare for your exams, are you?" he asks. His tone is intimate and friendly; at the same time I can see that he believes he is relieving my mother of a burden by asking the question. My mother seems ill at ease. I look at him and I am about to say: *What the fuck are you interfering for? You're not my father. I've got a father. He lives out in Store Ajstrup. Can you remember him, mum? The one you walked out on and wouldn't let me see – my own FATHER.* The words were queued up behind my teeth. And then I realize what Hans-Jørgen is up to. He split up with his wife seven or eight years ago and met my mother four years ago. He loves her flabby femininity, her caresses and devotion. He loves screwing with her and drinking wine and going to concerts with the Symphony Orchestra and taking city breaks in Barcelona and the whole shit. The only snag with my mother is me – the little brat who doesn't want to be a nice girl. Nothing would make him happier than if I kept well away so that he could have my mother to himself. She is one of those women who simply can't survive without a man – she can't piss straight and comes to a total standstill. The years from when she left my father until she met Hans-Jørgen were . . . desperate. Well, of course, it is good for her to have him. I can well understand that she is happy to have him around, but open your bloody eyes, woman; you are sitting opposite your own flesh and blood and you are letting the dweeby shmuck push you around.

Am I preparing for exams?

"Yes," I say. So everything in the garden is lovely, smiles all the way down the line, even if Hans-Jørgen's expression of pleasure is far from convincing.

It is written all over his face, the fear of having me back in the flat. Luckily, he has to go to work soon after and I make an excuse that I have to meet Asger at nine o'clock in front of the cinema.

Exploding Sun

I am sitting flicking through the instructions for the tattooing machine. Asger is out collecting old debts with Frank and the dogs are in the run in the yard because Tripper chewed up one of my tennis shoes.

I fetch a banana from the kitchen and tattoo small patterns on it. You dip the needle in the ink and tattoo the ink in. The machine gives a pleasant vibration in your hand and the ink smells good. I find an LP by Einstürzende Neubauten called *Halber Mensch* – some god-awful music I was given by Gorm. On the sleeve there is a little asexual figure, like a cave drawing – very trendy. I copy it but I give it a head like an exploding sun – it looks really great in blue-black ink on the yellow banana. In fact, I am better at tattooing than Asger. Then I draw little spunk men, the same shape as the salted liquorice pastilles you can buy; it looks like the pattern I had on my underwear when I was a child – a Paisley pattern I think it is called. The small figures were surrounded by rows of dots, so I add them to the banana, but there isn't enough room.

I would like to give myself a spunk tattoo on my ankle. After a quick read through the instructions, I change the needle and wind a couple of ordinary household elastic bands round the tattooing machine so that they exert pressure on the needle at the top. The elastic bands, together with the electric current which is regulated by the power supply, adjust the vibrations of the needle – that seems simple enough.

Before I start I shave my ankle and clean the skin with alcohol. I don't know if that is what you do, but it seems logical.

I draw the design for the tattoo directly onto my skin with a fine felt tip – it has to be unique after all. Finally I cover the whole area with Vaseline. According to the instructions the surplus ink is easily wiped off with a paper serviette. If you didn't use Vaseline the ink would stick to the skin and then you couldn't see where you were.

I am a little apprehensive about how much pain is involved. When I press the needle against my skin I receive a little shock. It *does* hurt, but not so much. I follow the lines and wipe the blood and ink off with a clean cloth. The pain is constant now – a smarting sensation, but I am relieved anyway. The fear of pain was greater than the pain itself. The burning feeling gives way to something like cramp, but it is restricted to the area where I am tattooing. The pain is uniform. In fact, it is pleasurable and I can feel my nipples hardening.

A good hour or so later I have finished. The skin is slightly raised and the pain is fairly constant, but it will probably soon go. And the *spunk* has turned out really well. No wonder there are so many bikers who become tattooists – it's a piece of piss.

I don't know how to go about taking care of a new tattoo, so I phone Ulla as she has a rose on her shoulder. She says I should put some transparent foil over it to stop dirt getting in. It has to stay there until the next time I have a bath.

She also asks if we will be seeing each other soon.

I just burst out: "Yes, I'd love to." Afterwards I tell myself that, of course, it doesn't mean we have to . . . well, as she herself said, it was only for fun and, anyway, she lives with Niels.

I pull my trouser leg down over the tattoo. I don't want to say anything to Asger – he will only be pissed off. He is so grumpy at the moment.

The Imprisoned Door

Asger tells me that Hossein is going to be his courier and will pick up the hash for us from Axel over in Christiania. Asger wants me to travel with Hossein the first time to introduce him to Axel. I am sceptical when he tells me, but actually I want to go even though I am a little frightened of Hossein. But then he is also exciting and I can sense that Asger respects him. And it is always good to go to Copenhagen and do some shopping.

Axel is an old Aalborg lad. I can remember him from the time when I was fifteen and started going out on the town. He was completely nuts. Always on magic mushrooms. There was a nice boy called Michael who told me about

Axel. In fact it was Michael who took my virginity one night down by Fjordmarken although I knew that he already had a girlfriend and she had galloping anorexia – something I simply don't understand. But Michael was one of the few guys at 1000Fryd whose mother had taught him about the basic rules of hygiene; he not only washed his hair regularly, he also used deodorant and so he was in fact a pretty attractive guy, though a little boring.

Michael told me that Axel was a great mushroom collector. There was a whole group of them, but Axel was the one who went out collecting. "Most of them are too lazy and too paranoid about nature to collect them themselves," Michael explained. I didn't know anything about those things at that time. According to Michael, it was *a very intense experience* taking mushrooms. "Everything changes," he said. It all went very psychedelic, very weird and very groovy. "The doors to perception," he said. "You have a house which is you and your ego; and what you do when you're on the trip is simply to open one door after the other, doors you normally have no access to, and you leave the doors open so there is a draught."

It made me think about my father. A total draught. I wasn't going to try anything, but I hung out with Michael for a while and we were up in Axel's flat where they were taking mushrooms – thirty each. And it was totally weird because they were not really talking to each other. They were just sitting there sending each other telepathic signals, nodding in agreement, and I sat there with a little baby joint and thought it was all so damn exciting.

Then Axel starts saying that the door is alive and it is a shame that it is imprisoned. I cast my eyes over to the door in the hall. It is an ordinary panelled door, painted white. "What do you mean by 'imprisoned'?" I ask.

"The wood isn't free. The paint impedes the door's existence," Axel says, looking at it with deep concern.

"It has fittings on," Michael says. "The wood grain is moving – can you hear it screaming?"

"We have to show our solidarity," Axel says and starts taking his clothes off, all his clothes. Michael begins to do the same. Axel is standing by the door as he throws off his trousers and I can see his pubic hair and his big, limp willy. "That helps. Can you hear it?"

"Yes," Michael says and then both turn and look at me with a kind of sorrowful wonder. What the hell, I think. I am smashed, and there is a living room table in teak veneer, and I too begin to think that it is alive, that the wood grain is undulating in a dancing rhythm, so I throw off all my clothes. Axel stands stroking the door, patting it, consoling it, as Michael starts removing everything from the table and lets his outstretched hands slide down the surface of the table. I am completely naked, and my nipples are stiff because it is chilly in the room. There is nothing sexual about it all, or only in terms of the wood that has to be consoled with our caresses, so I lie stomach down on the table and embrace it, and I can feel that there is sap in it, the sap runs through the grain and strokes my thighs, the skin of my stomach and my breasts and tickles my cheeks.

Not so long after Axel is admitted to the psychiatric ward at South Aalborg Hospital. He always ate mushrooms when he was out collecting because they talked to him, he said. Then he came home in the evening and strolled down Bispensgade, probably with an insane gleam in his eyes, and was stopped by the police. They confiscated his 700 mushrooms and a quarter of an hour later he attacked their patrol car with a meat cleaver.

Three days later he escaped from the ward at South Aalborg and six months later he turned up running his own wholesale business in Christiania. No-one knows what he did in the meantime and presumably he is still on the wanted list.

The Muslim Curse

"Come on, Maria. All you have to do is go with him to Axel's. He'll carry the slabs out of Christiania, you meet up at the main station and catch the train home," Asger says.

"Okay," I say. "Let me meet Hossein."

"You *know* who he is," Asger says.

"Yes, but I haven't met him. I'd like to be sure that he's an okay guy before going to Copenhagen with him and all our savings."

Asger shrugs his shoulders. "Ok, I'll ask him to drop by."

A couple of days later Hossein appears. He stands erect in the middle of the living room with his flashing black eyes and points to the coffee table.

"What this shit do here?" he asks in a heavy Iranian accent and with revulsion in his voice. Asger looks at him in total bewilderment. Hossein has occupied the space in the room to such an extent that Asger is finding it difficult to get air to his brain.

"What . . . shit?" Asger asks.

"Shit Palestinian head cloth," Hossein says. We use my old Palestinian cloth as a tablecloth. Actually, it probably is a bit tacky.

"They're your brothers," Asger says.

"They not my bloody brothers. Palestinians just scrounging bastards of dickhead Arabs. Make hopeless try to have good relations with Israel."

"Isn't Israel your enemy?" I ask.

"No, in Iran we happy for something called Israel. Arabs can waste time and energy on it." I look at Hossein in surprise. He tells me that Israel and Iran were good friends before Khomeini came to power.

"Aren't you Arabs? Or Muslims?" I ask. I don't know. I thought all of them down there were Arabs and Muslims.

Hossein looks at me angrily and speaks through clenched teeth: "I am not shit Arab and not pissing Muslim. I am Persian. My country, Iran, we are Persia. We hit by curse. Muslims occupy us. It is same problem we have in many thousand year." It seems that Iran has been occupied by Arabs, Turks and Mongols. "And Arabs did not stay, but they succeed to convert all rulers. Rest they killed." he says.

Asger interrupts him: "Okay, okay. Everything's fine, Hossein."

But Hossein is wound up – I have obviously touched on a sore point.

"Arabs wild people without reason to be – they just stand in way," he says and declares that it was a good thing Mohammed spread Islam among the Arabs because they were so primitive that even Mohammed was a huge step forward. "But since then not come further. Arabs should have relations with bloody desert and not interfere with rest of world."

"I thought Iran was on the Arabs' side against Israel?" I say, because that is what they always say on the TV news. I pass Hossein a mug of coffee. He calms down a bit as he explains to me that it is Khomeini's fault.

"He tried do mirror reflection – so Israel would be stupid bastard and Palestina liberated. Only because Israel lie in same bed as USA, like the Shah." Hossein lashes cream and sugar into the mug before sitting down in an armchair and telling me that the ordinary Iranian has no sympathy for the Palestinians. He says that many Iranians are tired of their children being lured to the Lebanon to fight against Israel.

"Many young Iranians killed. They been promised they liberate Palestine and instead they been cannon fodder in Lebanon."

Hossein does not seem at all like the kind of man who needs to work as a courier in Christiania to survive. There must be another reason for him to do so, I think, but I can't imagine what the reason could be.

"Why did you actually flee Iran?" I ask as casually as I can. He looks me sternly in the eye – all the casualness of my question is blown to the wind with his look.

"I am soldier. I come under suspicion for shoot officer during battle."

"And did you?" I ask the question completely without emotion. I am not afraid of his eyes. Then he smiles and, wow, what a set of teeth, two rows of well-proportioned, strong, white teeth.

"Yes, of course. He was stupid bastard," Hossein answers.

"Did you shoot him from behind?" I ask. I like him, but I would really like to see him lose a little composure.

"No, I turn round and shoot him in head from front."

"What were you so angry about?" I ask.

"Stupid bastard try hide from war, hide behind me."

Barbarian Bread

We agree to meet in the morning at Aalborg station two days later. On the day, the alarm clock goes off and I have only slept four hours. I almost arrive late because I want to shave my legs. I may have hippy parents, but that is no reason to go around like a complete dog's breakfast and I am not going to sit on the train in the company of a good looking foreign man with stubble on my legs.

And I have to remember to put Aloe Vera lotion on my tattoo to keep the sore soft and supple. It is best if the scab doesn't crack or fall off too quickly or there is a chance the colour will disappear and then there will be white dots left in the shape of the spunk man. The cream is soothing at the same time so I don't feel the urge to scratch, pick and play with the sore – that can leave white marks, too.

"AAASGER," I shout because, of course, he hasn't got up and because his misconstrued pusher machismo dictated that he wasn't able to give me the eight thousand kroner yesterday, so now I kick him out of bed and call for a taxi while he slouches to the window looking suspiciously over his shoulder. He doesn't want me to see where he hides the key to his small safe box. I go into the kitchen – the key is in the saucer under the potted plant on the window sill – I mean how difficult can that be to figure out? The taxi hoots, the money is put in my hand, I receive paranoid warnings as a send-off and then I am on my way.

Hossein is calmly waiting in the middle of the station hall and we catch the train without any problems. He finds our seats and points to one of them: "You sit facing train."

"Why's that, Hossein?" I ask, slightly taken aback.

"It's best for beautiful woman not sit with back to future," he says, apparently in all seriousness. He says that he will find the stewardess on the train and bring us a cup of coffee. "I'd like tea," I say, sitting up straight. Half an hour later the sun is flickering on my closed eyelids and there is an alien smell in my nostrils. I half open my eyes. I am sitting on a train beneath Hossein's large leather jacket; he is sitting opposite looking at me.

"Oh," I say, "I'm terribly sorry." A woman in her early fifties is sitting on the other side of the aisle. She has a somewhat huffy look on her face and keeps glancing furtively over at us.

"It's good you sleep if you tired," Hossein says.

"Yes, but it's not very polite," I say. My mouth feels sticky with dried saliva, probably because I've been sitting in the sun. I wish I knew what my face looked like.

"Who give monkey about polite," Hossein says. I reach out for the beaker of tea on the table between us.

"No, don't drink it – cold tea," Hossein says, diving down into his shoulder bag under the table from which he produces – of all things – a Fanta.

"Thanks," I say and drink greedily. The fizz loosens the saliva in my mouth and I feel both limp and tense because I haven't eaten a thing today.

"You hungry." The statement is intoned as a question.

"Yes, extremely hungry actually," I say, stretching. I also feel like a ciggy, but I think I will be sick if I smoke on an empty stomach. Hossein dives down into his shoulder bag again and comes up with two square packets wrapped up in foil.

"You have sandwich – Hossein made it," he says, passing me one and taking out a half-litre bottle of Fanta for himself.

"Hossein," I say smiling. "Are you sure you've thought of everything?"

"I hope I do," he says. "Old soldier always think about . . . provisions," he adds when he has found the word. I open the packet. There is a flat piece of white bread about the size of a quarter of a frying pan. The top surface is uneven, it has been glazed with something or other and sesame seeds have been sprinkled over it. I lift the top to see what is inside. Mayonnaise dressing has been spread over the bread and I can smell garlic. Between the pieces of bread there are slices of tomato, cucumber and feta cheese; there are also onions and jet black olives, pitted by hand. I wonder if he knew that I was a vegetarian. I can feel the woman continuing to stare at us. What the hell is her bloody problem? Has she never seen two people eating sandwiches before? Somehow I can sense that it is making Hossein uneasy.

"Did you make them, Hossein?" I ask. He nods.

"Please," he says. I take a bite. It tastes fantastic.

"Where did you buy the bread?" I asked. He raises his eyebrows and points to his chest.

"I baked bread."

"Is that right?" I exclaimed.

"Yes, it's right. You don't think Iranian man can do magic in kitchen?"

"Ummm," I say. "What's the . . . bread called?"

"It's called nune barbari – it means *barbarian bread*." He thinks the name originates from the time when this bread came to Iran with the Mongol hordes. I turn towards the woman and pass the big sandwich over to her so that she can't avoid my eyes.

"Would you like a bite?" I ask.

"No, thank you," she says.

"Okay. You were staring so much that I thought perhaps you were hungry."

"I . . . am not staring," she says, looking directly at the empty seat in front of her.

"Okay, but go ahead and stare. I think he's a good-looking guy, too," I say, winking at Hossein.

"You should be nice, Maria," he says.

"Yes, alright."

Then the woman suddenly turns towards Hossein: "Mmm . . . I just think you speak good Danish," she says.

"Thank you and the same to you," Hossein says, and I laugh so much that small pieces of bread, cucumber and feta cheese spray out of my mouth. The woman makes a little snorting sound through her nose and hurriedly pulls a women's magazine out of her bag and almost hides behind it.

No Problem

"Hossein," I say when I have regained my composure. "How do you feel when people stare at you like that?" He thinks about it for a moment.

"I am foreigner. I cannot go and act Danish like you other Danes. I don't want, either. And if you come to Iran you also will be foreigner." He pronounces the word with rolled 'r's and stresses the final 'r': forrrenerrr – it sounds like a parody.

"But what about . . . everyday racism?" I ask, indicating the woman with a flick of my hand.

"Most people I have problem with not because they racist but because they not happy with themselves and they try to find scapegoat – get rid of their aggressions. I don't want to be scapegoat."

"But what if they . . . harass you?"

"That not my problem. They make fuss – so let them. One said me: *I hate foreigners*, so I said him: *The same to you. We are the same, man*. Some of them after you talking to them, the only foreigner they like is you. I just say him: *It don't matter much if you like me*."

"But don't you think it was difficult, . . . well, to come as a refugee . . . here?"

"Yes, . . . only thing helped me to get on my life is I am sure of myself. I think I most wonderful person in whole world. First me, then me and then me again. It's *no problem*," he says, laughing disarmingly at himself.

We arrive at Copenhagen Main Station at two o'clock and it is just early enough to be sure that Axel is out of bed. I mean the pushers' daily rhythm in Aalborg is slightly out of synch but Axel is an extreme case. I have hung out at his place every time I have been to Copenhagen over the last few years and he has nothing less than the daily routine of a vampire. As a rule, he gets up between two and three o'clock in the afternoon. And then he drinks morning coffee with loads of cream – he always does that – and in the first few cups of the day he also puts a pile of sugar. It is just to get the system working; after all, he doesn't eat very much. With the quick rush of energy the coffee brings he feels as if he has had breakfast. So he sits making his morning mix so that he can smoke. It is not that Axel minds visits at the crack of his dawn, it is just that you must not talk too much, you can sense that. You have to sort of use your antennae, then he will make it clear himself when he is ready to communicate. But I don't think you should do any deals with him before late afternoon. There are also a couple of shops I would like to go to, so I tuck my arm under Hossein's and we walk over to the Town Hall square, then down Strøget and up into Pisserenden.

I soon blow my money and there is still some time left.

"Have you ever been to Istedgade?" I ask.

"No."

The Black Slug

A little way down Istedgade Hossein stops.

"What that thing?" he asks, pointing to a white inflatable sheep in a sex shop window.

"That's one of those . . . You can fuck it if you haven't got a girlfriend," I stammer. Hossein shakes his head and walks on so that I have to jog to catch him up.

"This place a disease," he says.

"Hossein," I say, placing a hand on his arm to stop him. "Look – a Turkish hairdresser." Hossein stops and looks at me.

"You need a haircut?" he asks.

"No, but you need to have the slug removed," I say, pointing to his moustache. "It makes you look like Saddam Hussein."

"You pay attention what you say," Hossein says, pointing sceptically at the barber's shop. "He Turkish hairdresser – I don't like Turkish village idiot. He not touch my head."

"But it's so *ugly,* that moustache," I say.

"Man has moustache. If no moustache, then you no man," he says. "All family laugh at you."

"What about a full beard then?"

"Never. Full beard only for religious. If I see on the street an Arab with full beard, I only want put my lighter to beard."

"What about sideburns?"

"No sideburnds. It for Iranian ferries."

"Fairies," I say. "Can't you see that a moustache makes you look like a Turk?"

"A *Turk?"* Hossein looks at me in disbelief. "You calling me Turk?"

"No, but you *look* like a Turk – with your moustache. And Saddam Hussein."

"I look like my father – he look good."

"In Denmark only fascist policemen have moustaches like that."

Hossein turns round and begins to walk: "I not listening any more that total rubbish."

I am not exactly clear whether he is angry or he is teasing. We walk back to the main station in silence. Hossein looks at his watch.

"We must get the thing now," he says, scrambling into a taxi to take us to the main entrance of Christiania.

"Have you been here before?" I ask, just to break the ice, as it were.

"Yes, many times," Hossein says.

Really?

Smugglers

We walk past the market square, through Pusher Street and out towards Dyssen where Axel lives in a builder's hut, but when I knock at the door a filthy little man with a long beard opens up and comes out. I ask to speak to Axel.

The little shit runs his eye over Hossein and says: "I don't know anything about that." I ask again. He denies knowing anything about Axel.

"What the fuck's up with you, you little shit?" I snarl. "When will he be back?"

"I don't know anything about that, but you could always try again in half an hour," he says, totally out of his head and anxiously clinging to his fragile psychopath façade, his vicarious power. He is probably looking after business for a couple of miserable grams while Axel is out grabbing some take-out and buying a paper or something like that.

"I don't know anything about any Axel . . . ," I say, imitating him with a grimace, then slam the door to the hut and walk back. "Fucking junkie."

Hossein laughs. "Take it easy, Maria," he says.

While Hossein gets into a conversation with a guy in a döner kebab stand, I have a look at the jewellery in the square.

At half past four we are back in front of Axel's hut. The filthy little pile of human refuse opens the door. I give him a stern look – I don't want any more crap.

"Err, come in," he says and we slip into the hut. At the furthest end there is a box mattress raised over the floor on a kind of wooden construction so that there is room for boxes and junk underneath. In front of the mattress on the right hand side of the hut there is a table placed against the wall on which there is a pile of smoking materials, coffee mugs, all the usual things, and five chairs surrounding it. On the left hand side, away from the table, a window with the curtains drawn and above the window a TV set on a shelf. Just inside the door there is a little kitchenette screened off by a partition wall. In addition, the hut comes complete with a large gas cooker, next to the bed, and several years' dirt and smoke on every single visible surface.

"Maria," Axel says, putting down *Ekstra Bladet.* I go over and hug him while he stays seated in his chair. He smiles, so he is happy to see me, but you can't expect the pusher literally to stand up – he sits on his throne while his subjects crave audience.

"This is Hossein," I say and Axel sticks out his hand.

"Good afternoon," Hossein says formally. Axel looks even more ravaged than the last time I saw him; his blond hair covers his cranium in thick, lifeless hanks and his skin is ashen grey.

Axel casts a glance to the numbskull who let us in. The little man thanks him and takes his leave. Axel offers us coffee. We can help ourselves to a couple of mugs in the kitchenette; needless to say, they have to be washed first. We run through the usual opening moves: how things are going in Aalborg, how Asger is and so on, but the formalities are soon over as who is actually interested?

Then the dealing begins. I explain to Axel that I have got 8,000 kroner, I want standard hash for the most part, but I also want some Moroccan black. The price for a kilo of standard is between 22,000 and 25,000 kroner. It is possible to get a kilo of Moroccan black down to somewhere between 45 and 55 kroner per gram, depending on the quality, on how good a customer you are and whether you know the people. So if you only buy 100 grams of black it may cost you 60 kroner per gram.

We agree on 200 grams of standard at 24 kroner per gram. So that leaves 3,200 kroner and for that I get 67 grams of black – which is a very friendly price. Based on a selling price of 50 kroner per gram of standard in Aalborg and 75 kroner for a gram of black, the 8,000 kroner would increase to 15,025 kroner. Of course, you have to deduct travel expenses, Hossein's fee, and Asger's and my personal consumption from that, so all in all it is no fucking goldmine.

"And a lump of hash to keep in your pocket," Axel says, pointing to Hossein. Without asking, Axel is aware that Hossein is there to transport the hash out of Christiania so there is no risk of me being busted.

"Sound good," Hossein says.

When you are stocking up with a relatively small amount, you put a lump of four to five grams in your pocket; it is the sort of quantity you can imagine someone would go out and buy for their own consumption.

Just the question of where to put the hash left. A hundred gram slab measures about twenty-five by ten centimetres and it is one and a half to two centimetres thick though it does depend on the volume – some hash is more compact than other hash. You put the slabs down the front of your trousers, just above the willy where a man should have a relatively flat stomach. That way, they can't be seen at all and you can't feel them in a quick body search.

And then you have to be cold-blooded. Sometimes the police run stop and search campaigns on people leaving Christiania. So you have to empty your pockets and the likelihood that they will be content to leave you alone is greater if you pull a good lump of hash out of your pocket. They got their bust. The hard-up fuck-ups who go out to Christiania to buy a gram or two often carry it out in their mouths so they can swallow it and get the benefit of it even if the police stop them. I would be loath to run around high on two grams of hash ingested through the stomach. That would be very unpleasant indeed.

Hossein manoeuvres the slabs into position and puts the lump of hash in his pocket.

"Don't you want a smoke?" Axel asks, pointing to his bong. On the table there is a bowl of bong mix, definitely a class A drug.

"I'm afraid not," Hossein says. "I am going to meet old soldier comrade." Well, I didn't know that, but perhaps he is just saying that so we can get away. We take our leave and we set off from Dyssen. It turns out that Hossein really is going to visit a friend. I ask him if I can join him. I can't. His friend was wounded in the war and is frightened of strangers. Hossein stops outside the café Månefiskeren.

"You go now. I meet you at main station at seven under clock."

"No," I say. "We have to go together."

"Why you think Asger pay me to come this trip? Not for you get busted."

"I won't be busted just because I am walking next to you," I say and put my arm round Hossein's waist. I know very well that Asger would have triplets if he knew, but I think it is safer for Hossein if we pretend to be a couple who have been for a walk around Christiania. "Come on then – put your arm round my shoulder," I say, giving his hip a squeeze.

"You sure?"

"Absolutely sure." So we walk towards the exit avoiding Pusher Street – sometimes the police have pigs posted in flats just outside Christiania with field glasses; they register who is dealing and pass the information on to police in the street via walkie-talkies. Actually, I quite like Hossein holding me tight, and to make it look more authentic I rest my head on his shoulder. We are not approached on our way out.

Homophobic Turdpackers

I have hardly stepped inside the door in Schleppegrellsgade at three o'clock in the morning when Asger starts trying out the black and the standard hash. I smoke a bit of black, but I am restless, so I get out the dog leads to take Twister and Tripper for a walk.

"By the way, your mother was here," Asger says as I am standing there with my hand on the door handle and the dogs are jumping up around me.

"When?"

"This afternoon."

"What did she want?"

"To see you."

"And how . . . was it?"

"Yeah, well, you weren't here, so she left."

"Mmm. But did she come inside?" I ask because if she did she would know that Asger was a pusher. She is not daft.

"No, no – just in the hall."

"Were you smoking?"

"No, I don't think so."

"Were you smoking or not?"

"Well, Butcher Niels and Leif were here for some stuff."

"Bloody great," I say and open the door. Twister and Tripper almost knock me over. Right. So my mother knows that Asger is a pusher because Niels and Leif always smoke some of their purchases before they go. What a prick.

The dogs jump around and entangle the leads and even though they are in a dreadful physical condition they drag me along. And have the runs in the middle of the pavement – it is so revolting. The dogs *are* totally weird. When I return I find out that Asger forgot to feed them of course – they are simply starving.

The next day I get in touch with Ulla and we go to the Scala in the evening to see *Goodfellas,* which is great, and we sit holding hands all the way through the film caressing each other's thighs and it is really nice, but I am not sure . . . . It doesn't go any further because the cinema is almost full.

Afterwards we go to V.B. – Vesterbro Bodega – where Svend comes to our table and is so sweet. I have heard a rumour from one of our customers that Svend made a girl pregnant, but I don't want to ask about it.

He tells us that Steso went down to *Huset,* the local community centre in Hasserisgade where Svend works occasionally as he is long-term unemployed. Steso had to go for a shit – apparently when you take drugs this is not a very frequent event – but the stuff he was on made him believe that the whole toilet was full of spiders, so Svend was forced to mix up a bucket of soapy water and wash the walls, ceiling and floor before Steso dared to go in. Now I hardly hear what Svend is saying; I just sit looking at his hands and chin. He just makes me go so moist that my underpants are dripping wet.

Svend has to move on, he is meeting someone and Ulla has to get up for work tomorrow. She is going the same way as Svend so they leave together, and I go home.

"For Christ's sake, why do they broadcast such shit?" Asger says as I let myself in. He is sitting gawking at the TV with Frank and Niels who asks where Ulla is.

"She's gone home," I answer and go into the kitchen. Pizza boxes are heaped up and I have to carry a pile out to the garbage before I can do anything. We eat almost exclusively junk food at the moment. Asger doesn't like the food I make. So I make myself a cup of herbal tea before going into the living room and sitting down beside Asger on the sofa.

On TV1 there is an American talk show with a very effeminate guy talking about his sexual relationship with his father who must be a senator.

"Bloody turdpacker," Frank says.

"Yeah, it's just bloody sick," Butcher Niels says.

"He should have a red hot poker shoved up his asshole," Asger says.

"You're probably the only person here tonight who has been finger-fucked by a guy wearing plastic gloves," I blurt out. As quick as lightning, Asger smacks me across the back of my neck and my chin hits the mug I am holding. I spill boiling hot tea down my angora sweater and I'm not wearing anything underneath.

"*You're bloody sick*!" I scream as I jump up, grab a newspaper on the table and throw it at Asger's face.

"Hey," says the idiot, looking aggrieved, but I am already on my way into the bedroom because I don't want him to see me in tears. Then he will just think I am crying, but I am not – it is plain fury.

"Take it easy, Asger," Niels says. Impressive statement when you have just seen a man hit his girlfriend round the head – bloody pricks.

And it is true. Four months ago Asger had another man's fingers up his ass. We were going to his cousin's wedding outside Stockholm – she is a sort of nature freak and got married to a Swedish climbing instructor who looks like a lithe, agile animal. When we landed in Arlanda airport we were stopped by a policeman with a sniffer dog who was well up for it. We were taken to different rooms where our baggage was searched and Asger was stripped to the skin and had fingers inserted up his ass. The only reason the dog freaked out was all the hash on Asger's fingers from the joint he had mixed and smoked in the parking lot just before we checked in at Tirstrup airport. The hash we were taking for the wedding was in his aunt's bag, only she didn't know and of course she sailed through customs.

I was also stripped and searched, but I said I had to go to the toilet anyway and so I was allowed to shit in a bucket.

I am simply so tired of listening to their derogatory comments about gays. What has it got to do with them? Why don't they just leave them alone? And none of them is above screwing a girl when they get the chance. I mean when Asger fucks me, or rather when he used to, he always put his finger up when he took me from behind. And when he licked my pussy he was always keen to lift up my bum and lick round my bum hole and a couple of times he sort of . . . fucked my ass with his tongue and it felt so wild and so good. And there was a time when he sat astride me and I licked him, then I put a finger up his ass and I could feel he liked it even though he removed my hand.

Now that I have stopped smoking so much I can't deal with all this stupidity any more. As I sit drying my eyes on the edge of the bed Twister and Tripper stare at me, wondering. Asger says it is too cold for them to sleep outside in their kennels unless he can find them some straw, and of course he hasn't managed to get his act together. It stinks of dog. They simply have to have a bath. And their claws are too long because they never go anywhere.

I tried cycling with them once: first of all, they were unable to run properly alongside me although they could when they were pups. Secondly, their physical condition was so appalling that after three kilometres they were on the verge of a heart attack

Twister scratches the bedroom door so I lock the dogs out in the kitchen and to remove the stench I end up hunting for a tea light with an aromatic ceramic lamp that my mother had made for me. The aromatic lamp consists of a ceramic base in which you place the tea light. You put a little ceramic bowl above it and fill it with water in which you add a drop of essential oils. I use lavender because it has such a relaxing effect. But, in fact, I am no fan of all this hippy shit.

I think about my mother. It might be best . . . well, perhaps, I should mull it over . . . move back home. It just seems like . . . admitting defeat. But I can't keep living with Asger either – it is just no good. I simply can't think straight . . . because I am stoned so much of the time.

Girl Music

Something happened to my father when I was twelve. That is the reason my parents do not live together.

He was on a tour with Tangerine Dream and took acid once too often. He came and talked in tongues to my mother:

"Decadence has taken hold deep in the wilderness we call our soul. Goodness is not just a moral gesture; it is also a spiritual act that finds huge resonance in the heart of every single person, at the very core of our humanity. This civilization may be about to grind to a halt, but we have to fight for good – those of us who are part of it. However, we must also comprehend how widespread the rule of evil is."

From then on he became weirder and weirder. Walking naked in the fields. Laying stones in symmetrical patterns around the house to "protect the angel"; I only realized much later that the angel was me. He ended up giving my mother electric shocks to "drive the darkness out of her." He stood yelling: "*The night has extended its territory – it gives the day its darkness. You have the day's darkness within you.*" He gave her 220 volts; it was a miracle she didn't die. So we moved out in a tearing hurry and my father stayed in the little cottage he rebuilt from a pile of ruins. My mother decided not to report him to the police, so all that happened was that he was left on his own – he wasn't even admitted to hospital.

Now my father has rented the house out to a nice young couple: a dull as ditchwater apprentice carpenter and a fat-assed nurse who works in an old people's home and stinks of perfume – Anaïs Anaïs. My father moved into the big workshop down at the end of the orchard. He put in the central heating himself and it runs off a large wood burner; there is electricity, running water, a gas boiler and a water closet as he calls it – he dug an old-fashioned cess pit out the back.

From the time my mother and I moved it was six months before I saw him again. My mother didn't want to let me see him, but I took the bus to Sebbersund, put my bike in the luggage compartment and cycled the last stage to Store Ajstrup.

He wept when he saw me. His breath smelt of beer, but he was not drunk, only intoxicated in a very controlled manner. I have never seen him drunk.

"I never thought I would see you again," he said and then I began to cry, too.

"Now I'll make you a cup of tea," he said, because he was nervous, I think. And then I asked him if he would play something on his old piano for me.

"Then I need some music," he said.

"Have you started playing from sheet music?" I asked.

"Yes," he answered and went to a shelf. He found an advertising brochure for Triumph ladies' lingerie which he put on the music stand.

"Is that your music?" I asked.

"Girl music," he said and I could see that he wasn't crazy. In some way or other it was the same as if he was playing piano to my children's books and singing silly songs about the figures in the pictures.

"But they're wearing underclothes, dad. Haven't you got any porn magazines?"

"That's not the kind of music I play."

"Can't they be naked?"

"The most they can show is breasts," he said, flicking through the brochure to a blonde girl in winsome lace lingerie.

"You turn over the pages," he said.

"But how will I know when to turn?"

"When I'm down to their knees," he said. "You just have to listen carefully." Then he played a melancholic yet somehow cheery tune; I really concentrated and I turned the page when I heard the knees.

"Yes, absolutely right on, my angel."

Echo Sounder

I stayed with my mother in Aalborg and she convinced me that it would be "healthy" to do my school leaving exams. So I went to Katedralskole while my mother was totally absorbed in making her holistic ceramics a success.

I begin smoking whacky baccy and hanging out with all sorts of weird types down at Café 1000Fryd, which is in a kind of consumer-orientated activity centre with practice rooms and so on – a bit punky and sort of underground. Then I get pregnant and I really don't know who shot his load and hit the bullseye. Well, I am seventeen years old, and I have sex, so what? But

I am stupid enough to tell my mother and she freaks out big time, forbids me to . . . do anything, without exception. Apart from having an abortion.

Then I begin going out with Gorm. The smoking escalates. I still go to school but I don't turn up. I can remember Steso-Thomas going there for a while but he is thrown out for dealing. And then I heard later from Pusher Lars that Steso had enrolled for the higher exam as an external candidate at Hasseris High School – in other words, he did the whole thing without going to a single class. He rolled up for the exam and was given the top mark in history and the second best in Danish. Yellow Tilly once told me that Steso wrote a review of Adolf Hitler's *Mein Kampf* in the fourth grade, and it wasn't anything he inherited from his parents because they were pretty ordinary judging from what people said.

I took my exams in the year before last at high school too; the last exam was an oral in biology. I was one of the last to go in. Nevertheless, I got up relatively early and smoked an early morning spliff before strolling up to hear how the others had fared. But someone had reported in sick and the teacher saw me in the corridor and said I could take their turn instead. And I was either too spaced out or too stupid to say 'no' and so we made a start.

"How is an amniocentesis carried out?" the teacher asked.

I considered a while before answering: "With an echo sounder."

"Let's just take a break, shall we," the examiner said.

Well, we made up again after the abortion, my mother and me. She gave me the silver snake I had curled around my forearm and I thought: *What the hell. Just forgive her.* And I did until she made me promise not to talk about my father when the francophile head stage designer was around. Now we haven't been friends since I moved in with Gorm.

Night Golf

Nowadays my father is a stable alcoholic. He lives off a big area of woodland he owns, which he lets hunters use even though he opposes hunting – but then he has to live after all. He has five crates of beer delivered every Monday. My father puts the bottles of beer in the wide spaces between the fins of the large old radiator he has in what he calls his living room. The radiator looks like a long wine rack with one layer of bottles. His stomach can't take cold beers any longer. He drinks the beer in the same way you read, from left to right. When he has taken the bottle of beer furthest to the left, over the thermostat which is always set to three, then he moves all the bottles, one at a time, one place to the left and concludes by taking one beer from the crate and putting it in the space that has now become free on the extreme right.

I asked him once if I could do it. "No, you shouldn't be doing that kind of thing," he said.

I have written a letter to my father telling him that I want to give up smoking grass and I tell him which day I will be out to see him to go cold turkey. There is no chance of me doing it at home. I mean there is a reason for being together with Asger: I am not far off becoming a hash head and I have caught the golden goose.

My father is relatively sober when I arrive and he has bought in a lot of red wine and food.

I cook and we eat, or to be more precise, I eat while he prods at his food. Then we listen to Otis Redding's *The Soul Album* and I begin to feel a bit pissed. Then he stands up with a very secretive expression on his face.

"What are you up to, dad?" I ask.

"I've arranged some entertainment," he says, going over to a corner of the workshop and throwing a golf bag over his shoulder.

"Bring the bottle of red wine along," he says.

"Ehhh?" I say.

"We're going to go out and play golf, my angel."

"How?" I ask in astonishment and stand up. I mean if he has arranged this just for me then I would like to go along with it, but it is pitch bloody black outside.

"We play to special rules – night golf rules," he says, stuffing his cigarettes into a trouser pocket. Then he fills the pockets of a large parka with beer and grabs hold of a plastic bag near the door. "We've got loads of balls," he says, holding up the bag.

"Dad, what the hell is night golf?" I ask, pulling on my jacket and taking an extra bottle of red wine and a corkscrew.

"You'll just have to wait and see," he says in a rather firm, fatherly way, which isn't at all like him. We go out of the door and begin to make our way towards the woodland path that runs behind the workshop. I ask if we have to walk a long way. We don't. Then I ask him where he got the golf bag and the clubs from.

"I saw them in a smart junk shop in Nibe. The woman who owned it wanted five hundred kroner for the set. So I went there one day when someone else was serving – a young girl. I went in with a hundred and fifty kroner in my hand and asked her what had happened to the lady who was normally in there. '*Why?*' the girl asked. '*Because the lady had promised me the golf set for a hundred and fifty kroner and I had just driven all the way from Skørping.*' So I got it."

"Da-ad."

"Yes, well, I'm not a wealthy man."

"No, but you did alright there."

"Oh, do you think so?" he says, with pride in his voice.

"What about the balls?" I ask. We are out of the woods now, walking along a path in the field beside the hedge. He tells me that he borrowed a book from the library to find out how to hit the ball, but he couldn't work it out so he went to the golf course by lake Sjørup to pick up some tips from them and was given a free trial lesson on one of those ranges they have where you just stand whacking the ball.

"And there are masses of yellow golf balls lying around, so I stole a few." We begin to trudge up a grassy knoll in the dark. I desperately need a joint and stop to take a swig from the bottle of wine.

"Are you okay?" he asks.

"Withdrawal symptoms, paranoia," I say.

"You can be as paranoid as you like, you're never paranoid enough for the imperialist world; it has such immense power," he says, standing up when he reaches the top of the hill. He points ahead. "Can you see the big black shadow in front of us?"

"Yes?" I say although I can't see a thing because not only is it pitch black, there is also cloud cover. It must be a barn of some kind.

"It's a greenhouse," my father says. So we stand there smacking yellow golf balls into the dark and I am getting more and more pissed. I am having difficulty getting the swing right while my father almost seems graceful.

"You've been practising on the quiet," I say.

"Of course," he says. "I've done it before." And then he tells me about one time in the seventies when he was travelling as a roadie with The Sweet. At night, when the trucks had been loaded up after a concert, they drove all the stuff to the nearest town. The drivers had a deal going whereby they had to stop if they passed an industrial greenhouse before it grew light. Then they played night golf to decide who would pay the bar bill on their next night off.

He hits the target. The sound of broken glass in the dark of the night is frighteningly loud. "Nice one, dad," I say. My paranoia rises to the surface, but I don't say a thing.

"Just relax," he says. "We're a long way from the owner's house and we can run into the woods if anyone comes." Then he gives me another lesson on how to position my hands and finally I hit the greenhouse. FUCK, it feels good.

For the next four days we have a blast together. I manage to get some solids down him, and he manages to pour a lot of fluids down me, and we borrow an old shit box from one of the neighbours. My father earns some money under the table as an electrician, especially on farms. He is handy with electrical things and well liked among the locals. Then we drive around the district, eating in wayside inns and although I am pretty paranoid the whole time my father is very calm and . . . he helps me. It is absolutely wonderful. And also a huge triumph. My mind is a total muddle, but I am proud of myself because I don't smoke.

Indefinable Fluid

"Where the fuck have you been?" Asger says upon my return.

"I've been at my dad's place."

"You can't just disappear for several weeks and leave me here to look after everything."

"Five days, Asger, that's all it was," I say as a stomach-wrenching weariness overwhelms me. Everything is in a mess. The living room looks like my house when I was a child, when it was at its worst. The Palestinian head cloth on the wobbly coffee table, the sickeningly sweet smell of smoke. Filthy mugs of coffee everywhere, bottles of wine, glasses, mixed nuts, unimaginable quantities of tobacco, cigarette papers, joint filters, chillums, pipes, a bong, a tjubang, a hookah as well as ashtrays full to overflowing. There are big balls of dust on the floor.

I turn to go into the kitchen.

"Your mother rang," Asger says behind me.

"What did she want?"

"Damned if I know," he says, "but she said that you should call back. She said that about twenty-seven times, as if I was bloody deaf."

In the kitchen there is a pan of rice with mildew growing over it. I take it into the living room and hold it in front of Asger.

"Do something about it, woman," he says. In the dogs' water bowl there are tufts of hair floating on the oily surface. It makes my stomach turn – we are a couple of total fuck-ups.

There has to be a clean-up and I decide to make a move the following morning when I wake up.

That night Asger wants a fuck.

"I'm sorry I lost my temper. I've just missed you so much, sweetheart," he says. We haven't had a fuck for several weeks and he doesn't make a very good job of it. Just about as exciting as the shipping forecast on the radio. In the end I have to see to myself to come and it isn't him I am thinking of when I get there. It would have helped to have a joint. Immediately afterwards he is dead to the world and begins to snore. What the hell am I doing? I could do with a cigarette . . . and a beer, strangely enough. Well, I suppose it is normal when you stop smoking dope. You smoke a lot more cigarettes and drink loads of alcohol to achieve a kind of high and feel at ease. To keep the lid on. It is not always the nicest things that come out of the pot when you take the lid off. The world seems a little frightening – unpredictable. I mean that is what it is really about. You deaden your emotional life when you smoke and the moment you give up, up it pops again. Being spaced out becomes the norm and not smoking for a couple of days is often a great deal more psychedelic than lighting up a giant spliff.

As I swing my legs over the edge of the bed my foot lands in something that moves. Rubber, lukewarm. A condom. I pick it up and hold it primly between my fingers – he didn't even tie a knot in it. I light up a cigarette in the kitchen. I don't turn the lights on, but when I hold the condom up to the window I can see the reservoir full of seed – Asger's bodily fluid. The colour is a yellowish pale grey; it looks disgusting and I am glad it is not inside me. After I have thrown it in the garbage can I put an empty carton of juice on top and press it down. I wash my hands and go into the bedroom, take my duvet and pillow and put them on the sofa in the sitting-room.

The day after, of course, my period comes on full blast.

"Yes, but can't you just watch the ones we've got, for Christ's sake?" Asger says because I send him down to the video shop to rent some videos. No, I bloody can't watch *Evil Dead II* or *Day of the Dead* – I don't feel like watching any of that splatter shit. In the end I manage to make him hire *Alien – the Eighth Passenger* and the second of the *Aliens*; it is just fantastic – Ripley kicks ass. The last one I saw made me want to have children.

The telephone rings. It is my mother. Instantly she starts crying. "Yes, but Maria, he's a drug dealer, isn't he," she says.

"Yes, mum. I'm aware of that," I say. "That's what we live off." She wheedles. Retracts all her demands. Simply wants me at home at any price. I am just about to tell her that I have given up smoking and that I have been out to see dad and that he is okay.

"Maria, you *know* how dangerous it is. Just look at your father," she says.

"Bye, mum." I put the phone down.

Doctor Hossein

The dogs start barking out at the back and I can hear footsteps on the garden path. Then there is a knock at the door. Asger has not come back yet and I am in too much pain to stand up and open the door.

"It's Hossein," I hear from outside. Okay, I don't mind opening up for him. So I stagger out with the duvet wrapped around me.

"Hello, the beautiful Maria," he says when I open the door.

"I'm probably not so beautiful today," I answer, walking stiffly back towards the sofa.

"You very serious ill?" Hossein asks with a grave expression on his face.

"No, it's nothing special. It'll go away again." With a feeble hand gesture I point towards the coffee pot on the table. "Asger will be here soon. There's coffee in the pot," I say, manoeuvring myself carefully into position on the sofa. Some idiot has put jagged metal pegs on all the organs in my lower abdomen. I can't really tell Hossein that. I mean the man is Persian. I don't know how they feel about us sailing with a red flag five days a month.

Hossein is standing pensively in the middle of the floor. "You have something make woman bear fruit? Make woman can . . . make fruit? Make the little person?"

"Ow, oooowwww," I laugh. "Yes, I have the fruit sickness."

"It not sickness," Hossein says, shaking his head. "It big miracle from Allah." He raised his face to heaven, to Allah, in whom he doesn't believe for one bloody moment, and then he winked with one eye. I smile at him – he is just so damn sweet.

"You can't get medicine for it?" he asks.

"No, only Panadol."

Sitting at the table, he puts his hand in his pocket and pulls out something. "You get Hossein's medicine," he says, taking out a little penknife.

"What's that?" I asked.

"It's good opium. Raw."

"Yes?" I say. Well, I would like to try that, after all it is only a painkiller. It is also the name of the perfume I wore when I was in the first year of high school. Now I use Chanel No. 5 which I pinched off my mother who got it from Hans-Jørgen – but I don't very often wear that kind of thing.

"This one," Hossein says, holding up a tiny bit between his fingers. I put out my hand, but he shakes his head and stands up. "First I make tea," he says.

"Why's that?"

"You drink tea afterwards. Tannin in – it destroy base in opium." He goes into the kitchen.

"But don't I just swallow it?" I shout after him.

"No, no," he answers. "You make powder in your teeth with spit – it much better."

Perhaps he means that it is basic, in other words alkaline as opposed to acid, something to do with the pH value, as in a brand of shampoo you can buy, but I have no idea what happens when you put something alkaline in your mouth.

He returns with two mugs of tea and puts three teaspoonfuls of sugar in each from the glass bowl on the table. Then he carries the mugs over to the coffee table and with a scornful look on his face he puts them down on top of the Palestinian head cloth.

Hossein moves a chair so that he is sitting opposite me holding a small piece of opium between his fingers. It is almost jet black.

"This very raw opium. Very strong," he says, placing the tiny piece between his front teeth, then crushing and grinding it. "You make powder," he says and passes me a small piece. "Get very dry in mouth."

I do as he says. It is incredibly bitter and my mouth tightens right up. I go completely dry in all the recesses of my whole jaw.

"You swallow it now," he says, passing me one of the mugs of tea. "Then you drink tea." And it is as if the tea removes all the dryness in my mouth – must be the tannin in the tea offsetting the alkaline.

"It help?"

"Yes," I say. "It was nice. What happens now?"

"You wait little. Perhaps quarter of hour, perhaps half hour."

"And then?"

"Then you become first little tired, quite horrible feeling, and then you feel really good."

I ask him to show me the lump of opium. It is completely black with a higher specific gravity than hash. It has a very soft consistency and Hossein tells me it is very temperature-sensitive.

"Because much oil in," he says. So it is the same as good hash which has a high oil content; if it is cold then it is rock hard and if it is warm then it is as soft as butter.

"Do you use a lot of opium in Iran?" I ask.

"No. Now people use – young people. They use opium, heroin, they smoke *hashish,* but not then. Just now they use intoxication drugs to keep people down."

"Do they give people drugs?"

"No, they let slip in, so young people can get. It is so bad that if you have child who do nothing . . . just sit and not smoke *nothing* . . . you are lucky man."

Hossein tells me that people used to say congratulations to a man whose child went to university. Now people say congratulations to a man whose child is not addicted to drugs. "It's very bad."

"Well," I say. "It doesn't sound that groovy."

"And so they say me why I don't like Muslims. This is good reason," Hossein says. "They're plague. First ruin brain because they fill you full Allah, who don't exist, in your head, then fill you with drugs so you not able think anything new, you must believe what they say."

"But I mean nowadays . . . they don't believe in God any longer . . . in Iran, do they?" I ask because . . . at least on TV it seems as if they are fervently religious.

"Most Iranians, they believe. But now they tired. It make everyday life difficult. Every time someone bad with them, they say it because of Islam. People believe in God but they tired of control. It have nothing to do with God."

"But what is it good for?"

"The Allah? For bugger all."

"No, opium."

"Ah, I see . . . In Persia we think it good for everything. Gout, stomach problem, back, sex. But not true. In reality it only super Panadol," Hossein says.

"Do you grow opium in Iran?" I ask.

"No, no, it come from Afghanistan." He tells me how during the Shah years it was smuggled across the Iranian desert to Turkey and to Europe. "The White Road." Everyone involved: Afghani drugs barons, Iranian border guards, police, other authorities." He stops speaking and gesticulates and looks at my face intensely instead. "You can feel now?"

"Yes," I say. It is as if my muscles fill with lactic acid, like when you work – I can feel all the big muscles becoming heavy and feeling hard even though they aren't. Like physical fatigue, but still not quite the same. It is not sluggishness, I just feel a little out of sorts.

"You soon through wall," Hossein says reassuringly. And just as I am about to find out what it is, the physical sensation begins to fade away. It is gradually replaced with a feeling of great well-being. It starts with a state of ease in my brain. I am carefree. It is no problem that Asger is an oaf. My mother can't give me a guilty conscience.

"It's so good," I say to Hossein.

"You feel good inside?"

"Yes, my body is so light," I say – almost in bliss. I smile.

"You see coloured carpets glide past your eyes?" Hossein asks.

"Doctor Hossein," I say, closing my eyes. I can smell the forest after a downpour. Then I hear Asger's key in the lock. He enters the living room.

"Hossein, man," he says.

"Hmm," Hossein says. I keep my eyes shut. There is no reason to open them now. It is so good.

"What the fuck are you doing?" Asger asks. He can say whatever he likes. I think he is a matter of complete insignificance. It is a really great drug if it can make me feel like this.

"We take the opium," Hossein says. "We feel better inside."

"Are you sitting together with my girlfriend taking opium?"

"It is good for pain inside," Hossein says calmly, like an oracle.

"Is that right, Maria?" Asger asks.

"Yes," I say. "It's perfect."

"Well, I'm fucked," Asger says to Hossein. "She always complains like hell when she has her period. Have you got any more?"

"I'm not pusher," Hossein says, shaking his head. I think he would only give some of his opium to me, as a present, but if it is Asger then he will damn well have to pay. I mean, even if Hossein is Asger's courier he will also have to pay if he wants some hash, though for a friendly price.

"No, no, damn it. For Maria's sake."

"I have a gram very raw opium. Strong as horse – you cannot get it somewhere else."

"Only a gram?"

"A gram enough for four, five, six time."

"What does it cost?"

"You can have it for 375 kroner – very friendly price."

"You must be barking mad. Do you think we're down in the bazaar? You can buy four grams of black for that."

"You don't think I know what black cost? I brought over from Christiania."

"But, for fuck's sake, Hossein."

Opium – it is fantastic. When I smoked I also used to think it helped to have a little joint whenever I had the sniffles. It dries out your throat.

Scars

There is a ring at the door. Asger pretends he doesn't hear, as if it is my job to jump up and answer it. Hossein looks across at Asger in surprise, who sighs – almost grimaces – before getting up and going out into the hall. Hossein glances at me with a strange, perhaps pensive, expression.

"Show me your money," Asger says, opening the front door. So it can only be Steso, but apparently he has some money because he comes into the living room, where he nods very respectfully to Hossein.

"Hossein. Good to see you – even among such white men." Hossein smiles at him. "Maria," Steso says, nodding towards me, and when he turns his head I can see a large weeping sore on his cheek.

"What on earth has happened to you?" I ask.

"Err, I fell, asleep against a wood burner."

"Really, Steso, I mean . . . ."

"Fell asleep my ass," Asger says and adds: "D.F."

"D.F?" I query.

"Dead face," Asger explains.

Steso shrugs his shoulders and gives a sweaty grin. "Yes," he confirms.

"You're so uncool," Asger says. You too, I think. Asger doesn't like Steso because he always shouts his mouth off. Pushers think they *are* somebody. The pusher holds court and buyers are at best tolerated; they have to show the appropriate respect or they will find themselves feeling the cold. Steso shows no respect, but I like him and that means something because I am called the *Pusherfrau* – always pronounced in German. *Pusherfrau* is the nice word. Others would say the *narco bitch* but I don't give a shit.

Steso remains in the middle of the floor. He screws up his eyes and peers at me. "You're on OPIUM," he confirms. The hypophysis inside him is totally geared to his junkie metabolism.

"Have you got any tattoos, Steso?" Asger asks. Steso grabs hold of his sweater and pulls both it and his T-shirt over his head in one. Then he holds out his forearms proudly to Asger. They are covered in multi-coloured abscesses.

Hossein sits there laughing. "Crazy junkie," he says.

"Bloody hell, Steso," Asger says.

"What do you get stuff like that from?" I ask.

"The pills work faster if I inject them," he says solemnly, by way of explanation. Now we are talking about important matters. "It's the preservatives that do it."

"What preservatives?" I ask.

"What holds the pill together – the binding agent. The physically and psychically active ingredients usually come in fluid form. Then it is mixed with all sorts of things – paraffin, calcium, potato flour, etc to form a pill that binds. When I dissolve the pills the binding agents come too."

"How . . . do you dissolve them?" I ask.

"With fire and water."

"But why don't you just swallow them?" I know what the answer is; I just think it is so amusing that he is a total junkie. He will take anything he can lay his hands on.

"It's a question of getting it into your veins – it isn't food, is it. The waste is too great when you use the stomach and it's too slow." He starts pulling his sweater back on.

Hossein is still sitting and smiling at Steso. Apparently they like each other.

"That's bloody horrible, Steso," Asger says.

"It's just like a roller coaster," Steso states. "You don't like it while you're on it, but when it's over you WANT another trip."

Asger thinks Steso is too weird, but actually there is nothing weird about him, he just has a higher ambition – an aim. He wants to experience the effects – and that is what he goes for 100 percent. I have been told that he also prostitutes himself with older men for money but for pills and medication, too. I was told that by Svend, who knows him. Yes, well, there are no women who would want to – Steso is simply too emaciated and his eyes are too possessed. I can see him in my mind's eye standing stoically against a wall being buggered by some fat old bastard. Steso has a higher aim and he will happily sink to any level to achieve it. There are some physical needs and some psychological costs. Something to be borne and something to be achieved. In his obsession there is a streak of . . . nobility.

"Hossein, my fine friend," Steso says, taking a seat. "Tell us about the Persian tattooing culture. Have you sullied your temple with idolatrous images?" Hossein smiles.

"Yes. Have you got any tattoos?" Asger asks.

"No. In Iran only sailor and long distance driver. And most of them who have it have been in prison for many years. So they bored and do tattoos on each other. Otherwise it is not popular."

"So you're a loser if you do it?" I ask.

"Yes. If you take them on street here and show them, so people come and say you: *Oh, that's cool*. If it Iran you go and say . . . ." Hossein lowers his voice and continues in an accusatory tone: *What have you done? Hide it, hide it – it is embarrassing*. It is for stupid people – criminals. Perhaps they have only one cross, something homemade."

"Is it correct to say that henna tattoos are very widespread in Middle Eastern culture?" Steso asks, sounding like a professor.

"Yes, we have the henna tattoo. Arabs do it – their women. Iranians do it – their nails. It disappear. They do it for fun. When they married, women have it do on hands, on feet because it bring good luck."

"Would you like a tattoo?" Asger asks. "In exchange for the gram of opium you have in your pocket?" When the word 'opium' is mentioned, Steso's ears prick up.

"I will not sully my temple," Hossein says.

"Aren't there any women with proper tattoos?" I ask because in some way or other I am frightened that Hossein will not like me if he sees the spunk I have on my ankle.

"Yes. My grandmother she had tattoo, real, on her hands. Some old women they have three dots tattooed on their chin, like a shield – it can protect against evil eyes. They are old-fashioned religious. My grandfather had too – he was half Arab robber. But people don't like seeing that."

"Was he an Arab?" I ask. Hossein points to his heart.

"Yes, I have the wild blood from *arab-e-kasif*."

I think of asking Hossein if he has any war wounds, but perhaps he will think it indelicate, so I drop the idea.

The Reader

Hossein has to leave, but Steso hangs around to smoke a little reefer. He walks over to two books lying on the window sill and takes them; Asger has borrowed them from Big Carsten – a primary school teacher who buys from us. *On the Road* by Jack Kerouac and *The Naked Lunch* by William S. Burroughs.

"Have you started READING, Asger?" Steso asks.

"Yes, of course. The two books have a lot to say about society's attitude to the drug culture," Asger answers in an almost word for word repetition of what Big Carsten said when he brought the books. Since then they have been gathering dust on the window sill.

Steso looks at Asger: "Are you aware that Kerouac was a psychopath who got off on beat poetry and alcohol and spiritual obfuscation out of FEAR that he could not cut the mustard as a middle class citizen? And Burroughs is just another American mythomaniac trying to put over his obsessive ideas with intellectual European finesse?"

"Burroughs saw through the whole damn established society's attitudes to drugs," Asger says.

Steso holds up *The Naked Lunch* in the air: "Are you trying to tell me that you've really read this?"

"Yes, for fuck's sake. Society is frightened of the drug culture because drugs allow us to see through the meaninglessness of society and gain deeper insights." Even though it is Big Carsten's sentence, that is the longest coherent statement I have ever heard Asger make.

"I don't think society is afraid of your cardboard hash," Steso says. "But it is in some senses true that society is a bourgeois woman who can't stand seeing her husband drunk because she can't CONTROL him in this state. Obviously: all societies at all times. At the same time I have to say that in itself this is of no importance."

"Why's that?" I ask.

Steso looks at me.

"It's all about trying everything you could imagine before you snuff it."

"And what's left that you haven't tried, Steso?" I ask with a giggle.

"Hell, Maria," he says with sudden enthusiasm. "I want to be here in twenty, thirty, forty years' time when the chemists come up with some FANTASTIC dope I can cheer myself up with." Steso stands there with a sensual and slightly embarrassed grin.

The Recreational Smokers

Hossein simply gave me the lump of opium in an unobserved moment and for the next few days I take a little when the pain is at its worst, though it is beginning to ease.

Now it is Friday afternoon, the high point of the week in fact because soon the recreational smokers will be here; they are people with very ordinary jobs – we receive visits from a wide range of people including a postman, a primary school teacher, a worker at Aalborg Portland, a printing press owner and a young woman with a shop in Gravensgade selling everyday items in steel and glass. She buys only from me.

On Fridays I have to keep a special eye on Asger because hobby smokers are customers you have to treat properly. They are not big customers, but they are dependable. They always come between three and five in the afternoon, always pay cash without any discussion, never smoke any of their purchases before leaving – and they always leave quickly. They have to return home to their families and only need enough for recreational use at the weekend. Some of them are ex-hash heads who have cut down and I actually envy them. I believe most people who smoke hash every day would like to smoke for recreational purposes, to have what is called *acceptable consumption* instead of being totally cleaned out financially.

Anyway, we have to tidy up and air the rooms when we get out of bed at half past eleven on Fridays. And I have trained Asger always to offer a cup of coffee; it is just a gesture and they almost always say 'no'. I don't want the regular punters sitting and hanging about on Fridays – I don't want it on weekdays either, but I definitely don't want it on Fridays. They can have permission to sit and sample their purchases – it would be bad etiquette to refuse them that and we would lose custom. But I don't want them bloody rolling up with a bag of beers and sitting around using our home as some kind of training camp while they rabbit on about all sorts of drug crap. And the dogs have to stay outside in the yard.

A singing sound on the tarmac comes through the open window and announces the first Friday customers even before we have finished mucking out. It is Zipper who comes trundling in on his skateboard. He is absolutely in his own league among our customers and functions as a kind of buyer for some hip-hoppers and skateboarders.

"Maria baby," he says as I open the door. He is standing there with his cap on back to front, a large sweatshirt, baggy trousers with the crutch round his knees and basic Converse trainers. The hottest hip-hop music comes belting out of a set of large old-fashioned headphones hanging round his neck. The skateboard is in one hand and the other is held out palm outwards so that I can do a high five. I clap hands as hard as I can and the tickling sensation on my palm is nice, because I have taken the last bit of opium to endure the house-cleaning. Zipper has come straight from the commercial college he attends in Annebergvej. He once went up to Leif during a concert at *Skråen* and said that he needed to buy "a load of joints." Leif introduced him to Asger who was of the opinion that they should buy a lump like everyone else and roll their own.

"We don't roll, man. We smoke," Zipper said, not budging. So now we roll joints for hip-hoppers.

"My man," Zipper says as I show him into the living room where Asger is sitting rolling joints because he didn't manage to get them done in time. Zipper doesn't drink coffee. He doesn't even sit down. He just puts the money on the table and says how many joints he wants. Together with his friends he gets smashed on pot, alcohol and skateboarding every single weekend at a sort of skateboarding meet in Vejgaard. Zipper always has huge grazes from falls – real *skateboarders* don't use knee pads. "Heavy," he says when Asger tells him that you can buy joints with black. They conclude the deal and Zipper puts the joints in a metal tin he carries around with him so they don't break if he falls. A handshake for Asger and a *"Maria baby"* and high fives for me, out of the door and then the singing sound of Zipper's skateboard skimming down the tarmac.

Reefer

Right, everything is ready: the ashtrays have been washed and coffee is ready in the pot. I lie on the sofa, watching *Aliens* and thinking that I bleed to flush out unfertilised eggs. In the film the mother monster lays enormous eggs. In reality Ripley would never have a chance. The monster eats people like her for breakfast.

Then the primary school teacher arrives, Big Carsten. It is the second Friday in a row that he has come; last week he mentioned something about some problems with his girlfriend so he has obviously increased his consumption.

"Yes, please," he says to the offer of coffee. Well, okay. He would like to sit and chat for a bit, that is quite alright. At that moment Marianne appears – the one with the shop. Asger lets her in. I have returned to the sofa because I am still in a little pain and I have run out of opium.

"Hi Marianne," I say. "Sorry I can't get up, but I'm a bit under the weather."

"Oh, what's the matter?" she asks sympathetically and sits on the edge of the sofa. I give her a look. "Oh I see, but that's over in no time," she says.

Then Big Carsten stands up and introduces himself. There must be so many problems on the girlfriend front that he is looking for a new one. Marianne looks terrific.

"Yes, Carsten is also a Friday customer," I tell her because I want to be nice and make sure that both know where they are in the smoking context. "And a primary school teacher," I add to make it clear that he is not a loser . . . or whatever you would call it. Primary school teachers aren't the icing on my cake, but someone has to do the dirty work.

Marianne immediately flushes. "Yes," she says. "I usually smoke a little reefer at the weekend." That is what she calls it – *a reefer*. She told me that she once went out with a Jamaican rasta type called Jones. He sold coke and sang in a reggae band in Aarhus. She went to Jamaica with him and there they call a joint a *reefer.* On Sundays they went out to the reef – the reef by a beach – and sat there smoking joints. In Aarhus, Jones had a BMW because Bob Marley had one, too. Bob had explained away this totally materialistic investment by referring to the car's name: BMW – Bob Marley and the Wailers. Right, but Jones had an accident in the stupid Bob Marley car; he was hurriedly drying the blood from his smashed nose before it stained the cover of the new bucket seat he had had installed in the car. Now he is sitting in a wheelchair somewhere in Jamaica and I remember how nonchalantly Marianne shrugged her shoulders when she told me about it. "Aren't you still in touch with him?" I asked. "He didn't stay the course," she said. Now I start thinking about that and cast a glance in Asger's direction.

Then Carsten starts telling an anecdote about his past life as a weedhead. It is never a good idea to sit and chat too much at the pusher's place, but an anecdote about a smoking-related area always goes down well. And he obviously wanted to impress Marianne.

He tells us that once he and his friends drove to Kjærs millstream to hang out, drink beer, smoke and have a good time. But the others were a little tight with their contributions to the hash that Carsten had bought.

"So I walked away to have a pee and that was when I got the fiendish idea," he says. There was hogweed growing down by the stream and Carsten knew he was immune to the toxins in the plant so he cut a large tjubang off the stem of fresh hogweed with loads of sap in. Well, a tjubang is similar to an air bong – a bong without water. You are supposed to hold it horizontally and there are holes at both ends. You put your hand at the end of the tjubang and suck until you have burnt the mixture in the pipe head and then you let go and have a lung full. It has more or less the same effect as a bong except that the smoke is not filtered, so it is dirtier. It works on the chillum principle: a dry smoke as opposed to a wet smoke.

Anyway, he showed the guys the fresh tjubang.

"And the ignoramuses were wildly excited of course. So we all smoked away and were absolutely smashed out of our heads. Then a little while later blister began to appear on their hands and round the mouths. They were horrified." Asger sits nodding, happy with the anecdote, while Marianne is giggling and holding her hand in front of her mouth. Then there is a knock at the door, an usually firm knock.

Powder

"It's the police. Open up." The living room is full of smoke because Carsten has just been sampling his purchases.

"Fuck," Asger curses vehemently. Marianne is already on her way to the toilet. Carsten stuffs his piece down one of his shoes. I have already left the sofa to open the windows. Asger has come over to my side.

"Take this," he whispers, passing me almost half a slab of hash. It is Moroccan black. It must be all we have and it shouldn't be in the house. He was too lazy to put it in his store, which is situated at the back and under the roof of the shed that functions as a kennel.

"OPEN UP OR WE'LL BREAK THE DOOR DOWN."

I can hear Marianne flushing the toilet – she must have dropped her lump down the toilet bowl.

"What shall I do with it?" I ask, taking the slab of hash out of Asger's hand.

"Stuff it up," he hisses. I raise my eyebrows.

"Why don't you shove it up your ass?" I say, holding it up in front of him.

"Come on, sweetheart," he begs. "That's worth four thousand kroner." He always exaggerates – the purchase price is a little over two thousand kroner. But the slab weighs just under fifty grams, it measures twelve centimetres by five centimetres and is two centimetres thick. He is such a prat. I couldn't have had that inside me however hard I tried. And it is not as if he makes much of an effort to expand the space there – he can hardly get the little fella up.

"RIGHT NOW!"

Asger curses and tears the slab out of my hand. I move to open the door as Asger sprints into the kitchen and throws the hash out of the window like a Frisbee. From the hall I can see it sailing into the neighbour's garden. Then he sprints past me again and I can see him turning one of the dining room chairs upside down, pulling the plastic stud off one of the hollow metal legs and stuffing the scales up out of sight. It is a set of pesola scales weighing ten grams, the type you use in physics experiments, long and thin. There is only one reason for having this style of scales in your home.

"OKAY, OKAY, FOR CHRIST'S SAKE." I shout.

"*Wait*," Asger says, digging down into his trouser pocket. I look at him. He pulls a little plastic bag up from his pocket filled with white powder and bangs on the bathroom door. "Hurry up," he hisses to Marianne.

"I'm having a pee," Marianne says from behind the door.

"Idiot," I say. He knows what I think about people on hard drugs. "Wash it down the kitchen sink."

"It's Frank's, for fuck's sake," Asger says, feverishly scanning the room around him.

BANG. The door and the door frame quiver from the blow and a chunk of plaster falls from the ceiling. Asger stuffs the plastic bag down into the point of my cowboy boots and makes his way into the living room as Marianne comes out of the toilet and follows him. The skin on my face tightens, that is how angry I am. If they find the bag I will tell them to check it for fingerprints. I am not going to be done for shit like that.

Short Measures

I open the door. A policeman is standing on the flagstones in attack position with a raised hammer in his hands, ready to strike. I stare at him with an expression of total tedium and raise my eyebrows. "Would you like a cup of coffee, love?" I ask. Behind him is Hr. Martinsen, the No.1 narcotics officer from the Aalborg police station, laughing.

"Hi Maria," he says, passing me the search warrant. The guy with the hammer is already past me on his way in. Martinsen's walkie talkie crackles.

"Would you be kind enough not to bother our guests?" I ask because that simply would not be so brilliant. I personally think it would be very embarrassing for Marianne, but it would be worse for Big Carsten as he is a weedhead and the rumour would spread like wildfire: Police raid Asger. In no time at all the coffers will be rattling.

"I'll see what I can do," Martinsen says, picking up his walkie talkie and speaking into it. "Yes?" He is informed that just before we opened the front door something came flying out of the kitchen window. Terrific. Then Martinsen goes into the living room.

Marianne is sitting on one of the chairs by the table and has elegantly crossed her legs. She is absolutely calm.

"Having a good time, Asger?" Martinsen asks with a laugh. He gazes around and says: "Hi, Carsten," then turns to the officer: "Give that one a light search and then throw him out."

"Fortunately, I haven't bought anything yet," says Carsten as he spreads his legs and places the palms of his hands against the wall. He has obviously seen too many films.

"Bloody hell, Martinsen, why are you harassing *me*? I have stopped dealing, haven't I." Martinsen raises his finger to quieten Asger and as he stands there, wagging his finger to and fro, he studies Marianne thoughtfully. She placidly returns his gaze. The dogs in the yard are barking – someone must be in the garden.

"You're the one with the shop – FLASH – in Gravensgade, aren't you?" Martinsen asks.

"Absolutely right," Marianne says as Carsten mouths "Bye" over his shoulder and is accompanied out of the house.

"Do you still stock those chrome garbage cans for bathrooms? The ones with the tip-up lid and pedal?"

"Tip-up – yes," Marianne answers.

"Fantastic. My daughter would like one."

"I don't deal any more, man. I'm going to be a tattooist," Asger says. Shit, he is so embarrassing.

"Welcome any time," Marianne says as another officer comes in carrying Asger's slab of hash in his hand.

"He threw this over to the neighbour's. It's a good sticky quality." The officer passes the slab to Martinsen who sniffs at it and looks across to Asger.

"Hmm, have you started importing?"

"Oh hell," Asger says, looking down at the tabletop. The officer stands waiting for orders. I bloody hope they are not going to turn the whole flat upside down even though I would actually like to see Asger being arrested for the powder in my boot.

"Have you got any more?" Martinsen asks.

"No," Asger says. "That's all I have." Martinsen chuckles.

"Are you trying to tell me you haven't any of the usual cardboard in stock?" Asger knows it is all in vain. At the same time he will do everything he can to prevent them from ransacking the flat and finding the speed or coke in my cowboy boot. If they do he is bound to end up spending the night at the police station and he will have them on his back for quite some time.

Asger sighs and puts his hand under the table where the hash is hidden in a little hollow between the table top and the sliding leaves of the table. He takes the hash out and passes it to Martinsen.

"Thanks," he says. "Have you got dog tags on those two beasts running around outside?" Resigned to his fate, Asger shakes his head.

"Make sure he gets a fine for that," Martinsen says to the officer and adds to Asger: "Just to get you going." Then he turns to Marianne:

"How's good old Jonesy?" I can see that Marianne is taken aback, but she doesn't try to hide it, she just smiles and looks Martinsen in the eyes.

"He does wheelchair racing in Jamaica," she says, unmoved. Very cool. It is odd that Martinsen knows about Jones when it happened in Aarhus. On the other hand, it is not every day a cokehead with enormous dreadlocks wraps his BMW round a lamp post fifty metres from Café Casablanca and has blood streaming out of his corroded nostrils. Perhaps it is a little anecdote told at the annual seminar for the narcotics division. "May I go now?" Marianne asks.

"Yes, just run along," Martinsen says as he casually continues the conversation with Asger: "Could you just take the dealer's scales out of the chair leg?" Asger rises, a beaten man, and pulls out the scales. Marianne puts on her coat while Martinsen digs out a coin from his pocket and puts it on the Pesola scales. He laughs.

"And on top of everything else you give short measures, Asger. Tut-tut-tut." Asger sits down, places his elbows on his knees and rests his face in his hands while shaking his head.

Marianne is standing shaking her head at him and turns towards me. I can't bring myself to look her in the eye. I really didn't think he was such an idiot. When you set Pesola scales, a twenty kroner coin should weigh 9.3 grams and ten kroner exactly seven grams. As a customer you have to be dead sure about your facts to accuse the dealer of selling you short. But you are a bloody idiot if you cheat your clients because many of them have Pesola scales at home from the time they had ambitions of becoming pushers. And then there is grumbling in the ranks.

"Bye, Maria," Marianne says. I writhe on the sofa because while there is sympathy in her voice, there is also a hint of condescension and it is just so unpleasant. Suddenly I have a flash of insight: Marianne must have put her purchase in her underpants when she was in the toilet. You would never believe it because she is so well turned out, but that is exactly why she can get away with a lump of hash in her muff. I should be able to do something like that, too.

"Shall we chuck this one in custody, Martinsen?" asks the policeman who has returned to the living room and is standing beside Asger.

"No. He only has to be interviewed, then we'll send him home," Martinsen says.

"What?" the officer replies.

"It's Friday – we need the room," Martinsen answers. The policeman looks cheated.

"Well, Asger," Martinsen says. He confiscates the hash, arrests Asger and charges him with possession and intent to sell in accordance with paragraph 191, clause 2 of the Criminal Code. "Do you admit guilt?" Martinsen asks.

Asger sits staring at the table top. He is unshaven and stinks of acrid smoke and stale sweat; his hair is dirty and bedraggled; and the thighs of his jeans are shiny with filth. The walls in the room have turned yellow with the nicotine. He doesn't say a word.

"We can easily hold you for twenty four hours, Asger. Or even longer if you don't plead guilty in front of the judge," Martinsen says. In fact, they can keep him in custody for four weeks, but I think they must have more on you than possession of a hundred grams of hash.

Asger grimaces and says: "Yes, I admit all this shit."

"Good boy," Martinsen says. "So let's nip down to the station and make that official."

When they have gone I close the blinds, switch off the light and turn on the TV with the volume turned down. I sit down on the sofa with a mug of coffee and pull my legs up underneath me. I ignore the customers knocking at the door. We have nothing for them.

Pushernoia

It is not long before Asger is back.

"Fuck, I'm bursting for a piss," he says, stepping in the door. Limpdick.

Oh fuck . . . the powder! The police raid has knocked me so far off kilter that I have forgotten all about it. I creep out into the hall. The bathroom door is ajar and I can see Asger's back through the crack as I crouch down and hoick the bag out of my cowboy boot. Asger's stream of piss splashes into the toilet bowl. The floor boards creak as I get up but I don't think he hears anything. I make a move towards the kitchen, opening the bag on the way. He has not flushed yet.

"Oh no, you fucking don't," he says, already right behind me. His hands close around mine which are holding the open bag only half a metre from the kitchen sink.

"I don't want to live with anyone on hard drugs," I say. Asger twists my wrist so that I have to let go.

"It belongs to Frank, for fuck's sake. I told you."

"And why do you keep Frank's dope here?" I ask.

"I got it for him."

"So you're dealing in speed?"

"It's for Frank. Just take it easy."

"I don't want anything to do with stuff like that, Asger. People go mental from that," I say. And I mean it. Anything that's stronger than alcohol and hash I want fuck all to do with.

"Move out then, Maria."

"And who'll fetch the hash from Christiania?"

"Hossein," he says, but he sounds a little unsure of himself. As if he is not sure Hossein will do it.

Asger sits down with the phone and calls around, talking about the so-called CDs, but he doesn't have any luck.

"Shit, shit, shit, shit," he curses to himself.

"What's going to happen now?" I ask. Asger says that he will receive a summons to appear in court before long and then he will probably get four months.

"Conditional?" I ask.

"Unconditional. I'll have to do a stretch," he says, with almost a hint of pride. "So you'll have to look after the place, sweetheart. Do you think you can manage that if Frank helps you?"

A quarter of an hour ago I was supposed to move out and now suddenly I am flavour of the month. "Of course," I answer because I can't be bothered to tell him where he can stick it. Besides, Frank will be behind bars – he has to do ten months for possession of amphetamines. Ulla told me that. Asger must have forgotten.

In the evening I can feel that my menstruation is over and it makes me think of the time my father told me that hens' eggs were in fact hens' menstruation – unfertilised eggs that we boil and eat. A few years went by before I ate my next soft-boiled egg.

At any rate, I soon want to be shot of the place because on Fridays an incredible number of wallies come to buy. And it goes on until late in the night. They are drunk and don't care how much they disturb the private lives that we almost don't have. Asger is as paranoid as shit now because the cops have been there, so all the people who knock on the door are sure to get a real going-over.

People always say that the police run these campaigns and raids to put the small-time pushers under pressure, but in fact you never hear of anyone being done. I mean how should the police get their hands on the small-timers and why should they be bothered with them at all? Pushers help to keep a load of emotionally unstable people happy whose self-medication may have got out of hand. Looking at it from established society's point of view, it is a perfect situation. Alright, I sound a bit like my father now when he is in a cynical mood, but there is a grain of truth in it. And today someone was busted – us.

Well, for the next few months people will probably have to buy at least three grams – or stay away. Or Asger may say that the minimum sale is for four hundred kroner; in that way he is indirectly making a few punters pool together. Actually, that seems fair enough when you consider the risk Asger is running selling the stuff – on the other hand, it *is* paranoid. I have not smoked weed now for almost two weeks so there is not much bloody point living with a pusher. It is not as if it is a goldmine. By far most of what the small-time pushers earn goes on dope. And what they don't smoke they spend on idiotic things like tattooing kits and frigid dogs. The interest in dope and this type of business do not appear out of nowhere – there are very few pushers who do not smoke themselves, it is *almost* impossible. Of course, they say they do it to make a fortune, but the real reason is that they want their own needs covered and they are too far gone to hold down a regular job.

I am simply dying to start mixing with normal people after spending five days on the sofa. I am dying to get plastered.

I call Ulla although I don't think I really know her that well. But we have similar problems – we both live with losers who are hash heads. Luckily Ulla has a day off from Matas tomorrow so we agree to meet at Café 1000Fryd at eleven in the evening. It is an okay place to start, a bit gloomy and punky maybe, but afterwards we can go down Jomfru Ane Gade and do some pulling.

Asger goes round grumbling. While I shave my legs I think about Svend. I have slept with Svend once, but it is a secret. He *swore* not to tell anyone. I shave under my arms. In the shower I stand playing with my breasts – I am as randy as hell; it is probably because I have stopped smoking joints. I am going to go out and look for a new guy.

When I have squeezed into my jeans I stand in the hall studying myself in the mirror. I stand in the same way I lean against the bar, with my ankles crossed and my legs close together. My pelvic area stands out like a small, compact, rounded triangle bordered by my soft stomach above and the curves of my denim-clad thighs on each side; they invite the onlooker's eyes upwards to the attractive swing of my hips and up again to my waist which is perfect, exactly two thirds of the width of my hips, just like Marilyn Monroe. And when the gaze has taken in my waist there are only two directions it can go: downwards towards the honey pot or upwards to the boobs and face. I am out for a kill. Up top I decide to wear a low-cut blouse laced down to the solar plexus with short broad sleeves. The blouse is raised slightly by my breasts and hangs loose over my stomach and then falls just short of my jeans.

It takes me half an hour to wrestle a measly three hundred kroner out of Asger.

"I've just been busted, man," he groans.

Hell, I am so sick of him. Normally you are well looked after as a *pusherfrau*. You don't lack for anything and don't have to do anything. I have access to all the hash I can smoke and I don't have to pay for anything, but I suppose in a way it doesn't matter now. And I also have to provide some sex (in Asger's case frighteningly little) and some maternal care. I have to go shopping, buy in the junk food, brew up a pot of coffee and run my fingers through his hair and say: "You really handled that situation well" every time there has been a microscopic problem. Otherwise, the deal is that I can sit sunning myself in his success and prestige. And so I regularly get my ass licked – I am conscious of that. Honestly. I realized all this one day when a guy called Bertrand sat telling me all this shit about my hair and I just lapped it up like a real sucker because Asger never says anything nice to me. Of course, Asger just sat there grumbling. The pusher is neutral when his woman is being entertained, but you can't try it on with her – those are the rules. You can entertain her with innocuous, cheeky, witty repartee – make her laugh. Punters do that of course because the woman has power over the pusher and they can hope that she will put in a good word for them.

Then Steso came in through the door. After forty-five seconds he raised his eyebrows looking first at Bertrand and then at me:

"Observe here a man who can lick a dead dog's asshole until it bleeds if he thinks there is any benefit to be gained. Fortunately, we know that you, Maria, are above such base flattery." Then I began to notice how often it happened and it soon became hollow when I realized why it was being done.

The Majestic Tongue

I leave home very early for my meeting with Ulla – I just want to get out of the house. I walk along thinking about Svend. But I don't think he has ever had a girlfriend, he just pounces on everything that is to his taste. I met him at V.B. the night we screwed. I was standing by the bar, hanging out with a gay boy I went to school with when Svend came right up to me and whispered in my ear: *"What about it baby? What about giving some pussy? I know you've got one."* And I was quite happy to, well . . . I wasn't getting a lot and I was very drunk. We went straight back to his place. I tried to hold his hand on the way but he didn't want to – it was obviously only a sex thing, and that was fine, too. We arrived and he went to the toilet; when he was finished I went to pee off whatever it was that had come out because I was dripping wet. I was so excited to see what would happen next because this is not something I do every day.

When I was finished he was sitting in the living room stark butt naked in a big green armchair with a huge boner. I went straight over, climbed up and sank down on him with my back to him. And well . . . he really stayed the distance. It was absolutely fantastic. I have never experienced it before . . . as fun.

"Yes. Yes," he said. "Fuck me." I was well into it. "YES. YES. You're *riding* my dick. It is SO good when you *ride* my dick."

They never usually say anything. After a couple of minutes when they can't hold back their load any longer they give such a sorry little groan. Svend roared with laughter when he came and that was *so* great. Then he fucked me up the back – well, he asked me first and in fact I like it – but then afterwards I asked him why he couldn't just screw a man from the back. "Men have got hairy asses," he said. Then, in a really deep voice, I said: *"What about it baby? Do you want big boy up the shitter? I know you've got one."* He was stunned, the poor boy, but he thought it was funny, too. And it was great having a screw and *talking* at the same time. Then he said my pussy tasted of honey and . . . well, I'm not naïve, I know that my pussy doesn't taste of honey and it is just a trick, but it is still great when he says it. Then we went for round two.

Afterwards we drank beer while he strutted round the living room saying something like: OH YES, MARIA. FUCK, YOU SCREWED MY ASS OFF."

He is so full of shit. When I got home to Asger's at five o'clock in the morning I was worried that he might be able to smell Svend on my body, but of course Asger was so smashed that he didn't notice a thing.

The next day I had a terrible hangover, but I was in a really evil mood, too. I hurriedly had a bath before Asger got up and then I almost begged him to lick me. And he did. He slid his tongue up and down my labia between which Svend had thrust his big, stiff cock eight hours before. Asger is not very good at licking pussy but still it was so wonderful that I started laughing and the clown thought his tongue was majestic.

Betrayal

I reach Café 1000Fryd at a quarter to ten. When I open the door, there are only the bartender and two customers in. They are sitting by the bar in their uniforms: military boots, filthy jeans and padded lumberjack shirts. It is much too early and I am just about to turn round in the doorway.

"Beautiful Maria," the sound of Hossein's voice carries from the other end of the room. There he is, all on his own, with a large draught beer in his hairy hand and a cigarillo dangling from his lips. He is wearing twill trousers, nice polished leather shoes and a kind of pitch black foreigner's shirt with white stitching on the chest. Iranian smart – I think he is good-looking.

"Hossein," I exclaim almost a little too enthusiastically and go over to him. "What are you doing here?" I ask as I sit down.

"I try to quench thirst," he says smiling and asks if he can buy me a beer.

"Yes please," I say, and being the gallant he is, he goes up to buy me a large glass of draught beer. He asks about Asger and watches me very attentively as I report back on the day's events. I am well aware that I shouldn't talk about it, but I am unable to hide my disgust at how badly Asger behaved. Why the hell should I?

"That very bad luck for you," Hossein says.

"Bad luck for Asger. For me . . . I don't know."

"For you Maria . . . you decide what you do."

"That's it exactly," I say. "Exactly correct."

"Skol to the happy future," Hossein says, raising his glass.

There is a gentle smile in his eyes and I can't help giving him a sly smile.

"Hossein, what are you doing?"

"I try to quench thirst," he repeats, screwing up his eyes. Then we light up our smokes, for me a cigarette and for him another cigarillo.

There are so many things I would like to ask him about. As he lifts his hand with the cigarillo to his mouth, I wonder what action his powerful, hairy forearm has seen. What movements and what actions it has performed, along with the rest of his body and brain, in the time before he came to Denmark. I would like to know that— how many people he killed, how many with his bare hands. I know already, however, that he is not so keen to talk about it although I have heard that the bikers respect him and that simply means that they consider him dangerous.

I take a deep breath. "Hossein, won't you tell me what you did during the war?" He gives me a slightly cold look. It is as if he is drawing the curtains inside his eyes.

"I did . . . war. Fight with the enemy."

"But . . . how?" He stares at me blankly, for quite a while.

"Why, Maria, you want know about this thing?" The coldness he somehow radiates makes me lower my gaze.

"Sorry," I say. "I shouldn't have asked." Then his hand closes over my hands which lie clasped together on the table.

"You not say sorry. But war very ugly thing." Now his voice is gentle again. Then there is a long silence in which he caresses my hands. "I will tell you the thing," he says in a weary voice. "I was soldier – professional in army. There was many betrayals during war."

Hossein tells me that he fought in southern Iran and that the front moved backwards and forwards.

"Iraqis mine the border areas and Iranians find a load of people along border – young people, volunteers. They send them across border to Iraq in the night to force Iraqis back."

He explains that all Iranian men are called up for three years' military service when they are eighteen. The volunteers come from schools where they are encouraged to take part in the war.

"Right down to thirteen years old – they got black headband and pistol. Then they sent over minefields. Many killed. They become *shaheeds*. The

. . . martyrdom." Hossein almost spits the word out. When the volunteers had found a path through the mines, the professional soldiers followed.

"But many times we . . . left in enemy territory without supplies, without support, and we slaughtered like dog."

Hossein says that Iran's religious leaders did not want to make peace. They used the war to weaken the army which might otherwise have rebelled against them.

"But . . . you fought inside Iraq?"

"Yes . . . I fought – only for my life and for my comrades." Hossein's intonation is such that I don't want to ask him about details. It is quite clear that he doesn't like talking about it. He crushes his cigarillo almost brutally in the ash tray and his voice is heavy with revulsion: "But they make so many children blind in their belief in the Allah and die martyr death – I think it too crazy."

"But . . . why did they want to be martyrs?"

"You become martyr, you come in the Islamic paradise – it is very wonderful." There is a glint in Hossein's eyes.

Paradise

"What do you mean, wonderful?" I ask to encourage him to talk about something other than war. I also retract my hands as I realize that more people have come into the café. We are sitting at the back by one of the small tables that are on the stage when it is not being used. Nevertheless, you can still clearly see the intimacy between us and it is well known that I am Asger's pusherfrau.

"In the paradise all man served by young maidens – *huri* they called. All man they drink wine and smoke Marlboro and Winston cigarette and every time they have . . . ." Hossein looks down at the table and lowers his voice: "When they have . . . fuck a *huri* , then she become virgin again. That is the Muslim paradise – Allah's paradise." My eyes linger on him for a while. Now all of a sudden we are talking about . . . fucking. Well, it is not unpleasant, but it is still strange.

"But what happens to the women?" I ask.

"Huris are virgin, so they raped and they become virgin again," Hossein says, avoiding my gaze.

"Are they . . . raped?"

"Yes. Muslim man want . . . rape the virgin to feel power. So he can do it in paradise. According to Muslim man, virgin is only good thing."

"Oh . . . yugh."

He looks up at me again, nodding.

"But where do women go when they die?" I ask.

"Koran say nothing about that." Hossein tells me that women are merely spirits, there to serve while they are on earth. Perhaps they become virgins in paradise so they can be fucked and become virgins again. Or perhaps they become the men who fuck virgins. "I don't know," Hossein says.

"It sounds a bit fruitier than God's heaven," I say.

"Yes, but if that the Allah's paradise – you fuck, drink wine, smoke Marlboro – why have not paradise down on earth? We must practise for paradise?"

"But . . . is it wrong to have sex, um, if you're Muslim?" I ask and I can feel the blood rising to my face. However, it appears to me that this is an important point to have cleared up. Hossein laughs.

"Yes, yes. You can, with your wife, all you want. And it is good for you and for her. You make each other happy. Not like your God – you are . . . you have . . . ." Hossein searches for the right word. "You are a guilty if you only have one time sex, It is crazy idea. In fact the only good rule in Islam is *imta*," Hossein says. "Woman has need for the sexual satisfaction in bed. It is her right – otherwise man, he is no man."

"Okay. So all sex with your wife is always a good thing?" I ask.

"No – not all. In Iran it forbidden . . . do it behind."

"Behind?"

"From behind – in the backside."

"Err, buttfucking?" I ask.

Hossein looks down in his glass and gives an embarrassed laugh. "Yes," he says before looking up with a cheeky glint in his eye. "You have to pay fine if you do. One of the holy persons in Iran has written book about that."

I laugh cautiously. Can feel my cheeks going red. A book about turd-packing. What *are* we sitting and talking about?

"It is right" Hossein stresses, holding up his hands. With the thumb and index finger of his left hand he holds the little finger on his right hand just below the top joint. "If you with your wife and stick your little finger in her asshole it depend how far it go. You must pay fine in gold. Book say how big fine you pay for different type buggery or frig. If suddenly you too wild and so hit wrong hole, OH DEAR ME." Hossein shakes his head in consternation. "If the head go in, you pay so much for fine, if it go *further* in, then you have to give camel. So it is expensive business in the asshole." We are both laughing. Hossein gives me a studied look, perhaps to see if I can take it. I can.

"We have the book in Iran, me and my brother, and we read and laugh when we bored. Everything in the book. Religious law for how you behave in bed."

"But why are you so bothered by anal sex?"

"You cannot have woman before you married. What you think we shall do?"

"But is this something that you talk about?" I ask, thinking that this conversation is really way out.

"Yes, we talk. Not with mother and father. But young people – they talk about it for fun. There is a town in Iran called Qazvin. In Qazvin they say: *you bugger or you be buggered.* There is no woman, only man. Even if there are women, you can't go to bed like that – you go to bed in other way. They say: *God has created the dick round like the asshole. If you want be in pussy the dick should be like this.*" Hossein draws a narrow, oblong shape in the air. The dick has to be shaped like the head of an axe to fit the pussy.

"The town lie north from Teheran," he says, getting up from his chair and putting his arm behind his back and covering his bum with one hand while flapping the other arm in the air.

"They say birds, when they fly over Qazvin, hold one hand on ass and fly on one wing. It's true. Mecca for buggery." Hossein sits down on his chair again. I laugh. I realize that we are flirting big-time.

"It is town with many religious." Hossein tells me about a mullah in Qazvin who went round during the month of fasting, Ramadan, and was starving. He had a sandwich in his pocket, so he went down an alleyway and started eating it. Hossein holds his hands up to his face and pretends to be munching away.

"So suddenly someone come by – it is embarrassing thing for mullah to do, break the fast. He become so frightened he stick head in dustbin – enormous dustbin – because he have to hide he eating the sandwich. Then a man come past and say: *'Oh, who have thrown such lovely ass in garbage?'* Hossein stands up again and looks lasciviously at the ass he has just told me about while rubbing his hands. Then he starts fucking the imaginary mullah. It is brilliant. People at the bar turn round.

"Better be buggered anonymous than be discovered eating during fast," he says, sitting down. I can't keep my eyes off him. He wants to get more beers in. I insist it is my turn. He is not keen on that. He keeps firing off all these dirty jokes – one after the other, but then he has to meet someone at eleven o'clock. I ask him what he is going to do.

"It is some business I must do," he says casually. He smells good and he looks very cool.

"Are you going to meet a girl?" I ask.

"No," he says. "Now I meet you this evening, all other women look ugly for me." I stand up and give him a goodbye kiss on the cheek. Then I sit at the bar and think about Hossein while waiting for Ulla.

A Modicum of Charm

I briefly greet Leif. He is a scaffolder and buys off Asger now and then. Actually he is a very nice guy, but at the same time he is just yet one more pothead in the making who performs the endless bouts of drunkenness and madness in a desperate milieu where getting wasted is the most important marker of status. It all seems so pointless.

The bar girl is a young hippy, and I haven't seen her before. She reminds me of myself a couple of years ago when I began coming here. She is not very tall, has attractive wide hips and a good bum on her. Her hair is thick and dark red with curls down to her shoulders. Her face is somehow very beautiful even though it is strikingly round; she has a broad mouth with a flat nose and large round nostrils – almost negroid. Her eyes are her best point; they are really appealing though she uses too much eyeliner. She may not even be old enough to work behind the bar, but she already has my vote because she plays some nice music. It is always the bartender who decides what music is played at 1000Fryd and most play Black Metal or loud punk music. I ask her what the music is.

"Cocteau Twins," she says with a smile. She is ripe for plucking by some shmuck with a modicum of charm. Just like I was. Only to be torn apart.

"Maja," Leif calls from the other end of the bar and she goes over to him with a smile to take his order. He starts chatting to her. She stands on the tips of her toes, leans over the bar and gives him a kiss. A shmuck with a modicum of charm. It is a miracle he doesn't fall off the scaffolding with all the alcohol and hash he consumes.

Ulla comes in the door swinging her arms coquettishly, but I can see immediately how she changes her tone when she establishes that there is not a single good-looking guy in the place. She gives me a quick hug and orders a large beer for both of us before taking off her coat and hanging it over the bar chair. She is wearing a very low cut satin dress, the empire cut with incredibly narrow straps and it moulds itself to her bosom to perfection despite the fact that she has small breasts. The four guys sitting at the bar send her furtive glances, but she is probably not the type of girl you can make a comment about and get away with it. When she has sat down I sneak forwards to get a better look down between her small round breasts – she is not wearing a bra. Usually you have to wear a bra or have half-decent prominent tits for a dress like that to sit well. Otherwise there is the chance your breasts might pop out – and that can be very charming – or they can slip right down so the stitching that is supposed to support the breasts cuts across them and that is just *so* embarrassing. I also have small breasts and I don't seem to be able to wear dresses like that although they really suit me – if I stand stock still, that is.

She tells me that Butcher Niels does nothing but play on the computer and smoke pot, and he is always evading work. So I tell her about Asger and the police raid earlier today. We agree we both suffer from a lack of satisfactory maintenance in the undercarriage department. As far as I can make out, there is no invitation for us, for Ulla and me that is, to do any maintenance for each other. But I think about it again.

In the meantime quite a crowd has come in and it looks as if a couple of the guys could deliver the goods.

"Shall we pull?" Ulla says.

"No, there are too many people here who know us," I answer. Luckily, the music is too loud for others to hear what we are talking about.

"I mean somewhere else."

"I don't think I dare today," I say, wondering if Hossein will return once he has finished his business.

"Rumour has it that you've been out with Svend, the one who buys off Lars . . . ."

"Who says that?"

"It's just something I've heard," Ulla says secretively.

"Ulla!" I say, slightly worried. "This is important. If Asger hears a rumour that I've been . . . then . . . ."

"You've said yourself that he's no bloody good."

"Yes, but I'm not sure what he might get into his head . . . ."

"I saw you myself coming out of Svend's place one morning," Ulla says.

"No!"

She puts a hand on my arm and squeezes it: "You looked very guilty."

"Yes, well, I was *so* nervous. But no-one knows anything about it?"

"Not because of me, at any rate."

"Whew."

"Well . . . ?"

"Well what?"

"Was he good?"

"Ooohh, you can't imagine."

"Yes, I can. That's what I've heard as well, you see."

"You've never had him?"

"No, but I can tell you it's not going to be long."

"He *really* can . . . ," I say with emphasis, ". . . move that tongue of his."

"It's strange he hasn't got a girlfriend," Ulla says.

"Yes. I think he goes with a lot of girls – really sexy girls," I say.

"I think he's in love with that Lisbeth, the one Steso knows." Lisbeth is a beautiful girl with a limp. I heard she was involved in a traffic accident and the driver died."

"Mm, could be, now you say so. But Lisbeth is with Adrian," I say.

"The small, rugged guy . . . I mean, the one with all the muscles?"

"Yes. That's what I've heard."

"He frightens me – but he's very exciting," Ulla says.

"They're a strange bunch," I say. I know Steso a little bit. Steso knows everyone a little bit if they have anything to do with intoxicating drugs. But then there is his gang: Pusher Lars, yellow Tilly, Svend, Lisbeth and a couple of others . . . and they all tend to be secretive. You see them and you know they are up to something, but you don't know what.

Duct Tape Tits

It has just turned midnight and the bar shift has changed. The new bartender plays deafeningly loud Black Metal. All this voluntary bar staff crap can make 1000Fryd a bit of a shit place. This is not a big night in town, but the café has a fair sprinkling of people in, sitting at tables and chatting. And then a little pseudo punk walks in and annoys everyone with his sad noise terrorism.

Now it really does irritate me how well that dress fits Ulla. We are sitting . . . and of course we have been kissing . . . and I am getting a little plastered too; I am not used to drinking beer.

Then I just ask her. I almost have to scream in her ear because the music is so loud and she leans over towards me so that the material of her dress hangs loosely around her breasts and I just catch a glimpse of her nut brown nipples, compact and stiff, but the stitching below her breasts stays where it is supposed to. She doesn't answer, just takes my hand and pulls me off the bar stool.

"Come with me and you'll see," she yells, pulling me to the stairs leading to the toilets. We giggle stupidly as we go into one of the cubicles and lock the door behind us. We can only hear the music now as muffled bass sounds and there are white tiles on the walls and a neon light; it is very bright. I stand opposite her feeling a little awkward.

"Now you'll see," she says, dropping the straps, and then she lifts the material down over her breasts, but the dress doesn't fall off her – it is as if it is hanging on the underside of her breasts.

"Duct tape," she says. On her skin there are two strips of duct tape which are folded over and stuck back, just where the lower curve of her breasts meets her ribs. They keep the dress stuck in the right place.

"Mmm, what wonderful breasts you've got," I say. She takes my hands.

"You can touch them," she says, placing my hands on her breasts. I enclose them with my hands and I feel the rubber-like sensation of stiff nipples against my palms. My heart races again. She slips her hands under my top, over my stomach and ribs while I caress the rounding of her breasts.

"Mmmmm," she says. Her hands press against my breasts and she holds the nipples between her thumb and fingers and squeezes them so that I gasp for breath.

"Do you want to kiss?" she asks.

"Yes . . . let's." I put my hand around her neck and pull her face down to mine. My tongue meets her slightly parted lips. Her mouth is so soft.

"Hey. Can a man get a piss here?" we hear from the other side of the door. I sit down on the toilet seat and pull Ulla down so that she straddles me. Then I suck her left nipple between my teeth and it feels good. I let the nipple go, dart my tongue up it, then down it, dab at it.

"Ooooh," Ulla says. "And the other one, too." When I change breasts I can see that Ulla's lips are slightly parted, but her eyes are open and she is watching what I do all the time. I can feel myself getting very wet between my legs. Then there is a kick at the door.

"I NEED A PISS." Ulla and I look at each other in embarrassment and quickly adjust our clothes.

"Okay?" Ulla whispers.

"Yes," I whisper and we unlock the door. Leif is standing outside, with a strained expression on his face.

"For fuck's sake, can't you get up to your lesbian perversions at home?" he curses as he hurries in. We giggle and go down the stairs.

Lars & Adrian

We take our seats back at the bar. Ulla drags her stool over to mine and then she starts caressing my thighs – and her hands move up higher.

"Hey, lesbo show," a drunken idiot says, and another says: "What they fucking need is some dick." Ulla looks at the guys hanging round the bar.

"You haven't got a hope in hell," she says, putting her hand around my neck, drawing my face to hers and nibbling at my mouth. She is a wonderful kisser. We let go and laugh at each other. It is all in fun. It is half past twelve and I think it is time to leave. We agree, but just at that moment Lars and Adrian come in the door. Adrian is a rugged bundle of muscle and a head shorter than me, and Pusher Lars is a bricklayer and in fact very well built. Pusher Lars nods over to me before saying hello to Ulla. Adrian stands beside them, opposite me, rocking to and fro on the soles of his military boots.

"Isn't Lisbeth coming this evening?" I ask, not because I actually know his girlfriend, but just . . . to say something. He leans over to me: "Lisbeth? She's doing her studying. She's bright, you see, not like the rest of us." He looks at me with a devilish grin to see whether I have enough self-knowledge to know how dim I am. Today, it has been shouting me in my face. It seems you can see it in my eyes even though I try to strip all emotion from them. Lars moves away from Ulla and presses against the bar to catch the barman's eye.

"Yeah," Adrian says, leaning over to me. It is as if he whispers with completely normal intonation, as if he is not as psyched out and high on acid as he always gives the impression: "Maria, not being bright is simply a terrible misfortune, but we have the colossal advantage that we are aware of our condition." As he withdraws his face he looks me gently in the eyes for a second and then he turns away and shouts: "*Lars – my metabolism is getting impatient.*"

Shortly afterwards Lars comes over to Ulla. "Do you want to come outside and do some weed?" he asks in a low voice. She looks at me, raises her eyebrows questioningly and motions towards the door with the side of her head. I nod. Why not? It is Friday night after all and though I am no longer a heavy user, what harm can there be in smoking in moderation – being a recreational smoker.

"Yes," Ulla says with a smile as she slips off the bar stool. We go out, first Pusher Lars, then Ulla and I, then Adrian. Anyone can work out what we are going to do, but fortunately there are no hangers-on – I don't think Lars is the sort you can scrounge off.

We go through the arched passage and continue down the narrow, darkened street to the building on the opposite side of the Kattesund, the back wall of the Ambassadeur dance hall which is plastered with the remains of old concert posters and old graffiti, and there is refuse everywhere. We go up the staircase leading to the fire escape of the Ambassadeur and sit down so that we are hidden by the low wall surrounding the landing on the stairs.

"Will you toast the tobacco?" Lars asks.

"Of course," Adrian says, taking a cigarette by the filter tip from the pack. He puts all the tobacco-filled part in his mouth and sucks it until both paper and tobacco are thoroughly moistened. Then he toasts the cigarette over a lighter. At regular intervals he places the filter between his lips and blows a cloud of smoke out of the end of the cigarette. It is a slightly more practical method for outdoor use than setting things up with silver paper. Actually, I don't mind smoking a joint with untoasted tobacco, but it is obvious that you can taste the hash better if the majority of the nicotine has been toasted out of the cigarette. Then you get a pure high, instead of one adulterated by a nicotine kick.

No-one says a word and I don't really know what to do. Perhaps I could tell them that many Americans are supposed to smoke hash on its own – without tobacco – but I simply don't believe it. You get an unpleasant, cloying, slightly nauseous sensation in your throat if you smoke pure hash. That is why there has to be tobacco in it, but you make it as neutral as possible by toasting it first.

You are always in the spotlight when you talk about something dope-related, but I drop the idea because they know everything about dope already and I don't want to seem banal. I sit looking at Ulla. Tomorrow I am going to go out and buy myself a new dress – and a roll of duct tape.

Stesolid

"What have you done with Svend?" Ulla asks.

Lars produces his lump of hash together with roll-up paper and a jet black joint filter – I think it is ivory. "Svend's in hospital," he says.

"But what happened?" Ulla asks. Adrian begins to laugh and passes Lars the toasted cigarette.

"Weeell – difficult to say," Lars drawls.

"He's probably been arrested or something like that," Adrian brays.

"But . . . what do you mean?" Ulla asks in some confusion.

Lars is sitting taking the paper off a cigarette and sprinkling the tobacco onto the rolling paper for the joint.

"Well, he walloped Steso over the head, then Steso fell over a sort of iron framed table and went out like a light."

"And leaked his contaminated blood all over the floor," Adrian adds.

"And then . . . ?" Ulla asks. Adrian continues:

"Svend calls for an ambulance, of course, and goes with him to the hospital. But the paramedics think that the whole thing is a bit suspicious so they call the police who turn up and interview Svend while Steso is having his skull sewn up. Then they talk to Steso who reports Svend on the spot for assault – you know what Steso is like – then I don't really know what else happened."

Lars is warming a corner of the hash with his lighter. Instantly there is an incredible smell of pollen – it is fantastic hash.

"But why . . . did Svend wallop Steso?" Ulla asks.

"Well, it all started yesterday," Adrian says, smiling to himself for a second before carrying on:" Steso came over to my place and gave me twenty Stesolid – about forty milligrams. He thought I should try them and that if I took all of them at once it would be the right kind of dose for me." Adrian puts his hand on Lars's shoulder: "I rang Lars here to make sure the dose was correct. I know Steso and I know he would love to see me in my death throes from an overdose. He would think that was great because then he could sort of . . . *choose* whether he would save me or not. But it was okay and so I took them."

Lars switches off the lighter. If you warm the hash oil it makes it incredibly easy to crumble. Lars picks the warmed part off with his fingers and sprinkles the hash over the tobacco. Then, with his fingers, he lightly mixes the tobacco with the hash before rolling the joint paper so that it closes tightly around the mixture and the joint filter. Finally he licks the adhesive edge of the paper and sticks it down. His movements bear the mark of an old hand.

"Was it fun being on Stesolid?" Ulla asks.

"Nooo, not fun," Adrian says, looking at her. "But it was cool. It just took away all your feelings. All except one. I was standing on Lisbeth's balcony looking over the town and after a while my mouth began to go dry and I went to get a glass of water."

Lars cautiously taps the mouthpiece of the joint filter against his thigh to compact the mixture before twisting the end of the joint paper with two fingers so that the end is hard up against the mixture.

"What did you feel?" Ulla asks.

"I was standing on the balcony so I could feel how it grew inside me and I looked out over the town thinking: "*Shit, man. All this – it's mine.*

YES." Adrian laughs. "A feeling of total omnipotence, that was the only thing left inside me."

Lars appraises his workmanship. At the tip of the joint there is a little twist of paper.

"Was Steso there at that point?" Ulla asks as Lars takes his key ring and looks for a three-in-one nail-clipper to cut off the little paper tip of the joint which is now ready.

"Yes indeed," Adrian says. "We went to town and everyone kept well clear of us because we owned the world. But then we got home in the morning and Lisbeth had gone to the university and so . . . well Steso has been friends with Lisbeth since they went to kindergarten – so I let him sleep on the sofa. Then Lisbeth comes home and wakes me up. Of course she doesn't know that Steso has been there, but she thinks there is something odd about her bookcase and it turns out that seventeen first editions she inherited from her uncle have gone missing. They had just been stolen."

"Yes, he always knows what has most value," Lars says, passing the joint to Ulla and nodding: she should light it.

Adrian continues:

"Books worth twelve thousand kroner. And Lisbeth lives over the Limfjord in Nørresundby so it takes a little time to get to town and there was no way of knowing when Steso had split. So I rang Svend and said he should shoot over to Pilegaard's in Algade as that was the only antiquarian bookshop in Aalborg with any understanding of first editions."

Ulla is now lighting the joint. The smell is delicious; she inhales deeply.

"Did he get there in time?" I ask.

"Yes, just in time – at the counter. And Svend had to bloody stand there in the shop threatening to call the police before Steso would admit that the books were not his rightful property."

"Was that when Svend hit him?" Ulla asks nasally as she is holding the smoke down in her lungs to allow it to take effect.

"No," Adrian says. "Svend brought him over to Lisbeth's and my place to hand over the books and then they went to see Lars because Svend wanted to buy some hash.

Ulla breathes out, then takes another drag and passes the joint to Lars who motions that it should go to me first. He seems a little reserved towards me, probably because he and Asger are competitors.

I draw on the joint. The hash goes straight to my brain, absolutely perfect. I don't know if Lars has a special relationship with the bikers, but what we are smoking is way above standard.

Lars takes over the story: "Yes and Steso is a bloody strain when he's not on something. The way he whinges, it's almost an art form, so I gave him some Rohypnol I had lying around."

I have heard rumours about Lars's sideline as a pill-pusher. There is a huge market for it among bikers and a variety of psychopaths. Of course, GPs prescribe medicine for people who need it – Methadon, Rohypnol, Stesolid, all sorts of sleeping tablets and anti-depressants. But they vary a lot. Some doctors are prescription factories pure and simple; you just have to show your face and you can get prescriptions for things which you don't really need. The only requirement is that you have to be getting on a bit. So young drug addicts can go and buy the goods at some sleazy pub or a local community place where pensioners and invalids hang out. Pensioners also like to earn a bit of pin money and their doctors hand out prescriptions to avoid hassle.

"So Svend went to Westend to get a couple of beers down him," Lars continues. "Little knowing that Steso had taken Rohypnol, and then they go to Svend's place to have a little spliff."

I pass the joint to Lars who passes it on to Adrian – it is very unusual to let all the others smoke your own joint first. Lars looks at me in a slightly weird way. It makes me think that he must have heard about the police raid already, but perhaps he is too kind to mention it. But maybe there is something else behind it. He is not bad-looking. Well, he is a brickie – he is very well built.

Lars takes the joint from Adrian who has smoke wreathing out of his mouth as he speaks:

"And then Steso sinks his teeth in Svend's arm. Total mayhem. I told Svend he should have an injection against rabies to be on the safe side." Adrian laughs.

"So it was my fault in a way," Lars says.

"No, it bloody wasn't," Adrian says.

"Well, I shouldn't have given him the Rohypnol," says Lars.

"Yes, but you couldn't have known that he would be crazy enough to drink Carlsberg Gold on top of it," Adrian says.

"I could have guessed," Lars says.

"Can't you do that?" I ask.

Adrian explains to me that mixing alcohol and Rohypnol makes people go totally insane. You can do the most bestial things and not remember a thing afterwards. "Like murder and GBH," he says.

"And Steso is sort of . . . it's like he's doing research into incompatible substances," Lars says.

"But what happened then?" Ulla asks impatiently.

Adrian laughs at her. "Yeah, well, when Svend felt his flesh tearing and he was in danger of having a chunk bitten off he remembered a report he had read about hand-to-hand fighting in the Second World War. It said it was very effective to place the tip of your thumb over your opponent's eyeball and press downwards as if you wanted to pop the eye out. It is so painful and is so frightening that the other person stops doing whatever they're doing."

"Why didn't he just kick Steso in the balls?" I ask, wondering if Lars actually has a girlfriend.

"Steso is an agile little bugger and hard to hit," Lars says.

"But what about Svend?" Ulla asks.

"I don't know," Adrian says. "He rang up from the hospital, but at that point the police were still discussing how to deal with the incident. They also know Steso, of course, and they know he's full of shit."

We finish the joint.

"Thanks for the smoke," Ulla says to Lars. He nods to her with that sluggish and slightly coked up expression in his eyes that all hash heads acquire after a long day in the service of hemp and a thought flashes across my mind: *No, two pushers has got to be enough.* We go back into 1000Fryd and sit down at a table.

Slut

After a while Lars leaves – he has to go home and sleep. Actually I am sleepy as well and 1000Fryd closes in half an hour, but I had agreed to go out on the town with Ulla.

Then Big Carsten comes in the door with a real hard-smoking slut called Nina – she tried to pull Gorm when I was living with him. Carsten's relationship with his girlfriend must really be blown to smithereens. Adrian is at the bar talking to Loser who has just slipped in. Nina catches sight of me. She comes over to our table and stands in front of it. Ulla and I look up at her. I realize that Carsten must have told her everything about the day's events.

"Seems things are not going so well for you, are they, you little narco bitch," Nina says. Her face is like an asshole tired of shitting. I can feel my whole body tensing up.

"You are so full of shit inside," I hiss at her. "I know what you're made of. I know what you're like." At that moment she steps forward and slaps me in the face. I throw over my chair and scream at her; I take a swing at her face and hit her neck. I can see Adrian moving towards us as arms clasp me from behind. Adrian is holding Nina's neck with one hand and pulling her backwards away from me. I am so angry that my muscles are trembling.

"Now, now, take it easy now," Ulla whispers, holding me tight from behind. Adrian has taken Nina all the way up to the bar.

"Let's go now," Ulla suggests, loosening her grip. I take my jacket off the back of the chair. I want to go out because I can feel I am on the point of tears and I don't want anyone to see me cry.

Ulla and I go to Griflen in Vesterå. I am completely sober now and feel miserable – if I had just torn the filthy slut's eyes out I am certain I would have felt better. We have a beer and smoke a couple of Ulla's cigarettes – I have run out.

"I'm going home," I say.

"Do you want me to come with you?" Ulla asks.

"If you feel like it, yes, I would really appreciate that."

"Of course I feel like it, my lovely," she says and we walk arm in arm down Borgergade and Kastetvej. If we go down Reberbansgade there is a chance we may bump into people we know and we don't want that. Ulla gives me a big hug in front of the garden gate.

"You've got to leave him," she says. I can only nod in agreement. But where shall I go? I drag my steps to the front door, suddenly very tired.

Punctuated Bleeding

Already before I put the key into the lock I can hear that we have visitors. They are playing *Sabrewolf* on Asger's Atari computer which is linked to the TV. Frank stares at the TV screen with wide, vacant eyes while drumming his fingers on his thighs. Asger is sitting on the edge of a chair with the joystick between his hands, completely engrossed in the killing.

"Hi," I say in the doorway.

"Errr, hi," Frank says, almost without looking up.

"Bloody hell," Asger says as he dies – unfortunately only in the game. "Maria," he says, rising from his chair in a slightly manic way, all jerky movements. The idiots are on amphetamines. I go over to the table to find a cigarette. Asger is standing in the middle of the floor fidgeting and staring at the TV screen. Then I see Loser stretched out on the floor behind the sofa. Shivers run down my spine.

"Asger, what's the matter with Loser?"

"Oh, he's just gone out cold. I'll chuck him out, don't worry."

"How cold?" I ask.

"Cold. How the fuck should I know?" Asger says with a shrug, continuing to concentrate on Frank's game.

I switch on the main light. "Hey," Frank says. Then I go over to Loser and move the coffee table aside so that I can crouch down.

"Did he just lie down to sleep?" I ask.

"No. Heh, heh," Asger chuckles. "He was sort of standing when he fainted."

A thin film of sweat covered Loser's pallid grey forehead.

"What did you do?" I ask, trying to find a pulse in his neck.

"Hey." Asger is beginning to sound irritated. "I'll chuck him out before I go to bed." Loser's neck feels like cool, damp rubber against my fingertips – his pulse is racing. Then I open one of his eyelids. His eyeball is rolled up almost into his skull; it is trembling and the white of his eye appears to have been whisked up with lumpy blood. Punctuated bleeding.

"Asger!" I screech, giving Loser a stinging slap on one side of the face and then on the other. "He has to come round NOW." Asger comes over and stares at Loser.

"He just has to sleep it off."

"NO," I say. "There's no life in his eyes. I think he's in a coma. How much did he take?" I ask.

"Take?" Asger asks in mock innocence. He knows I don't have any time for people who take amphetamines. Well, I tried it once and it was really wonderful, almost too wonderful. You have the whole world served up on a silver platter and your brain penetrates EVERYTHING. You can explain how things interconnect and the shit from your mouth simply streams out. You smoke all the time, the cigarettes taste simply incredible and you drink without getting drunk. You are a world champion. What a night! By ten o'clock the next morning you have worked your way through at least forty cigarettes, a large handful of joints and twenty-five bottles of beer – and that is as a girl. And then suddenly it hits you all at once – your mouth freezes and you are like dead for the next forty-eight hours. Unhealthy and bloody dangerous, I think. At least in my case, I was up for more, to feel so on top of things again, but when it comes down to it is just "hippy self-deception" as my father calls his LSD experiences when you ask him now.

It must have been some bad 'a' Asger and Frank took because they don't talk much; their motor functions are just a bit too frenetic. Baker's speed: stuffed full with flour and sugar, crushed tranquilizers and finely ground glass.

"Yes. How much speed did he take?" I ask.

"Hey, what do you want me to do?" Asger throws up his arms in despair. I slap Loser two more times. My fingers sink into his face; it reacts in the same way that wax does and the indentations remain, no rush of blood.

"He has to go in the shower," I say and begin loosening his belt and the buttons of his trousers.

"What the fuck's going on with Loser?" Frank asks casually as he turns his head and looks at us over his shoulder.

"TURN OFF THAT FUCKING TV NOW," I shout at him and go back to Asger: "Pull his shoes off." Frank switches off the TV so that he can concentrate on the events in the room. Strange.

"Maria wants Loser's body," Asger says to Frank. I push Asger to the side and tear Loser's shoes off myself. Then I try pulling Loser's trousers off, but he is surprisingly heavy so first I have to edge the waistband down over his bum. He is not wearing any bloody pants underneath and his dick and balls give off a smell of frost damaged onions and ammonia.

"Fucking hell," I mumble.

"Yes, his hygiene isn't quite top drawer," Asger says. We are standing there with a guy in a coma and the twat is trying to be funny. His trousers slide off now without any trouble.

"Carry him into the bathroom," I tell Asger. Amazingly, he immediately bends down and begins to lift Loser off the floor. It suddenly occurs to me that I am standing there with legs akimbo, my hands on my hips and a very angry expression on my face.

Asger puts his arms under Loser's shoulders from behind and starts dragging him towards the bathroom. The soft clunk as Loser's heels go over the door bar of the door frame almost reduces me to tears. It is not until now that I think of calling for an ambulance. Asger has got Loser into the bathroom and is about to put him down on the floor.

"Hold him up," I say as I scramble past and snatch the shower head down from the wall.

"I'll get wet, for Christ's sake," Asger shouts. Indifferent and fascinated, Frank stands gawking behind us in the doorway.

"Wouldn't you rather call for an ambulance?" I ask between gritted teeth while turning the hot tap full on. I decide to call the emergency number if nothing happens in the next two minutes.

"Right," Asger says meekly. I hold the shower head in front of Loser's face so that the jets of water squirt into his face.

"I'M GETTING WET, FOR FUCK'S SAKE," Asger shouts.

"Slap his face a few times," I shout to Asger. "NOW." I can see in his face that he is about to lose his temper.

"Okay, okay," Asger answers coldly. He lets go of Loser with one hand, which means that he has to move even closer to keep the body up against the wall so that it doesn't flop down onto the floor. Now Asger really does get wet. He systematically slaps Loser about the face.

"Not too hard," I say as I shower Loser's body up and down. His T-shirt sticks to his skinny pigeon chest. His eyelids tremble. They open, the eyeballs roll down in their sockets and come to a halt in the correct position. Jackpot.

"Harrrrumph," he mumbles.

"Okay, sit him down," I say. Asger lets go of Loser so he flops down on the floor. He looks up at us with disoriented eyes.

"Ohh, hell," Asger says, turning round and leaving the bathroom. He is soaked to the skin. Loser looks up at me, speechless, as I continue to spray him with the shower. I realize that my top has got wet and it is sticking to my tits, ribs and stomach. My trousers are tight up against my mound and cling to the curves of my thighs as if all my clothes are made of duct tape.

"Maria," he says in astonishment.

"Hi Loser, "I say. "Enjoy the sight." He opens and closes his mouth a couple of times – a stranded fish.

"Thanks," he mumbles. I start laughing. He sits there examining me from top to toe and actually appears to be extremely happy. "Did I go out cold?" he asks with his great staring eyes.

"You were completely gone."

"Maria . . . I'm very sorry."

"Don't worry about it." He rubs his face.

"Ohhh," he says, suddenly holding his hands in front of his private parts.

"It's a bit late now, Loser, but I think you should have a wash. Take your T-shirt off and I'll find another one for you." I put the shower head back on its rest on the wall and turn to go out of the bathroom.

"Okay," Loser says, "Oh beautiful . . . ohh." Loser nods and devours me with his eyes. I look back at him before leaving.

"Yes, aren't I," I say.

Jesus

Asger and Frank are back in the living room. They are only bloody playing their game again. I pull off my drenched clothes and put on an undershirt and underpants before looking for one of my old T-shirts for Loser. I find a worn one with Jim Morrison standing in a Jesus pose. No. I want to keep that one. Then I realize that I don't like Jim Morrison any more and actually it would be perfect for Loser. One loser with another loser. I go back to the bathroom and place it on the toilet seat together with a hand towel.

"Thanks, Maria," he says and switches off the shower. Then I go into the living room and sit down at the table where I find a ciggy and light up.

"Is he okay now?" Asger asks.

"Yes."

"Hmm. The little shit." A little while later Loser comes into the living room with a towel round his waist and Jim Morrison on his chest.

"Umm, sorry," Loser says. Asger turns round to face him.

"Get out right now," he says.

"Alright," Loser says – his face is still as white as chalk.

"No," I say in a matter of fact voice. I am not sure Loser has anywhere to go and his body is completely out of synch so he is bound to be ill.

"What!" says Asger.

"He's sleeping on the sofa."

"You can bloody . . . ," Asger starts.

I interrupt him. "Otherwise I'm leaving you . . . *right now*."

Grumbling, Asger goes back to his computer game. "Women," he says in an attempt to pass off my insubordination as a joke in front of Frank. Asger ignores me. And he is wise to do so because he knows that I mean it. I smoke the cigarette to the end, then stub it out. What a day.

Loser pulls his trousers on as noiselessly as possible. He looks across at me dolefully. I point to him, point to the sofa, point to the plaid rug at one end of the sofa and gesture to him that he should lie down on the sofa and pull the rug over him. He gives a nod of gratitude. I take two more cigarettes from the packet and light them both. Asger and Frank are sitting with their backs to the sofa. Loser's body seems even frailer now that it is under the rug. I pass him one of the lit cigarettes. He mouths the word 'Thanks' – in total silence.

I go into the bedroom. Asger's wet clothes lie in a pile on the floor. I throw them into the laundry basket with mine and open the curtains so I can see into the back garden. Twister and Tripper are slowly walking around the run with their heads sunk low. They look immensely dejected. I switch on the tiny TV we have in the bedroom and turn down the volume. I sit back in bed and zap through the channels. I miss Ulla.

On the Discovery Channel a peacock struts around proudly; it thrusts its chest out – pea green, self- important, imperious and proud. In the dusk it goes to rest after graduated hops from the ground to a fence post and finally up onto a high branch.

It carries its plumage behind it and the plumage is caught under a car tire in the drive because it refuses to hurry. It is so vain – it seems to be trying to manoeuvre itself into a good position so that it looks regal in front of the camera. Comical peacock chicks practise with their small feather dusters.

Finally, there is the ultimate display when the male of the species vibrates and shakes his feathers in a kind of ecstasy – hundreds of richly coloured eyes spread out in a fan behind his body. He pumps up his chest and stretches out his long, shiny neck. The eyes are haughty, eternally penetrating like small glass beads in the ugly, yet profoundly aristocratic head. I imagine that the sound the tail makes is similar to when you shake a young deciduous tree bearing almost desiccated leaves. It would be really great to have one of these peacock feathers tattooed on your shoulder, or perhaps on your back. Or on your *buttocks*. Yes.

The next morning I have a hangover. I force my mouth open. It tastes as if someone has been burning car tires in it.

All 107 kilos of Lone

"Stupid woman" I shout at my case officer – all 107 kilos of Lone – when I find out that she is going to force me to see a doctor of their choice to have my neck injury examined. If I don't, they will stop my social security money. Naturally enough the doctor doesn't find a bloody thing wrong with my bloody neck.

"So we're assuming that you will be at school at nine o'clock on Monday or we will be forced to stop your payments," the 107 kilos say to me at our next meeting. Who the fuck is "we" and who is doing the forcing? School – oh, fuck, no.

Asger grills me thoroughly when I return home from the social security office. Not because he is interested, but he wants me to keep receiving money of course so that I can pay my share of the rent.

"You'll have to do it, Maria," he says with an Olympian attempt at empathy. Up yours. He walks round looking pathetic, sets the alarm clock, orders an early morning call and wonders whether I shouldn't go to bed soon.

I have slept a measly five hours when the alarm clock goes off. Asger shoves me out of bed; he even gets up himself to make sure I don't lie down on the sofa. And he calls for a taxi for me.

First lesson on the timetable is English. Some nerdy young woman with glasses and stiff body language stands by the board. Her job is to make us – the clients, the riff raff, the detainees – think. Society deems that we are in need of social rehabilitation. The young woman is party to that and she wants us to analyze Pink Floyd's song "Another Brick in the Wall." Is she being patronizing? Should we take this as humiliation? Is it irony? Or is she trying to make me conscious of my role in the social machinery?

I put up my hand.

"Yes?" she says, standing up on the tips of her toes, peering down at me and nodding encouragingly. I stand up.

"This," I say, "is simply too pathetic for words." I take my denim jacket from the back of my chair and leave the room without closing the door. No-one utters a word behind me. So there I am in East Aalborg at half past nine in the morning. Asger hasn't got up yet and I am a little high – it is a long time since I got up so early and it is actually really cool. I buy rolls and coffee at a cafeteria. What shall I do? I consider that while flicking through an old copy of *Ekstra Bladet.* Hossein. Of course. I ask for a telephone directory and find him: Hossein Kalvâti, 14 Finlandsgade, fourth flat on the left, close by Østre Anlæg park. I think about calling him first, but it isn't very far and I would rather surprise him.

Entry Holes

Twenty minutes later I am standing in front of his door in an old-fashioned, red brick block of flats. He must be up – I am fairly certain it is his flat the music is coming from. Grace Jones – I would never have guessed that.

"One moment," I hear from inside the flat. One moment later the door is opened.

"Beautiful Maria," he exclaims in surprise – his broad smile is wreathed in shaving cream and his powerful, hairy chest is staring me in the face. He is only wearing is a towel wrapped around his lower body. I can see two round scars at the bottom of his abdomen on one side – they must be gun wounds.

"Oohh, I didn't want to disturb you," I say a little nervously. Hossein steps to the side and waves me in.

"You never disturb, Maria. Welcome."

"Thank you," I say and go in.

"I soon finished," Hossein says, making his way to the bathroom. I can't see the exit holes when he turns his back to me – they must be covered by the towel or else the bullets are still inside him. At the top of his back he has three jagged bits of scar tissue. They are too irregular to come from a bayonet, I guess. Perhaps he was hit by shrapnel from a grenade.

The flat smells of Hossein's cigarillos, but there is a smell of dough, too. While taking my jacket off and hanging it on a hook I survey the room. It is clean and austerely furnished except for a number of large green plants.

"Don't forget to remove the slug," I shout in the direction of the bathroom door.

"The what?" He sticks his head out of the door. I put my hand up to my face and run my index finger under my nose.

"This," I say.

"No, Maria, it become ugly," he says.

I go into the living room. White walls and a light parquet floor, no curtains. There is a dining table with four chairs, a sofa, an armchair and a coffee table, all in teak, simple and clean lines, from the fifties perhaps. A standard lamp beside the armchair, a clean ash tray and a copper dish on the table, a couple of Aladdin lamp-like jugs and boxes on the window sill. Finally there is a TV set and a little book shelf with some books and a ghetto blaster on. And then there are the plants, all in big pots on the floor; there is one on each side of the window looking out to the street, one in each corner of the room and one beside the TV. Seven in all, the smallest of which is one metre, thirty. On the walls there are only two photographs, in mosaic frames and covered with glass, which you can see if you are sitting in the armchair. One is of two middle-aged people standing on either side of an old woman in front of a white house – maybe Hossein's parents and grandmother; the other is of a thin young man in military uniform with a huge slug and a machine gun. It has to be Hossein as a very young man – it doesn't really look like him. The Grace Jones CD has finished. I turn round when I hear Hossein coming out of the bathroom.

"I'm ready in a moment," he says, going into what must be the bedroom. I catch a glimpse of him – he also has thick black hair on his shoulders and back, and his muscles are clearly defined under his skin.

"You didn't take it off," I call over to him and somehow feel a little embarrassed. After all, I didn't come to talk about his bloody moustache, for Christ's sake.

"Hossein must not look like chicken's ass, like Danish man," he says from inside the bedroom. I go into the hall and try to catch a glimpse of him through the bedroom door, which is ajar, but all I can see is the corner of a bed which has been made, straightened and smoothed over, with the quilt cover tucked under the mattress at the top and sides.

I go into the kitchen where my eye is caught by a large golden samovar with loads of intricate designs and embellishments standing out in relief on the holder and lid. Otherwise the kitchen is spartan and tidy. On the table there is a bowl with dough in, covered with a damp cloth.

"You're baking," I shout to Hossein.

"Nune barbari," he shouts back.

Then he comes into the kitchen wearing loose fitting khaki canvas trousers and a white shirt of a soft material which he wears outside his trousers. There is a wonderful smell of after shave.

"A cup of tea? Coffee?" he offers. I lean up against the tabletop feeling awkward because we are standing so close to each other in the small kitchen.

"Only if you're having one," I answer.

"Yes, I going to have tea, but first I have to roll bread – otherwise it go wrong," Hossein apologizes.

"Oh, well, I would like to watch."

"Okay," he says, tipping the dough from the bowl out onto the table where he flattens it and rolls it out into one large piece which he puts in a roasting pan he has greased earlier.

"Don't you know any jokes, Hossein," I ask, because I don't know what to say.

"But Maria, I know only dirty stories," he says while poking holes in the bread dough with the tips of his fingers until it is covered with indentations.

"Okay," Hossein says. "I tell you the story from North Iran. They say that North Iran people they not religious actually. People say they very earthy. And the man he limpdick and woman, oh dear, they are wild – have many lovers."

Hossein has finished working with the dough and washes his hands before going to the fridge for eggs and yoghurt, all the while continuing to tell the joke:

"Once upon a time there was North Iran man, he had to go on trip and so he tell his wife: *I have to go on trip. I come in a week.* And the wife she say: *Okay, have a good trip.* But the husband, he suspicious – he think: *Hmm, let me test my wife.*"

Hossein breaks an egg, pours off the egg white into a glass on which he places a lid and then puts it back in the fridge. He mixes the egg yolk with yoghurt.

"So the man he go under bed and take a bowl full of milk, he put it under bed, then he hang iron rod from bed, so if a person lie above in bed, iron not touch milk, but if two persons lie above in bed then iron rod touch milk so you can see iron is dip in milk – so you can see it on iron."

Hossein has spread the mixture of egg yolk and yoghurt over the bread in the roasting pan and is about to sprinkle sesame seeds on it. He puts everything down and looks me in the eye.

"So the man – he come back after just one day and the milk become butter because so much rod went up and down." He stands there holding my gaze when he has finished and I can feel my cheeks getting warm – so warm that I have to turn away.

A Woman's Touch

Hossein opens the oven door and pushes the roasting pan in. "Now we have tea," he says and asks me how strong I like it while locating two glasses in a cupboard.

"Strong," I say. Hossein takes the little jug standing on top of the samovar and pours a very black liquid into each glass. It is almost like tea extract – I can smell the tannin in it right away. Afterwards he opens the tap at the side of the samovar and fills the glasses almost to the brim with boiling water.

"You want have milk?" Hossein asks. I say no and he arranges the glasses with the tea in, a sugar bowl and a plate of Bastogne biscuits on a round tray made of beaten copper which he carries into the living room and places on the coffee table.

"You live in a nice place," I say, "but isn't it a bit bare?"

"Yes, I'm old soldier." Hossein says with a flourish of his hands: "It need the woman's touch."

"What kind of tea is this?" I ask.

"It is strong tea – very bitter. You should take sugar. I will show you."

I take the lid off the sugar bowl which contains irregular sized lumps of sugar candy. Hossein has put the glass of tea in front of me but he has forgotten teaspoons. I take a lump of sugar candy with my fingers to put it in the tea.

"No, no, I will show you Iran way," he says.

"Okay," I say, putting the sugar back.

"But it very difficult if you haven't done before," Hossein says, taking a piece of candy and placing it between his front teeth. Then he drinks the tea *through* the sugar, which remains positioned between his teeth.

"You try it now," he says and I do, but I immediately wash the sugar into my mouth with the tea.

"Try again," he says. "You must practise." The second time I pour the tea down my front because I am concentrating on not pouring too much tea into my mouth at once. Then I start laughing.

"Oh no," Hossein says. "I'm sorry."

"It's okay," I say, lighting up a cigarette. "That's the kind of tea to drink if you've been taking opium."

"Yes," Hossein says slowly. "But the opium not something you should take often."

"No, no," I say, and a small awkward silence follows, not because I wanted to take any opium, it was just, well, to say something.

"How things going at home?" Hossein asks.

"Asger is . . . ," I make a gesture of indifference with my hand and my facial expression indicates how hopeless I think he is.

"Yes, he is the . . . infidel dog," Hossein says slowly.

"Haven't you got any Persian music?" I ask because I don't really feel like talking about my home life – I mean, it's not going that great.

"Yes, I have it," Hossein says, raising his eyebrows. "You want hear it?"

"Yes, of course," I say. He gets up and puts a cassette in the ghetto blaster. The tones that emerge are unfamiliar, but it sounds fine until a man begins singing in such a sad, sentimental way that I think it is . . . tedious.

"What's he singing about?" I ask.

"About love. Always they sing about love," Hossein says.

"He doesn't sound very happy."

"No, it is very sad."

"Can you translate it?"

"Yes, perhaps a little. He unhappy because she play with his heart, but now she will not have him – she stay with the other man."

"Is that always unhappy?"

"Like in reality. Often the love is unhappy."

"Yes, there could be something in that. Who is that?" I ask, pointing to the pictures. Hossein smiles.

"It is my father and my mother and in middle my grandmother," he says, pointing. "And that is my little brother, Mahmad."

"What does he do now?"

"My little brother? He live in Copenhagen. We can go visit him. He live with his wife – they get married last year in Greece."

"Is he also a . . . refugee?" I ask.

"Yes," Hossein says. "He made political activity at university – the religious police come after him."

"What does he do now?"

"Now he work at laboratory – Novo Nordisk," Hossein says with obvious pride.

"But wasn't he a soldier?" I ask, glancing towards the picture where he is standing with a machine gun.

"No," Hossein says," not a real soldier. Only the conscription after war."

"What about his wife?"

"Marjân. She still learn Danish. She wants be . . . a nursy teacher?

"Nursery teacher?"

"Yes, the one look after children." He tells me that Marjân is their cousin and the families arranged for Hossein's little brother to meet her on holiday last year in Turkey. "It is prestige for parents when daughter come to Europe," he says and explains that Iranians think that relationships are easy with Europeans because they are civilized. "With European you can discuss about things and if you not agree you can just discuss more. But you don't *need* agree. You don't need go to war just because you don't agree."

"So all Iranians want to come to Europe?"

"Very important, yes," Hossein says with a glint in his eye. "There was a man, he tell people he going to Europe but he can't afford. So he tell his wife: *If anyone come, ask you where I am, you just tell them I am in Europe, and I go hide under bed.*" Hossein starts smiling. He is taking the bait.

"Next day a man come into house and go to bed with her. Her husband under the bed and say to himself: *Just wait, when I come back from Europe then I know what I do with you.* Very important to travel to Europe."

I smile at him. "But what about love?" I ask.

"What do you mean – what about love?"

"Do they love each other, your brother and his wife?"

"Yes, they are lucky because they love each other – really," Hossein says.

"Wasn't there a cousin for you?" I ask.

"A cousin for what?"

"A cousin you could marry?" Hossein gives a cheeky smile, but then he is serious again.

"I not try to build Iran here. In Denmark I can live with a Dane, easy."

"You want a Danish wife?"

"Yes, Danish wife, Danish children with black hair – but the children they must speak Persian with their father because he come from Iran. Then it is good."

"Are you on the lookout for a Danish wife?"

"Almost – perhaps. *Insh'allah* – God willing. I am looking for the wife. You don't just take random woman to have woman. You must have right woman, so you have respect."

"But what about Marjân . . . does she wear a veil?" I ask. Hossein suddenly sits back on the sofa.

"No, no, – never. She is free woman. My brother is not Muslim. According to Islam a man can be divorce his wife if he just say three times he want it. *Thalak, thalak, thalak* – then everything over. It crazy religion. The veil only there to repress woman."

"I don't suppose that is the priests' explanation for women having to wear a veil, is it?" I ask.

"No, no. The priests say it because they want protect woman from suspicion that she flirt by show her hair to other men."

Hossein sits smiling at me and I realize that I am in fact tossing my hair; put my hands up to tuck my hair behind my ears.

"What's so dangerous about hair?" I ask.

"A man can be horny when he look at woman's hair," Hossein says. There is a little teasing smile in his eyes and I simply don't know where to put myself.

Terrorist

"Have a good day, sweetheart," Asger says from bed as I am on my way out of the door next morning. He thinks I am going to school. This man couldn't catch a cold. The whole situation is deeply depressing. So deeply depressing that I consider whether I should move in with my mother and Hans-Jørgen and improve my school-leaving grades. But what good would they be? Well . . . what the hell shall I do? And all the time I am walking around with a really strange sensation inside me. It is not hash paranoia because that has gone and it doesn't feel like the paranoia I had when I gave up smoking but it is still a paranoia or . . . only a feeling that something is lying in wait, trembling just outside my field of vision.

I go to my mother's studio. When she sees me step inside the door, she knocks a container of pastel coloured glaze over a whole table covered with beads.

"Oh no," she says and stands there wringing her hands as she alternately looks down at the flooded table and at me with a hangdog look. "Maria . . . ." she starts but comes to a halt.

"What's up?" I ask.

"Oh dear, I'm just . . . ." she says. She makes a half-hearted gesture with her arms and then folds them around her waist.

"Dad says 'hello'," I say and the accursed trembling gets stronger and stronger – I can almost taste it, whatever it is.

"Oh," she says. "Is he alright?" She looks at me with eyes full of expectation – a little frightened, I think to myself.

"He's an alcoholic," I say.

"Oh . . . I didn't know that."

"You should go out and see him one day," I say.

"I am . . . ." she says and comes to a halt.

"He's still got all your books and knick-knacks."

"Maria . . . he went insane."

"Perhaps you should have got some help instead of simply taking off with me. And perhaps you should have made sure that he could come and see me, his daughter."

"He tried to kill me," my mother says.

"He didn't mean to."

"No." She looks around the room. There is no-one else there. Then she faces me. "How's it going with . . . Asger?" she manages to ask before her gaze wanders off again. Suddenly it all fits into place. I remember a scene in a gangster film I once saw.

"Does it give you a feeling of power when you report someone to the police?" I ask, walking over and stopping in front of her.

"It wasn't me who . . . ." my mother says, but stops in mid-stream. She stands quite still looking at me tensely, to see if she has given herself away.

"Did what? Tell me what you didn't do? How do you know what I'm talking about?" I look into her eyes. She looks down at her hands. Begins crying.

"Yes, but all I really want is you to . . . ," she says. I stare at her for a long time until she raises her head and looks me in the eyes.

"I know who you are," I say. "I know what you're like." I let the words hang there and then I speak slowly with marked pauses: "I never want to be like you." I see the skin tighten on her face just as the slap hits me across the cheek, and then her hands are up in front of her face – she is shocked by her own actions. I hold her imploring gaze. Then I quietly shake my head. "Tut, tut," I say. And turn away from her. I make my way towards the door. Feeling that there is still hope, oddly enough. My mother almost screams when I leave.

"Maria . . . ?"

I don't say anything to Asger when I get home.

Kûn-é-morgh

Again I am walking towards the station, this time with only five thousand kroner in my pocket. Asger will not tell me where he got the money from, but he is desperate for some hash to sell. Hossein looks quite strange when I catch sight of him in the station. *He has shaved off his slug.* I run over to him and stand up on the tips of my toes so that I can kiss him on the side of his mouth.

"Thanks," I say. Hossein raises his eyebrows and points to his mouth.

"You aware you kiss the chicken's ass?" he asks.

"I like it," I say, giving him a smack on the bum. Firm bum. I go in and buy the tickets and then we stand on the platform waiting for the train.

"Why you come too if I know Axel?" Hossein asks.

"Well, Asger is pretty paranoid. He thinks it might occur to you to steal his money. I can hear in my voice how drained I feel.

"I will tell you the story," Hossein says.

"A joke?" I ask hopefully.

"The story about paranoid wimp," Hossein says smiling and tells me about a man who goes on holiday and asks his neighbour opposite to keep an eye on his house while he is away.

"He say his neighbour: *Keep eye on my house and my wife while I not there so nothing happen.* And neighbour say: *Alright, I do that.* Then man come back – go straight to neighbour. *Well, what happened then while I was away?* The neighbour is little nervous: *First day a man, he come and talk with your wife.* The husband put his bag down on the floor. *Well?* he ask. Neighbour answer: *Yes, but they just talk. Then he went. The day after he went in hall,* neighbour say. So the man put his hand in pocket and say: *Yes?* Neighbour say: *But they just talk and then he went. So third day he came, he went in living room.* The husband take his knife out, say: *Yes?* Neighbour say: *But they just talk. So he went. Fourth day the man came, he went in bedroom.* The husband open the knife in hand, say: *Yes?* Neighbour say: *Curtains were closed, I couldn't see very much.* So the husband say: *Ooohh. You have bad thoughts about my wife, neighbour.* So the husband he put knife back in his pocket and go home to his wife."

In the train Hossein tells me that we have been invited by his little brother and his sister-in-law to dinner at six.

"But how will we get home?"

"We take night train," Hossein says.

When we have finished business with Axel I call Asger and tell him we will be late because there are extra police out around Christiania, so I will have to take the night train back.

"Ring when you're out of Christiania," Asger says and I can hear the paranoia rising. "What about Hossein?" he asks.

"He has to visit some cousin or other," I answer.

"Fuck his bloody cousin. He hasn't got cold feet, has he? "

"No, no, for fuck's sake. He'll get the stuff out alright," I say.

We take the number eight to Brønshøj, better known as the Dope Express as it goes directly to Christiania, but we go the opposite way, with people who have made their purchases.

In the taxi on the last part of the way to the address, Hossein tells me that his little brother's name is Mahmad which is the shortened Iranian version of Mohammed. Mahmad's wife calls him Mami which is an affectionate form. Her name is Marjân which is a Hebrew name from the Old Testament. "But you can call her same you – Maria. She called that by her Danish friends."

I feel slightly awkward. "What have you told them about me?" I ask.

"That you lovely girl," Hossein says. I ask him if they know where he knows me from. "No," he answers." I have met you in town at discotheque." I want to ask him why it is that we are in Copenhagen together, but what the hell – it doesn't matter.

The sister-in-law opens the door. "*Bâ khodet chekâr kardi*?" she asks and holds her hand in front of her mouth. Then she shouts: "*Mami, Mami*," takes Hossein's face between her hands and kisses him on both cheeks. As she lets him go she runs the thumb of her right hand along his shaven top lip and giggles.

Hossein looks up at the ceiling. "Why I have taken it away?" he mumbles.

The sister-in-law stands in front of me a little undecided. She is dressed like an Italian woman. A dark blue blouse in a soft shimmering material with a lace collar and the letters CD embossed on golden buttons the size of large coins. Christian Dior. Slacks and court shoes. Armband, necklace, earrings, dripping in gold. I stand there in my bleached jeans, patterned leather boots, Jaguar vest with batik print, tight-fitting denim jacket and a large red postman-style coat that goes well with my hair. Perhaps I should have toned the colours down a little. Then she offers her hand and says tentatively," Hello . . . welcome."

"*Salâm*," I say. Hossein taught me that in the taxi – it means 'hello' in Persian. Then she breaks out into a big smile and embraces me and I receive kisses on both cheeks.

"*Hossein*," comes a shout from the other end of the corridor and Mahmad, a younger, smoother version of Hossein – with slug – comes hurtling out. He hurriedly shakes hands with me. "Welcome," he says and then he goes into a bear hug with Hossein.

"*Kûn-e-morgh*," Mahmad says, grabbing Hossein's chin with his hand. "*Mager mardo nito az dast dâdi, bacheh sosûl shodi*?" he says, continuing to turn Hossein's face from side to side, staring at it in wonder and astonishment. "*Kun-e-morgh*," Mahmad repeats.

"What does that mean?" I ask.

"Chicken's ass," Hossein says. "He ask if I'm still man."

"*Bebinam, Bache ye sosûl shodi, nakoneh mikhâi beri Qazvin*?"

Hossein raises his eyebrows and looks at me reprovingly:

"Now he asks if I will move to the town where the birds only fly over on one wing because they must cover asshole."

Mahmad bursts into laughter. His wife tries to steer us out of the hall.

"Come inside," Mahmad says in perfect Danish with very little accent. Marjân disappears into the kitchen while we are led into the living room and are shown to two armchairs, obviously the best two seats in the house. Just like in Hossein's place there are lots of green plants; some are creepers and coil round wires screwed to the walls to ceiling height. There are Persian carpets on the floor and on a couple of the walls there are woven tapestries with motifs that must originate from Persia. You can clearly see the woman's touch – there are masses of ornaments. At the other end of the room the table is already set for dinner. On the coffee table there are dishes of fruit and nuts, some cream-filled biscuits and cookies.

Mahmad asks if we have had a good trip, if things are going well in Aalborg and if we are staying until the following day. He produces an old picture in which Hossein is standing in front of a tank with three others – all with slugs. He says that he has the same type of cowboy boots as me but his wife won't let him wear them. Then Mahmad looks deep into my eyes and says in amazement: "They are so blue they're almost silver."

Hossein sends him a look and says something in Persian which makes him slap his thigh and laugh out loud.

"The little brother, he dangerous," Husssein says, shaking his head.

Then Marjân returns from the kitchen carrying an imitation silver tray on which there are floral pattern coffee cups and a bowl of sugar lumps and sugar candy. There are also teaspoons and the tea has already been poured. We each receive a dessert dish and a little knife so we can peel the fruit and have somewhere to put the nutshells.

Hossein and Mahmad sit cracking toasted pumpkin seeds between their front teeth. It is only Hossein who drinks the tea through a lump of candy; I am not going to be caught spilling it all down my front today.

Marjân has already dashed into the kitchen again, but now she is back and standing in front of the coffee table. "Take more," she says again and again, and Mahmad does, too. We eat for gold; it is just like Denmark in times gone by – the hosts have to show that they lack for nothing. Now she has rushed off into the kitchen again and a delicious aroma wafts in.

Khoresht sabzi

"Um, would it be okay to look in the kitchen?" I ask, glancing at Mahmad.

"Yes, of course," he says, inviting me with a sweep of his arm. Mahmad and Hossein move closer together and before I am even out of the room they are quietly speaking in Persian as if they are on speed.

I intentionally make a sound with my boots on the floor as I enter the kitchen. Marjân stirring a pot but she turns round when she hears me.

"Hi," she says with a hesitant smile while looking around worriedly to check that whether everything is alright.

"That smells good," I say, moving over to the stove. There are lids on two of the pots. The smell comes from the third.

"Almost done," Marjân says. I lean over the pot. It is a kind of stew made with small cubes of lamb, vegetables and red beans. It smells slightly sourish and is greenish-black in colour.

"What's it called?" I ask, pointing to the pot.

"*Khoresht sabzi*" she says. She nods and calls for Mami; she keeps nodding as she points to the door, but no-one comes. I take a step into the corridor. They are no longer in the living room.

"Hossein?" I shout.

"Here," Hossein shouts, apparently in the bedroom behind the closed door. I don't know if to knock or just go in, but then Hossein opens the door.

"What are you doing?" I ask.

"Mahmad is showing me his new suit," Hossein says. I look past him and see Mahmad pushing the drawer into the bottom of the bed, turning the key, taking it out and discreetly dropping it into his trouser pocket while turning round with a smile.

"Right, we're coming now," he says and accompanies me into the kitchen where Marjân natters away to him in Persian, then gestures for me to come. She wants me to hear what he has to say.

"Now I'll tell you what it is. *Khoreshti sabzi*. 'Khoresht' means that it is a kind of stew and 'sabzi' that it is made with fresh herbs and vegetables. And then there is chilli and dried limes which give the meal a sour flavour. In addition, there is lamb and beans." Mahmad nods. Marjân says something to him.

"Well, let's eat now," he says and he goes to the fridge for some fizzy drinks. Marjân is busy ladling the food into bowls and I can feel that I am in the way in the kitchen so I go to the living room and sit down beside Hossein.

"What was that about?" I ask. He leans over to me.

"He owe me some money, but it not good idea for Marjân to know about it."

"Oh," I say and suddenly Marjân is in the room calling us to the table.

Each place is set with a bottle of Fanta. They have already been opened. It looks bizarre and actually I would prefer to have water or wine, but I don't want to say anything. There are two large dishes on the table with smaller dishes and flat plates of yoghurt, pickled garlic and cucumber, boats of raw onion and a salad with everything finely diced. Lastly, there is a dish of white rice mixed with large flat pieces of something else, something yellow. Mahmad tells me that there are two kinds of rice: rice with beans and dill, and the rice in the dish which he pronounces as *ta-ah dic*. "*Ta-ah dic* is what was at the bottom of the pot – the yellow stuff," he says. "It consists of slices of potato and oil."

Hossein and I are asked to help ourselves first and it tastes really good. The white rice has a slightly perfumed flavour and the yellow pieces from the bottom of the pot are crispy and delicious. As soon as Hossein starts eating he says something to Marjân which immediately makes her blush. Mahmad laughs. I send him a questioning look.

"The rice," he says, pointing to my plate. "This is how we judge whether a woman is good at cooking or not."

"How can you see that?" I ask.

"The bottom must be firm and crispy while the rice over it is fluffy with long firm grains," Mahmad says.

"It is absolutely good," Hossein says.

"It tastes really good," I say to Marjân.

"Thank you," she says, nodding and smiling. "Thank you, thank you."

The meat dish, khoresht sabzi, is delicious, too – sharp and sour. Even the lettuce has a special taste – I think it is called Roman salad. The only things I don't eat are the boats of raw onion, but Hossein carefully separates the layers of onion and takes the film between them off before he puts them in his mouth. I ask him why.

"Membrane give a . . . ." He searches for the word. "Bad for digestion." Mahmad says something to Marjân who shakes her head at Hossein.

"It's just a superstition," Mahmad says to me.

Foreigners

In fact, Fanta goes very well with the food. As soon as the bottle is finished it is replaced with another, also opened and ready, so it is difficult to say 'no' and I make sure to not finish it during the meal as I am not used to so much sugar.

"Are you a couple?" Mahmad asks. Hossein studies the ceiling.

"No," I say.

"When will you be?"

"Difficult to say," I answer coyly and Hossein gives me a smile. I ask about Mahmad's work. He likes it, but he is looking forward to Marjân learning Danish so that she can get a job. She would like to be a nursery teacher. He would like to buy a house.

"But don't you like living here?" I ask. "It's a wonderful apartment."

"Yes, but there are too many Turks and Muslims here. It's almost a . . . ghetto," Mahmad says.

"Don't Iranians like Turks?" I ask. Perhaps it is the same sort of relationship as we have with the Swedes.

"Yes and no," Mahmad says. He tells me that Iranians in the north western part of Iran are of Turkish origin and well educated. He says that Iran has been controlled by Turks for many generations. They live in the best part of the country in attractive, efficiently run towns.

Hossein interrupts him: "That is why it go wrong in Iran. Because of Turks. They take all wealth to their part and they have many mountains and apples." I look across at Mahmad.

"There's something in that," he says. "The part we come from, in the south, there we had masses of oil but people live in terrible poverty. Near the border to Afghanistan many people still live in the stone age."

"So you don't like living with Turks from Iran?" I ask. It seems very prejudiced to me. I mean the man is an Iranian, he is a refugee and he is dark-skinned.

"You misunderstand," Hossein says. "Iranian Turks not see themselves as Turks. If they see Turkish Turk in the street, they think: *Oh no*. So, they a kind of Iranian and speak Turkish at home. But they have no connection with Turkish village peasant who come to Denmark in seventies – those peasants they orthodox religious."

Mahmad nods: "That's right. Iranians in Denmark never go to the mosque."

Hossein's face darkens when the word 'mosque' is mentioned. "The mosque is like cancer in town," he says. "When I go by, my hairs stand up."

"But can't everyone follow their religion as they want?" I ask, because that was what my religion teacher at secondary school always said.

"Everyone must also have freedom from all religion," Hossein says. "It can be positive for person in private life, but official religion, regime religion – it is tumour of cancer."

I stare at them in amazement. We have finished eating. Marjân stands up and starts clearing the table. When I go to help her she puts a hand on my shoulder and gently pushes me back onto the chair while firmly shaking her head.

"When Palestinian come to Denmark, it is embarrassing . . . ." Hossein says, collecting the plates, ". . . to have to call them foreigner and to call ourself foreigner. It is too much – they live in hole in ground." Hossein shakes his head and walks into the kitchen with the plates. Marjân comes back and asks a question in Persian. Mahmad answers her. Then she says something in an angry tone to Mahmad and Hossein – who has just come back from the kitchen – before turning on her heel and going back.

She doesn't like us talking badly about other foreigners because we are also guests here in Denmark," Mahmad says to me.

"I'm not guest," Hossein says, sitting down. "I soon have Danish passport."

"White men," Mahmad says. "You can enjoy yourself with them, but black men – they're upsetting, they're too dark. You don't know how to behave with them." He has a glint in his eye while he is saying this and I can't work out how much they mean and how much is a joke.

"Iranians in Denmark, they both love and hate the local people – in other words, all of you," Mahmad says, pointing to me with a smile. "Because on the one hand they just want to be normal, but on the other hand they know very well they are labelled foreigners. We know that and we are extremely put out by it."

Marjân has come back to the table. She stands looking at Mahmad and Hossein before turning to me and rolling her eyes to the heavens.

"Yes," Hossein says. "We in same pigeon hole as the bloody village idiot or shitbag with four or five kroner who circumcise his daughter so he can enjoy sexual thrill. What the hell is the idea?" Hossein laughs.

"Iranian man," Marjân says slowly. "He thinks he is so clever." She returns to the kitchen.

"Don't take us too seriously," Mahmad says.

"You can take me very serious," says Hossein.

I hope that Marjân is not upset, so I go into the kitchen to help her do the washing up, but I am only allowed to carry glasses into the living room.

Besalamat

Hossein and Mahmad have made their way back to the three-piece suite. We light up cigarettes and cigarillos and shortly afterwards Marjân arrives and places an ice cold bottle of Stolichnaya – Russian vodka – on the table and we drink it neat. Marjân drinks too even though she puts a hand over her glass at first when Mahmad tries to pour her a drink. She also takes a couple of drags from Mahmad's cigarette. I knock the vodka back just like the men. It is fun getting drunk when all you have experienced for a long time is getting stoned. It is quite different and it reminds me of my father and night golf.

Mahmad teaches me how to toast in Persian. *Besamalat* we say – 'To your health' – and knock back another vodka. You can also say *nush* which just means 'skol'.

I ask Hossein why we are drinking vodka because I had no idea that Iranians were allowed to drink alcohol. He says they know vodka from the USSR as they called Russia at the time of the Shah. There is a common border with what is now known as Turkmenistan. And during the Shah's time you were allowed to drink. I ask if women drink in Iran.

"Yes," Hossein says."some of them do."

Then Mahmad raises his glass and says something in Persian. I look across at Hossein as if to ask what we are toasting.

"Our grandmother," he says. "My father's mother. She is in picture I have at home, between my father and mother."

"Okay," I say and raise my glass. "*Nush*."

Then Mahmad says something in Persian which makes Hossein laugh and prattle away. Marjân smiles at me and shakes her head at what they say. I put my hand on Hossein's arm. It is really difficult being the foreigner, not understanding a bloody word of what is being said.

"My grandmother," Hossein says. "She is very superstitious." Mahmad nods and says something to Marjân – he must have told her what Hossein is about to tell me.

Hossein continues: "When I come home from school, she always ask very serious . . . ." Hossein grabs hold of my arm and looks deep into my eyes: "*Hossein, what happened today? Who talked about you? Who saw you?* So if I tell her something, some names, then she write the names on a chicken egg, then she throw it on embers until it explode in air. Then she say: *Oh, the evil spirits, they been killed*." Hossein puts one hand over my head and makes circling movements while Mahmad explains the whole thing to Marjân.

"Then she had herbs," Hossein says. "She move them over my head and after . . . ." Hossein makes a movement with his hand as if he were scattering herbs. ". . . after she throw them in the fire to catch evil power. Poor woman, I tease her so much." Hossein is laughing and shaking his head with glee; a single tear rolls down his cheek which he quickly wipes away and this makes Marjân point to him and say something which sends Hossein into fits of uncontrollable laughter. I want to hear more – my own grandmother is a bitter old woman in an old people's home.

"He's always been the big troublemaker in the family," Mahmad says to me, nodding towards Hossein.

"How did you tease her?" I ask.

"For example, I say to her: *Today a man look right in my eyes and say to me: 'You have beautiful eyes'.* Then she say: IS THAT RIGHT? And she go completely bananas. And then she fetch own grill and put coal on and lights. Come with egg. Come with incense too, runs round house mumbling about evil spirits, mermm, merm, merm, mermm-merm, and give me good food so I can fight against the eyes. And sometimes sit and mumble all the names she know while egg is in fire, and then the name she say when egg explode, she jump up and shout: AAGGHH, THAT WAS HIM."

Then I ask Hossein to interpret for me. I tell them that my father is an alcoholic and that we played night golf, whacking golf balls at a greenhouse. Marjân looks at me in disbelief, but laughs too. We all get really silly and the strange thing is that I feel that what they say will be funny afterwards too because I will be able to remember it. Well, I can remember when I have been high too – except that when the high has gone, so has the humour.

I am a bit sozzled as we arrive at the main station and get on the night train at 11:30. We have a sleeping compartment all to ourselves with two beds. Hossein asks if I would like to have some opium. I would. At some point we are fantastic. More than naked.

The Pig

In the compartment Hossein gently wakes me up. We have arrived in Aalborg; it is half past six in the morning . . . and I don't know where the hell I am. Well, it was wonderful, but I don't know if I can . . . sort of . . . live with an Iranian man. Hossein is very cool about everything, but it is written all over his face that he would like me to say something about . . . it. Um – and I don't know what else I can say other than that he is absolutely wildly gorgeous.

We go into the station and Hossein buys two cups of coffee for us at the kiosk. I am already onto my second cigarette when he comes out.

"Shall we drink coffee in the square, Maria?" he asks, motioning towards John F. Kennedy Plads.

"Yes," I say. That is all I can say. Hossein is quiet now, too. We sit down on a bench. There is the clear sound of birdsong in the otherwise silent early morning air.

"I . . . ." I stammer and get no further. Hossein puts his hand under my hair round my neck. He massages it. I close my eyes. It feels really good and a little "mmmmm" escapes my lips.

"Maria," he says and I can feel him studying my face. "I hope for you come in my life." I open my eyes. This is no good, we are sitting in the open in Aalborg and Hossein is stroking my neck. Not that I know many people who are up at such an early hour, but I know some who could be on the way home to bed. I flick the cigarette end away with my thumb, stand up and look at him.

"I'll think about it, Hossein." My voice sounds shrill. Then I turn and leave; I force myself not to look back.

It is an odd smell that greets me as I enter the house. Asger is fast asleep and snoring. I go into the kitchen but that doesn't seem to be where the stench is coming from. In the living room I get a shock. There is a huge pig's skin spread out over the table we eat off. On it there is the outline of a Valkyrie in full armour with enormous balloon-like tits on the coat of mail.

The pig has been slit open between the belly and the breast and the skin has been cut off the carcass in one piece. The way it is placed on the table there are two rows of eight teats on the outer edges of the skin.

A black line has been tattooed on part of the outline and you can see that there the skin is slightly raised where the tattooing has been done. The room smells of wax that for some reason or other has gone rotten.

My first impulse is to throw it out before Asger wakes. On the other hand, we have not been getting on that fantastically well for some considerable time so there is always the risk that he would throw me out. And as for Hossein . . . I will simply have to have a good think about that.

In fact, I had wanted to have a sleep on the sofa, but that is out of the question now. Well, I mean to say, I am not bloody sleeping in the same room as a dead pig's skin – I would rather sleep next to a living pig.

Imprisoned

I wake up to Tripper and Twister wandering into the bedroom and sniffing around the bed. Asger is standing in the doorway.

"It's only started snowing outside," he says. "They have to come in." Snow? We are much too close to spring for snow. Does nothing work properly any more?

"Well, put them in the living room," I say.

"The tattoo," he says. "They'll eat the tattoo." It begins to dawn on me. Oh no.

"The pig's skin," I mumble.

"Yes, for fuck's sake. I got it off Butcher Niels. It'll be bloody great," Asger says with a large smile and closes the door after him. The dogs stay by the edge of the bed and sniff at me. They seem . . . weird. Almost frightening. And they stink. They stare at me as if they can't understand why I don't do what I have to do, but I don't have a damn clue what it is they want me to do. Hossein's smell is somewhere close by, probably in my underwear. I push the duvet aside – it is sodding cold because of the snow. I hurriedly slip on clean clothes, shoot out of the door and into the bathroom. I can hear some sad heavy metal coming from the living room, a band called Kings X – Asger thinks they are absolutely fantastic. As I shave my legs and under my arms I think about . . . yes, guess what. Wow. But then I catch sight of my nipples in the mirror and I am reminded of the long row of pig's teats. Yuk, disgusting.

I can see by the clock in the kitchen that it is only eleven o'clock. Asger must be off his nut. The mail box clatters as the postman arrives. I go out into the hall. There is a fat letter from my mother on the floor. I consider whether I should just throw it out, but then I stuff it into the pocket of my coat hanging on the hook. I might read it later. When I have put on a fresh pot of coffee I go in to see him. He is crouching over the pig's skin and I can hear the characteristic buzz of the tattooing machine."

"Hi sweetheart," he says without looking up. "Isn't it good?"

"Mm," I say tonelessly and sit down on the sofa. He asks me about the trip to Copenhagen.

"So we can have roast pork with parsley sauce," he says, sitting down, and then adds: "You probably won't be able to taste the spot of ink."

I never eat pork – he knows that – and he almost never does either, although of course I know for certain that he does when he goes out, but that is pretty seldom because he has to take care of business.

The dogs are being driven crazy by the stink of the pig's skin as it sags and flaps nauseatingly from the edge of the table as Asger pulls it round to add another detail to the picture.

I am on the point of becoming hysterical because the stench of the meat mingled with the hash smoke makes me feel as if I am in prison. My life is about to go off the rails entirely because of Asger who simply does not function as a human being. And – yes, I am well aware of it – because yet *again* I have allowed myself to be trapped in a situation where the man I am with is in total control of what happens. Because I have no fucking life that I can call my own. Because I am a bloody fool.

Customers start appearing again. This time we have only bought standard hash. That was all we could afford. And I sit there smoking like all the other idiots. I simply don't know what else I can do with myself. Pig's skin in the living room, dogs in the bedroom and me – totally out of it – in the kitchen. The air is thick and suffocating and I feel a void . . . I am dead inside. I can't get my head round the business with Hossein. Perhaps I should just go to him? Fuck Asger and all his shit? But I need to do something *myself* . . . I just don't know what. I feel disconnected and drained. And I have no idea who I can talk to about it.

The first night we sleep with the dogs in the bedroom as the snow outside has not melted yet. During the night Asger holds my breasts and sucks one of my nipples between his teeth. I usually enjoy that but now I just can't take it, both because the pig is lying in there with sixteen teats and because the dogs are in the bedroom and are weird. It totally psyches me out.

In the morning Twister is standing astraddle Asger on the bed and making copulating movements.

"Um what . . . ? Whaaat?" Asger mumbles, still half asleep. When I half sit up in bed I can see Twister rubbing his stupid pink prick feverishly up and down against the duvet Asger is lying under. Tripper is sitting and staring at the spectacle in wonder. And I always thought that the dogs were like their owner – almost completely devoid of any sexual urge.

"WHAT THE FUCK IS THAT FUCKING DOG DOING?" Asger shouts. He grabs hold of Twister's collar with both hands and throws the dog off the bed so that it hits the dresser which is up against the wall. Then Asger flies out of bed and it is so funny because as he stands up in fact he has an erection himself – piss proud, I think you call it. But when he hits Twister it is not particularly funny. He packs the dogs off into the kennel run.

When I go into the living room he has draped the pig's skin over two telephone books placed on top of each other. "Well, I need to have it at a level I can work at and it has to be as close to the rounding of shoulders as possible."

"Couldn't you have put them in a plastic bag?" I ask.

"The shoulders?" he asks.

"The telephone books," I answer.

The following night the dogs are allowed to sleep in the kitchen. Asger is concerned about the state of their health after all. "They represent a certain value," he declares gravely. Perhaps Twister's obvious demonstration of some kind of sexual urge has awakened Asger's hopes of becoming an affluent dog breeder.

In the night I wake up and go into the kitchen to smoke a cigarette. Now the dogs have scratched the kitchen door, too. As I light the cigarette they stand prodding me with their snouts – it is very unpleasant. Afterwards Twister starts snarling at me and his lips curl up and he bares his teeth. I grab a spatula out of the sink and smack him over the snout with it, which only makes him snarl even louder.

"Hey," I shout and hit out at him, hard. He retreats marginally and I hurry out of the door while I have the chance. The dogs are beginning to go crazy. Perhaps we should have them put down. I remain standing in the corridor with the spatula in one hand while I finish the rest of my cigarette. I don't want to go into the living room because . . . and it is too revolting to smoke in the bathroom. I am homeless in my own home. The dogs have already started scratching on the door again.

Shaving

When I get up on the third morning Asger is bent over the pig's skin whistling the way he does when he shaves. I assume he is washing it until I see that he is shaving round the teats with my Ladyshave.

"*You uncouth pig,*" I shout.

"What?" he says, totally at a loss.

"That's my Ladyshave. Why the fuck don't you use one of your own?" Asger uses those yellow disposable razors.

"I've run out," he says.

"Then bloody well go down and *buy* some," I shout. Now he turns to face me.

"Sweetheart, stop putting me under pressure." His eyes are cold. I am a small step from having no roof over my head. But . . .

"Pig," I repeat – he is not fucking threatening me.

"Hey," he says. "I'm not the pig here." He laughs and starts slapping the pig's skin the way he slaps my buttocks when he takes me from behind. It is just *so* unsavoury to think about the two things at the same time. I don't know what to say . . . or do. My brain is totally addled from all the hash I have smoked over the past few days. I stand there thinking about a TV program I once saw about there being a direct connection between the nerves in your buttocks and the sensitive areas in your honey pot and that is why women come much quicker when they have had a few good slaps on the bum. I do, anyway. In fact, it is an unbelievably long time since I had a plain little pat on the ass.

"It's the same with bodies," Asger says as he continues to shave the outer edges of the pig's skin which he has covered with shaving foam; those are the only areas he hasn't tattooed. I haven't the faintest idea what the fool is taking about.

"The beard keeps growing for several days after death, so if the bodies are on display the undertaker has to turn up every morning and shave them."

To my ears that sounds doubtful. You don't usually get hairs growing out of a joint of pork if you leave it in the fridge for a few days before you roast it – I mean, I don't think so. If you did, Philips would have a new hit on its hands for Christmas: *Pork joint shaver, now battery driven.* In my mind's eye I can see a housewife in an ad on TV2 humming while removing the stubble off a joint and her husband coming and kissing her on the cheek before she puts the clean-shaven roast in the oven. The skin might have been cut off the pig's carcass before it was scalded and that is why the hair follicles keep functioning. When I was a child growing up in Store Ajstrup I often saw them slaughtering pigs on the neighbouring farms and there was some connection between scalding and the bristles on pigs.

"It's my Ladyshave," I repeat. He just keeps shaving, pressing the Ladyshave hard down against the pig and dragging it along the skin; he rinses the foam off the shaver by whisking it round in a bowl of warm water which he keeps on the table.

Careful you don't cut the teats, I think, but I don't say anything – it is not the right moment.

The pig's skin smells of shaving foam, but the stench of putrefaction prevails. Asger wipes down the skin afterwards with a moist cloth to remove the hair and the remaining foam.

"Aren't you going to put any after shave on?" I ask. He stands there with his hands on his hips contemplating his work.

"It's certainly beginning to smell a bit unpleasant," he says. I go into the bathroom and get his Old Spice. Then I return and sprinkle it onto the pig's skin. I also give Asger a quick dab – he doesn't often have a bath.

"FUCKING STOP THAT NOW," he shouts.

Narco Bitch

Two hours later we are sitting at the table and for the sake of peace in the house I am rolling joints for the hip-hoppers. Asger is sitting tattooing. I have rubbed some tiger balsam under my nose so that I can't smell the pigs, nor the putrefying pig's skin, nor the Old Spice.

I make the filters for the joints out of some Aurora advertising leaflets for organic flour in Hjørring. I found them in the health food shop in Frederikstorv when I was buying some elderberry juice; they have exactly the right thickness. I cut the leaflets into sheets measuring five by one and a half centimetres. Then I roll the small strip of paper into a sausage and place it at one end of the joint roll-up paper. The rest of the paper I fill with a mixture of standard and Petterøes no. 3. Some people start by wrapping the rolling paper round the joint filter and securing it so that they have an empty shell which they gradually fill with the mixture. That is only for amateurs. I roll joints in the same way you roll cigarettes, the only difference being that I add a filter and that my joints are three times bigger than a ciggy. You have to have first-rate motor co-ordination skills. The idea of the filter is to allow you to smoke the joint right to the end and to stop you getting tobacco dregs in your mouth.

Leif, the scaffolder, drops in to buy a couple of grams. "Asger, you smell like a bloody tart," is the first thing he says. Asger gets up from his chair and from across the table he aims a slap at me with the back of his hand. I manage to lean back and avert my head so that the brunt of the slap misses but his knuckles catch me at the side of my eye. Leif grabs hold of Asger's arm.

"Asger, what the fuck are you doing?"

"The little narco bitch is trying to sabotage me," he answers savagely. Okay, that is the famous final straw. Now I'll just move out, but before that I'll damn well find some way to hurt him so that he never forgets.

I go into the bedroom and call Ulla and Niels, but no-one is at home, so I call Matas and tell them that there is a family crisis so that Ulla can be allowed to go to the coffee room and answer the phone. I tell her about the bristles on the pig's skin – is that normal? She may know since she lives with Butcher Niels.

"He's already explained that to Asger," she sighs and tells me that Niels stole the pig's skin after it was scalded but before it was scorched. There was something about not being able to get the hairs and the hooves off without first scalding the skin. And after the scalding the pig goes into an oven at 1200 degrees for fifteen seconds. "That's how you burn off the last hairs and there's also something about it removing bacteria and giving the hide a firmer consistency," Ulla says. That partially explains why the pig's skin seems so rotten.

"So there may be some hairs left on it if it hasn't been scorched?" I ask.

"Well, Maria, *I* don't know, but there could well be," Ulla says and continues in quite a different tone: "But what about Copenhagen? And Hossein? What happened there?" What does Ulla know about Hossein? I don't think I have told her anything. Not at all. Aalborg is just a bloody village – gossip gets round in no time at all. I don't know what to tell her, so I whisper:

"Ulla, I can't speak freely now, but I'll tell you about it some time."

"Okay," she giggles, "but couldn't you come over to my place tonight? Then we could . . . well, Niels isn't at home . . . ."

"I can't, but Ulla . . . ." I say, chewing my bottom lip.

"Maria?" she says when she hears nothing.

"Yes," I say.

"But . . . do you want to?" she asks.

"Yes, well, I really like you Ulla, but . . . I'm not really . . . I don't feel like . . . well," I whisper.

"Maria – calm down," Ulla says. "That's fine. I just think you're so great and I'm sort of up . . . for everything."

"Yes, but I hope we won't fall out," I say.

"No, no, of course not. I'll have to go and work now," Ulla says and we say goodbye. I hope I haven't pissed her off because she might tell someone about Hossein and then I'm really in deep shit. How the hell could she know? I can't work it out.

The dogs keep scratching at the bedroom door, but when I take them out they don't do any business. The door is totally scratched to pieces, but Asger takes no notice and I don't give a damn. It is his deposit that will be lost if the house is damaged.

In the evening Asger is wasted and I think he has forgotten his anger. Real anger requires intelligence and stamina to maintain. I nag him to roll the pig's skin up and put it in the freezer. The stench is almost suffocating.

"But don't you think that might . . . well . . . do something to the ink?" he asks nervously. The dogs are almost going catatonic in the bedroom. The telephone books under the skin are totally ruined from the pork grease. "Couldn't we use the fridge?" he asks.

"No, but we could just open all the windows instead," I answer because I don't want to have rotting pig's skin next to the food I eat.

Customers pop in all the time and Asger gives lectures on tattooing and basks in their admiration. And their admiration is no sham. I mean, how often do you see a grown man in intimate contact with parts of a dead pig for days on end? But they disappear quickly with the stench. Some ask for a reduction in the price. Others threaten to change their pusher. Asger is beyond caring.

"I'm going to be a tattooist," he says.

Polaroid

On Friday he is finally finished and goes into town to buy a Polaroid camera. The picture actually comes out pretty well, but the pig's skin is a dreadfully unhealthy colour and the teats look like dried abscesses.

"Hold the lamp at more of an angle," Asger says excitedly, taking the first picture. The pig's skin is spread out over the dining table. Then he stands in the middle of the floor with the picture in his hand like a little boy, waving it around madly to dry it quickly.

"Soon be ready," he says and his excitement is almost touching when he tears the protective cover off the photo. Then disappointment is etched in his face: the picture is much too dark.

"I'm going for a slash," he says, thin-lipped. This could become a long day so I go into the kitchen and make a bucket of coffee. There is the sound of scratching on the other side of the bedroom door. Twister and Tripper are in there, but the snow outside has melted and it is just crazy if they are allowed to ruin the door completely. I close the door to the living room and let them out. They stare at me in expectation the whole time as I shoo them out into their run. What the fuck is up with them?

"Maria, now I know what we'll do," Asger enthuses on his return. "You hold the pig's skin up to the window so the light shines through and then I can get a good picture."

"You want me to . . . touch that?"

"Hey, sweetheart," he says with forbearance, and condescension too. "It's not fucking poisonous."

"Yes, well, I'm not so sure about that," I say. Asger stands with the camera in his hand watchfully waiting for me. He is so close to throwing me out; perhaps he knows that Nina, the hash head I had the set-to with at 1000Fryd, is creaming her pants to take my place as the narco bitch. I don't give a shit, but I haven't had time to think up my revenge for the two times she hit me, so I am not going yet.

"Okay," I say on my way to the kitchen where I find a pair of pink plastic gloves in the cupboard under the sink. I grab hold of the skin and sink my fingers into it before lifting; it feels like it is going to fall apart. I have to squeeze tighter so that it doesn't slip out of my fingers – it is a ton weight. But it seems too flaccid, probably because it is so rotten.

I hold the pig's skin up against the window. Yes, and I can't smell anything either – tiger balsam has become my loyal companion. He takes his picture and again he is not happy; he walks around grumbling and kicking the furniture and is generally a pain in the ass. What did he imagine? That it would look good? It is a bloody pig's skin he has tattooed.

So I go for a walk and as I approach the house I see Hossein coming along the pavement from the opposite direction. He waves and I stand waiting for him by the garden gate.

"You look so lovely," he says, but then he catches sight of the discolouring beside my eye. Well, I tried to cover it with make-up, but it is still visible. "What is thing on your face, Maria?" he asks sombrely.

I look down at the pavement.

"It's nothing," I answer.

"Something have happened, I know."

"He's off his nut," I murmur.

"Perhaps you and I, we have to find some thing new," Hossein says in an ice -cold voice, casting a sombre glance across at the house.

"You might be right," I whisper.

We go indoors. The air is thick with smoke – it is like going to the Månefisker café in Christiania; you get high from just breathing in. Hossein looks at the pig's skin in disgust. Asger sulkily pours cream and sugar in the coffee. He greets Hossein perfunctorily; Hossein sits down in one of the armchairs and lights one of his cigarillos. I light a cigarette. Asger lights the dog-end of a joint from the ashtray. Time stands still. The smoke gets thicker. No-one says anything; nothing happens.

Mecca

Asger jumps out of his chair and stands with his back to us, crosses his arms over his stomach, grabs hold of his T-shirt and pulls it right up to his shoulder blades. Has he completely lost it? He looks at Hossein over his shoulder and says:

"If you sort of . . . pull the skin around your chest and stuff the end of it into your trousers and stand as if you're about to pull your T-shirt off and Maria kneels in front of you and pulls the skin in tight around you, then I can take a picture of it while it's on your back and it'll look alright," Asger gushes with enthusiasm.

He reaches out for the camera and signals to us that we should stand up. I glance across at Hossein. He stays put, completely unruffled. In fact I have never seen anyone so unruffled before. He takes a long drag on his cigarillo, holds it up in front of him and slowly blows out a thick cloud of smoke; you can see the temperature in the glowing tip of the cigarette rising under the ash. When he has exhaled he flicks the cigarillo with his thumb and the ash flies off the cigarette in an arc and lands on the floor.

"You take picture of pink tattooed pig and I stand with hairy dago hand holding up T-shirt – not look right," Hossein asserts dryly.

"Then Maria holds the T-shirt and you hold the skin," Asger suggests, changing his idea – he is obviously having one of his more lucid moments.

"Me, I am Muslim," Hossein says, pointing to himself and staring at Asger with heavy eyelids. "You understand I not touch pig. Illegal. Pig very dirty animal . . . unclean. Filthy. Go to the Allah's hell forever. Eternal torment with fire and spear."

"Okay, well, I'm sorry," Asger says confused, staring at Hossein with a look of resignation. Hossein is making the sign of the cross like a catholic.

Asger looks baffled and obviously doesn't click that Hossein has just used a Christian gesture.

"Jesus, Maria," Hossein mumbles when Asger turns round and slaps his hand against the window frame.

"Where is the . . . East?" Hossein asks in a grave voice while looking at me with a highly amused glint in his eye. Asger turns round.

"Um," I say, pointing in the direction of East Aalborg. "Over there, I think."

Hossein looks at his watch with a grim expression on his face before announcing gloomily: "I must pray to the Allah now – it is so important."

Asger throws up his arms in frustration. "For Christ's sake, Hossein, do you have to now? I'm sorry about the pig. You'll have to excuse me – I wasn't thinking."

I was suddenly reminded how much he needed Hossein. Copenhagen and Christiania would take Asger's paranoia to boiling point – I imagine the train journey on its own would probably do the trick.

"But . . . ," I stammer innocently."Why don't *you* do it? I could hold the skin around you and Hossein could take the picture."

Asger looks daggers at me.

"Yes," Hossein says," I can take that picture with pleasure – but not picture of the Allah."

"I'll take the picture *myself,*" Asger says, sulkily taking a seat at the table. Time passes. Then there is a knock at the door. It is Loser in my old Jim Morrison T-shirt; he must have scraped enough together for two grams of standard. He stares with disgust at the rotting pig's skin as Asger explains to him that Hossein is too dark-skinned.

"Why don't you do it yourself, man?" There are limits to how accommodating Loser is, especially when he has got money in his pocket, and Asger's standing has slumped considerably since he was busted by the police.

"*I'm* taking the picture," Asger answers.

"Uh-huh," Loser says indifferently.

"Loser, he's more pale than pig skin, too," Hossein says.

"And I'm no bloody pig either, for fuck's sake. I'm a vegetarian," Loser says. Oh really – I didn't know that. Clearly he was not to be tangled with today. Loser only agrees when Asger offers him five grams of standard. Then he asks for another T-shirt and permission to take a bath afterwards.

"Yuughhhh," Asger says as he helps manoeuvre the pig's skin down into Loser's trouser waistline. There is only one pair of plastic gloves and I am wearing them.

The Third Cleverest Animal

Loser stands puffing away on one of Hossein's cigarillos to ward off the stench. "The pig is an intelligent animal," he mumbles, staring up at the ceiling. "Very clean. After the human and the dolphin the pig is the cleverest animal in the world." Asger stops struggling with the skin.

"Shut up, Loser," he says and goes over to the table to light a cigarette. I have my tiger balsam.

"This is conduct unbecoming to carcasses," Loser states philosophically. "Perhaps it's worse than eating them."

After quite a struggle we get the pig's skin tucked into Loser's waistband. While Asger is out washing his hands I kneel in front of Loser and pull down the ends of the skin; the two rows of teats look like dried abscesses . . . or perhaps types of button and I am a seamstress working with a raw infected pig's skin, fitting a jacket for a client. Asger has returned and is standing ready with the camera. At last I manage to get the skin tight up against Loser's frail chest while he holds up the T-shirt so that it only just covers the top edge of the pig's skin. Hossein moves the dining table lamp so that the light shines on the tattoo.

Asger snaps away until the film is finished. He tries every possible angle: from the front, from underneath, from the top and from the sides. He may have immortalised a whole row of the pig's teats along with the tattoo. I suppose it is conceivable. There are people who have an extra set of undeveloped nipples situated slightly below the ribs, on the stomach in fact, and they are called accessory nipples. But a young man with eight sets of nipples – now that is simply sensational.

Asger is wildly excited about the pictures even though it is obvious, even to a blind man, that it is not Loser's skin. I put the pig skin down on the ruined telephone books; Loser uses Jim Morrison to wipe the worst gunk – left by the putrefying pig grease – off his chest. Asger goes into the kitchen and returns with the washing-up bowl and throws the pig skin in it.

"I think it'll be alright for the dogs," he says and puts the bowl in the middle of the floor. I don't bother to remind him about what happened when he gave them the raw pork with the crackling.

I go and find one of Asger's T-shirts – a faded black number – and give it to Loser. Then I pack him off to the bath and throw Jim Morrison into the garbage with the telephone books.

"Yes, come on then," Asger says gently, bringing in the dogs. Both Twister and Tripper sniff at everything and Asger is almost knocked over when Tripper jumps up him. They both turn their heads towards the washing-up bowl and look at the pig's skin from about a metre's distance without showing the slightest interest. Then they go back to Asger.

"They've missed me, that's what it is," he says in surprise, stroking them and scratching them behind the ears. They are unimpressed. They just keep looking at Asger in wonderment, confused almost in a stressed sort of way, slightly aggressive. I sit watching, feeling ill at ease.

Loser comes in, freshly bathed and wearing his new T-shirt. "Now I could do with a joint," he says.

"Loser," I whisper in a low voice which only he can hear and then I pass him a ready-rolled joint from the pile in the box for the hip-hoppers.

Tripper is standing by the table sniffing at Asger's sour-smelling old leather bong. In the meantime Twister has switched its attention from Asger to Loser and me.

"Thanks," he whispers and sits down opposite Hossein who has been quiet for some time now, observing local customs.

Peace of Mind

Loser receives a gentle smile from Hossein. "Time for *tundah*," Hossein says. "Peace with yourself."

Loser nods, puts the joint in his mouth and fires up his lighter; he sucks in greedily and retains the smoke in his lungs. Twister stands next to him. Tripper stops sniffing at the leather bong and looks over towards Loser. As soon as Loser breathes out, Twister puts his front legs on his lap and begins hyperventilating while Tripper hurries over to join him. So both dogs have their front legs on Loser's lap and their snouts are close to his mouth. They must be heavy for such a frail figure of a man – together the dogs must weigh a good ninety kilos.

"Um," Loser says with a quiver in his voice, but the dogs don't really do anything, they just stand still and seem profoundly weird. Then Loser takes another massive drag and holds it down in his lungs.

"What the fuck is up with them?" Asger asks out loud.

"Your dogs are junkies for *hashish*," Hossein says as Twister and Tripper start hyperventilating again when Loser breathes out. It seems as if the truth suddenly dawns on Asger, as indeed it does for me.

"They lie always here when you smoke. Lie on back," Hossein says, leaning well back in the armchair limply waving his arms and legs as if in ecstasy to illustrate how the dogs usually lie on the living room floor when people are smoking pot.

"*Oh fuck*," Asger says. He goes over and kicks them so they whimper and back away from Loser, but not very far. Tripper stands right by the chair while Twister bares his teeth and snarls at Asger. Hossein shakes his head.

"Hey," Asger says menacingly, but retreats, away from Twister, and when he does that Tripper puts his feet back on Loser's lap.

"That not dog's fault," Hossein says.

"Fucking junkie dogs," Asger says in disgust. Hossein eyes him, angry and resigned at the same time, and shakes his head.

Poor animals. They have been going cold turkey while Asger has been tattooing. It is obvious that they have had a bad time. At least I had loads of alcohol the last time I did it.

Hossein gets up and starts putting on his jacket.

"What . . . er Hossein . . . didn't you want to buy something?" Asger asks. Hossein glares at him.

"No. I going down to see Lars and buy from him. I buy from man who not hit the woman, not hit the animal."

"What the fuck are you talking about?"

"Hossein don't like things he see here, Asger. Soon we will have the serious conversation." Hossein waits to see if Asger has anything to add. Nothing happens. Hossein leaves.

Perhaps he was waiting for me, too. But I don't know what to do.

Muscles & Sinews

"Maria, shall we invite Hossein to come with us on a trip to the West coast?" Asger asks the following day. Amazing. I mean it is certainly true that the weather has improved, but Asger has not been outside the city limits in all the time I have known him.

"Why?" I ask.

"I was just thinking . . . drive to the sea . . . take the dogs with us. Make a day trip out of it."

"And what would we, as it were, drive?"

"I can borrow a van from Frank," Asger says. I can't fathom what goes on inside him.

"But Asger, why go to the West coast?" I ask.

"I've just told you, Maria. A trip. A drive."

"Is Frank coming too?"

"No."

"But Hossein is?"

"Mm, I'd like . . . well, I don't want to fall out with him." Asger almost looks convincing.

"Okay,call him."

"Wouldn't it be better if you rang him, sweetheart?"

I shrug my shoulders: "Okay." So I do. Hossein says 'yes'. We agree to go on Monday at one o'clock. Asgercalls Frank who drops the van off late that afternoon. Asger goes out to feed the dogs and give them fresh water. I am busy tidying up and cleaning round the kitchen sink and, a little mystified. I stand watching Asger stroking Twister and Tripper. Is he suffering from a softening of the brain? I remind myself that he hit me. When I entered puberty I swore to myself that I would *never* put up with a man hitting me . . . and now I have done just that and I simply have to get my revenge. Well, I will have to see what happens, I think to myself, and I continue the cleaning.

At eleven o'clock at night I have something else to think about. When there is a knock at the door I automatically get up to answer it, but this is no normal visit. They may be dressed casually – sneakers, jeans, and bomber jackets – but they are obviously bikers. The brain is at the front: a thin, sinewy guy in his early thirties. Behind him towers the brawn: a man whose wrists are each the width of my neck.

I swallow quickly. "Come in," I say, stepping to the side and holding the door wide open.

"Thanks," the sinewy one says and walks past giving me a polite nod. I reckon he is the big brother of Pusher Lars, the builder Hossein visited yesterday. It is as if the mountain of muscle folds in half as he goes through the doorway – he just fits through. The sinewy one stops to look into the living room.

"Good evening, Asger," he says.

"Konrad," Asger says nervously. I can hear him getting up from his chair. "Come in. Fancy a joint? A cup of coffee?"

"A cup of coffee would be excellent," says the sinewy one, going into the living room. If his name is Konrad, then he must be Lars's brother.

"*Maria,*" Asger barks. "Bring some coffee in."

The mountain of muscle has stayed by the front door.

"I'll have to make some fresh," I say.

"Get a move on, woman," Asger shouts from the living room. Give me a break, will you. The mountain makes a little gesture with his hand towards the kitchen and I scuttle off – he follows. As I put the kettle on I think to myself how lucky it was that I cleaned up today. Then I measure six spoonfuls of coffee into the coffee filter that I place on the coffee pot. The mountain clears its throat. I turn round nervously.

"My name is Kurt," he says, holding out a giant paw.

"Maria," I say in a strident voice and then I only *curtsey* in front of him! My hand disappears in his huge bear paw; his skin is dry and rough.

"Put two more spoonfuls in," he says in a friendly voice. So I do. The water boils and I can hear Asger agitatedly explaining something about the police raid.

"Yes, that was nasty for you, Asger," Konrad says. I have heard he has become a Hell's Angel prospect and is high up in the new hierarchy which is establishing itself in Aalborg. When the water has boiled I go to pour it on the coffee but Kurt the muscle mountain places one of his enormous maulers on my arm and stops me.

"Wait a second," he says.

"What. . . ?" I ask.

"The temperature," he says. "The water mustn't be more than 96 degrees when it meets the coffee or else the coffee tastes bitter."

The only response I can come up with is "Ah."

"You keep a nice kitchen, Maria," Kurt says while I am straining to hear what is going on in the living room.

"Thank you," I say.

Asger repeats for the third time that it won't happen again, at which Konrad chuckles and says that he is aware of that.

Blanco ' Negro

"It's okay now," Kurt says and I pour the water over the coffee. Inside, I am cursing that it takes so long because I want to go to the living room and hear what is going on.

"I understand that you know my good friend Hossein?" Kurt intones the statement as a question and speaks in such a way that he can't be heard in the living room which I am very happy about. I am also quite sure that he is making a conscious effort to speak softly.

"Yes," I answer.

"He's a good man," Kurt says and gives me a meaningful nod.

"Yes," I say and start looking for coffee mugs.

"An excellent character," Kurt says.

"Shall we go into the living room?" I suggest when I have found two clean mugs and the thermos. Kurt waves one of his huge hands and steps to the side so that I can lead the way.

I put the mugs on the table and pour the coffee. I notice the sickly film of sweat on Asger's face and the two rows of cocaine Konrad has arranged on an LP cover: *Life's Too Good* by the Sugarcubes, one of my records.

"Do you want anything in it? Sugar? Cream?" I ask. Konrad gently shakes his head.

"*Blanco ' negro,*" he says. White powder and black coffee – Colombian breakfast.

"Kurt?" I ask, turning to him. He is just inside the door and sticks a paw out.

"I'll take it black," he says, adding a 'thank you' when I pass him the mug. I scuttle over to the sofa and then keep quiet so that the only noise to be heard in the living room is Konrad sucking the cocaine up his nostrils through a little silver pipe.

Asger is sitting uneasily in his chair. Quite obviously he needs to pee. I can see by his face that he is summoning up the courage to say something.

"But I have also decided to stop dealing," he says in what is supposed to suggest a casual tone, but the words tumble out so quickly that they almost trip over each other.

"Oh, have you?" Konrad says in a relaxed manner after which he sniffs, closes his eyes, frowns and jerks his head backwards several times while rubbing his nostrils with two fingers. It must be good cocaine.

"Yes, I want to be a tattooist," Asger says, fumbling around on the table to find the Polaroid photos of Loser. "I'm doing intensive training."

Asger cautiously passes two photos over to Konrad. I can see Asger's hand shaking as Konrad slowly lowers his coffee mug and accepts the pictures.

"Yes, just look at that," Konrad says with a gleeful smile, all teeth and his eyes alight. A real summer smile. "You should see these, Kurt," he says with a smile and a nod to Asger. He passes the pictures over his shoulder to Kurt.

Asger doesn't get it. He has a foolish grin plastered all over his face. "Yes, isn't it just a fantastic idea!" he says.

Konrad sits quietly nodding. "Yes," he says with a smile and continues in the same tone: "If you tattoo anything living, I'll remove your kneecaps."

He doesn't say: "If you *ever* . . . ." He doesn't have to, he would rather enjoy the four seconds of bewilderment in Asger's eyes until he digests the message.

"Aaahh," Asger says.

"Nice chatting to you," Konrad says, getting up. "Maria," he says, giving me a little nod. Asger is stunned.

"Thank you for the coffee, Maria," Kurt says.

"Pleasure," I say and follow them to the door. And then they have gone.

I sit in the kitchen for half an hour before going into the living room.

"No more independent shopping trips to Christiania," Asger says. "And there are three errands I owe them." He looks over at me as if I had something to do with it.

The Stench

The water is trickling through the coffee filter and we are almost ready to go. The weather is great; it is the first spring day with anything resembling sunshine.

"Are you taking the dogs?" I shout to Asger.

"Just a sec," he answers from the bedroom; he sounds a little strained so I go out into the corridor to see what he is doing. He is half lying on the floor reaching under the bed. Then he heaves out a blue sports bag. I ask him what it is.

"It's just something I have to deliver to Frank with the car." Right.

In the kitchen I screw the cap on the coffee pot. "Could you put the coffee pot in the bag," I ask because all three of us have to sit on the front seat and it is impractical to put it on the floor and have it rolling around between out feet. Twister and Tripper have to be at the back and I don't feel like drinking coffee covered with dog saliva.

"No," Asger answers in an irritated voice. "There are a few things I've got to deliver." That is just so bloody typical of Asger. I stand by the van and wait.

The neighbour comes out to the pavement from his front garden and walks towards me. "Can you smell it?" he asks.

"Spring?"

"No, the stench of all the shit from your back garden," he answers. Now he says it, I can. All the dog shit inside the dogs' kennel run steaming in the sunshine. Asger should have dug it in – that is his job. At that moment he comes down the garden path.

"Asger," I say. "We'll have to move the dogs' . . . mess from the run. The whole area is stinking of shit because of us."

"The problem will soon be solved," Asger says, jumping in the van without gracing the neighbour with a glance.

A Walk on the Beach

We pick up Hossein, who brings a shoulder bag full of food. Then we shoot off listening to pop music on Aalborg local radio. The dogs are completely calm and enjoy the ride; we smoke a large joint I rolled at home and the dogs both stand up by the metal caging separating them from the driver's compartment. The sun shines through a dusty sky. We drive past the turning to Blokhus, go up through Saltum and down to the beach by the summer house area known as Grønhøj. Asger parks the car in a parking lot right behind the dunes.

"And now?" I ask when he has turned off the engine and Hossein has opened the door, so you can smell the sea. There is only a slight breeze causing the dune grass to ripple lazily.

"Hossein let the dogs out," Hossein says and goes round the back of the van to open the rear doors. Asger sits down and looks pensive. The odds that he wants a pee are overwhelming.

"Shall we go for a walk along the beach?" I suggest. The dogs have started barking and trot around the car sniffing inquisitively.

Hossein comes over and leans against the passenger door.

"You're coming now?" he asks.

"Why not have a cup of coffee and a bite to eat first?" Asger asks.

"You're hungry?" Hossein asks and adds: "We can do that," unpacking the sandwiches. I pick up the coffee pot from where it was wedged under the seat and find the three plastic mugs I put in the glove compartment. We sit slurping coffee and chewing at a home-made Hossein-sandwich.

"We are going long walk, aren't we?" Hossein asks.

"Yes, yes, of course," Asger replies in a strangely vacant way.

At last we get out. Asger locks the van. Hossein has lit a cigarillo, I have lit a cigarette and we begin to walk towards a path that twists along the top of the little dune between the parking lot and the broad sandy beach. It is a weekday and there is no-one about.

Then Hossein knocks me flying in the sand as a big bang rings in my ears. Hossein is half lying on top of me and staring intensely behind him.

"WHAT THE FUCK YOU DO?" he shouts and jumps up. I raise my head and can see Asger standing with a sawn-off shotgun that he must have had in his sports bag. Twister and Tripper run round the dunes about twenty metres away from Asger, dazed. They sniff at the wind, turn but can't work out what is going on. I sit in a crouch and look up at Hossein who is looking at Asger with what can only be described as intense hatred.

Asger shoots again. The back of Tripper's body is torn sideways, she lets out a howl and then falls. She whimpers as she tries to stand up and I can see a dark red stain on her hindquarters as she collapses again. Twister shakes his head in his distress, runs over to Tripper, peers at us and runs in zigzags. Then Twister suddenly sprints towards the beach, barking with all his might. I can see Asger breaking open the double-barrelled shotgun by the car and digging deep in his jacket pocket for more ammunition.

"You stay here, Maria," Hossein says. Then he runs across to where Asger is. I have got to my feet. Twister has reached the foot of the dunes. By the edge of the water, a little further down the beach, I can see three people walking, two adults and a child. They seem to be looking up at us. Twister is running at full speed across the broad expanse of beach. Asger raises his shotgun to his cheek.

"NOOOO, STOP," shouts Hossein who has almost reached him. A shot rings out. I cast my eyes over to the edge of the beach and see the man raising his hands to his face and falling to his knees at the same time. The woman screams and holds the child close to her. Twister storms across the beach and closes in on the three of them. I turn my head in time to see Hossein tearing the shotgun out of Asger's hands.

"Distance too big," yells Hossein. He hits Asger on the side of the head with the stock of the gun, knocking him over. The man on the beach lets out a piercing cry – in German, I think. I glance across at him. The woman is holding the child in her arms and screaming hysterically. She wades out into the icy cold water. The man has stood up. He is standing stock-still, paralyzed by the sight of Twister approaching fast. I feel completely numb. Hossein's hands are behind his back, up under his jacket. His right arm moves back towards the front of his body. Hossein has a revolver. My stomach churns. What is going on here? Twister gallops gracefully; I can see the small gusts of sand swirl up as his paws hit the beach and the spray of sand as he moves into his stride. The wind in his coat. A few metres away from his goal now. There is the muffled sound of a bang and I see Twister's front legs almost snap beneath him; he begins to fall about three metres from the man, but he has so much momentum behind him that his body keeps rolling. I see Twister's back strike the beach and rise up again in slow motion, his black coat spattered with sand, a red stain on the beach behind him. Twister comes out of his *salto mortale* on his side and rolls on involuntarily until he limply smacks into the man's legs. Now I can hear the woman again. She is sobbing and holding the child's face against her bosom. I look across to Hossein who is stuffing the revolver into his waistband. Asger is on his feet; he is standing quite still, holding a hand to his head where he was hit. He says nothing.

Tools

"The dogs have name tag, on the collar?" Hossein asks, making a gesture in front of his neck. To me it looks like he is showing Asger where Asger's throat has to be slit.

"Um, yes," Asger says, because they have. They got one after the drugs cop, Martinsen, raided the house.

"Get it now," Hossein commands in a voice that simply brooks no discussion. "Run," he adds and takes two steps towards him to deliver a stinging blow with the palm of his hand. "Otherwise you go jail for weapon, killing animals, shooting at civilian. NOW." Asger lopes half-heartedly down the dunes towards the beach. The German has waded out into the water to bring back his wife and child. Hugging each other, they make their way through the breakers.

"I really don't like man who wants kill, but cannot do it proper," Hossein says.

"Tripper?" I exclaim. She is still whimpering faintly. "What shall we do?" I ask. My voice squeaks and I can hardly get the words out. I stand there hugging myself, suddenly extremely cold. Hossein goes over to Tripper and crouches beside him in the sand. He talks to him gently in Persian; I follow him and stand behind him. He has a revolver. The dog is bleeding profusely from the hip and hindquarters, her eyes wild with fear. Hossein strokes her head while talking to her gently; he lowers his face to her head and fondles her ears. The sand under Tripper is stained red and some of the dune grass has red streaks across it. Her coat has become sticky with the thick blood seeping out of her.

"Can she . . . be saved?" I ask. Hossein doesn't answer, instead he places his right knee against her shoulder, tightens his grip on her head and twists it diagonally up and back in one abrupt movement. I hear a dull crack. A squeal of anguish escapes my lips.

"No," he says. "It never will walk again." He looks up at me with his gentle, dark eyes. I cry; my eyes are fixed on the beach. The woman is screaming hysterically at Asger who is jogging along and has almost drawn level with Twister now. The man says nothing; he stands there slightly bent over as if he is in pain, holding the child close to him.

Asger grabs the collar and opens the buckle. I can faintly hear him hissing at the woman: "Shut up, will you." Then he stands up, casts a last look at the dog and starts back on his way towards us.

"*What the fuck are you doing*?" I shout at him finally.

"*I don't want any bloody junkie dogs,*" he shouts back.

"I don't like man who kill his dogs because he make them junkies," Hossein says. He stands there with Tripper's collar in his hand watching the Germans on the beach. "The woman have mobile phone," he says. I take a look and the woman is holding her mobile phone up to her ear. Asger is half way up the dune.

"The man had some gunshot wounds in his face," he says almost enthusiastically.

"Go and sit in car," Hossein orders. I am already on my way to the van.

"How the fuck did you do that? There was a huge hole in the dog's chest, man," Asger says.

"If you want kill, you have to use right tools," Hossein expounds flatly. If you want to kill? Who is this man exactly? I stand waiting by the van because I do not want to sit next to Asger. Hossein is aware of that without me having to say anything. He scrambles in, sits in the middle and I follow. But I don't really know how I feel about sitting next to Hossein. I mean, why does he carry a gun when he goes for a walk on the beach?

Asger sits down behind the steering wheel. "What bloody weapon was that, man?" he asks.

"Bullets. Dum-dum."

"Let me see the shooter, man." Asger starts the van and we trundle off, away from the parking lot, away from the corpses of the dogs.

"This not thing to play with. Only for people who know how to kill. Only for soldier."

"Hey, come on, man. Show me the bloody shooter."

"I don't like you any more."

"What the fuck do you mean by that?"

"You shoot your dogs. Innocent animals."

"They were junkies, you said it yourself."

"You perhaps not junkie?"

"What the fuck are you talking about, man? Shit, I'm no fucking junkie." Asger glowers at Hossein instead of keeping his eyes on the gravel track through the summer house area. The car moves ominously towards the ditch. Hossein puts his right hand on the wheel and straightens up the van while putting his left hand round the lower part of Asger's head and neck and banging his cranium against the side window once, hard. Hossein says in a calm voice:

"Are you very stupid idiot? Is there nothing brain in your head?" he says before letting him go.

"What the fuck are you doing?" Asger says, offended, frightened. "There'll be no more trips to Copenhagen from me, man."

"Hossein not need your shit job."

Double Idiot

We drive out onto the main road. There is silence for some minutes. Then Asger pulls into a gas station. I can sense that he is on the point of asking me to jump out and fill up with gas, but then he catches himself, sighs and does it himself. I don't say a word until Asger has gone to the kiosk to pay. Even then it is an effort for me.

"Are you . . . at home this evening?" I ask.

"Yes. Why, Maria?" There is a teasing tone to Hossein's voice, which I don't like in fact. He has turned round in his seat. I keep looking straight ahead.

"Hmm, no reason really. Just if there should be . . . well, any bother." I suddenly notice how shaky I am. I am sitting next to a foreign man who carries a handgun. Twenty minutes ago he used it to kill – he handled the gun as casually as if he were a cook using a whisk. And the van smells of dog, but the dogs are dead. Hossein killed them both because Asger was not up to it and afterwards he was humiliated into the bargain.

"You okay?" Hossein asks.

"Yes, of course. I just wanted to know if you were at home." I can see Asger coming out of the kiosk.

"You always welcome in my home – you know that," Hossein says. "Always." There is no sign of the teasing in his voice now.

"I know," I hasten to say, sinking down further in my seat and lighting a cigarette. But Asger goes round the back of the gas station – he has to have a pee, it seems.

I look up at Hossein and hesitate – after all, I don't know how far he is prepared to go, with the pistol, that is. Perhaps he only took it to do a bit of shooting practice, for fun. But . . . .

"I don't know if he'll freak out if I leave him," I say.

"That no problem," Hossein says. "He owe me fourteen thousand kroner." I have a sudden inspiration.

"What about the bikers? Do you lend them money?"

"Yes, couple of them. At cheap interest – it make good relationship."

"Hossein, you're a loan shark," I exclaim.

"Yes I know it," he says with a smile as Asger opens the door.

We are on our way again and I consider my situation. I have to get away from Asger – that much is sure. I could have Hossein – I think that is sure, too.

But . . . well, where will it all lead? Leave a pusher for a loan shark with a gun? That doesn't seem like a particularly good idea. And I don't want to live with a . . . have children with . . . well, live in a home with guns. No. You mustn't do that Maria, I tell myself. Not bloody likely.

It begins to pour down. The windscreen wipers can hardly keep up. The drops hit the tarmac so hard that they bounce up. I wind the side window down a little and stick out a hand. The rain lashes into the driver's compartment.

"Hey, there's a draught," Asger complains. Hossein lights a cigarillo. He doesn't care.

When we drive up to the bridge over the Limfjord it is pitch black. Hossein reaches over me and winds the window right down. He yanks his gun out of his waistband and hurls it over the balustrade as we drive past.

"Why did you do that?" Asger asks.

"Police can trace bullet."

"They're not going to dig a bullet out of a dead dog."

"You know nothing about nothing," Hossein says.

"What about the shotgun?" Asger asks – a mite nervous now.

"You think shotgun put mark on every small shot?" Hossein says dismissively.

"Umm . . . no, I suppose it doesn't."

"And bullet you used – you leave them on beach?"

"Umm . . . yes."

"And shotgun – it used before?"

"I don't know," Asger answers.

"Where it come from?"

"Bloody hell, I borrowed it. From one of my friends."

Hossein shrugs his shoulders: "Never have weapon you don't know history of."

"What the fuck can happen, man? I have to give it back again, don't I."

"Perhaps it come out that dog shot with same weapon as bank robbery and then they find out you shoot dog so it is you who do bank robbery. So you double idiot. Or you snitch on your friends – in prison you get big goods train go right up your asshole." Hossein is enjoying himself. "Now you drive me home."

Where to go?

We are driving down Vesterbro. "Um, Asger," I say. "Couldn't you drop me off here? I want to go home." Asger doesn't say anything, but pulls into the side by the bus stop in front of the statue of the Goose Girl.

"Bye," I say jumping out and slamming the door behind me. I rush home via Ladegårdsgade and the short cut through the parking lot behind the North Aalborg hospital. In Reberbansgade I quickly check to see if I have enough money in my pocket before jumping into a taxi that has just dropped some people off at Café Ib René, Cairo. It won't take Asger long to run Hossein up to his place and I am not sure if he has to go to Frank's and return the van or if he is going straight home.

As soon as I get into the house I start throwing my clothes into a big bag I generally use for washing when I go to the launderette. I also turn up a black garbage bag in the kitchen in which I stuff my duvet and pillow. I drag the garbage bag into the hallway and on top of the bed wear I sling my shoes and my jackets. I press it all down and hurl my toilet things on top, then find some duct tape in the living room, tear off a strip and seal the bag. I drag my laundry bag into the living room and stick a handful of LPs down beside the clothes. Then I open the stash box and take my bamboo joint pipe and a couple of ready rolled joints which I put in my inside pocket. I glance at the potted plant which my mother gave me as a housewarming present when I moved in with Gorm. I go over and lift it up, take the key from the saucer, unlock the safebox and pocket seven hundred kroner, about half of what is there. Otherwise I have got fuck all. Dazed, I stand in the hallway with the laundry bag and the garbage bag. I peer into the kitchen which I furnished with all kinds of groovy things I found in second-hand shops, church rummage sales and loads of recycling shops. Fuck it. I go into the living room, find a scrap of paper and write a note to Asger. *Good luck with the tattooing business* is all I can think of. I put the note in the middle of the table on top of the stash box so he can't miss it. Then I go out through the hall, slam the door and slip the key in through the mail slot. I pick up my two bags and hurry down the garden path to the pavement and round the corner towards Hasserisgade. I know that Asger doesn't take that route from Hossein's. My body gives a shudder and there is a hollow in the pit of my stomach.

I arrive in Hasserisgade, absolutely exhausted. It is heavy work carrying the garbage bag over my shoulder. Some of my toiletry things cut into my back or perhaps it is my shoes. I cross Vesterbro and walk down Prinsensgade towards John F. Kennedys Plads. There are always taxis waiting outside the station. So all I have to do is go up Jyllandsgade towards East Aalborg and up to Hossein's. The man with the gun. I walk past the taxis and sit on the steps in front of the station. The bus station is on the right. I could also take a bus to my father's house; he would be happy to see me. But what the hell would I do out by Halkær Broad? My head aches. Hossein is at home and I would certainly be welcome there, but how great is that? I land on his doorstep like a fucking tramp and he carries a gun. I could also go to Ulla's, but I don't know her that well and her guy, Butcher Niels, deals with Asger so I would be in the shit in no time at all – it would take about seven seconds. My mother – *never*! I suddenly remember her unread letter in my coat pocket, take it out and shred it, then shove the bits down between the bars in the drain.

Sitting back down on the step, I pull up my trouser leg and look at the spunk. The sore is healed now and it is a fabulous tattoo. At least I am happy about that.

My hand rummages around in my inside pocket and pulls out one of the ready rolled joints, puts it in my mouth and dives down again for a lighter. It flares up and almost burns my hair off, so I have to lean back before I can put the joint carefully to the flame and inhale.

I smoke it like a cigarette without holding the smoke down in my lungs for very long. It is a mix of standard with Petterøes no.3, untoasted. It doesn't taste very good, but nevertheless it does shift the headache to the back of my skull where it disperses. Unfortunately, in its place I have a slightly smashed sensation and the thought of lugging the laundry bag and the garbage bag anywhere is inconceivable. In fact, things are not that great.

THE BRIDGE

1992

He walked 'til morning.

The high wore away; the chromed skeleton corroding hourly, flesh growing solid, the drug-flesh replaced with the meat of his life. He couldn't think. He liked that very much, to be conscious and unable to think.

—WILLIAM GIBSON: *Neuromancer*

1

"Can I come in?" The new ship's cook lingered in the doorway, undecided. There had been a knock at the door. I had shouted 'yes' and then the door into my cabin opened.

At sea, it is a deadly sin to lock your cabin door because then people can't get in to save you if there is a fire. But it shows a lack of respect to knock on a closed cabin door. If the door is open visitors are welcome, but if it is closed it is equivalent to saying you aren't at home. On ships, this rule is respected. You only knock in emergencies.

Perhaps he didn't know. I lay on my bunk and looked up at him – I didn't even know his name at that time. He had signed on two days before, when we were docked at a jetty outside Lagos in Nigeria taking on 300,000 tons of crude oil, and I had only briefly greeted him the evening before in the TV room. Our former cook had become pregnant. The captain had refused to have her on board even though she was only in her fourth month.

Yet again we were on our way up through the Atlantic off North Africa on course for Rotterdam – our sailings were as regular as the bus departures from Aalborg bus station.

It had vaguely occurred to me that the new cook may be the kind of person I could hang out with. On the other hand, after two and a half years as second engineer on oil tankers, friendly social intercourse on board was no longer something I believed in.

The time was 22:45 and I had just finished the last round in the hole. All the tanks were full, the pumping off had been completed, there were no leaks and the readings were as they should be. Even through the ear protectors the noise of the Burmeister & Wain diesel engines had been deafening; at fifteen metres in height they constituted the heart of the huge engine room in the ship's aft. I had set the alarm in the engine room to ring in my cabin in case of a problem during the night. With the day's active work done, I had left the 53°C and 98 percent humidity of the hole behind me and had gone up through the accommodation section – the superstructure in the ship's aft where the crew lives.

Now I was in my cabin enjoying the little bit of private life that I had before having to turn in so that I would be able to start work at eight o'clock the following morning. I had closed the cabin door behind me, as always. There was no-one I wished to receive a visit from. Several members of the crew had had their leave cancelled by the shipping company and there was a lot of muttering going on in dark corners – also because the new captain was pious, so the rules were interpreted in the strictest manner possible. The daily ration of two pilsners was served already opened.

For myself I had been at sea now without a break for eight months – I didn't know where else I could go.

When I was finished in the bathroom, I lay down on my bunk and picked up my novel. The air-conditioning in the cabin kept the temperature at a constant 32°C, which seemed cool in comparison with the 34° outside. And with humidity down to only 40 percent the air in my home felt pleasantly crisp.

And then there was a knock at the door.

"Have you got any . . . magazines?" the new cook asked from the door.

"What sort of magazines?" I asked.

"Well, magazines for . . . men's magazines?"

I put my novel face down on the floor. He was still dithering in the doorway; tall and gangling.

"I haven't got many," I answered, swinging my legs down from the bunk. "But you can have the ones I've got," I added and motioned him to come in and close the door.

"Allan," I said, pointing to my chest to make it clear that it was my name I was referring to.

"Allan," he repeated, taking a step into the cabin and proffering his right arm. "Chris," he said. I shook his hand – long white fingers, strong though. He held his right elbow in his left hand and he continued to do so after we had shaken hands, as if he was deciding to show respect because he still hadn't figured out the hierarchy in the crew. His eyes, however, betrayed no embarrassment as they searched my room.

"James Lee Burke," he said with the air of an expert, nodding towards the book I had put down.

"Yes," I said.

"Is it good?"

"Better than the film." I opened the cupboard, crouched down in front of it and rummaged through the dirty linen at the bottom.

"Perhaps you prefer to use your imagination?" he asked with a touch of irony – boldness – in his voice.

"What do you mean?"

"Since you don't have many men's magazines," he added.

"I suppose you could say that," I answered.

"Do you think about your girl back home?"

I wanted to laugh, but instead only a snorting sound emerged from my nostrils.

"No, I wouldn't like to say that," I answered.

"So you just think about a . . . fantasy person?" he asked. Again there was an edge to his voice, this time of . . . scorn, I think. It seemed a touch ridiculous to me. He was too thin, too anemic to make fun of me. I sent him a look.

"Sorry," he said, as if dropping the tough guy act – his shoulders slumped. "It's just that people don't seem to speak on this ship. I've never sailed before and it seems so . . . it's just so . . . boring," he said emphatically.

"That's right," I said from the cupboard where I was still searching. I knew I had three porn magazines; I had bought them just in case.

"Why the hell do they do it?" he asked in desperation and started pacing the cabin. There wasn't a lot of room – approximately fourteen square metres.

"Why do you do it?" I asked as I found something that felt like glossy paper. Bingo.

"I got caught up in a little . . . what would you call it?" he said haltingly as I straightened up. He was searching for the right words. ". . . bit of trouble at home. Problems," he added.

"That sounds like an excellent reason," I said unsympathetically and put the three magazines in his hand. I wasn't in the mood to listen to his problems – I reckoned that I had had the same ones myself. I stayed on my feet – hoping that he would leave.

"I just can't do that . . . use my imagination," he said with disgust in his voice, but caught himself and sent me an apologetic look. Perhaps he thought I had taken offence at what he had said. I could recognize myself in his eyes. We were at sea. He was alone – he felt trapped. No-one can predict how they will react.

I decided to be decent, to thaw; I grinned at him. "Can't you think about some girls you've been with instead of these . . . paper pussies?" I asked, sitting down on the edge of my bunk. Chris took up my invitation and sat in the armchair, perching on the edge. He shook his head.

"No, I don't like to do that," he answered.

"Why not?"

"It seems a bit . . . ." He shot me a quick glance that was intended to take the edge off his comment, indicate that this was his own personal opinion, and that if I had a different view of the matter it shouldn't come between us. ". . . foolish. It seems foolish . . . to me."

"What's foolish about it?" I asked. He looked me in the eyes and laughed – almost dirtily. He made an obscene movement down towards his member as he looked up at the ceiling with a pained expression. Then he studied me again with a static, blank expression in his eyes – this stood in absurd contrast to his right hand which was beating – audibly, jerkily, rhythmically – against the crutch of his jeans.

"A man struggling to remember something he would rather forget," he said tonelessly.

"Hmm," I said. His behaviour was familiar to me. A man trying to return to reality as if nothing had happened, but his personality had changed. Too much white powder.

"I don't know . . . ." Chris said with a questioning gesture of his hands. Then he looked around the cabin as if his surroundings had only now attracted his attention and he was trying to interpret them. "Do you smoke?" he asked. I pointed to the ashtray, the cigarettes and the lighter which lay on the little table beside the bunk.

"No, I mean . . . ." Chris hesitated. I nodded my head slowly and narrowed my eyes. I don't like smoking on my own, either. He pulled a joint out of his shirt pocket and made the same questioning gesture with his hands.

"Yes, that'd be fine," I said.

It is people staring that makes me feel out of place in the room. Their eyes sweep systematically across a crowd of faces, searching – they must all be hoping to find someone they know. It is Saturday evening in Jomfru Ane Gade; everyone has come to have fun, but it seems merely desperate, meaningless. I am in Rock Nielsen where I am leaning against a small wooden panel fixed at chest height all the way around one of the columns supporting the roof. I haven't seen anyone I know and in a way that suits me fine – there are some people I don't feel like meeting. But the eyes . . . they glide past me, searching, then stop and go back, examine my face – frightened, confused eyes – and I become self-conscious. The skin on my face tightens, more than usual. As if it is burning red again – it feels like parchment that is on the point of bursting and I turn towards the column in the discotheque to watch people dancing, take a swig of my beer, light another cigarette and feel empty inside. My bottle of beer is empty too, but I don't want to leave yet. I rub my hand across my forehead and feel the uneven surface just above my eyebrows where the burns were so deep that they had to graft skin from the inside of my thighs. The rest has grown together naturally, but the pigmentation of the skin has a strange appearance.

I have to get used to it – that is the way my face is. I turn towards the bar where there is a dense throng of people; some are drinking, others are trying to attract the attention of the barman.

Then I see her. I *see inside* her. It is not like . . . like the twenty times in the course of the evening I have seen a girl who was fuckable. My eyes are drawn into her, see through her . . . outer shell; frightening. I can only vaguely make out a round cheek – her face is almost obscured by her dark red hair which falls in curls onto her shoulders. She is standing with her back to me, up by the bar, and my eyes are drawn into her. On tiptoe in a long, blue-black velvet dress cut tight at the waist, emphasizing her waistline; the slight curve of her back, nicely proportioned hips, beautifully rounded buttocks. She is trying to catch the barman's attention, but nothing is happening; she is not tall enough. Without a moment's thought, I walk over towards her and wedge myself in between her and another customer. I don't touch her; she smells of earth, warm living flesh. I can see past the hair and briefly take in a round face with a broad mouth – full lower lip – and eyes heavily lined with black eyeliner; a broad nose with a slightly saddle-shaped bridge and almost completely round nostrils. I think to myself: Allan, she's one of those alternative types – your eyes have been drawn to a hippy. Don't think about it, I tell myself. It's just prejudice; you've never known any alternative types.

I push the guy to the left of her away so that I have room – not brutally but firmly. Now I am facing her and have my left arm on the bar, which she is leaning against. My presence, in the form of my arm, catches her attention. The tattoos. She looks up from my arm to my face and her eyes change almost imperceptibly when she sees my skin. She breathes in and is about to say something but stops herself. The skin tightens as I flash her a smile. She is turning her head away again.

"Come on, say it," I say. She looks up at my face again and nods downwards at my arm.

"Nice tattoos," she says simply, almost as if she were bored. I look at the starfish, crabs, snail shells, anchor and chains, fish, seaweed and sting-rays.

"Thank you," I say, and add," We need some service here." With my right arm in the air I call the barman. He leaves the two girls he has served and comes straight over to me past several outstretched arms waving notes and credit cards. It is the face that does it again.

"I hope you don't mind if I buy you a beer," I say to the girl.

"Tuborg FF," she answers, nothing else. We are given the beers and change.

"What happened to your face?" she asks.

"A fire," I answer. Notice that isn't satisfactory, so I elaborate. "At work . . . where I last worked." This is not particularly informative, but I don't feel like going into details.

"What do you do?" she asks.

"Engineer . . . I'm an engineer." My profession seems to surprise her.

"What happened then?"

"A whole load of oil caught fire because someone wasn't paying attention."

"But you weren't seriously injured." It is a question.

"No," I answer. "Burns, but not much more than you can see. There are some burns on my chest and shoulders, but I got off lightly."

"Did anyone . . . ?"

". . . come off worse? Yes," I answer. Much worse. My back goes cold.

"But no-one died?"

"No," I lie. I don't want to go into it. "This is not the right place to talk about it. My name's Allan," I say, stretching out my hand. She looks at it. She seems to find it ridiculous that I should want to shake hands; she seems amused, but she takes my hand anyway and squeezes it briefly.

"Hi," she says and adds, "Maja."

"Maja," I say. I nod. She tilts her head.

"Why did you buy me a beer?"

"I . . . it seemed like the right thing to do."

"Why? I was going to buy it myself." A slight smile plays across her lips.

"It was just a . . . ."

". . . gesture?"

"Yes," I answer and bite my tongue, kick myself. This is why I am here; I am here to talk to her; there are 250 people pulsating around me, but it is her I am talking to. So speak up, man, I tell myself.

"I . . . ." I begin, take a deep breath, breathe out. "I was standing over there," I say, pointing. "And then I saw you – your dress. I thought I had to stand next to you, because I think it is such an attractive dress . . . that you look attractive in it."

She peers up at me for a while with serious, thoughtful eyes – she is working something out.

"Thank you," she says finally. "Who are you here with?"

"I'm on my own," I answer and I can hear that it sounds like an invitation, and it probably is as well, but it is not what I meant. "I've just moved here," I say. "Well, I grew up in Klarup, but I've been away for a couple of years . . . working in other places . . . to learn a bit more."

"Where?"

"Yes, where . . . ? Around. Boring places and then after the fire I decided to drop it all. Been on the move too long. And well . . . my family lives here," I venture as an explanation. The girl called Maja is about to say something when our attention is caught by a noise coming from where the staircase leads from Jomfru Ane Gade up into the room. The doorman, a bodybuilder type wearing a tight-fitting white T-shirt, has grabbed hold of a young guest and is pushing him up against the banister and shouting in his face. The guest tries to fend him off and is pushed down the staircase. From where we are standing I can't see if he falls.

"And stay away from here!" I hear the doorman shout, wagging his finger in the direction of the staircase. An attractive girl, looking terrified, hurries down the stairs, from where a tall, erect figure emerges, stirring something in me. I feel a hand on my arm, it is the girl's – Maja's – and I realize that I have become tense, that I have instinctively pushed myself away from the bar during the spectacle and can't tear my eyes away from the top of the stairs where the tall, erect figure is talking in a very business-like manner with the doorman.

"Do you know him?" she asks. I don't know either of them, but on the other hand I do know him – the doorman. I know what he is like, the kind of girls he goes with, where he lives, how he talks to his friends, what he does in his holidays, how he treats his dog and how much shit he is on.

"Steroids freak," I say.

"What?" she asks – Maja, that is.

"He takes anabolic steroids. That's why he's so aggressive," I explain.

"How do you know that?"

"It's . . . obvious. Paranoid. Psychotic. Stupid. It's clear – from his behaviour."

"Are you sure?" she asks a little tentatively and I am conscious that she is wondering if this is something I have personal experience of.

"Look at the size of him," I say.

"Mm?" she says, peering over.

"If he were to train himself up to be that big, he would have to be in a fitness centre several hours a day – all the time. For years. It's very unlikely he's done that." She gives me a questioning look and I have to explain myself: "I used to train at Jyden some years ago at the time when all the pills and syringes came on the scene. I trained just as much as the guys who were twice as big as me."

"What about the one standing next to him? What kind of person is he?" she asks. I take another look at him. He is a pusher. Not drunk at all, seems quite clear-headed – perhaps too clear-headed. He isn't out to enjoy himself. He is at work. He briefly surveys the crowd around him. He is not a plainclothes policeman – a policeman comes in search of something, investigates problems. This guy simply comes, and he is approached by the needy. Everyone can see that he is working, that he has something to sell and it is a seller's market.

"What do you think?" I ask.

"Pusher." She almost spits the word out.

"Agreed," I say and at the same time I wonder if the girl now thinks that I am some kind of biker – because of my tattoos, my build, the things I know, my line of work. I hope not. I point to her with a smile: "Much more important, what do you do when you aren't here?"

"I work for an upholsterer who restores rustic furniture and sells it to rich Americans."

"Okay," I say, surprised. "So you put new covers on sofas and that sort of thing, or . . . ?"

"No, I paint the furniture and then I rough it up so it looks old."

"Why . . . rough it up?"

"So that it's sold as an antique."

"Okay. People think they're buying antiques then?"

"Yes, of course. I'm a swindler," she laughs. "And I also make dresses."

"Did you make this one?" I ask.

"Yes."

"Wow!" I am thrilled, but automatically stop myself. Never show too much enthusiasm. It is deep in my psyche.

"You'll have to get hold of the barman again," she says. "I was supposed to buy beers for a couple of my friends."

I make a sign to the barman. He comes up, turns to me: "What's it to be?"

"Three Carlsberg Hofs," Maja says, putting a handful of coins on the bar. The barman counts it up. It is correct.

"Beer money," I say as the man opens the bottles.

"You're a funny one, you are," Maja says to me. She takes the beers in one hand and makes a move to go.

"Will I see you again?" I ask.

"Perhaps," she says. "If you try." We nod to each other and I follow her with my eyes as she winds her way through the crowd to a table. A gazelle-like girl is sitting there with short black hair around her skull like a helmet, together with a pale, scrawny guy, a little older – with a hunted expression in his eyes. The guy takes a quick swig of the beer which is pushed into his hand and talks away, gesticulating excitedly with his arms. Maja laughs, says something and points her hand towards the bar. The gazelle girl raises her eyebrows in surprise and looks over towards the bar. I turn round and rest my arms on the bar. Light a cigarette. My bottle is empty. I am a little drunk, but I decide to have one more beer – a Fine Festival brew, the same as she had. I buy the beer and search out their table again. They haven't got very far with their beer. I can't take my eyes off her and I am irritated by the people who obstruct my field of vision. Look at me: I think. Turn around, for Christ's sake, and give me a sign – but she doesn't. I quickly reject my idea I have of going down to her table. I am not a dog, I tell myself, but without much conviction. She is telling the others something and gesticulating with a serious expression on her face. Then the scrawny guy says something and she gives him a smile, which I hope is more indulgent than inviting. Then she makes a brief comment and all three of them laugh – the guy less than the girls; apparently it was at his expense.

How can she not look at me? That is what goes through my mind and it makes me realize that I am getting drunk, so I turn away and resolve to go home as soon as I have finished my beer. Above the bar, there is a slanting window running the whole length of the roof; the people sitting at the tables behind my back are reflected in the glass. I stand facing the bar watching the reflections of the people walking behind my back. A shiver runs down my spine; Frank walks past and I spin round, but it isn't him. Relax, I tell myself – there is no unfinished business with Frank even though he may see the matter differently.

I turn to face the bar again and search out Maja's reflection in the glass. I have almost finished my beer when she gets up and makes her way to the toilets. Out of sight from the table, she stops and turns round. She stands staring at my back and I know it is absurd, but I do it; I try with all my might to make my back look good. She stares at it for fourteen seconds, I think, before moving on. So I am happy. I leisurely finish my beer and keep my eyes off the reflection. When I leave I can feel her watching me and I shoot a quick glance in her direction and nod, and even though I am not in a position to see, I know that her expression changes because the scrawny guy is suddenly very busy looking over towards the place where I was. But I am on my way down the stairs and out into the streets where my legs carry me home to East Aalborg. It is beginning to get light and as I lie down on the sofa in my grandfather's living room there is a pleasant heaviness in the whole of my body that I try to hang on to, but I am already asleep.

The sun is shining in my face through the door out to the little balcony in the flat. The warmth is good although I feel dehydrated. Carl, my grandfather, has opened the door, perhaps to remove the foul air I have breathed out. I take a cigarette from my packet on his tiled coffee table and light up before shifting my feet to the floor. He has gone down to his boat. There is a note lying on the dining table – probably for me. When I am in the shower I think about the girl – Maja. I eat porridge oats and drink coffee in the kitchen and then I remember the note. Carl has written that he knows someone in the harbour, a property landlord, who has an apartment for me – also in East Aalborg – and I can move in this coming week. He also says that he is down at the boat in Vestre Bådehavn, the harbour on the other side of the town centre. He is getting it ready to go in the water, but he is behind because his rheumatism plays him up when he has to clean the bottom of the boat and he is too proud to ask me directly for help.

Okay, I drive down there in the sinfully hideous Ford Mustang I had up on blocks while I was away. The car could do with a date with a car re-spray man – the red paintwork has lost so much of its gloss that in parts it looks almost white. I briefly consider whether to sell the car and to buy something more practical. But the roar of the engine makes me feel good as the radio drones on about the murder of a biker on Zealand, and I watch the girls cycling in their fluttering flowery dresses even though there is still a chill in the air.

The boat is chocked up for over-wintering in the boatyard. Carl is sitting on deck having his lunch, some sandwiches and a beer. He hasn't advanced very far with cleaning the bottom of the boat.

"Carl," I say, scrambling on board.

"Idle, drunken scamp," he says with a grin. "Meet some girls, did you?" he asks.

"Decide in haste, repent at leisure," I answer and wink at him – so that he believes that I have met a girl, but I don't want to talk about it because it is too early or it was just a one-night stand. And perhaps it is too early, and perhaps it was merely a single encounter, but I believe I will meet her again – I hope so.

"Your mother rang," Carl says. I look at him; don't want to ask what she wanted. He knows I have been to see her and that it didn't go well.

"She's your mother," he says, without looking into my eyes – she is his daughter. We are both up to our necks in shit.

"One mother and many fathers," I remark. All the men my mother has lived with while I was growing up. The name of my biological father is Jens Simonsen. I have seen him once that I can remember. I was thirteen and we were in Bilka supermarket. I was pushing a shopping trolley with my eight-year-old mulatto half sister, Mette, towards the cafeteria when my mother put a hand on my shoulder to stop me. She pointed to a man whom I recognized from some photographs I had found in a drawer. My father. He has one arm casually wrapped around the waist of a pregnant young woman while pushing the trolley with his other hand.

"Allan," my mother says, nervous but with hope in her voice, as I begin to walk towards the man. Who the hell can tell what causes people to act in the way they do, or not act for that matter? I stand in front of him and his new model so that they have to stop. I look at the woman. With a flick of my head in the direction of my father, I say:

"I'm his son." Then I lower my gaze to her stomach before looking into his eyes: "I hope your kid gets cancer." Then I walk away. I felt justified in saying what I did. Now I am not so proud of it; it wasn't her bloody fault that he had behaved like a bastard towards me.

My mother met Jens Simonsen when she started working as a secretary in the accounts department of Aalborg Portland where he was the boss and of course he was spellbound by her beauty, and she took him. She led him with a sure hand, too. My mother was a very beautiful woman – she still is in her own way, although alcohol has left its marks. And she can make a man feel like he rules the world. I have seen her do that with all my mother's boyfriends. And men believe she is easy to live with because she is so totally in love with them. They are right. What they overlook, though, is that she has enormous, razor-sharp ambitions on their behalf.

She was twenty years old when she married Jens Simonsen and one year later they had me. Five years later she had worn him down – he couldn't stand the pressure and they got divorced. Then my mother took to drink. I don't remember it very clearly, but my grandmother told me about it. My mother felt that victory had slipped between her fingers and now her options were limited because she had a child – me.

"She's still your mother," Carl says.

"Stop worrying about it."

"You have to stop being bitter, Allan," he says, slowly shaking his head. It is difficult to tell off a weather-beaten old man with speckled grey hair and muscles like steel cables – especially when, by and large, he has brought you up.

"That may well be," I say, reaching out for a dust mask. "But it won't happen today." I hop over the railing and start sanding the bottom of the boat with an orbital sander.

Yes, I am bitter about that woman. I visited her when I had been back in Aalborg for a couple of days. Rang her doorbell half an hour after she had finished work – I wanted to avoid meeting her when she was sozzled. And she was – I think – almost painfully sober when I arrived. On the other hand, she can carry off being drunk better than most, but the frenetic way she was making coffee seemed convincing.

She chatted away. "Now look what a nice place Mette has got with Peter. Allan, I don't understand how you could leave Janne like that. She's married now and has got a child, and they live in lovely Hasseris." She stopped and looked up at me, but avoided my gaze. "You also need some decent clothes," she said as she stretched out her hand towards the cupboards for some coffee mugs. Dyed hair, sunglasses perched on her forehead, short tight skirt, sparkling-white blouse, stocking seams as straight as a die, high-heeled shoes, solarium-tanned skin and gold jewellery. She works as a secretary for Customs & Excise. "Just you go into the living room and I'll pour the coffee," she says, shooing me out of the kitchen. I was on the point of reminding her that I only want coffee and not coffee laced with alcohol, but I stop short.

"You look good, mother," I say as we sit down with lighted cigarettes and coffee – hers both weaker and stronger than mine.

"Really, thank you. Do you think so? Yes, well, I try to look after myself." She adjusts her hair, almost as if she were flirting. Pull yourself together, mother – you are too easy.

"Allan, you couldn't lend me four thousand kroner, could you?" she asks me a little while afterwards, looking into my eyes.

"No, but I can give you two." She won't take it. Now she is offended. A woman with principles. She wants me to lend her four thousand kroner and forget about it, but I can't give her two.

"All the years I've taken care of you," she says into space. And I know full well that she has chased wealthy men all her life to give Mette and me a good upbringing. Everything had to be *right*: the house, cars, furniture, clothes, wine, holidays. There was nothing wrong with her intentions; things only went wrong because booze took over.

If I stayed there another five minutes we would begin to squabble and then it would definitely turn into a shouting match. I stood up.

"I just need a glass of water," I said. I went into the kitchen where I stuffed two one thousand kroner notes into her bag before leaving the flat. Feeling like a total idiot.

On Monday morning I start the second week of my new job at the Limfjord Repair Yard in Skudehavn – the harbour right next to Vestre Bådehavn; again thanks to Carl. After the boss has checked me out and seen that I know my stuff I am given my own ship's engine to work on and an apprentice, Flemming, who gives me a hand. I feel that I have some perspective over my life. Everything is simple and in order, my aims clear and well-defined, the distracting elements of no real significance. Until I come home and Carl tells me that my old pal, Frank, dropped by and was put out that I hadn't contacted him.

"Uh-huh," I say – and that is all. Carl studies me carefully – the silence seems almost tangible. I can see by his face that he is not happy. I keep my mouth shut.

"Don't get caught up in all that again, Allan," he says.

"No – we can agree on that," I say. Again there is a silence as I take out a cup and pour coffee into it from the jug in the coffee machine. Frank . . . it had to come sooner or later. I sit opposite Carl at the little dining table in the kitchen and light a cigarette. We smoke and drink coffee in silence in the tense atmosphere with the radio droning away in the background.

"You don't owe him a thing," Carl says.

"I don't think he sees it that way," I answer. Carl plants his right elbow on the table and waves his cheroot around close to my face."

"That's his problem, Allan. Do you hear me?"

"Yes," I answer. "Loud and clear."

When I come home from work on Wednesday, Carl has got hold of the keys to my flat so we go down to the car and drive out to see Mette, my little sister, in Gammel Hasseris. Unfortunately, she and her husband are not at home and that makes Carl impatient. I open one of the two doors in the double garage with the key that I have been carrying around with me for three years and begin to load the Ford up with the few scant belongings I have, while Carl puts on the roof rack so that we can take my box mattress.

At one point I stop to look around the garage. There is loads of room here; my brother-in-law is not the type to accumulate tools. By the end wall I would put a long workbench with a couple of clamps. On the left I would have a lathe, a column drill and some shelving space. On the right I would hang my tools on the wall and have my welding equipment in front. With a little wood burner in one of the corners and a couple of strip lights in the ceiling it would be perfect. It happens every time I see an empty room with a concrete floor. Immediately my mind turns to how I would equip my own workshop – it is a regular obsession. I resume my work.

"That's what happens when I persuade you to go to sea," Carl says when I arrive at the car carrying a box.

"What happens?" I ask.

"That you live on your own and don't possess a stick of furniture."

"But I got away from all that shit," I say.

"Yes, but you lost Janne in the process," he says.

"Janne was a bitch," I say.

"She was a lovely girl," he says. I won't lower myself to answer that; I just glance across at him with raised eyebrows.

"Look . . . you're a grown man and all you've got to bloody well show for it is a couple of cardboard boxes and nothing else," he says.

"You never went in for that kind of thing, did you."

He stares at me. "No, I had your grandmother to see to all that, until she passed away." Then the old buffer gets a faraway look in his eyes. He turns his back to the wind to light a cheroot, but the thing is: there is no bloody wind. The air is still. With his back still to me, he strolls off into the garden. He has gone sentimental in his old age, seventy-six years old.

"But I've got you, Carl," I shout after him. "You're my manager." He doesn't answer, doesn't turn round, merely throws his right hand, the one holding the cheroot, up in the air in a dismissive gesture. It is most unusual to see him behave like this. He wants to see his grandchildren well set up in life. He wants to have great-grandchildren before he snuffs it, as he phrased it himself when I had just arrived home overloaded with duty-free booze. We were sitting having a tipple with Mette and all three of us were in a good mood. "I want to see results," he said, pointing to her. "The oven is heated. Put the bun in."

He doesn't utter a word on the way to the flat. Sits there filling the car with cheroot smoke. "It's draughty," he says tersely when I wind down the side window. I wind it up again and keep my mouth shut. Slowly, we carry the things up to the third floor. I make sure that I time my trips so that he doesn't have the opportunity to help me with the box mattress. I took four beers from the crate in my sister's and brother-in-law's garage. I open two and pass him one.

"Skol, grandad. Thanks for your help," I say, sweeping my hand around the flat.

"That's okay," he says. When I offer to drive him home, he declines and says that he can walk, that I have to organize the flat. I offer him the car keys.

"I can walk," he says again. Really rubs it in, whatever *it* is.

"See you, Carl," I say in the doorway and again he merely raises his hand without turning round, without saying, "Yes, bye," as he usually does. I really think he is sorry that I have moved off his sofa.

I walk around the flat to get an overview. Two small rooms, a little kitchen and a microscopic toilet with a hand shower. It is great. And recently an entry phone and cable TV have also been installed.

The view from the kitchen offers a little chunk of the fjord through a gap between the blocks of flats. A view of the fjord – if you are lucky. Then I realize that I can also make out one of the buildings in the now defunct Aalborg Shipyards. Where I did my apprenticeship. The summer of 1981 after I left school. There were eighty 15 and 16 year-old guys sitting for the exam in the canteen. Had to write an essay and do some maths – they didn't want anyone who was too feeble-minded; you had to be able to learn to follow a diagram and read a technical manual. Those that got through had to turn up one bright sunny summer morning and we were given a tour of the shipyard – huge, a complete society of its own. Filthy, noisy, fascinating; all that steel – getting all that to float. Enormous machinery. We were only there one day and then we had to spend three months at the technical school where all those who had fooled around at primary school because they wanted to be metalworkers regretted it big-time; we had to do reading, writing and arithmetic.

The first day after the tour we sat scowling at each other in the shipyard canteen, not saying a great deal and chewing away at our sandwiches. I had made my own – my mother did not trouble herself with that kind of thing. The other mothers, however, had got up early – lunch packets had to be made for the son and the father (who often sat in a different part in the canteen among the eight hundred men, and said 'Yes' when asked if the kid was starting that day, and inwardly hoped that the kid would behave himself and wouldn't bring any shame on him) and most fathers were wise enough merely to greet their kid from a distance with two fingers to the forehead as they passed – you don't mess with the sensitivities of teenagers.

There was a twenty-minute lunch break. The big clock hung on the end wall. The minute hand moves – clunk . . . clunk. Just before ten minutes past there was a light shuffling sound of people moving, then came the clunk, sharply followed by the massive scraping and rasping of hundreds of lighters – the fluted wheel passing over the flint and afterwards the hissing of the gas flames mixed with the smell of the controlled burning of fuel from lighters. Eight hundred men inhale. At precisely ten minutes and seven seconds past twelve an enormous cloud of smoke rises towards the canteen ceiling. If you light up before, you are severely taken to task – by the other smokers as well; you don't smoke when other people are eating. They have ten minutes for that. It isn't written anywhere. You can smoke everywhere in the canteen. Smoke-free zones – they didn't exist in those days.

No-one over-exerted themselves during working hours. You could sit on your backside for days, stranded, because a carpenter hadn't removed three boards from your working area and you weren't allowed to take them away yourself of course – there were strict rules governing job demarcation, and there would be trouble with shop stewards; there is a community spirit in the trade union movement: we don't steal each other's work and we light our cigarettes at the same time. And while waiting we undertook small tests of our manhood: we put our forearm right up against our opponent's, lit a cigarette and placed it in the crack between the two arms; the first person to move his arm had lost. It was an honour to have your forearm disfigured with cigarette burns the length of a green Cecil.

I stand by the kitchen worktop recalling the morning the police swooped on illegal mopeds outside the yard gates. I had to kiss goodbye to the fastest Yamaha in town. Three days later I was on my way to the shipyard at a hundred kilometres an hour on Janne's Puch Maxi – tuned, bored, notched, honed and re-geared. Maximum voodoo. She wasn't wildly enthusiastic about what I had done to her moped. And it was no bloody joke being the person who didn't drive to work on his eighteenth birthday in his own car.

The situation becomes more and more grotesque as I unpack my bags and boxes. I don't have anything. Fortunately, in the bedroom there is a fitted wardrobe with large teak sliding doors where I can put my clothes. The box mattress and the clock radio on the floor; a naked light bulb hangs from a wire in the ceiling as if my existence were a caricature – lonely gentlemen, twenty-six years old.

The living room: my old TV set on the floor, the few books I possess divided into two equal piles, one on each side of the TV. A stack of LPs up against the wall – no stereo set. I have to screw the clamp of the office lamp onto the window sill, there is basically no other option. A box of odds and ends: soccer trophies, model boats, a cracked glass bong, beer glasses stolen from pubs, foreign cigarette packets, lighters, a silver-coloured metal pipe. I start putting all the things on the window sill. Then I get down to a picture of Janne in an imitation tortoise shell frame, bought in Bilka. She is sitting in the garden of our rented row house, smiling happily. Her skin is smooth and golden, her frock flimsy. It does nothing for me. I remember the day. It is Saturday. We are going to have a barbecue. A couple we know – or, to be more precise, *she* knows – come over. I have worked every evening for a week putting new tiles up in the bathroom in a complex pattern. I didn't even like the tiles. I put the picture back at the bottom of the box, place the loose items on top and cover them with my various papers before putting the box at the bottom of the cupboard in the bedroom.

One box left. I know what it contains and I want to leave it until later. It is late and my stomach is rumbling. I go down, find an Iranian pizzeria, order a family pizza and buy a few things from a convenience store: milk, instant coffee, porridge oats, currants, beer and cigarettes. Pick up the pizza.

I switch on the office lamp and turn the light to the windowpane so that the people living in the building opposite can't see in. Then I sit in the middle of the floor in the living room eating pizza, drinking milk and watching cable TV. I switch to the Discovery Channel. They are showing a program about something that could be mistaken for the Olympic Games for tanks and armoured vehicles. It is taking place somewhere in the Middle East. All the major military powers are represented. Someone has produced a grenade that can penetrate armour plating and knock out tanks. But then someone else has developed an extra layer of armour, consisting of small linked boxes the size of an old-style dial telephone, which is hung on the outside of the tank. When the grenade hits the extra armour the detonators in the small boxes explode and thus counteract the detonation of the grenade by forcing it outwards – away from the tank. So someone has developed an armour-piercing grenade that starts with a smaller explosion, thus activating the explosion of the small boxes, and only then does the real detonation of the grenade take place, penetrating the tank's armour. Another strategy against the small boxes (which the Russians are said to have developed – at least they developed counter-strategy number two) is based on the idea of firing grenades towards the tank with such a high trajectory that they land from above, in other words, on the turret which traditionally has the thinnest armour in the tank (and you can't make it any thicker because the tank would then weigh too much, the commentator says) and then the grenade bursts through and toasts the soldiers inside. There is something about the temperature inside the tank increasing to 6,000° within one second. Fried.

But then the Americans or the Hungarians or someone else have developed a defence against aerial grenade attacks. They have mounted two infrared lasers on the turret of the tank. The lasers take an exact cross-section measurement of the path of the grenade and fire a small grenade which explodes in the air. The commentator on the program says: "*It confuses the incoming grenade, so it explodes in the air above the tank without damaging it,*" or something like that. What crap rhetoric because the grenade isn't confused. It can't think; it only does what it is built to do. Anyway, this tank get-together in the Middle East continues. The commentator is very enthusiastic. His stock comment is: "*What can be seen can be destroyed.*" It should be an Olympic discipline, I think to myself.

The kettle has a strange smell, so I boil some water in a pan for coffee. It is a little late for coffee but there is one more box to do, the most important, and I don't think I will be able to sleep, anyway. I feel like a joint and that makes me think of Frank. But I am done with being a pothead and I don't owe him a thing. He was caught carrying just under a hundred grams of bad amphetamines which we were selling in small portions so that we could cover our own consumption. Along with the other minor matters Frank had on his account, it resulted in him being given ten months in the shade and, yes, that could easily have been me. It was just very hard luck – hard luck for Frank. For me it was a wake-up call. I paid the 5,700 kroner we owed the ex-Bullshit biker we had bought the shit off and went to sea. Before Frank was released I had already moved from coasters to super tankers. I have seen Frank since, but the last couple of times I have had time off I have avoided him. When I have been in Aalborg I have limited myself to visiting my sister and Peter, Carl and my mother.

I manage to get all thoughts of Frank out of my mind as I spread the sea charts out on the floor. First the oldest ones of the Limfjord, the Kattegat and Skagerrak with Carl's inked-in lines on and the date and the year written in his angular sloping handwriting. The trip to the islands of Læsø and Anholt and all the way down to Helsingør in the summer of 1976. Later trips through the Göta canal to Stockholm – Carl at the helm in the middle of Lake Vänern: "Water, water everywhere and not a drop to drink."

He chewed tobacco when we went sailing because "it didn't matter if it was wet – that's practical at sea."

"Don't you want one of your cigarettes?" he asks one wind-still day when we had just eaten lunch and he had lit up a cheroot.

"Cigarette?" I say, trapped.

"The ones you smoke when you think I'm asleep," he says.

"Er – yes."

"Don't drop your ash on her." He is talking about the boat.

My eyes follow the line marked 1980 – the tough trip to Oslo. I returned to school two weeks late because the mast broke and we were stranded in Strömstad and Carl said that you couldn't catch a ferry home if you had sailed out. I was entirely in agreement, while Carl had his task cut out to explain the educational value of his plans to my head teacher. To my great pleasure, the conversation ended up being an opportunity for the head teacher to hear the richness of Carl's seaman's vocabulary.

Later, my own ink lines criss-crossing the Baltic – sailing in a coaster as junior engineer after I left the school of marine engineering. I hang all the charts up on the end wall with masking tape. If you place them adjacent to each other there is just enough room. Then I go into the bedroom, open my travel bag and take out the packet with the latest charts in. I bought the big charts two and a half years ago before I went to sea. Carefully, I unfold them on the floor. They are creased and stained with dried sea water. I have taped the charts together so that they cover an area stretching from the North Sea, down through the English Channel, out into the Atlantic and right down to the equator. From Rotterdam to Lagos. Over and over again. From oil jetty to oil jetty, without going ashore, unless the machinery broke down completely and we had to take on an emergency engineer. Day after day of grinding our way up the shipping lanes along the North African coast, into the Gulf of Guinea, past the Ivory Coast and the Gold Coast to the Bay of Benin off the Slave Coast and Nigeria's capital, Lagos.

And finally the latest line: the ink path through the Atlantic to the English Channel ending abruptly a little before Rotterdam in the middle of nowhere: no more, date and year – three months ago. I hang it up on the other end wall, above the TV. Then I sit down and drink beer, looking at the chart and smoking cigarettes. I like that chart. It is almost two o'clock and I have to get up in a little over four hours. It doesn't matter. It is my chart. I sit thinking about the things that have happened. It seems as if I have distanced myself from them – at any rate, I don't feel uneasy.

It was strange. I have always thought it was ridiculous when people talked about having hunger attacks after they had smoked a joint. I had never had a hunger attack in my life. And then when Chris had smoked the joint with me I was just so bloody hungry. My whole mind was focused on my stomach which was the size of a cathedral and equally empty. Okay, I thought, you're hungry and there's a ship's cook sitting right in front of you.

"I'm hungry," I said to him and then we both started laughing. It was the most fun I had experienced since I was in an Athens bar eight months earlier with a Serbian first engineer eating whole raw onions and drinking Slivovitz; he kept winking at the waitress, holding his crotch and raising his balls, saying: "Good for thiizz" *before taking another bite of the onion. The tears were rolling down our cheeks.*

We went into the ship's galley. Everyone had turned in except for the watch on the bridge. I sat on the steel worktop while Chris pulled things out of cupboards and drawers. Even along the west coast of Africa we have the galley stocked with fresh produce from Denmark, everything from meat and potatoes to eggs and milk. The Chief Steward doesn't go ashore in countries along the route to go shopping at the markets – all that is a thing of the past. Everything you eat comes from Denmark even if it was grown in Spain or South America. The goods are packed in refrigerated containers and dispatched to the ships in trucks *so that seamen never have to eat anything that is any more exotic than whatever is on sale at Bilka.*

"A certain casualness is required," Chris said.

"What?"

"To be a good cook. Well, of course, you don't chuck the ingredients together," he said, pointing at me with some sort of aubergine, "but you have to have a perspective and a routine which is so consummate that you can instinctively feel when something is right. I'll give you an example you can understand," he said as the knife in his hand flashed down onto the chopping board: chop, chop, chop.

"The amount of salt you need between your fingertips is obvious when you taste the sauce – do you understand what I mean?" He glanced up.

"Yes, perhaps," I answered.

"What about engines?" he asked.

"It's more exact," I answered.

"In what way?"

"It's not . . . a creation," I said. "It's . . . maintenance, repairs." I was still high. Chris had told me that he had bought a whole load of joints in Lagos. The end product was wonderful.

"Can you feel the engine?" he asked.

"Yes, but . . . ."

"Sort of feel how much salt – so to speak – it needs?"

"No," I answered. "It isn't something you should be casual about. That is taboo. It's more of an exact science."

"Oh," Chris said. "Yes, but there are also cook books, aren't there. They can't cook, though – cooking stands or falls with the person juggling the pans." He had taken two pans out and was juggling with them. He held one handle while throwing the other in the air. I was spellbound.

"Yes, okay," I said slowly, choosing the words with care. "It may sound sentimental, but it's all about love."

"Love? . . . you have to love the engine?" He was astonished.

"You have to be focused, to know what it needs, keep listening to it and taking care of it so that when you ask it to do some work for you, it will do it. But with a new engine like this one . . . ." I swung my arm around and pointed down to the floor. ". . . It doesn't need so much."

"That's almost the same as when you have fresh ingredients and the meal almost makes itself," Chris said. *The bottom of one of the pans was sizzling; it smelt of fried poultry, hot oil and exotic herbs.*

"But this is when you set the pattern for whether the machine will give you good service or not," I said. *"I mean, it can easily work perfectly well for many years even though I might be sloppy with the maintenance . . . ." I hoped he understood this. It was important for me that he understood.*

"But then it will punish you in later years?" Chris asked, *staring at me intensely. I chuckled.*

"Yes, well, I don't know if it will punish you – after all it can't think, but it seems as if it's disappointed," I ventured.

"It loses its self-esteem and becomes bitter," Chris said.

"Ha, ha, yes . . . it's certainly harder to pull the wool over its eyes."

2

From Føtex supermarket I walk down to the harbour front where I have parked my car. I load up my shopping. Even though it is warm and the sun is bearing down directly on the car I decide that I still have the time to go and have a look at the tugs before the food goes off. I stroll towards the bridge where they are moored – magnificent in all their rugged power. Mjølner, Goliath Fur, Goliath Røn. Bulldogs of steel. They are also used as icebreakers in the Limfjord when the fairway freezes over. They seem so relaxed: the sun shines on their black painted hulls, floating on water that is probably ten degrees. I imagine them sailing towards an expanse of unbroken ice to crush it with their weight and create a fairway. Gigantic diesel engines. That is a job I have thought about before – being first engineer on an icebreaker. You work all through the winter. If the ice is not frozen over you are on call and are paid 'waiting money' and then if the wind turns and the weather comes from the East with the continental climate and Siberian temperatures you work twenty-four hour shifts to keep the fairways open. On the other hand, you can have quiet summers, unless you are greedy.

The water gurgles against the wharf. I light a cigarette and a shiver comes over me – an image in my mind's eye: the surface of the water covered with twenty centimetres of ice, the night is pitch black; I stand there in an engine room – locked in – the engine thrashes, the hull creaks. There is no-one in the vicinity. No-one can move forward. The water outside is a killer. Involuntarily, I take a step backwards, away from the edge of the wharf. My upper body trembles. I am . . . I am simply afraid of the water. I spit – it is not pleasant to admit. Stub the cigarette end out with the toe of my shoe. I am not bloody going to be out in the middle of the sea in some fragile tub. Light another cigarette, inhale deeply, peer up towards the bridge and there – just as I look up – is Maja cycling with an erect back on an old black ladies' cycle; her dark red hair flowing after her like glistening newborn snakes, her face radiant like a figurehead on a galleon cutting through the air. I gasp, then finally shout out: "*Maja, Maja, hey*!" She seems to gently turn her head and look in my direction, but she makes no sign. Perhaps she can't hear me? The din of the traffic is too loud. I turn, run towards my car, throw away the cigarette and pull the key out of my pocket before I get to my car. And as I unlock I think that it takes an incredibly long time, my movements are quick and automatic, but at the same time it is as if my thoughts are trudging through heavy water:

Key in, turn, take it out, pull the door handle, open the door, put one leg in – followed by the body and the other leg, close the door, put the key in the ignition, turn it and press the clutch and accelerator, release the hand brake – I glance up at the bridge, can't see her any more, she must be half way to Nørresundby. Smack the gear lever into first – fortunately the car is parked with the nose outwards – the glide as I slip the clutch, press the accelerator, indicate to turn, eyes scour the road and I turn the wheel. Absurdly, I am disgusted by American films and TV series in which actors can always jump into a car, start up and go in a fraction of the time it really takes. It irritates me like hell as I scream out onto Strandvejen, shoot the red lights, turn left into Toldbogade, roar the short distance up to Vesterbro and then go to turn right up onto the Limfjord bridge and, *of course*, the lights are red and there is too much traffic for me to squeeze in. I smack the palm of my hand against the wheel.

Finally I am out onto the bridge. Line up – the cars are being overtaken by cyclists. I could have run faster. Naturally, I don't catch up to her. I drive around the centre of Nørresundby, but it is pointless. Shit.

The week is endless, I have a pile of overtime; the days seem draining – quite different from being at sea even though working hours are much the same. But the context is missing. The simplicity. I dash around completing a variety of tasks: transport, work, shopping, cooking and washing up. Household chores are a large part of the problem. My cooking is dreadful – the kilos float off. And the telephone rings, my sister wants me to go over, Carl wants to go sailing – and I want to do these things, but when? And there are women everywhere and not one of them is mine. Monday, Tuesday, Wednesday, Thursday, Friday, it is hopeless. Where are the two-three months between trips when you are paid and can do whatever the hell you like? On land, people only seem to be sane from Friday evening to Sunday evening – me too – and that is when I live my life. The rest of the time we go around in a peculiar daze. It is Monday again and you look forward to Wednesday because the week is half over. You don't think like that on long voyages; you have a different rhythm – longer and . . . more rounded.

The telephone rings one day when I am having half an hour's shut-eye after work. I wake up disoriented, look at the clock: two hours have passed. It is Carl.

"I'm almost ready to put her in the water," he says. It is an invitation.

"May I bring a girl with me?" I don't know why I ask – I must have been dreaming.

"Yes, of course you can. This weekend?" he suggests.

"Well . . ." I start. "I'm not sure if she wants to come. I haven't . . . asked her. I just wanted to know if it was alright." My voice is heavy with sleep.

"Of course, Allan," he says. "Um, is anything the matter? Are you ill?" he asks.

"No, I was just asleep." Carl grunts – in his book this is no time to sleep. He clears his throat a couple of times, probably because he is going to say something he doesn't want to say.

"Oh, Allan . . . that Frank rang," he says.

"Uh-huh, okay. What did you say to him?" I ask.

"That you had moved," Carl says, as if that was all there was to say about the matter.

"And what did you say when he asked for my new address?" I ask.

"Ummm," Carl hesitates. But then his voice regains strength: "I said that he should keep away if he doesn't want to get his ears boxed."

"Uh-huh, so you did tell him," I say.

"Yes, and I mean it," Carl says.

"Right, well, that's absolutely fine," I say.

"You have to get stuck in, my boy," he says.

"What?" I ask.

"Take her by storm." Then I realize what he is talking about.

"She's no pushover, Carl."

"No, no, of course she isn't. But a boat trip always impresses a young girl – mark my words," he says. I have the impression that almost too many of his words have marked me.

Every day. Turn the alarm off at seven o'clock. Pull the thin boiler suit over my underpants and my T-shirt. Breakfast in the mess room where work clothes are permitted. Whizz round the cabin, brush my teeth, have a dump, drink another litre of water, swallow a couple of salt tablets. Down to the fitness room. A quarter of an hour on the exercise bike; a quarter of an hour with dumbbells. Get a bit of exercise to kick start the sweating before going into the hole. Otherwise you go dizzy – something to do with your metabolism. Everyone feels unwell for the first few hours. Your intestines boil. You can't get away from the heat. 50-60 degrees down by the centrifuges. Between 90 and 110 degrees up at the top of the engine room by the exhaust boiler and the oil boiler. It is only when your clothes are totally soaked in sweat that you feel alright again. People working on the deck are equally exposed; the sun burns down on them all day. The engine guy started at seven. He cleans the turbines and the turbo-chargers by throwing in nutshells to eliminate all the furring up. They used to use rice, but it didn't seem right with respect to poor people. Or else he cleans one of the fuel centrifuges that the diesel oil is pumped through to remove impurities; two to four hours in the oil steam at 50-60 degrees. The working day starts with a meeting. The first engineer distributes the tasks as we smoke cigarettes. Perhaps the chief engineer is there too. He also smokes cigarettes. We are all deathly pale – we work in the hole. We smoke cigarettes. We sweat. We drive the ship forward. All the stuff about getting out in the sun is for bridge-watchers and so on.

Daily maintenance. Things have to be repaired. Planned maintenance. You take machines to pieces and replace worn parts before the machine breaks down. Programmed maintenance: the shipping company has issued a schedule, more like a book, which we follow – tasks with dates are listed for several years into the future. An auxiliary engine, a fresh water pump; tightening of bolts, cleaning, replacing of bearings, linings, gaskets. Adjustments, tests. Changing of oil. Emptying and filling of tanks. When the tasks have been allocated the duty engineer follows the schedule of his round. All the machinery is checked; to see if it has the right pressure, temperature and air filtration. Watch in the hole is for twenty-four hours at a time. Seven in the morning until seven in the morning. The working day is standard. Eight until half past four – we pay for our own lunch break. Evening free. Shower. Perhaps put a wash on. Write a letter. Sew on a button. Supper in the officers' mess. Video in the TV room. Read news cuttings from home. The weather in Denmark is always good. Either because they are having good weather at home or because you aren't at home in the foul weather. A round of cards. A novel. A sort of sleep. You can always hear it. Unconsciously you listen for the noise of the engine. Even if you are not on watch and the alarm is silent. If the main engine changes tone or stops then you hurtle out of your bunk and race down into the hole.

I start work at seven on Thursday because we are behind. A few minor repairs have come in which have to be finished for today and by Friday afternoon the pistons in an engine from a coaster have to be replaced; you take the cylinder head off, loosen the piston from the piston rod and lift it out of the cylinder. There is enormous power at work here; a piston of this kind can easily weigh a ton. There is absolutely no chance of us getting this done in time. Perhaps I am too thorough? Flemming – my apprentice – is tired. He always seems to be tired. I set him the task of overhauling the outboard motor on a lifeboat. He doesn't know how to assemble the parts and, instead of asking, he does it the way he thinks is right, which results in a bang and an ensuing silence after he starts the motor up. Sounded as if something had gone through the side of the engine. He stands staring at it with an expression of concern, for my benefit, and I stare at him speechless – anyone can see that he couldn't give a damn. I walk over and inspect the motor. The connecting rod has shot off the piston and made a hole the size of a small coin through the engine block. I already have my hands round his collar and I knock him down onto the oil-stained floor, my knee on his chest. I don't know what I shout at him, but afterwards there is a conversation, me and him and the boss in the office. I am seething. In the end I am obliged to shake hands with him – the boss's idea of making things right again. So I have to drive to Frederikshavn to collect the parts we need. I sit in the car thinking. He is just like I was eight years ago – Flemming; he comes to work smashed after long nights out on the town. I have a short fuse, I know that. But I was never slack with my work like him. It is wrong. When I return I go over to Flemming and apologize. I talk to him before starting from scratch again on the outboard motor – without Flemming. The boss has given him the job of cutting threads into pipes – he should be able to bloody manage that. Anyway, by the end of the day I have repaired the damage and the boss manages to have the coaster job put off till Monday. So a working weekend. That is okay.

Skip the shower, drive home, park outside the block of flats. There is something familiar about a man getting out of a car some way in front. Frank. Fuck. Well, it has to be faced. I am not against Frank; I have simply finished with that lifestyle.

He walks over to me with a big smile on his face.

"Why the fuck didn't you tell me you were home?" he says loudly. I have swung one leg out of the car, but I am still sitting back in the seat.

"Didn't know where you were," I answer.

"I'm, you know, – everywhere," he says grinning as I get out of the car. We shake hands. He holds mine a little too long while putting his other hand on my shoulder.

"Allan, for fuck's sake, you look a bit grilled," he says, examining my face.

"It's not much. Do you want to come up for a cup of coffee?" I ask. Not because I want him to come up, but I don't want to go to a pub and although I have finished with that lifestyle we are still friends – I mean, after all, we were in the same class from the seventh grade on.

"Have you eaten?" he asks. In fact, I am bloody starving so we go towards town in his car, a nippy Golf. "Old Carl was a bit grumpy when I phoned him for your new address," Frank says – he must have found it through enquires.

"Carl is a bit edgy," I say.

Frank laughs. "He had a go at me – threatened to beat me up. Said I should keep well away from his lad."

"He's afraid I'll have the police on my back again," I say.

"It was *my* back the police were on and they won't do that again," Frank says. "We are old enough now to use our heads." I don't say anything even though I am not that fond of him saying 'we' and I am not at all sure that he is any better at using his head.

We go to Vanggaards Cafeteria in Vesterbro – you can eat well there and wear filthy work clothes. Frank's mobile phone rings as soon as we have sat down and he walks over to the billiard tables to take the call. While we are eating I ask Frank what he is doing at the moment. He says he is still at Aalborg Boilers; otherwise we talk a little about the accident, about my younger sister, about the survival trip we went on in my little rowing boat when we were twelve. We shot seagulls on the island of Egholm with Frank's saloon rifle and roasted them over an open fire. The meat was hellishly tough and we felt like men.

"What about a beer?" Frank asks when we have finished the rissoles and we have had a cup of coffee. I tell him I have to be up for work next day at six.

"Okay," he says. "I'll drive you home but I just have to make a pit-stop on the way – bit of shopping." It is obvious we are going to see his pusher; it is the casual way he passes on information that tells you.

It is nine thirty. Frank drives through the streets towards East Aalborg while I turn on the radio and try to find some music. The mobile rings again. Frank switches on and listens.

"Right, well, I'm on my way," he answers. "Yes, I'm ready . . . got a guy with me . . . guy called Allan . . . three minutes. See you." He switches off the phone.

"Asger, his name is. Good contact," Frank says.

"I've stopped all that stuff," I answer.

"Is that right?"

"Yes, it is."

"Completely?"

"Yes."

"Not even a bit of recreational?" And of course he is right.

"That's not absolutely out of the question," I say with a grin even though it is not my intention, but what the hell . . . you only have one life and you have to have some fun.

"Asger's cool. Friendly prices," Frank says. "We could perhaps work something out. I fix a few things for him now and then."

"No, thanks."

"You'll soon get tired of heaving that machinery around."

"I really like my work," I say

"Not much money in it," Frank says. I have enough money, but that is none of his business. "I think you should consider it," he adds.

"What's the deal?" I ask.

"Oh, you know, it's a job in sales and customer care," Frank says, grinning.

"I'll think about it," I say, even though I have no intention of thinking about it. I am tired – just want to put the lid on the topic of conversation.

Frank parks the car outside an entrance only a few hundred metres away from my place. We go upstairs. A long-legged, dark-haired girl opens the door.

"Hi Frank," she says, looking at me with suspicion.

Frank nods, says: "Nina." She leads us into the living room; by the dining table there is another girl as well as the man who must be Asger, the pusher. He is wearing jeans and a lumberjack shirt with rolled up sleeves so that he can show off his biker tattoos. It is fortunate for his self-esteem that I am wearing a long-sleeved jumper. We stand in the middle of the floor and Frank raises his hand, points to me and says, "This is Allan, a school friend from primary school days and my partner until a couple of years back." Frank introduces Asger. I shake his hand. There is something strange about one of his eyes. "And Nina is Asger's girlfriend," Frank says, pointing then to the girl Asger was sitting talking to when we came in. "And Lene . . . umm, she's a friend of the house," he says.

"Hi," Lene says – she seems embarrassed or, perhaps to be more precise, a little cowed.

In fact, the room is tidy although the familiar ingredients are in place on the dining table: ashtrays, rolling tobacco, joint filter, king size cigarette paper, hash, pot, silver paper, tea-lights, bottles of wine, a painted wooden stash box containing the goods and digital scales. It reminds me of the old days when I used to be blasted at Frank's and we played casino; when the game was over we always started weighing our tricks to see who would receive points for their cards.

"Any requests?" Asger asks, turning to me. He is very thin.

"Coke."

"I haven't got much."

"A little is more than enough."

"Coke?" Frank says with raised eyebrows.

"As I said – only on very rare occasions," I say to him.

Asger takes the digital scales in his hand, stands up and motions me to follow him. Frank gets up, too. I notice the Amiga computer next to the TV – after all the long trips at sea I can beat anyone. We go into the kitchen – I don't know why, but paranoia is always an ingredient in these situations. He takes out a bag with a little powder in it from a cupboard, puts a little plastic bag with a press stud on the scales, sets it to zero and begins to scoop. "Stop, stop, I just need to get high once, that's all I need," I say.

Frank shakes his head, pointing to me, and he says to Asger: "I've seen this man break into a dentist's clinic and he took so much laughing gas that we had to call for an ambulance."

"That was then," I say.

We negotiate, after which Asger invites us to coffee. We sit down at the table again. He piles cream and cane sugar in his mug – the pusher's diet – and lights a hash joint which begins its circuit round the table. I steal a furtive glance at Asger's eyes. One iris is blue-green while the other is almost jet black.

Asger's girlfriend, Nina, talks to Lene about a third girl who doesn't know who the father of her child is and has therefore taken eight men to court on a paternity charge.

"Hurray for DNA profiling," I say.

"Why?" Lene asks cautiously.

"Damn sight better that one guy takes the rap for it than all eight of them have her on their back," I answer.

Asger chuckles. "Yeah, what a tart," he says.

Nina gives him a look. "You should be happy that you haven't been summoned to the trial," she says.

He looks at her. She holds his gaze. Obviously it is the pusherfrau who wears the trousers here.

"Take it easy," Asger says, turning his gaze to the table. He starts rolling some joints with clumsy hand movements.

"Haven't you got any punters?" I ask.

"I deliver," Asger answers, pointing to Frank, then seems to re-consider and adds, "It's different with him. We're partners."

"So if I need anything, I should ask Frank?"

"Yes," Asger says.

"It's because of the neighbours," Frank says, passing me the joint. I can manage a single drag – then it is easier to go to sleep after all the coffee.

"Sensible," I say to Asger, leaning back, inhaling and listening to the conversation. The police don't want to waste their time busting small-time pushers, but they are forced to if neighbours complain. It is fantastic hash.

"It was no good having all those people coming round, anyway," Lene says. She seems to be trying to harden her voice and her facial expression, but it doesn't really suit her. Perhaps she is playing the role of the pusher-frau's puppet. "People coming with their dogs and never having enough money – so gross," Lene added, looking across at me and giving me a cautious smile. I pass her the joint. It goes straight to my head which becomes light and airy – no heaviness or lethargy.

"No," Nina says, looking at me. "People came here wanting tiny bits of hash on the slate."

"And then they always had to sit here smoking," adds Lene with an aggrieved expression.

"What about your eye?" I ask Asger. He raises his head from the little pile of joints he is rolling.

"It doesn't hurt," he says.

"What happened to your eye?" I ask again. High, disoriented in an interested way, or vice versa. Ought to go home to bed.

Asger, resigned, laughs: "It's all a bit stupid." He says he went out for a drive one night with a guy called Leif: "On speed, of course. We had to go to a gas station to put air in the tires. And Leif was standing there messing about with the compressed air pump while I was fidgeting with the air jet and for fun I put it in my mouth, as if I was going to blow my brains out. Just at that moment he switched it on and my eye popped out of the socket and sort of . . . rested on my cheekbone."

"Christ," I say. "What did you do then?"

"He was so alarmed that he simply pressed the palm of his hand up against my face and put it back, but his ring somehow got caught up and made a hole in the pupil and that started a discharge." Asger smiles.

"Right. Are you still good friends?"

"No, Leif is dead," he answers. He let it hang in the air as if that was the price he paid for injuring him. But it turns out that Leif was a scaffolder and fell from the fifth floor while he was putting up railing.

"He survived," Nina says. "It took him four days to die."

"Tough," I say.

"Childhood friend," Asger says, nodding slowly while continuing to look down at his work.

"The worst thing was those girls, Susan and that other one," Nina says, glancing across at Asger again. He is concentrating on toasting more tobacco.

"Girls?" I ask. I don't know which girls she is talking about.

Frank interrupts: "Asger was living with another girl then, Susan. And Susan's girlfriend – I can't remember her name – she was with Leif, the guy who died. They were a couple of alternative types who hung out at 1000Fryd." Asger seems to be concentrating even harder on his work.

"They completely freaked out, particularly Leif's girl . . . ," Lene starts and checks with Nina as if for approval. A second passes, then Lene turns round to me and explains: "Well, Leif . . . after he died the girl went to his funeral in a long, dark dress with a veil. She stood there sobbing, her eyeliner was caked round her eyes and it ran down her cheeks. It was simply unbearable." Lene seems indignant. Frank has picked up a car magazine and nods absent-mindedly. I don't understand it, cast a glance over to Asger who still isn't saying anything and has started putting around thirty ready rolled joints in a plastic bag with a press stud.

"It was too much to take," Nina says. I look across to her.

"Was she was his girlfriend . . . I mean, Leif's?" I ask.

"No." Frank raises his head from the magazine. "You see, Leif was with her, but there was nothing in it. They weren't a couple. No, no." Frank shakes his head dismissively. Asger slowly gets to his feet. Packs things into the painted wooden stash box. Makes his way out of the living room.

"So the miserable one sat up here with Susan . . . and mourned. They lit tea lights and incense and all that shit until Nina chucked them out," Lene says. I discover that the cigarette I am smoking tastes awful; it has burnt right down to the filter. Not used to being stoned. It is too much. Stub it out in the ashtray. Apparently look bewildered, so Lene explains: "Yes, Nina used to come up here then . . . I mean, as a customer." Meanwhile Frank has stood up and followed Asger into the living room. Perhaps he needs to go to the toilet.

Nina looks angry. "Yes," she hisses. "And that hippy's still going round town as if she's carrying a huge sorrow, all black around her eyes and mysterious expression on her face."

"Who?" I ask.

"The girl . . . I can't remember what she's called – the one Leif was with," Lene answers.

"And the girls weren't even aware of what was going on," Nina says.

"They probably believed in love," I suggest.

"Love," Nina spits the word out. "It's got fuck all to do with love, ruining other people's business like that."

"Oh right, I thought you meant that they hadn't understood that they weren't welcome."

"No," Nina says through gritted teeth. "They didn't understand that they were frightening the customers away with their ridiculous morbid romanticism."

"But they realized or . . . ?"

"Nina made it clear to them," Lene answers.

"And Leif was only with her for the fun of it," Nina adds. She lights a cigarette, turns towards Lene and says: "I always have this urge to go over and slap her."

"Yes, and she's not kidding," Lene admits. I don't understand this anger towards a girl who was friends with a man who is dead.

"And what about Asger's girlfriend . . . Susan?" I ask.

"Ex-girlfriend," Lene adds hastily.

"I threw her out," Nina says. "She was just a young girl who thought it was exciting to live with a pusher. She had no backbone."

Asger appears in the doorway. "Nina has been chasing me for years," he says, leaning against the door frame.

"Aw, shut up," Nina says, angrily.

"She's a heavy smoker," Asger explains. "She has to be with a pusher to get her own needs covered."

"You'd never bloody get out of bed if you didn't have me to kick you out," Nina says, still angry, but there is a touch of caution in her voice.

"Possibly, but your continual abuse of people is beginning to be tiresome," Asger says.

"But . . . ," Nina says.

"I'm off," Asger says, disappearing from the doorway. Franks pokes his head in.

"Allan, let's get going," he says. I nod to the girls. Lene gives me a cautious smile.

"Bye," she says, taking my hand and giving it a little squeeze. Take it easy, I think. Maybe. For sex. I make my way out of the living room.

"If I hear that he is running after her one more time . . . ," Nina says behind me. Menacingly, but so low that Asger won't be able to hear it. He is already on his way down the stairs.

When we are in the street I tell Frank that I want to walk home. He talks about meeting up again.

"Beer," he says.

"Any time," I say. They take Frank's car. I start walking. Why the hell did I buy cocaine? Okay, once in a blue moon is no problem of course, but this is not a groove I want to get into. Probably because of the bad day at work. Walk slowly, the silence does me good after the two girls' . . . well, almost spiteful gossip. There was something callous about it all . . . their attitude – there was also something else I could not quite put my finger on. My brain is clouded – I am not used to smoking dope. I arrive home, undress and fall asleep immediately.

We face each other in the chilly room, naked, and I slip my right hand round her hip until my thumb rests by the crack between her buttocks. The alarm clock goes off. It is five o'clock. The duvet has slipped onto the floor. I am alone.

Maja. She is on my brain all day while I work for thirteen hours. It is Friday, but I also have to work on Saturday. Nevertheless, I take a long shower, shave, drink coffee, stay awake until eleven o'clock when I go to town to see if she is there. She isn't. I hang around the bar and drink beer until half past twelve. She doesn't come. I feel like an idiot. Drive home. Pass out with exhaustion.

Saturday. We finish the coaster job in the middle of the afternoon. I just manage to do my shopping. Sleep two hours. Cook, eat. As I screw my expectations up several notches I tell myself to stop.

Towards midnight I go up the steps, and there she is. By the bar. Like the first time. I feel I can breathe as I walk towards her. Consciously tense my facial muscles so that I do not smile too much. Suddenly I know that . . . that I am . . . that I feel a lot for her.

I smile and say hello. Shall we find a table? And then it is . . . it is all . . . wrong. She seems angry, but also it is as if she is talking to a child:

"I'm no good for you. Not at all," she says emphatically.

"I think you are," I say – and that is all I can find to say. "I definitely think you are," I repeat. With one hand I have lightly touched her elbow. She looks down at my hand, her elbow, and then looks up at me – a questioning expression – ironic – framed in red, shiny curls.

"I think you should go," she says. Inside in my – in the whole of my upper body – I feel bad. Scan her face for signs of . . . something else.

"Are you okay?" Who spoke? Force my eyes off her. My brain is not getting enough blood and oxygen, same feeling when you step on dry land after a long time at sea – the dizziness – only in a negative way. Everything stands completely still. There is the scrawny guy from last time. Behind him the gazelle-like girl with the helmet hair style. The scrawny guy gives me a hard stare, then turns to Maja.

"Is he bothering you?" he asks. It is depressing and at the same time rather amusing that he asks her this, amusing in a sad way.

"It's okay, Valentin," Maja says.

"I . . . ," I begin, falter, let go of her elbow, need a cigarette. "I'm sorry," I finally manage to say as I bring out my packet of cigarettes. I put one in my mouth while I consider whether to offer the packet to her – so grotesque. She doesn't move, I don't move – happy to wait for the possibility of . . . another outcome. The scrawny guy is still standing there – and the gazelle girl. I consider whether to offer him a cigarette or knock him over.

"Perhaps we could have a cup of coffee one day?" That is what I say without knowing where the hell the question came from. There is a touch of mockery in my facial expression – I can feel it in the way the skin tightens.

"I don't drink coffee," she answers, pushing the scrawny guy ahead of her. The other girl follows and they disappear.

"What can I do for you today?" It is the barman standing in front of me – obviously recognizes me. My evening meal moves, my back feels sweaty – it must be the exertion from not hitting the guy. Shake my head, turn around, go down to the street.

Am still . . . dizzy. My stomach slowly calms down, somehow out of synch with the many people there, the lights from the bars, the loud noise and music. I am only too conscious that I have cocaine in the pocket of my jacket and now I curse myself for not having bought speed. Who am I?

Stand in the gap between two pavement cafés and scoop it up my nose with the help of a nail file on my penknife. People stare. Up yours. Rub my nose, shake. Walk on. Everything is . . . teeth like steel in my mouth. I have bite. Go into Grøften. Frank is sitting at a table with the one called, I think, Lene – she looks a bit anaemic. Frank calls me, the girl raises her arm – meekly. A passage through the swarm of people automatically opens up in front of me; the force of my aura frightens them away. Make it clear with a look, gesture with my hand, minimal movement of my head that I am going to the bar for a drink. I have a thirst on me. People dancing, bodies in tight clothing. I am at the bar, I drink, take my beer to the table. Sitting, looking at the dance floor, living flesh – it is finding its way through. I have control.

"Have you thought about my offer?" Frank asks after I have sat down. I look at him, silent. For a moment my high takes a dip and hovers over the Earth's surface, the pit of my stomach hollow. Maja, I think. Why would you . . . reject me? I make myself busy by lighting a cigarette so that Frank can't see my eyes. Frank's offer? Put Maja out of my mind, inhale the smoke deep down into my lungs, focus my gaze on Frank as I breathe out.

"I haven't finished thinking," I say.

"You're here anyway . . . and you're flying," Frank says. Of course he can see that I am affected but . . . there is something that makes me uneasy about Frank, there is something rumbling around just out of my reach. Wished my brain was clear so that I could work it out instead of being strung out on coke.

"I haven't finished thinking," I repeat and flick my head towards the dance floor. "Tasty ass on her."

"Which one?" Frank asks, turning round in his seat to follow my gaze.

"The blonde," I say. The girl has a hole in her jeans at the bottom of each cheek. Her arms are raised above her head, rhythmically she rotates her bottom, each of the holes opens and closes in turn according to her movements and reveals the luminous skin. Invitations – eternally there.

"Perhaps ought to dance today," I remark.

A smile from Lene: "I'd like to dance," she says.

Frank is serious. "Take care," he says, pointing to a table. "Her bloke is over there – he's no joke."

I follow the direction of his finger, eyes cut through the air. Biker.

"Okay," I say, understanding the point. "She's only out there to shake her fanny and get him going."

"Don't be so coarse," Lene says with an embarrassed smile. Frank laughs.

"Face up to it," I say to Lene. "She is out there rubbing herself up against the crotches of the young males and in the end the big guy wakes up and chases them all away, and then they go home and screw."

"Allan, you're too much," Frank laughs. Then he turns to Lene: "He's always been like this."

Tasty biker girl comes over and stands at the end of the table.

"It's bloody true," I say. "And if he can't make it because he's taken so much shit that he can't get it up, then he beats her up instead." The girl has sat down next to me, close. Bleached blonde, perm, heavy make-up, tarty perfume; the two demi-globes protrude from her low cut blouse. Lene peeks nervously at Frank who is trying to catch the biker girl's eye – he is clearly interested.

"You're called Allan, aren't you?" she asks.

"Yes, that's me," I say. "Who are you?"

"I'm Lykke, sometimes known as Joy."

"You *are* a joy," Frank says.

"Is that right?" I ask.

"Sometimes," Lykke answers coquettishly, moves position so that her thigh is tight up against mine. "What are you talking about?"

"About the mating ritual," I say.

"Mating ritual?"

I point to the dance floor: "What's going on out there."

"What do you mean?" Lykke asks.

"It's like watching wildlife programs on TV," I say. "The males swagger and the females preen themselves."

Lykke laughs. "There could be something in that."

"That's enough of that," Lene says from the other side of the table. "They're just dancing."

"I fail to see what point there is in dancing if you haven't already decided to take the girl home and give her a good screw afterwards."

"Aren't you the one who was in that accident?" Lykke asks.

"Yep."

"I read about it in the paper. It must have been terrible."

"It wasn't that groovy," I answer.

"Were you afraid?"

"Not a bit of it, "Frank says. "He's a tough bastard."

"Of course I was frightened," I say.

"Do you mean that?" Frank asks.

"One night, just try jumping into a burning sea knowing that you have to swim twenty to thirty metres under the water to avoid being fried and to get air."

"Yeah, right," Frank says. Lykke has put her hand on my thigh under the table.

"There were also some people who died, weren't there?" she asks, curious.

"Seven," Lene says. How the hell did she know that?

"It's fear, of course, that makes the adrenaline pump in situations like that," I say to Frank. "That's what enables you to survive."

Lykke nods and says: "Yes."

Lene asks about my burns. I give her an offhand answer and drink my beer.

Lykke's hand is squeezing my thigh. "Oh, I'm just crazy about this tune," she says. "Do you want to dance?"

"Of course." I stand up and follow her with my hand at the bottom of her back. I can feel Frank's eyes. Of course she wants to copulate with the survivor of a disaster at sea – it is almost a principle.

She is wearing tight-fitting denim shorts – very short, almost hot pants. There are men hanging round the bar, cigarette and beer in hand, speaking to each other and pointing to the dance floor. I pull her close to me, her pelvis grinds against my crotch. Hold her tight, my left hand at the base of her back, my right hand firmly gripping her ass. Her arms round my neck.

"Fresh boy," she whispers huskily.

". . . my impression you like it."

"Oh, you think so, do you." She clings to me. I slide my right hand up the front of her thigh, between our bodies, concealed. Manoeuvre a finger under her shorts inside her thigh. The smooth, wet touch of vaginal lips.

"Ooohhh," Lykke murmurs.

"Let's go now," I answer.

"I live nearby." She is out of breath. We can't keep our hands off each other as we walk. I loosen the knot at the front of her blouse. Black, shiny bra. She is in front of me in the stairwell. I pull her blouse off her, run my hand up the inside of her thigh to the crack between her cheeks, the pussy – warm, wet. The bra off in the hall, my mouth round a nipple, rubbery hard under the light pressure of my teeth, my tongue licks round, the other breast in my hand.

"I just have to go to the bathroom." She tries to say it with composure, but she is too excited. I go into the living room, take off all my clothes. My dick is so hard it hurts. Take the last of the cocaine. Light a cigarette, sit down on a dining room chair with my hands on my thighs. She comes in.

"Is that for me?" she says; laughing.

"Take your clothes off." She obeys and comes over. There is a pair of sunglasses on the coffee table. I put them on her. Don't know why but it is necessary; I don't want to see her eyes. She sits on top of me. When I look down I can see the base of my dick come into view and then dive out of sight like a piston as she rides me, her abdominal muscles clearly defined under her very thin skin.

"Oh yes, fuck me," she says, her mouth open, groaning, almost jumping up and down on me, sinking her nails into my shoulders as I am getting closer. I think she draws blood. My face hideous in the reflection of her sunglasses – it halts my orgasm.

"Oh, haven't you come yet?" Her voice is like damp rust when she has got off me, and my dick stands erect in the chilly air. She kneels down and devours it. The plastic of the sunglasses is cold against my stomach. She is anyone. I can smell her pussy. Pull her up by the shoulders, sit her on the sofa, kneel down, spread her legs far apart, her pussy gleams, wide open, heavy with wetness. I enclose it in my mouth, lick, the smooth taste like glass, let my teeth rub against her clitoris, create a vacuum, suck it in and out between my teeth loudly, play with it with my tongue. The shock waves run through her. I peer up; she is pulling hard at her tits. I take my face away from her pussy, let the cold air in. My cheeks are wet. The insides of her thighs are wet. I lift her legs higher up. The bum hole – a pink imploded scar; that shines with wetness, too. I run my tongue around it.

"Ooohhh," she says.

"Turn over."

She places her knees on the edge of the sofa, bum in the air and holds the back of the sofa.

"Fuck me, Allan." I do.

"Are you my screw?" I shout.

"Oh yes, yes," she groans. I smack her on the bum. She groans, deeper. Slap harder. Now she is whining, the imprint of my hand remains. I can see her ass hole; the muscles are contracting. Lick a finger, play with it, massage it until it is open enough, insert my finger.

"Ooohhh," she says again. I look down. My dick is pumping in and out of her pussy. This is where I am. This is why I am here.

"Fuck my ass."

I do.

"Yes, fuck that ass. Fuck it." She puts her arm through her legs and slaps herself on the pussy.

"You like that," I say.

"Fuck that ass. Harder," she says and slaps her cheeks with the back of her hand until I start doing it. She slaps her pussy again. Screams. Now she likes it. Finally I come. My balls ache – small, hard, unripe plums. Move to the bed. Continue.

In the end, she falls asleep. The smell of sex hangs in the air in the flat. I smoke a cigarette and as the smell becomes older it becomes colder or simply tired and begins to reek, to stink. Joy, oh Joy, oh Joy unconfined. I put on my clothes and go down to the street. The cinders set in; the body fills with sand. The insides of my eyelids scratch the cornea every time I blink. Take a taxi home, go into the shower. Hit the sack. Empty. Get up. Drag the box mattress into the living room, lie down and stare at the sea charts until it is day and I am consumed by sleep.

3

Sitting in Cine 5 on Sunday evening watching *The Abyss* – part of a science fiction cavalcade they are running. Great visually, but utter rubbish. In the film a woman is on the point of drowning and I have to squeeze the arm-rest tight not to throw up. I don't take in the rest of the film – I shake and I have the shivers; luckily no-one is sitting next to me. When the film is over I calm myself down watching the credits so that I can go out on my own, and then I see her. She is sitting a few rows down from me with the girl who looks like a gazelle who was also in Rock Nielsen. They stand up. Maja is wearing a black V-neck woollen jumper with pre-washed army pants that fit tight round the backside. What the hell do you do with a girl like her? Why not just go for one of the others? I ask myself that question and curse myself for trying to fool myself. The others are anyone. She is twenty-five metres in front of me on the pavement when I leave the cinema and as well as being annoyed I feel strange walking behind them without making my presence known. But I have to walk in the same direction and have every bloody right to be there.

I concentrate on my cigarette and the shop windows until I look up. She is standing waiting for me; the gazelle girl has gone.

"I think you need a haircut," Maja smiles uncertainly.

I look into her eyes and in fact I don't know what to say. Fortunately she says 'sorry' and lowers her gaze.

"Hi Maja," I say.

"It was just because . . . ," she says, fidgeting with her hands. I want to tell her it doesn't matter.

"Because . . . ?" I ask.

"I'm sorry if I hurt you," she says. Fortunately I remember how easily I am to con.

"That's not what it's about. I don't like being . . . well." I gesticulate vaguely, start walking down the pavement, for a second she is behind me. "I came looking for you . . . and then . . . then a . . . guy . . . comes up . . . I mean it is just too grotesque for words." She walks behind me.

"He was . . . well, we . . . were drunk and the atmosphere was a bit . . . ."

"So you had to piss on me because I wanted to say hello to you?" I don't know if I am going a bit too far here; I don't know her type of people, but I know what I want, so . . .

"I know. I can't buy you a beer, can I?"

"Why?" I ask.

"So that I would feel better."

"A gesture?"

"Yes – a gesture," she smiles.

"Okay." I say , and she takes my arm and, strangely enough, already seems happy again. She walks close to me and says something about the film. I don't know if she realizes what she is doing. I tremble as if electricity runs through my whole body. As we walk she talks about how much she loves being at the coast and swimming in the sea. We go into Queens Pub in Vingårdsgade, a classic pub with a high ceiling. I take my jacket off and sit down on one of the corner benches with my arms casually spread out across the top rail, aware that she can see the build of my body. I like the way she stands at the bar with her back slightly curved and her bum sticking out as she gets us a beer.

"But I mean it," Maja says as she sits down at the table. "I think you need a haircut."

"What style?" I ask.

"Very short – I think that would look good."

"I'll think about it," I laugh. My hair has only just properly grown back in the last couple of weeks.

"But will you though?" she asks with a broad smile, and I can see the tip of her tongue peer out from between the two rows of teeth in mid-smile and a little bubble of saliva which bursts on one of her front teeth. She grins at me and because I don't know why, I grin back and say: "I really like your smile. I liked it from the very first time I saw you."

"I've got a pair of scissors here," she says, taking hold of the strap of a little military knapsack she has hanging on her right shoulder.

"Do you know how to cut hair?"

"Yes," she says. "Do you dare take the risk?"

"On one condition."

"What's that?"

"That you cut my hair in the middle of the Limfjord bridge."

"Right, that's what you want, is it?" she says, studying me closely.

"Yes, that's what I want," I answer. She drinks slowly and even though I slow down I quickly overtake her. We sit talking about this and that; feel our way towards topics we can share. It doesn't seem to be strenuous.

I ask about her work.

"I paint rustic furniture. Everything used to be painted with oil-based paints, so that's what I use. First a primer and then rustic style patterns and motifs and the real colours they used at that time. And then sometimes I paint the year on because they often did that in the past, for example 1867. Or if it is a bridal chest I add a signature. And then I rough it up so it looks aged."

"But the furniture you buy – isn't it antique?"

"No, they're copies. And mostly they're one colour, and if they really are originals they're usually worn and . . . lack charm."

"Do you strip them first?"

"No, you mustn't do that. It's like with panelled doors when the panels are made with off-cuts; furniture often is too, so if you strip it the paint remover makes the wood warp and then the joints come loose. We sand the paint off or have it sandblasted at a car paint shop."

"And when you've finished painting you rub dirt in?"

"Yes, that's the whole secret," she says, winking at me. I look at her hands. They are clean enough, but I can see paint deep in the pores of her right hand. She notices my gaze although I try to be discreet. All the girls I have known freaked out when flaws in their personal hygiene were pointed out. She lifts up her hand.

"Wood stain. Sometimes I rub a stain into the fresh paint and push it right into the corners and when I have let it settle for a while I dry most of it off again, from the surfaces that are easy to get at."

"What else do you do?"

"I rub the furniture down with fine sandpaper, especially where it tends to get worn. Like the backs of chairs, where you hold the chair to pull it out and where your thighs rub against the edge of the chair. And on cupboard doors, where you open them. All the corners and edges generally. I often sand right through the paint, but the wood looks nice and bright, so you have to dirty it up."

"With earth?"

"Coffee and tea."

"Do you pour coffee on to it?"

"No," she says as if I were stupid.

"How the hell should I know?"

She smiles. "I take some moist coffee dregs or tea leaves – they're also good for rubbing into cracks and crevices, then I brush it off when it's dry. Where the dirt collects it looks very natural. I give the corners a going-over with a leather rag – that gives them a definite sheen. You can put several layers of dirt on so that it looks authentic. I also scratch it with sand and gravel to make it seem *genuinely* worn." As she talks she waves her arms around energetically. She is fantastic.

"It is a whole . . . art form," I say.

"When the furniture has the false patina I rub it down with a waxed cloth so that it is a little greasy, as if it has been used. The wood that has been sanded down must not seem too dry, you see. And then it's finished to all intents and purposes."

"And then the Americans buy chairs and wooden trunks?"

"Yes, and wardrobes, cradles, chests of drawers and linen chests. Mostly wardrobes. So we pack them into a container and there are whole loads of rich people in the US who furnish their houses in a style they call "Scandinavian country" which they have seen in a large catalogue put together by a Swedish-American interior designer. Something from *the old world* – like this," she says, pointing downwards to the floor.

"So you're good at painting . . . ?"

"Yes, I've always painted. Though I never thought that I would use painting to screw people. But it seems I'm good at that, too." She smiles at me in a slightly odd way.

"And you live off it?"

"Yes, there's good money in fakes and forgeries," she says.

She asks me what it is like having a tattoo done. I tell her a bit about that and she starts telling me a story – without me realizing how we actually got onto the subject: about how she and her girlfriend collected snails in the garden when they were children, and went into their playhouse where they pulled their underpants down, lay on the wooden floorboards and put the snails on each other's bottoms and let them crawl around, and about how the snails left shiny lines on their skin. I am sitting there thinking more and more how I would like to sink my teeth into her bum. I tell her. She smiles, but merely goes on with her story and concludes by saying: "I only wished we had found a black slug." I sit there for a while smiling at her.

"Shall we do it?" I ask.

"Play with snails?" she asks with a smile.

I smile. "The haircut?"

Maja nods. I finish my beer. With one eye on the barman, she slips her bottle of beer into an outside pocket of her knapsack.

She steps up onto the knee-high, foot's width, metal railing that separates the pavement from the cycle path over the Limfjord Bridge, with the bottle in one hand and her other hand on my shoulder. Spring is so well advanced that it is not really dark in the town at night. She keeps passing me the bottle of beer until it is empty and we are close to the tower before where the bridge opens.

"Why do you want a haircut out here?"

"It seems fitting, in the middle of the bridge, high above the water."

"Do you know that I live over there?"

"I guessed as much, yes."

"How's that?"

"I've seen you cycling across." A pause ensues.

"Well, there you go," she says.

The back of my head rests gently against her stomach as she holds one hand on my skull, to stop it moving, and cuts my hair very short with the scissors. I am sitting with my shirt off on a concrete pier situated in a little area overhanging the water on the far side of the moving sections of the bridge. Every time a car goes past, the slipstream gives me goose pimples and I try to sit upright even though my teeth are beginning to chatter.

"I think I'm almost there," she says. She steps out in front of me, stoops, moves my head from side to side with her hand to make sure she hasn't missed anything, lets go and then straightens up.

"It looks good," she says. I stand up and put my hands underneath her armpits to raise her up; she puts her legs around my waist and we go into a tight embrace. We kiss each other, tentatively and clumsily; our front teeth collide. She leans back and touches my cheek, and then she shakes her head, and we both grin self-consciously.

"So what do you think should happen now?" she asks.

"I take you home," I say.

"And then . . . ?"

"I hope I will be allowed to stay."

"You can't because Susan – the girl I went to the pictures with – she's sleeping over at my place."

Susan?

"That's fine," I say. "I would like to take you home, anyway." I am allowed to do that, and Maja threatens me, in fun, because I want to go up with her for a glass of water, but I mean it – I am thirsty. We go up the stairs to the hallway by her room. A faint snoring sound comes from the bed. I stand in the doorway as Maja pours a glass of water in the kitchenette. She returns.

"May Iphone you?" I whisper.

"I haven't got a phone." I think she can sense my disappointment. "But you can drop by," she says.

"I'll go back to my car now."

"Your car?"

"My car's parked down by the harbour."

"You mustn't drive. I don't like that. You've had too many beers, Allan," she says. My chest sort of swells with warmth at the way she says my name.

"I won't. I've got a blanket in the car so I'll stay there for a couple hours."

"Okay."

"I'll be off then." She immediately grabs hold of me and presses up against my body, kisses me passionately, almost brutally, after which I let go, step outside the doorway and close the door between us. For a little while I stand gazing at the door. I feel . . . I am very happy. A . . . calm, a feeling of satisfaction inside. She is inside, behind the door, we don't know each other, but I feel that we have something in common – something good. I smoke as I walk and realize that I am not going to sleep at all this night. I am too pleased, too happy. When I am back by the concrete pier in the middle of the bridge, there is still some of my hair on the tarmac, so I bend down and sweep it into a pile with my hands, then throw it over the railing and watch it float down into the fjord. I stand there for some time sending gobs of spit into the water as my desire for her rages through my body.

I have Monday off so I decide to go to Valhal and play billiards.

The pub is fairly empty. There are a couple of people playing and a couple of sad girls at the bar. The barmaid pours me a large draught beer and I make my way to the left of the L-shaped room and round the corner, to the billiard tables. The two guys playing seem vaguely familiar.

"Hey, Nazi hair. Are you out to roll a few dagos?" One of the two guys speaks – an overweight biker-wannabe with typical bodybuilder muscles and a layer of fat on top, as well as bad tattoos. Perhaps he went to the technical school at the same time as I did – I think he did.

"The length of my hair has nothing to do with Nazism," I tell him. The other guy doesn't say a word, he just calmly measures me up – I have seen him before, too.

"You look just like a neo-Nazi with that hair," the overweight one jeers.

"Don't use the word Nazi about me."

"Aw, take it easy, man."

"Did you hear what I said?"

"Sensitive tart, ain't he." He bends over to take a shot.

"Better a tart than a turkey," I say. He straightens up again, without playing the ball. Stares me in the eyes – his are far too glacial, in an animate kind of way.

"Are you calling me a turkey?" he asks.

"Did you hear me call you a turkey?"

"Answer me!"

"What do *you* think?" I ask. Most of the billiard table stands between us. But then he has a billiard cue in his hand.

The other one – a rugged, alert-looking guy – raps his knuckles on the edge of the billiard table. "We're playing for money," he says to the overweight one. "Move it."

The overweight one bends down again to take the shot. He turns to me: "One false word out of you and . . . ." he says menacingly, high-handedly, contemptuously.

The rugged guy puts his hand out. "Adrian," he says. I shake hands and say my name.

"You used to play in Vejgaard in the old days," he says. Now I can remember him – good soccer player.

"That's right," I answer, "but not as well as you." He nods in acknowledgement of the compliment, says nothing about my face, but still stares at it for a little too long. "Fire," I say.

"Uh-huh," he says. The overweight one smacks the ball; it cannons around the billiard table noisily but to no effect. The one called Adrian steps up to the table. I sit down on a chair by the wall.

"I went to school with your little sister," Adrian says. "Who is it she moved in with?"

"Peter, a dentist," I answer.

"Bourgeois?" Adrian asks.

"In fact, he's very nice," I say.

"Nice . . . that's what I mean," Adrian says, calmly potting a ball.

"My sister likes tidy arrangements," I say, trying to work out where he is going with all this. He straightens up, grinning.

"She looked so bloody good. She could have had anyone she wanted."

"And so she took a dentist," I add.

"Yep." Adrian shakes his head and pots another ball. "It makes you think when you have to come to terms with something like that."

"Don't hit any more heavy metal speed balls," I say. The overweight one stands there with a crafty expression on his face – it doesn't suit him.

"Is it legal to bang your half-sister?" he asks no-one in particular. He is standing at the end of the table, two metres away from me. Adrian is on the far side of the table and is considering his shot. Out of the corner of my eye I can see that he is surreptitiously changing the position of his hands on the cue so that he can quickly bring it round.

"I don't like the tone of your voice," I say.

"That might be a question that means something to you," the overweight one says. I am still sitting on the chair, but tensed and ready.

"Shall we go outside right now?" I ask. Adrian hits the ball. It rebounds off the corner, but he stroked it so softly that it pulls up at the edge of the hole. Adrian bangs the end of the cue on the floor twice, one after the other, to intervene.

"Jøns," he says – that was the other guy's name apparently. "I couldn't care less what you do, but there's 400 kroner at stake here." He sweeps his arm across the billiard table. "So first finish this sodding game." Reluctantly, Jøns returns to the table.

"It wouldn't bloody stop me if she was *my* sister," he says.

I don't say anything. I can easily take him, I reckon – his type of musculature is useless in a scrap. He is standing with a billiard cue in his hand;

I am sitting on a chair with a beer glass by my hand. If he carries a knife, he is probably too arrogant to have learnt how to use it.

"Afterwards . . . ," Jøn says. Bloody hell. I can't go now. I have to wait to the end of . . . .

"Weren't you with that . . ." Adrian interrupts my thoughts. ". . . Janne?" he says, completing the question.

"Yup," I answer.

"Where have you . . . ? Have you been in the nick?"

"I was at sea."

"Oh, right," Adrian says.

"No, literally – on oil tankers."

"Well, no guff. What was that like?"

"Educational."

"SHIT." It is Jøns shouting. He put the black ball down by mistake. Angrily, he slings 400 kroner down on the billiard table and stomps off to the toilets at the back of the room. Adrian smiles wryly and picks up the money.

"Play?" he asks.

"100 okay?" I ask. He isn't any better than me, but I am very rusty. We start. Fat man hasn't come back yet.

"You must have good teeth," Adrian says.

"He's not the type to do anything for free – that's why he's well off. What about your friend?" I ask with a flick of my head towards the toilets. Adrian shrugs his shoulders.

"Too much . . . ," Adrian raises his hand and taps his nostril with his index finger twice. "Don't take any notice of him – he'll be out there for a while."

I lose slowly but surely; it is a good game and we both play with a defensive strategy. The 100 kroner note changes hands. Adrian asks if I can give him a lift.

"What about Mr. Snowman?" I ask.

"Screw him. He's a biker lackey – no significance," Adrian says. We move towards the door to the street.

The barmaid is now alone in the bar. She looks concerned.

"What about your friend?" she asks.

"Who?" Adrian asks as I pull open the door.

"The big guy you came in with."

"He's gone," Adrian answers and walks past me onto the pavement.

She looks relieved, and then her worried expression returns and she begins to say something that I can't hear over the noise of the street traffic. The door closes behind me and through the window I can see the barmaid leaving the bar and walking around the corner where she sees that the room is empty. But the Valhal toilets are famous for being junkie hideouts; on a good day you can see people sniffing snow at the tables. She glances at the closed door with a worried expression and tentatively makes her way towards the toilets. We walk to my car. Adrian has to go to Vejgaard. It is only a little detour. He invites me to join the old boys' soccer team. I promise him I'll give it some thought.

The discussion has been churning around in my brain. Monday or Tuesday would indicate desperation while Thursday or Friday would indicate too much casualness and it is too close to the weekend which would mean that she has already made plans. Today is Wednesday; I can't wait any longer; that is my conclusion.

Go over to hers in the evening, but she isn't at home. I trudge back to the car – I don't feel like going back home. I walk over to a convenience store and persuade the assistant to give me a plastic mug of coffee from the machine he has at the back of the shop. I buy a magazine called *Boat and Motor* because there is a long article about sailing in the Arctic seas around Greenland. Then I sit on the hood reading, smoking and drinking coffee. The paintwork is so worn that it is almost embarrassing – an invitation for rust. On the other hand, the appearance of the car does not interest me the way it used to. I begin to get an aching bum from sitting on the hood of the car and also feel a little foolish – as if I was trying to . . . show off. I sit in the passenger's seat reading with the door open.

"Hi, Allan." I get a shock. She is standing right next to me.

"Hi, treasure," I say, stretching my arm out for her. She lets me take her arm, but looks sceptical.

"Do I get a kiss?" I ask.

"I don't want you to call me 'treasure'," she says.

"Why not?"

"I don't like it."

"You're a treasure and I've been lucky to find you," I say.

"No. It makes me sound like . . . savings or something you can buy with money."

I peer up at her. "It isn't meant like that . . . beautiful."

"That's more like it," she says and squeezes in onto my lap, her face close to mine.

"I really mean it," I say.

"I know you do." She kisses me briefly on the mouth. "My father always calls my mother 'treasure' – that's why I can't stand it. The man's a numbskull."

"Do you mean that?" I ask.

"Yes." She doesn't say any more, just looks into my eyes. She doesn't appear to be pleased or happy, but still it feels as if she is glad in some way that I have come. I tell her that I can take some time off in lieu on Friday and I wonder if she would like a trip to the coast. She would very much like that – she presses me into her with a smile. Then she gets off my lap.

"Wow," she says. "I really like your car." She walks round, kicks one of the tires and rubs her jaw as if she were critically examining the vehicle. I lean against the door.

"Well, beautiful – have you decided whether you're going to invite me inside?" She comes over and takes my hand.

"Allan, it's . . . too early," she stammers.

I wait for her to say more.

"A little," she adds. "It's a little too early." Fair enough, I don't agree, but don't want to pressure her.

"That's fine," I say. We make a date for Friday, we kiss, I drive off. In reality I am flying.

"You smell absolutely great." Her fresh fragrance fills the car. I breathe in deeply several times. She pats my thigh. Our bodies are weary after a whole day by the water. She gives a squeal of delight when I spin the wheels in the gravel parking lot by the dunes. We drive to Aalborg. She doesn't like my music and finds a cassette in her knapsack. A group called the Cocteau Twins – it is really good. She draws her legs up under her on the passenger's seat and lays her head back against her intertwined fingers on the head rest. She asks me how you drive a car and I explain it to her. We decide that I will give her a driving lesson. Her eyes are fantastically beautiful today. I am amazed, until I realize it is because she is not wearing make-up; no black around her eyes. I am about to tell her how beautiful her eyes are, but I catch myself in time – I don't want to shoot myself in the foot with any suggestion that I don't like the way she uses eyeliner. She is a girl – they have dangerous patterns of behaviour when you start talking about their appearance.

Then it begins to rain. The music and the noise of the tires on the wet tarmac, the windscreen wipers, the scent of her in the car, the feeling of dried salt on your skin – everything is perfect.

"Shall we wash it?" she asks.

"Wash what?"

"The car."

I take a look at the hood. The dust is caked on it now.

"It's raining – that'll clean it," I say.

"Then it'll just look like a . . . spotted place." She is wearing a sceptical expression.

"I'm game if you fancy it," I say.

"Good."

I turn into the next big gas station. She takes her sweater off and is only wearing her undershirt underneath and shorts.

"Don't you want to keep your sweater on?"

"No, I'll keep it dry for afterwards." We get out and start cleaning the car. The rain continues unabated. I stop working. She works energetically even though she must be tired, too. The rain drives in from the side. She attacks the car with brush and soapy water until she discovers that I am not doing anything.

"What's up?" She glances downwards and starts giggling. She has just won my personal beauty competition. Her stiff nipples are clearly outlined against her wet clothes.

"It could do with a lick of paint, too," Maja says. She is right.

"What colour?" I ask. She has a think.

"Beige, and very shiny."

"Okay," I answer.

"Will you do it?"

"Yes, of course. It needs it," I say.

We finish the job and jump into the car again. Her pert breasts quiver as she tears off her undershirt and replaces it with her sweater. They are perfect – I just catch a glimpse before staring at the roof of the car.

"Shall we go in and have a hot cup of cocoa," she says. We run to the door because of the rain. The cafeteria doesn't have many customers. We sit opposite each other in one of the bays. She has cocoa and a tart; I have coffee and a sandwich.

Two tables down in my sightline is a little family. The parents have their backs to me, the father is on the outside and the young son sits opposite – he is looking out of the window and smiling.

"What is it, Jesper?" his mother asks. He takes the cigarette out of his mouth and turns his gaze on his mother.

"I'm happy," he says. "I'm looking forward to the whole of next year."

"That's good, Jesper," the mother says, a little warily. No-one says anything for a while, but the silence at their table seems charged.

"You might at least have spoken to me before phoning Uncle John," the father says to the son.

"You might at least have spoken to me before planning my future," the son says to the father.

"We had a deal," the father says.

"No, *you* had a deal. I told you ages ago that I was going to Norway to work and snowboard and then you still go and fix me up with an apprenticeship . . . in Silvan – God forbid."

Maja looks into my eyes: "Fight coming," she whispers.

"Preben, it can't be changed now. Can't we just . . . ," the mother says to the husband.

The father interrupts her: "You were supposed to start at commercial college in September – that was the deal," he says.

The son gesticulates – says with some heat: "That was *your* deal. I didn't bloody go along with it. It's obvious I want to go to Norway."

"And what good's it going to do you?" the father retorts angrily, authoritatively. "I went out on a limb to get you the place." The mother lays her hand on the father's arm.

"Preben, I'm sure it's a good thing he's taking a break. He's tired of school."

"Tired of school? It's only one more year – it's nothing at all. Just a question of knuckling down."

Maja rolls her eyes at me; we eat our food while concentrating on the conversation.

"It's not one more year, it's one more year plus forty years in Silvan and certain death," the boy says, glaring at his father, disgust written all over his face.

The mother makes another attempt: "Anyway, John said it wouldn't be a problem finding a place the year after."

The father turns in his seat to face his wife: "I pressured your brother into giving me the place. And afterwards I have to go to him hat in hand and ask him to undo everything."

"That's what it's all about, isn't it?" taunts the son.

"Now come on, Jesper, you mustn't . . . ." the mother starts.

"Don't sit there defending him, mother," Preben says to his wife.

"Preben," she groans.

"Er, dad, if she's your mother, who am I then – your elder brother?" the son says cleverly.

The father gets to his feet and raises his finger: "Don't be so smart or you'll have me to deal with," he says.

"Just try it," the boy says. His eyes have narrowed, he is still sitting but he is as tense as a spring. The father has risen to his full height. It is a time bubble with the father and son glaring at each other. Maja bares her gritted teeth, winces and gives a light shake of her head. I am mesmerized – the whole situation . . . First of all, to have a father at all and then on top of that to try to have any kind of will; I have always found that deeply fascinating. Then a sniffle comes from the mother.

"Oh, stop it, please," the son says, desperate.

"You're frittering away your time," the father says to him, then turns and leaves the cafeteria, moving mechanically and staring stiffly ahead of him.

"You know how angry he gets," his mother says into a paper serviette.

"Frittering away your time," the son mumbles. "What the hell does he do? Put it in a ring binder?"

"He's only concerned for you, Jesper. He means well."

"Yes, that's what all the dictators claim as they crush their people," the son says.

Now Maja is sitting there with a broad beam on her face.

"What?" I ask. She points over her shoulder to the table with the family.

"Putting time in a ring binder. I liked that one," she says.

"Yes," I laugh. The son smiles at me, shrugs his shoulders and makes the victory sign.

The mother pushes her chair back. "I'll have a word with him, just stay here."

"You don't have to do this on my account, mum. I've had it with the silly fool."

Maja shovels the last large mouthful of the tart into her mouth and chews with slightly open lips. I can see some of the crème fraîche on her front teeth. "Like my father," she says through the food in her mouth.

"Is he like that?"

"Yes," Maja answers, taking a swig of cocoa. "The time . . . well, I was at high school last year – in Hasseris. Then I stopped and he wouldn't let me in the house.

"You've got to be bloody joking."

"I'm not. It's true. He stood on the other side of the door – one of those with frosted glass in."

"The front door?"

"Yes. He stood there telling me that I could come in when I had promised that I would go up to the high school and re-enroll the next morning."

"Bloody hell."

"Mmm. It was in the middle of winter and I was freezing."

"What did you do then?"

"Told him he should open the door and tell me that to my face."

"What did he say to that?"

"That I could come in when I had promised and so on . . . So I smashed the window."

"You're joking!" I can see her doing it. She is fantastic.

Maja grins at me.

"No," she says. "Then he came running out and walloped me round the head."

"He didn't."

"He did.

"What about your mother?"

Maja points to the mother who has just left the cafeteria to pacify her husband.

"Stood there screaming."

"Shit," I say.

"Lots of it."

"Did you get in?" I ask.

"No, I moved out."

"The same evening?"

Maja's brow darkens and . . . she seems saddened.

"Yes. I went round to a guy I knew at that time." She stares vacantly into empty space.

"And what now?"

"I don't talk to him – my father, that is."

"How does he get on with that?"

"Badly."

"What does your father do?"

"Sell insurance."

"It all fits," I say.

Maja shakes her head. "Yes," she says wearily.

The sound of the shower comes through the wall as a faint, variable buzz. I am lying, freshly showered, in her bed with the duvet pulled up to my hips. It is only ten o'clock, but it is almost dark here because the curtains are drawn. We have had something to eat, we have . . . nothing in particular, just worked our way towards the point where I am lying in her bed waiting for her and I am nervous. I am very nervous. The shower is turned off. The waiting is unbearable, the thudding of my heart audible. Maja comes out of the bathroom. She doesn't say anything; she comes over to the side of the bed. Stands there dressed in undershirt and underpants. My breathing is hacked into tiny fragments every time a heartbeat breaks the flow – like driving across the furrows of a frozen ploughed field.

"You're beautiful." I manage to say that even though my voice is unfamiliar. Can't think of anything else. She lies down and coils up against me, kisses me gently. We caress, cautiously. She kisses my nipples; the hair on my chest rustles faintly under her hands. I am incredibly worked up. Her skin is . . . she is simply so delectable. She pulls my boxer shorts off my dick and I reach down to wriggle them off from under my bum. She grabs my hand.

"Wait," she whispers, sitting up in a kneeling position and pulling them off me. She sits across me, reaches behind her, to between my thighs and softly encloses my scrotum in her hand. She straddles me and rocks gently to and fro, massages my dick as she slowly peels off her undershirt. I can feel myself stiff against her mound – even through her cotton underpants I can feel her pubic hair scratching against my shaft. I pull her down towards me, lick her breasts – the small, hard nipples glide across my cheek, wet. She reaches out and takes one of the condoms I put on the bedside table. I reach out my hand for it. "No, let me," she says. I can feel her smiling. Carefully rolls it on before she lies on her side, peeling her underpants off in one quick awkward movement, kicks them away and then she is back on top of me. Even before she sinks down on me I can feel the moist heat radiating from her sex. She takes my hands and leads them to her breasts. My back arches and I thrust myself deeper inside her. "Easy, young man," she says and with both hands presses my chest back flat against the mattress. I am much too close. She spears herself on me, dangles her breasts over my chest again and again. I come in a blinding blue flash, but it is much too soon. She isn't with me.

"Sorry," I murmur, removing the condom, tying a knot in it and letting it fall between my fingers over the side of bed. She says nothing. Only kisses me, and I kiss her breasts and her stomach, paint patterns with my tongue as I approach, until I am lying with my head between her legs and she lets out little noises and presses her hands firmly against the base of her tiny belly.

"God bless you," she says in the dark. We land in a timeless void, an infinity. The insides of her thighs are strong and wet against my hips.

"Are you hungry?" Maja asks. She leans against the door frame to the small bathroom. I feel strangely vulnerable as I stand naked in front of her in the light, drying myself. But also powerful. I dry my neck; the smooth white upper arms contrast with the hair and tattoos of my forearms.

"I could eat a horse, beautiful," I say, putting the towel over the rail that holds the shower curtain. When I see my face in the mirror I am taken aback. I . . . my hand shoots up beside my cheek and stops there. It looks quite . . . different. I feel exposed because she is standing beside me, so I run my hand across my cheek as if checking the growth of my beard and then take it away.

"What's up?" she asks.

"I don't know."

"I haven't got a great deal of food in," she says. "Perhaps we could . . . ." She doesn't finish the sentence.

"Shall I go . . . umm – to the bakery?"

"Do you mind?"

"Of course not," I say. "Is there anything particular you want?"

"Have you got any money?" she asks.

"Hell, yes, it's no problem."

"Fruit yoghurt, if they have any."

"Course." I put on my clothes, follow her directions and find a bakery by the market square in Nørresundby. I stand in the shop with a foolish grin on my face when I see the trays of six eggs piled up in the cooling cabinet.

In the evening we stood in the engine room. I was on duty and Chris was free. He was anxious for me to explain to him how a combustion engine worked. I had to put my mouth right beside his ear so that he could hear me over the noise.

"It would be easier if we had a car," I said.

"A car, a boat – what's the bloody difference?"

"This is a diesel engine, isn't it."

"Diesel?"

"There's a difference in the way diesel engines and gasoline engines work."

"Really? Come on then – you explain the difference. Let's do this properly," he said and so we walked around the Burmeister & Wain diesel engine which was three floors high.

"With gasoline engines," I shout, "the fuel is sucked into the cylinder and then compressed by the piston. When the fuel is compressed, a spark passes from the spark plug and combusts the mixture. The combustion forces the piston down. The piston is on the end of a pole called the piston rod – that transfers the power to the crank pin." I try to show him how the crank pin, the crankshaft and the counterweight work together on a four cylinder engine so that there is a continuous transmission of power, but I lose him instantly – I am not a great teacher.

"And so what's so different about a diesel engine?"

"There are no spark plugs – there's no spark to ignite the fuel. The air in the cylinder is compressed with such power and becomes so hot that the oil that's injected into the cylinder under high pressure simply combusts.

"Okay," Chris shouts, nodding seriously – I can see that I am losing him again.

"The advantage of a diesel engine is that it uses less fuel than a gasoline engine even though they have the same piston area. The disadvantage is that a diesel engine is a lot heavier."

"Yes, but how much power has this thing got? Say, compared with a car?" Chris asks, pointing to the engine.

I point to the main engine: "This has 48,000 horsepower. If you take a big car – a Mercedes Benz, 3.2 litres, like one of the big taxis – it probably has about 200 horsepower so the performance of this engine is roughly the same as 240 Mercedes Benz taxis banging away."

Chris is well into this. He is also smashed – running round feeling the parts and sniffing at the engine in various places and patting it. It makes me happy.

"But this one is a two-cylinder engine with 80–90 revolutions per minute. It's one of the most simple and reliable you can get because there are not that many sensitive moving parts compared with a four-cylinder engine," I explain. I would like to explain to him how uniflow scavenging operates because it is so fantastic, but it is hopeless. Chris is already looking at me sceptically.

"You've lost me now, man," he shouts. "I'm not on that trip at all."

"You know what the cylinder is, don't you?" I try again. "The chamber the piston rod moves up and down in – on a moped it's about this wide . . . ." I put my thumb and forefinger together to show the circumference.

"Yes, yes. Of course. I know that," Chris says.

I point to the engine: "Well, this engine has twelve cylinders and three men can easily stand in each of them." Chris comes over to me so that we can hear each other better.

"Mmm, that's big, but . . . ," he says with a look of wonderment on his face and points to me, ". . . what do you guys do?"

"What do you mean? We keep an eye on the machinery," I say.

"Okay, so you run around, four or five full-time employees, keeping an eye on the engine. It's as if all motorists had their own mechanic with them every time they went out for a drive."

I chew this over. How can I explain to him how tough the conditions are under which these engines work.

"You have to consider that a ship like this is never in the garage. We're always at sea. And we use a kind of diesel fuel that is actually a waste product."

"Is diesel waste?" Chris asks.

"No, not the diesel you fill your car up with – that's a product that has gone through several processes of refinement. But we use something called 'heavy fuel'; *it's almost tar. Imagine taking a pick axe to a road and breaking up the tarmac, then heating it up to 120-130 degrees, removing the gravel and then running the engine on the oil you're left with." I check to see if he is following.*

"Tarmac, man" he says with a nod.

"We've also got something called marine diesel oil, which is a bit better quality; that's what we use on auxiliary engines. But you would never put that in trucks on land. The consistency is a bit like the bitumen you paint plinths with. Finally there is the stuff you use in diesel engines on land. This diesel oil is so refined that you never use it at sea, it's much too expensive."

After the engine lesson he took me up to the galley. He wanted to teach me how to make an omelette, but first I had to learn how to fry an egg.

"This is the basis of Western European cooking," he said.

It took me five eggs before I had fried an egg more or less properly and another eight to make an omelette – two eggs each time. Chris put a note on the fridge saying that he had dropped a tray of eggs on the floor and he was sorry. The next evening I found him down in the engine room where he was sitting playing his harmonica while reading a booklet about playing techniques.

"WHAT THE HELL ARE YOU DOING?" I shouted. He held the harmonica out towards me.

"I'M PRACTISING," he shouted.

"BUT YOU CAN'T HEAR ANYTHING."

"NO, IT'S AMAZING," he shouted back, then continued to concentrate on his playing while holding the music book in front of him so that he could see what to do.

We eat breakfast. I tell Maja that I have arranged to drive out to my sister's. She is smoking a cigarette and looks serious, but she doesn't say anything.

"Do you want to join me?" I ask and I have already regretted it – I shouldn't be in such a hurry. She shakes her head. "When will I see you again?" I ask.

"I . . . ," she starts, breaks off, sighs, takes a deep breath, then continues. "I'd like to see you again . . . but we can't be a couple. Not right now. I don't think I . . . can do that." I am silent for a moment.

Will you tell me why?" I ask.

"No." There is a pause. "Can't we just . . . see each other?"

"Yes, of course, but . . . ."

"No. I'd like to see you, I . . . like you but . . . ."

"One step at a time?"

"Exactly, yes," she says, relieved.

"Okay." I look at my watch. "Got to go now," I say and start doing up my laces.

"What are you doing this evening?"

I tell her that I have promised to look in at Grøften and have a beer with some workmates: "You know – new job and all that . . . ," I say. Maja is going to Rock Nielsen to meet Susan – the gazelle girl.

"Is she your best friend?" I ask.

"Yes," Maja says with a smile.

"Did you go to the same school?" I ask. Maja gives me this enquiring look. "I'm not prying, I'm just curious," I say, grinning. "I'm just hugely . . . interested in you," I add.

Fortunately, Maja smiles. "Aha, well, I know her from 1000Fryd and then both of us have worked at the post office," she says.

"And you're always together – bosom pals?" I ask.

"Yes," Maja says, hesitating. "I'm taking care of her for the moment because . . . she's been having a few problems with a guy and so she isn't in the best of moods." I can hear that I shouldn't ask any more questions.

"But you two are going to Rock Nielsen," I say.

"Yes," Maja says. "You can pop by if you have time."

She writes down my telephone number; the whole situation seems a little awkward because we were so close during the night. As I am about to leave she gives me a hug that is like from friend, not a lover, so I hold her tight and tell her about my feelings for her, then let go and walk down the hall. Discuss with myself whether I did the right thing, said the right thing and so on, but then I am outside and see my clean car in the parking lot and tell myself that I mustn't think too much.

4

Her breasts swing freely under her loose-fitting blouse and her tight leggings emphasize the rounding of her bum as she reaches up for glasses for us from the high cupboards. My younger sister, Mette, has always been a looker. The foreign features come from her father. Mette is the result of one night in Viborg. My mother went to a party for NATO personnel working in Karup and she slipped between the sheets with a black American officer. She didn't want an abortion, but she couldn't bring herself to contact the soldier during the pregnancy, either. There was a second man who might have been the father, so she had to wait for the birth: "That was *very* exciting," as she puts it when she tells the story. Mette is light brown with freckles and jet black curly hair. When my mother tried to contact the father she discovered that he was back in America where he had a wife and children, so she just let the matter rest.

I have been sat down at the dining table in the large, bright all-purpose kitchen and Mette says:

"Have you found yourself a fancy woman?" and "Have you heard that Janne got married and has a child – so you lost out on her."

"To tell the truth, that doesn't matter," I say, pouring out a beer for us both.

"Really, why do you say that?" My sister laughs – she was never very fond of Janne, who was my girlfriend for almost three whole years before I went to sea. In fact, we were together for most of the time from the seventh grade onwards.

"She always thought she was doing me a favour when she gave me oral pleasures," I state flatly. My sister's husband, Peter the dentist, has been cutting the grass. He just catches my comment as he comes in through the utility room, grinning, and says 'Hi'.

"Girls from Klarup remind me of our mother, but they're even more obvious."

"Yes, we have to assume you're like your father even though it's impossible to know," I say.

"The way I've turned out, he must be a great guy," Mette says as Peter sits down and opens himself a bottle of beer. We are going to have a late lunch in the style of an evening meal – Mette has never really grasped the concept of fixed eating times. It is wonderful to be able to sit talking to her again. We're always on the same page.

"We can be sure that he was great as far as the discipline of logical thinking goes," I say.

"Why do you say that?" Peter asks.

"He saw through our mother's thin veneer of charm within one night." Peter stands up and goes over to the worktop, shaking his head. He comes from a healthy, orderly background and would have nightmares if he talked badly about his mother.

"Good thing you haven't seen through my charm yet," my sister says, sending him an affectionate look as he fiddles around with some vegetables at the sink.

"He didn't have a chance," I say.

"Because I'm not so easy to see through," Mette says.

"What about you?" Peter asks.

"Me? Well, luckily my father's genes didn't make it," I say. "I'm like Carl so I'm almost perfect."

"Right, of course. And otherwise?"

"My teeth could do with a clean-up, but otherwise they're fine."

"Yes, it's incredible how much like him you are," Mette says.

"Stop messing about, Allan. Aren't you going to settle down soon?" Peter says.

"We can talk about me when you've put my sister in the club. I think it's about time and Carl is waiting impatiently." Peter lets out a deep sigh by the sink. Mette runs her hands across her flat stomach and hips:

"He's frightened of ruining this terrific figure."

"You must have earned masses of money at sea. Don't you want to settle down?" Peter persists with his question.

"Don't you worry about me," I say, thinking abut Maja. She could settle me down, no problem.

Mette looks at Peter with a feigned serious expression: "My brother has been out in the world – he doesn't want any more Klarup girls."

"Think you're a cut above the rest now, do you?" Peter asks.

"A cunt above the rest. Yes, perhaps."

Peter groans.

"Okay, sorry," I say. "I've been de-toxicated – in all sorts of ways."

"Well, it suits you now you mention it," Mette says, serious now.

"Mmmm," Peter concedes.

"Can you see it?" I ask.

"Yes, you seem calm, healthy . . . ?" Mette has a question on her lips.

"What?" I ask.

"But . . . ," she begins, taking a deep breath. She continues:" What about . . . Frank?"

"I've met him," I say.

"And . . . ?" Mette asks. I take a deep breath. Actually, I think to myself, I don't want her to be mixed up in my affairs. She is only twenty-one and is living with a nice, solid guy of thirty – a choice I can completely understand – and she doesn't need my problems.

"Frank thinks that I owe him a favour because he ended up in the nick. I don't agree."

"And what does Frank say to that?" she asks.

"He'll have to get used to the idea." I say.

"But . . . you have to be careful, Allan. I think Frank is in with the heavy mob," she says. Mette still has a couple of friends in that scene so she hears the rumours going round.

"I will," I say, taking her hand which is lying on the kitchen worktop. "Calm down, Mette. I've finished with all that." She takes my hand between hers and squeezes it.

"I hope so," she says, as Peter concentrates on the meat he is cutting. Fortunately it isn't pork – I can't eat pork any more . . . just the smell makes me feel sick.

"But I can always use a bottle of laughing gas," I say and Mette laughs. Peter starts laughing too, while shaking his head. He has only had his fingers in my mouth once. I kept telling him it was hurting so that he would turn up the gas. In the end I couldn't speak, that was how good it was. "He doesn't reply," the dental assistant said. "He definitely mustn't have any more then," Peter said.

"Skol," my sister says. "Our mother's children are upwardly mobile, socially speaking."

"Could you go any lower?" I ask.

"Not without a spade," Mette answers and Peter asks us to stop.

"Are you aware that you've been used as a social springboard?" Mette asks him and I sit there waggling my empty bottle of beer.

"Is there any more beer or is this as good as it gets?"

"Hell no," Peter says going into the utility room to collect a fresh supply.

"Well, in fact she's picked up a bit," Mette says.

"Really?" I say – that is news to me. Mette is a good person. She is training to become a health worker and she is making an effort to ensure that our mutual mother stays our mother.

"Have you visited her?" she asks as Peter puts a cold beer in front of us.

"Yes – she was desperately sober, asked if I could lend her some money."

"Did you?" Mette asks.

"You can't buy an abuser out of her abuse," I say.

"But you can try to keep them at a distance," Mette says.

"Okay, you two, thank you very much, "Peter says. Mette stands up and puts her arms round him from the back.

"Sorry sweetheart," she says. "How were you to know that the girl you fell for grew up with an alcoholic?"

"It's beginning to smell good," I say.

"Yes, he can also cook," Mette says proudly.

"Yes, well, you certainly can't, can you," I say and Peter nods at me with an earnest expression on his face. He joins me at the table.

Mette hugs him again as he sits there. "No, but I'm very beautiful and I'm very good at talking on the phone," she says, kissing him on the cheek and neck. Peter shakes his head.

"What *have* I done?" he asks, feigning melancholy.

"You have felt the full force of love," I comment. Mette winks at me across the table and coos as she bites the lobe of his ear making him blush and I go to the toilet to give him a chance to get things under control.

The noise of the engines was driving me mad despite the fact that I was wearing earplugs and ear guards. The sounds were beginning to change into metallic music; so uniform that my nerves were screaming. Why had I gone to sea? I knew all too well why – to flee from myself and my old life. But why had the rest of the crew chosen to go to sea? I didn't understand – there was no sense in spending your life isolated from . . . everything.

I went up to the accommodation quarters to rest my ears and to find a porthole so that I could look out to sea as I smoked. The thought of smoking outside grew on me, even though it is highly dangerous because the oil in the tanks gives off inflammable gases which can seep out and hang over the decks if the tanks have not been properly ventilated. The worst is an empty oil tanker because there is always a little oil at the bottom of the tanks, and it evaporates so that the tanks are full of inflammable gases, bombs waiting to explode. It has happened that a charge of static electricity has been generated which has ignited the fumes and the boat has simply been blown out of the water and there is nothing left. You aren't even allowed to take gas lighters, metal lighters or merely metal objects outside. If they should happen to fall out of your pocket they could cause a spark when they hit the deck and then you would have an explosion of enormous dimensions. But I wanted to feel the wind and the sun on my face, suck the smoke down into my lungs together with the fresh sea air; it was becoming an obsession. I wondered if I was nurturing a secret urge to be sacked.

I dismissed all this as I went up into the silence and walked along the gangways in the cool, crisp air. Chris was already there with his hands buried deep in his pockets and his shoulders hunched up round his ears. We said 'hi' and smoked in silence.

"I miss . . . girls. I miss some girls. Just to look at," he said.

"You're the only person on the ship who has the daily company of a girl," I said, thinking of Lone, the Chief Steward.

"Lone is a woman."

"We all have to pass that way."

"We all become women?" Chris asked.

"Look around you."

"Wonderful," he said. He tightened his lips around the cigarette filter, sucked in slowly and noisily a couple of times, then blew the smoke out in thick rings through his nostrils, keeping his hands in his pockets all the while. "Have you got um . . . a girl?" he asked.

"No."

"Why not?"

"We fell out," I said.

"How?"

"I . . ." I couldn't find the right words so I said, "I probably wasn't enough of a lapdog for her."

"What did she want you to do?"

"Acquire things: house, furniture, car, money, clothes, shit." I shrugged my shoulders; 'obey' that was the word I was after. "What about you?"

"Me?" he said, laughing out loud. "It was hard enough getting into the sack with them."

"Why was that?"

"A film had got to them," Chris said.

"A film?"

"The Unbearable Lightness of Being. *Have you seen it?"*

"Yes, but that's such an old film."

"Right. But they showed it at the film club at the high school in Vejle."

"Did you go to high school?"

"Not for very long," Chris said.

"Lena Olin. Could drive any man crazy."

"Yeah, Lena Olin is just too tasty," he said, spitting onto the palms of his hands, and was going to demonstrate but instead dropped his hands by his sides, took another drag of his cigarette and said: "Girls at my school had about as much magnetism as a tin of non-perishable liver paste. But they all thought they were Lena Olin."

"If that could do the trick for them, that's fine in a way, isn't it?" I said.

"The problem was that several of them bought themselves a large mirror and a bowler hat and that was what you were confronted with if you got as far as their bedrooms."

"Seriously?"

"Yes," Chris said. "That was the props you needed. If you didn't have them you simply weren't sexually advanced enough."

"But a mirror and a bowler hat – you can live with that, can't you?"

"Yes, but then you had to be thin and black and sombre like that actor . . . ?"

"Daniel Day-Lewis?"

"Yes, exactly. You were only COOL if you were sombre and I simply wasn't very good at it."

"I can see that must have been irritating," I conceded. "But you're thin enough."

"Yes. It was worse for the guys with soccer-players' legs – they NEVER got anything."

I looked down at my legs.

Chris shook his head. "No chance," he said. We smoked on in silence. Then he said dryly: "The outrageous thing was that they always hid one of your socks . . . ALWAYS."

Grøften is becoming noisy. My workmates have left. Only Flemming is still here – my hopeless apprentice. He is a mirror image of myself years ago: drunk and on something – not speed, perhaps some kind of tranquilizer. Or ecstasy – I haven't tried it, don't know what the effects are. I am no good at judging people's state any more. Years ago I could tell you exactly what someone had taken. Fortunately, Flemming joins some friends. That suits me fine. Today he was supposed to be cutting threads into a couple of pipes I needed. At some point I went over to see how he was progressing. I stand behind him and shout over the noise: "It doesn't sound as if it is getting enough grease." No reaction. I move around in front of him. He doesn't see me. I study his face. He has a completely blank look on his face; his mouth moves but he is abstracted. Then I realize that he is wearing a Walkman – the man is cutting threads without listening.

Some people want my table so I go to the bar to finish my beer. I see Frank coming towards the bar; behind him is the pusher type I saw when I met Maja for the first time at Rock Nielsen – he and Frank seem to be together. I haven't time to slip out of the back door, he has already seen me.

"Well, did you have any Joy?" he says loftily, with an undertone of anger.

"I did," I say simply.

"Yes, she's not exactly my style, but she can suck, swallow and gargle," Frank continues. The pusher type says something in Frank's ear. Frank says: "Okay, I'll fix that," and the other guy leaves.

"Lene is sitting at a table over there," he continues – pointing to somewhere in the room, turns to go down there and takes it for granted that I will follow. I don't. When he sits down he casts his eyes around, perplexed. I turn my back on him, face the bar. The mirror on the back wall shows people dancing, but there are so many bottles in front that it just looks like wallpaper with moving colours. Shortly after, Frank is back.

"Hey," he says. "What the fuck are you doing?"

"I'm not interested in sitting next to her," I answer.

"Come on man, just let's sit down."

"Got better things to do."

"She's really nice, you know," Frank says. I give him a cool look.

"I'm off," I say and start forcing my way through the crowd; can sense Frank behind me on my way to the exit.

"I'm going with you, man," he says and adds: "Where to?"

"Rock Nielsen," I answer. "Don't take it personally, Frank, but there's something I've got to do there – I'm meeting someone."

"Allan," Frank says, spreading his arms while walking. "That's fine. I've got a couple of errands to sort out there, too." We emerge onto the street. I know what is coming now. "Have you thought about my offer?" he asks, putting his arm round my shoulders. He indicates the whole of Jomfru Ane Gade with a sweeping movement of his other arm. "Easy pickings," he says.

I send him such a look that he reluctantly removes his hand from my shoulders. "Frank, I'm not interested," I say, turning into the staircase and starting the climb into Rock Nielsen. Music, smoke, human voices hit me.

Frank makes a push for the bar with me. We buy beer.

"You owe me a favour, Allan," he says.

"Why's that, Frank?"

"I took the stretch for both of us," he says.

"And?" I say.

"So you owe me," Frank says.

"It could just as easily have been me, Frank. You know that perfectly well. It was just tough shit."

"Yes, for me. You got away," he says.

"Chance," I say, scanning the room.

"You don't get off that lightly, Allan. I consider that you owe me a favour and I need to call in the debt now."

I spot Maja on the opposite side of the room. She is standing by a table where Susan and the scrawny guy are sitting with a couple of others. "I'm going over to the girl I've arranged to meet," I say and discover that he was following my gaze. He grabs my arm.

"Hey, which one is she?" he asks.

"The one in the black dress."

"Wow, great legs."

"No, the one in the long dress," I say and suddenly everything falls into place. Of course. Maja and the dead scaffolder, Leif. Asger, the pusher, and

Susan – she really doesn't seem like Asger's type – she is too innocent. But perhaps that is precisely the reason for a flirt with something she thinks is exciting and has a hint of danger.

"But that's bloody . . . ." Frank stammers, then breaks off. He looks extremely thoughtful. Examines my face as if he could read something from my expression.

"What?" I say.

"That's bloody . . . her," Frank says and stops in his tracks.

"Who?"

"Yeah, she was going out with Leif when he fell off the scaffolding."

"So they were going out?"

"Well, call it what you will."

"Her name's Maja," I say.

"That's right. Maja. How do you know her?"

"She cut my hair."

"Did you know it was her?" Frank asks. I can't work out his expression. Is he angry? Frightened? Defiant?

"I had a feeling," I answer, wondering whether Maja was with the scaffolder when he was dying – it took him four days. Wonder whether he was conscious.

"But you haven't asked her?" Frank asks.

"I'm not interested," I say.

"Are you going out with her?"

"Call it what you will." I raise my hand to indicate my departure, but Frank grabs my shoulder.

"We haven't finished yet," he says.

"Yes, we have, Frank," I say, lowering my gaze to his hand which has a firm grip on my shoulder, then raise my eyes to meet his. He lets go.

I make my way through the packed room to Maja. Susan, who I now know is Asger's ex, is sitting with a group of people including the scrawny guy – Valentin, I think his name was.

"Hi," I say, putting my hand on Maja's hip and try to force a smile, but it is difficult under her gaze. What is wrong now?

"Do you know him?" Her question sounds like a command.

"Who?" I say, telling myself not to become defensive – I don't have anything to defend.

"The guy you arrived with?" Maja's voice carves a clear path through the music and the noise.

"Not very well," I answer almost truthfully. "I went to school with him. We were both apprentices at Aalborg Shipyards."

"Are you out on the town together?" At the table behind Maja everyone is stealing furtive glances at us except the one called Susan, who fixes her cold eyes on me.

"No," I say. I return Maja's gaze. I shake my head. "No," I repeat. There is nothing to hide – or almost nothing.

"You came here with him."

I pause for two seconds before answering. "What's the matter?"

"*You came with him. You arrived with him. I saw you coming up the stairs with him.*" She is almost screaming.

"Yes."

"So you're out on the town together."

A deep breath. Stay calm.

"I was in Grøften meeting friends from work. He was there and came on here with me."

"Why did you let him?" she asks, with a touch of puzzlement in her eyes.

"For Christ's sake, Maja." I try smiling, lean over so that she can hear what I say without my having to shout. "He was already there. He came over and sat at the table and started talking about the old days and so on. Then he joined me when I said I had to leave to come on here."

From behind, from where she was sitting, Susan has put Maja's hand in hers and keeps her eyes fixed on me.

"Why did you do it?" The words come out of her mouth in a snarl; make her appear beautiful in an intimidating way. Do what? My anger is beginning to take hold of me. Things are moving fast.

"We had an agreement – do you remember?" I can't restrain the edge of sarcasm in my voice.

"*You know him,*" she screams in my face, so close to me that I have the full aroma of her skin in my nostrils. The look she gives me; there can be no doubt about what she thinks and she is totally mistaken. She tugs at Susan who immediately gets to her feet and Maja turns round to distance herself from me. I catch her shoulder with one hand; she swirls round so quickly that my hand is shaken off.

"SHOVE OFF!" she yells, turning again and running into the crowded dance floor. Susan pulls at her, they bump into people – then they are swallowed up. My brain mists over, I shiver. Turn. Scan the bar for Frank. She . . . ? He has . . . there is something wrong. Frank has . . . vanished. Clench my teeth. I manage to find my way out . . . don't exactly know how.

Stand in the street, smoke cigarettes, draw breath, tensed up. All things I want to keep away from . . . he is barging into my life again; dragging me down in his filth. Slowly my self control returns. Frank, Asger the pusher, his pusher-frau – Nina, who threw them out; Susan and . . . Maja. Something . . . not right. But what? I have to know. Perhaps Frank has gone back to Grøften. I walk there.

Frank is sitting at a table opposite Jøns, who recognizes me. That is awkward – not what I had anticipated. I put my hands on the table and lean over so that Frank can hear me over the music. "I have to talk to you," I say, and with a movement of my head indicate the door.

Franks bares his teeth – his version of a smile. "Talk away," he says.

"Outside," I say. Frank pulls the corners of his mouth down, slowly shakes his head. I can feel how steamed up I am. Jøns gives me a condescending look.

"Well, wasn't she happy to see you?" Frank says. "That was a shame, wasn't it," he adds casually. The red ball in my chest grows; the sensation of my knuckles bursting through the skin.

"I don't think he's got the balls," Jøns says to Frank. What?

Oh yes, he has," Frank says. "Sit down, Allan. Let's talk about things." With the flat of his hand he pats the space beside him. The blood is rushing in my ears. I push myself away from the table, turn, my body is pointed towards the door. For a moment I am unsure whether my legs can move. They are numb. Mechanical movements – I find my way out. Cold drops of sweat run down over my ribs under my shirt.

On Sunday I drive over to Maja's. The car seems lifeless now that she is not sitting in the passenger seat. She isn't at home. I sit outside waiting, in the car again. It isn't the same feeling as last time and I have to fight hard to resist the temptation of burrowing my face in the seat to inhale her smell.

I know Frank, or I knew him – at that time. It is several years ago. All over now. Well, we were the same, but not any more. If he is still doing the whole thing – that is his business, it has nothing to do with me.

I register a movement, look up and see Maja jogging past the car. I open the car door. "Maja," I shout, but she is already up the stairs. I break into a run, but stop. Walk. Up the stairs, along the corridor. Stand in front of her door. Knock.

"Go away," her voice says, muffled by the door between us.

"Maja," I say calmly but loud enough for her to hear me. "I beg you to . . . I would like you to explain to me what the problem is."

"I do not have anything to do with people who know him . . . Frank," she says firmly from behind the door. "He is a bastard." I have no doubt that Frank can be a bastard, but . . . ."

"What is it with Frank?"

"You know perfectly well," Maja says – I can hear from the sounds inside that she has moved away from the door. A door opens behind me. A young girl sticks her head out to see what is going on. My glare is enough to send her back in. I ask Maja again to open the door. She doesn't respond.

"I'm interested in you," I say. "I'd like to see you again. You've got my telephone number – I hope you'll give me a call."

It takes me a long time to locate Frank. On Monday I finish early and phone around from home. I phone Aalborg Boilers too, but he was dismissed four months ago. That wasn't what he told me when we were eating in Vanggaards Cafeteria. I consider visiting Asger, but reject the idea. It could be sticky if both of them are there. The urge to take a hit grows stronger inside me – all too strong. I pour myself another cup of coffee. No – I'll have to solve the problems. Stand up. Go.

Nina opens the door. "Is Frank here?" I ask.

"No," she says. Asger isn't there, either. I ask for Frank's address, a telephone number. She claims she hasn't got them.

"What's it about?" she asks.

"That's between me and Frank," I say.

"Perhaps you should have a little chat with me?" she suggests with a self-important expression on her face. She thinks she controls Asger, who controls Frank, and together they will draw me in with their ridiculous little intrigues.

"Bye," I say and go down the stairs. I drive out to Frank's parents in Klarup. I should have made do with a phone call, I think to myself in the car, as I make a wide berth round the house where I lived with Janne. Instead I drive past the street where we lived with Bjarne with whom my mother shacked up when I was in the seventh grade. I turn into the street and pull up in front of the detached house. It doesn't look any different, except that the plants in the front garden are better established. One of my mother's sober periods – up to a certain point. Bjarne was a widower and had money. She simply seduced him and took possession of him because he had the status that could give her the life she desired – for her children, too.

I can remember the last day in the house all too clearly. I had signed off in Kolding after my first stint – four months at sea on a coaster. I took a taxi to the station where I jumped on a northbound train after phoning my mother to ask her to tell Mette when I was due in Aalborg. But when I arrived at the station in the evening there was no Mette. The drunken bitch has probably forgotten to tell her, I thought, and jumped into another taxi.

When I arrive at the house, one of Bjarne's big tourist coaches is standing outside. Both the idiots are apparently at home. Well, I can always go to my grandparents – take Mette with me if she isn't already there. I simply don't have the energy to confront Janne until the following day.

I am met by the noise coming from the area around the swimming pool. I walk through the kitchen. Chaos. Leftovers on the dining table, empty bottles of wine. Through the living room and out towards the swimming pool through the double sliding doors. Some of the glass panels surrounding the pool have been opened to the garden. The furthest section of the roof is also made of glass and tucks under the flat roof which covers the rest of the pool with the aid of an electrically operated system that I installed two years before.

The shallow end of the square swimming pool is open on one side while the water in the rest of the pool is covered with long strips of thick, insulating plastic which are there to reduce the heating costs. It seems they couldn't be bothered to remove all of them. A couple of plastic chairs are floating in the water in the uncovered area – the idiots celebrating must have been sitting on them.

There is a three piece suite and Bjarne is sitting there with four young men. Soldiers – that is obvious even if they are in civvies. Before running his own company, Bjarne worked at the barracks and he still gets occasional jobs up there. There are always loads of soldiers willing to drink his booze, stuff themselves on his food and swim in his swimming pool.

"Come and have a beer, Allan," he shouts when I make my presence known. Bjarne's bloated face is shining – his skin blotchy from the booze, food and high blood pressure. Mette isn't out there with them.

"Where's Mette?" I ask.

A couple of the soldiers give each other a funny look. They seem drunk. One of them is sitting with a bottle of cognac in his hand and pestering Bjarne for permission to open it.

"There's no more bloody beer – and no wine, either."

"Open it then," Bjarne replies. No more wine? If they have emptied the wine cellar since I was last here then they have really gone for it.

"Mette?" I repeat.

"Try upstairs," Bjarne says.

I go upstairs to find Mette, happy that she is not taking part in the binge by the swimming pool. My mother's strident laughter rings out from the large bedroom. The door is ajar.

"Just see if you can find the key in his jacket pocket then . . . and hurry back. Then mummy will be nice to you," she says. I push the door open. Henrik is on his way towards the door. He is stuffing his shirt down in his trousers, but stops and takes a step backwards when he sees me. Henrik is a steward on the bus trips to Prague and is apparently fucking my mother. I doubt that a human being can sink any lower.

"Oh, hi, Allan," my mother says with a quick glance down at herself and round the bedroom. "We've run out of beer and cigarettes. Henrik is going to get some," she tells me.

"Piss off," I say to Henrik and step to the side so that he can come past. Mother's eyes are swimming. She is wearing a silk dressing gown; the cord around her waist is coming undone. There is a low neckline and you can see the top of her tits and the shiny skin-coloured lace bra.

"How's my big boy then?"

"Where's Mette?"

"I don't know, she must be playing with the boys," my mother says. A fury shines through the inebriation in my mother's eyes. She becomes ugly. "The little cunt was doing a fashion show by the swimming pool – in my fur. Making up to the soldiers like a real little whore."

"Don't talk like that about my sister." I leave her and walk down the corridor to my sister's room. The sound of a coach starting up makes me stop and look out of the roof light. Henrik is sitting behind the wheel and one of the soldiers is sitting in the guide's seat – they are obviously using the coach to buy beer. Bjarne can't have given them the key to his Mercedes.

The stench of vomit hits me in the face on opening the door to Mette's room. The sound of movement from under her duvet reaches me as I round the door and see her on the bed with a swollen face and reddened, surprised eyes; her eye make-up has left a trail down her cheeks. She is holding my mother's fur tight around her with both her thin child's hands. "Allan," she says, sounding happy but also frightened . . . or embarrassed. There is a large splat of red vomit beside the bed; there are almost no solids in it and the stench is like sour wine.

"Mette," I say. Walk over and sit down on the edge of the bed. Her body shakes as if with a sudden shiver or a convulsion and then she is racked with sobs as she wraps her arms around me and buries her face in my chest. There is dried sick on the lapels of the mink coat.

"What happened?" I ask.

Mette sobs. Hiccups. Gasps. Is quiet.

"There, there," I say, stroking her hair and lifting up her face so that I can see into her eyes. She is still drunk, but also . . . afraid. "Come on. Tell me what happened." She hides her face again. Says nothing.

"Let's get you into the shower," I say to her and as we sit there on the bed I move the upper part of her body away from me so that I can take the fur coat off.

"No," she says. She hugs the fur tighter around her, turns away from me and buries her face in the pillow. I can feel a red anger growing in my chest. Stand up. Take hold of her shoulders, pull her to her feet. She stares down at the floor. Weeping uncontrollably.

"You can tell me, I won't be angry," I say to her as calmly as I can while looking into her eyes and holding a hand on each shoulder. She howls and I can feel all her strength ebbing from her shoulders. Her arms drop down by her sides and she looks across to the window with desperation in her face as if everything that happens from now on is inevitable anyway. She is silent. I push the fur off her shoulders and it falls to the floor. Her bra has been pushed up over her small breasts and it hangs rolled up across the top of her chest and under her armpits. Her arms jerk upwards and she begins to tear at it to put it back in place while sniffling again.

"Did . . . Bjarne touch you?"

"No," she says. I hold her bare shoulders with one hand and with the other I reach out for her sheet on the bed and drag it off. Mette stands there with hunched shoulders feverishly trying to pull her bra down over her young girl's breasts while shielding them with her forearms. But the bra is twisted and she can't disentangle it. I hold the sheet up in front of her.

"Put this around you." She takes it from me and turns her back on me. She reaches back and undoes the clasp of the bra and I think to myself that her bashfulness in front of me – her elder brother – would be touching if the situation were different. But the red anger inside me keeps working away – gathering momentum.

She winds the sheet around her and despondently sits down on the edge of the bed.

"Are you sure he didn't touch you?"

"No. He just patted me . . . on the backside. I mean, when I was walking . . . doing the fashion show."

"He can't do that," I say. She cries again. Soundlessly. I sit on the edge of the bed and put my arms around her. "What about the others?" I ask.

"Yes, well . . . it was me who started it," she whispers.

"Did you say 'stop'?"

"Yes." Now she is sobbing, burrowing her head into my chest so that she doesn't have to see me.

"Did he stop?"

"No."

"I have to know if he went too far, Mette," I say. She sobs. "Just nod or shake your head. Did he go too far? Yes or no?"

She shakes her head.

The glowing red ball in my chest is still trembling.

"So he stopped?"

She nods. "I was sick over him," she says.

"And then he stopped?"

"Yes." I can hear from her voice that she is chuckling although she is still sniffling.

"Well, that was something, anyway," I say. "Which one was it?"

"It was me who started it," she says.

"Tell me."

"His name is . . . Kim, I think." Mette sits slumped on the edge of the bed. She is going to have a hangover, I muse.

"You need a shower," I say, getting up and taking her pyjamas which appeared under the duvet when I took the sheet off. "Get up," I say. She does and I take her by the shoulders and lead her out into the corridor. We can hear singing from downstairs. An army song. Bjarne sings loudest of all. We walk down the corridor to the bathroom, but the door is locked. I bang on the door with clenched fists.

"Yes. Who is it?" says my mother and there is a giggle. Hopeless. "I'm coming out now."

She opens the door and looks at us in astonishment as she pulls down her tight mini-skirt. I slap her across the face. See the white outline on her cheek before she covers it with her hand. I have wanted to do that for some years and I don't even have time to think. It . . . happens. Her open mouth. Speechless. "What . . . ?" she says, stepping back a pace in shock – her mouth like a landed cod's. I take Mette in and let her go, grab hold of my mother's arm.

"Your husband paws your daughter's bum. Your guests get her drunk and grope her tits," I say, leading my mother out of the bathroom. It is as if she is . . . on medication.

"Yes, but I . . . ." she says.

"Yes, you're a drunk," I say and go to close the bathroom door after me.

"Aren't you staying with me?" Mette says.

I let go of my mother. "I haven't finished with you," I say and join Mette. She is already in the shower. I ask her which toothbrush is hers and put toothpaste on it before passing it into her. "Try and drink some water," I say. Then I sit on the edge of the bath and mull over what I am going to do.

"What are you going to do, Allan?" she asks when she has turned off the shower and swathed herself in a towel.

"I'll think of something." She doesn't say another word. Just takes her night clothes in her hand and goes to her room.

I curse myself for not having intervened before. Taken her away from here. But where would I have taken her? Things weren't so bad when I left. But I should have known where it was all leading.

My limbs feel hollow as I walk downstairs. Pop music is coming from the swimming pool. My mother is sitting in the kitchen, on her own at the breakfast table, hunched over, cigarette in hand, a glass of wine. "Allan," she says. I walk past, towards the swimming pool. Now there are only three soldiers – they are my age, possibly a bit younger. They are sitting with Bjarne – they all have a glass of cognac in hand and are smoking cigars – Henrik is obviously not back yet with more beer. I only realize afterwards that I tackle the events in the wrong order. I stride over, grab a fistful of Bjarne's shirt in my left hand, drag him to his feet, the cognac splashes, the glass is smashed, my fist is like a piston rod in his face, one, two, three times. There is the clatter of armchairs as the soldiers try to get to their feet. I drag Bjarne away from the sofa as two of the soldiers stand up – one seems sober. I knee Bjarne in the testicles so he is bent double. My hand holds his shirt tight. His mouth is bleeding profusely. "Kim?" I say, but it is too late. I should have found that out before – my violence renders their reactions worthless. I can't see which one Kim is.

"What the fuck . . . ?" the sober soldier says and moves towards me. The other one seems paralyzed on his legs, the third immobile – still sitting. I let his shirt go while I sink my other fist into Bjarne's kidneys and follow through. He wobbles; he is half a metre from the edge of the pool, in front of the covered part at the shallow end. He topples over. The pain in his testicles does not allow him to control his fall. He hits the tiles and flips head first over the edge onto the plastic covers which give way under his weight so that the water seeps up between the strips. He thrashes around wildly. The plastic is forced under the level of the water, with his fat body on top. Screaming penetrates my consciousness. My mother in the room, coming closer. Screaming. The soldier takes three paces and jumps in with his legs together, next to Bjarne. The soldier presses the plastic down under the water with his legs so that it doesn't wrap itself round his body. This act of charity seems entirely unnecessary to me. The soldier manages to raise my stepfather into an upright position. They both stand in the shallow end absolutely soaked. Bjarne is spluttering.

"You're crazy," the soldier says. To me. I look at my stepfather, waiting for him to draw enough air to speak.

"I'll report you to the police," he says, an offended expression on his face – comical with his thin hair plastered against his skull, blood running from his mouth, his shirt stuck to the rolls of fat, struggling to pull himself out of the pool with his feeble arms weighed down with fat.

"I really hope you do," I say, turning and walking past my sobbing mother, through the house, up the stairs, into my sister's room. I pull a chair over to her bed. She is still awake.

"Give me your hand," she says. I cast a quick glance down at my hands. The left one is covered in blood. Grazing on the knuckles of my right hand. I wipe my knuckles on my trousers and pass her my hand. She doesn't notice anything. Hugs the whole of my forearm tight into her. "You won't go, will you," she says sleepily.

"I'll stay here, don't worry," I say.

A little time passes. There is a bang on the front door downstairs. It is opened. My mother's shrill: "*What*?"

It is the police. The bus has been in an accident – drove into a traffic island on the way to the gas station. The driver is on the operating table – unconscious, the passenger severely injured.

"He must have pinched the keys to the bus," my mother says instantly.

I can hear Bjarne shouting downstairs. "Her psychopath of a son attacked me." I light a cigarette. Not long after I hear steps coming up the stairs and a policeman opens the door to Mette's room and he looks around. The smell of vomit hangs in the air even though I have opened the window.

"Allan?" he says.

"Yes."

"Who's that?" He nods in the direction of my younger sister, who is now asleep.

"My little sister."

"Is there . . . something the matter with her?" he asks, probably because both of my sister's hands are holding my forearm tight, although she is asleep.

"They got her drunk and someone groped her," I say.

"Who?"

"One of the idiots downstairs."

"The one that's been beaten up?"

"Possibly," I say.

"What's that on your hand?" he asks.

"Blood," I say.

"Where's it from?"

"The one that's been beaten up."

"That was you?"

"Of course."

"He's reported you for assault – do you realize that we will have to take you with us?"

"Then first of all you'd better get hold of my grandmother so she can be here when my sister wakes up. Otherwise you won't be able to take me."

"I can't . . . ," the officer begins to say, but then the tear-stained face of my mother appears in the doorway. She looks frightened, seems composed, but there is rarely any depth to her composure.

"If you don't leave this house now I'll report your husband for abusing Mette," I say to her.

"Has he . . . ?" the officer asks.

"But Bjarne hasn't . . . ," my mother starts, but she pauses and gulps once. "But what will I do?" she whimpers.

"Go downstairs and call a taxi, then phone grandma and say you're both on your way."

"But I don't want to . . . go away." She tries to muster some authority.

"Otherwise I'll have Mette forcibly taken away from you. It won't be difficult – there's always alcohol in your blood."

My mother looks down at the floor. "I'll phone," she says, leaving the room.

I was taken to the police station and thrown in the sobering-up cell. The day after I was taken into custody. Two days later Bjarne withdrew the charges. According to my grandmother my mother had threatened to report Bjarne for rape, if I wasn't released. My mother had added that she would make sure that everyone heard about it. That would have been the death blow for his business.

Mette was sent to boarding school a couple of months after and I was still living with Janne at that time even though the relationship was in its last throes. My mother completely went to pieces and stayed in Carl's and my grandmother's cellar until she put her life together again.

I start the car and drive down all the familiar streets in Klarup. Frank's childhood home hasn't changed, either. I walk up the garden path as I had done countless times before, completely demented. Frank's mother is suspicious when she sees me.

"I don't know what Frank's doing," she says discouragingly, but I can still sense that she wants to chat.

"Are you still . . . ?" she asks, leaves the question hanging in the air. Am I still on speed half the time.

"No," I answer. She remains standing in the doorway, studying my face.

"It was a terrible thing, that accident," she says sadly. Then I go in and am given a cup of coffee. She doesn't know where Frank is, she thinks he is involved in all sorts of things, she is at her wits' end. She has an address.

"But he's never there," she says, and she doesn't have his telephone number. I drop by the address on my way home, but no-one answers the door.

Together with a couple of the deck guys, I had hoisted some iron sheets up onto Monkey Island – the top of the living quarters – and welded them together so that we had a swimming pool three metres square and half a metre in depth. We pumped sea water into it, and then you could float around in an inflated rubber inner tube in water that was 32 degrees, with a little pilsner on your stomach. We had had a minor outbreak of fire in the hole, in an oil heater. Nothing serious. It was put out quickly and no-one was hurt. But I had started going to the swimming pool every evening. Just lying there quietly and watching the sun go down under the horizon. The stars appeared, I scanned the sky for satellites and I could hear the throb of the engine in the background. It used to have a soothing effect. It didn't any more.

You start the engine with 30–40 bar of compressed air and an injection of fuel. Some people say that the engine doesn't have the dimensions for that kind of pressure. A year earlier the whole caboodle blew up on our sister ship. Now I was thinking about it again. A fire in the engine room. One of the worst things you can experience at sea because the fire can only be tackled from above where it is hottest – there is no way you can get down to the fire at the bottom of the ship. You can fill the engine room with halon and try to suffocate the fire that way, but there is no guarantee it will succeed. So the whole of the engine room and the living quarters burn down. And when the fire in the engine room is well alight, it burns a hole into the cargo hold, the oil gushes out into the engine room, the oil catches fire – a massive liquid fire. The oil becomes hotter and hotter and it breaks down into its smaller constituents, it distills; the volatile materials burn off, the heavy materials slowly sink to the bottom of the engine room. You try to extinguish the fire with foam until there is none left. Then you use water. The fire is in the engine – from the moment the alarm sounds it is the guys from the engine room who have to try to put it out.

The huge quantities of water immediately find their way to the bottom of the engine room which is now a gigantic receptacle. The heaviest constituents of the oil are immensely hot and over the course of a couple of days they sink to the bottom of the engine room where they meet the water that has settled there. Explosions of steam; a 100–150 metre high column of steam and fire blasting out towards the sky. I thought about fires and I continued to think about fires.

5

On Tuesday my hopes turn to dust. In the afternoon I grab *Ekstra Bladet* in the canteen, go to the toilet and read the sex ads. After work I park the car outside the Marine Museum at the western end of the small craft harbour. A telephone box is there. I walk past it and on to Fjordbyen. The allotment cottages are lived in all the year round despite the frequent rumours going around that the council will clear the area. Someone has opened an illicit bar. I have a couple of beers. To drink Dutch courage or . . . no, it isn't courage; removing the worst of the jagged edges – coming to terms with my defeat. Walk back to the telephone box,phone and drive straight there. Afterwards drive home. Although I haven't eaten a thing I feel bloated, as if I were almost fat. I take a long shower, but it doesn't change anything. So I go down to a convenience store and buy a bottle of gin which I mix with a bit of lemonade and drink until I throw up. Only then do I feel sort of alright.

On Wednesday morning at work they say I look ill and send me home. I drive into town and buy a telephone answering machine from Fona. I stroll around the centre of town, and the sun is shining. At least twenty girls arrest my searching eyes and I believe for a nano-second that they are her. I can see from the way people stare at me that the expression on my face is repugnant.

I lie in bed dozing. Late that afternoon there is a ring at the door. Nervously, I grab the entry phone.

"Yes?"

"Hi . . . it's Lene – you know . . . ? May I come in?" the voice says in my ear.

"Um, yes," I say, pressing the button to open the door downstairs. While she is coming up I hurriedly put on a pair of trousers and a T-shirt. The thought goes through my head that Lene is exactly the kind of girl who will always fall for me. Always. She sees a man who is solid, has training, a job and can give her security, but at the same time he is strong – there is a hint of . . . something dangerous about him that can raise her out of her deadly tedium. And she sees herself as the woman who can give me something I lack – make something of me. And perhaps it is true – that it might be okay. But there is no life in it – no fire. I could never respect her; she has nothing that is . . . her own.

Lene steps through the door. She is visibly on edge, but tries to display an air of superiority.

"Cup of coffee?" I ask before she can say anything. Already there are cracks in her façade.

"No – um, I just have to . . . say something."

"Say it over a cup of coffee," I announce while going into the kitchen and fetching a mug. She goes into the sitting room, looks around inquisitively and sits on one of the two dining room chairs that I bought with the table from a second-hand dealer. I also managed to acquire a roller blind before going cold on the whole project. I pour some coffee for her.

"What can I do for you, Lene?"

"Yes, um, . . . Frank wants to talk to you."

"Yes? He knows where I live."

"Yes, but he's got an . . . offer for you."

"And what's that?"

"Some . . . work. He said you knew what it was about."

I sit down facing her, place my elbows on the table, put my fists together and rest my chin on them.

"What sort of jobs are we talking here?"

"That's . . . ," she hesitates. "What he'd like to talk to you about."

"Lene, I'm an engineer," I say. "That's what I am. I don't want to work for him." She gives a deep sigh – relieved somehow.

"Are you his girlfriend?" I ask.

"No. No, I'm not," she answers – with hope in her voice. It is so . . . sad. Then she giggles. I look at her, puzzled.

"He certainly wasn't very happy when you well . . . I mean, when you went home with Lykke."

"That was obvious. But you're not together?"

"No," she repeats. "What makes you think that?"

"Well, I had the impression there was something between you."

"No." She stares at the table. "We were . . . a couple once. But that's a long time ago." She looks up. "I have to be off now," she says and gets up. I have to know something. She tentatively makes her way to the hall. I am right behind her. She stands still, looks up at me, as if expecting me to let her out, open the door for her.

"Lene," I say, putting my hand on her hip. "I want . . . ." I turn her round so that she is facing me, pull her to me and kiss her hard on the mouth. Feel a light headiness, almost hollow inside. Her lips feel like plastic. I know it is wrong . . . it *feels* wrong. And at the same time I want . . . to have a release inside her. I want to . . . use her. I can't see any other option.

"Noooo," she cries, struggling, and immediately surrenders, like an actress, I imagine. We are in bed in a flash. Afterwards we smoke a cigarette. And everything has gone. I can't touch her any more. She is used. My body is dirty inside. The bedding will have to be changed. I want to have a shower. She has to leave. I want to lie on a clean sheet – feel coolness on my skin . . . and hunger. Her presence somehow makes me miss that hunger.

I compliment her on her body – and I mean it at that. Feel obliged to say it.

"Yes," she says without feeling. It is very strange.

"I need some information from you."

"What about?" she asks.

"About Leif, Asger, Frank, Susan, Maja, Nina and maybe about you yourself."

"Why?" she asks.

"That doesn't matter," I answer. "I know what Frank and Asger do. You don't have to tell me anything, but I'm asking you – I would appreciate it."

"What's in it for me?" she asks.

"Nothing."

"What's the idea then?" She sighs.

"Perhaps it can help you to see that you are . . . driving down a blind alley, so to speak."

"Why . . . did you go to bed with me?" she asks – her voice right at the top of her throat. Fuck. I want to apologize, but it makes no sense. What for? Less than nothing happened here – way below nothing. I did it because I could. Goose pimples appear on my arms, my forehead hurts. And I don't want to ask her why she went to bed with me; I know – her wretched, miserable hope. Two lonely fools, together alone.

"We wanted . . . to go to bed with each other," I say and add: "I don't know why."

"What do you want to know?" she asks in a flat voice.

"What went on with the two girls – Susan and Maja – before Nina threw them out of Asger's place? That's what I want to know, exactly that."

"Why?"

"That's my business," I say.

"Do you know them?"

"Kind of."

"There . . . ," Lene stammers. Then she takes a deep breath and says: "They gave them something – I don't know what – without them . . . knowing."

"What was the something?" I ask. Lene hesitates.

"LSD, I think." Then it is me who hesitates. How crazy can you get?

"Why?" I ask.

"I don't know . . . that's the way they *are*."

"Then what happened?"

"Then . . . well, I wasn't there. Nina says that . . . ." Lene falters again.

"That. . . ?"

"That Asger tried to . . . get into bed with Susan and she completely freaked out, I mean, went completely ballistic, and the other one did too, and then Nina chucked them out. That's what I heard."

"And what did Asger do . . . ? When Nina chucked them out?" I ask.

"Nothing."

"Was Frank there?"

"Yes," Lene answers.

"What did he do?"

"He gave them LSD – that's what Nina said, anyway."

I don't feel anything, or I don't know what I feel, but I clearly seem to be expecting more.

"That's all," she says, standing up and putting on her clothes. As she does so she starts sobbing. The walls are bare. Clothes strewn over the floor. The digital numbers on the clock radio change soundlessly.

"Lene," I say.

"Mmm." She stands with her back to me in the dark room, pulling on her trousers, almost toppling over as she tries to guide in leg number two.

"Thank you," I say.

She says nothing. Goes out into the hallway. I can hear her putting on her shoes. The door opens, the steps down the stairs die away.

On Thursday I get up a bit earlier and drive by the address I have for Frank. No answer. On the way home from work I buy a piece of fish which I throw into the oven with a few vegetables and a shot of white wine. As I stand in the shower my body feels amazingly strong and I have a cool sensation on the skin around my head despite the hot water. I have to possess her. I tell myself that I can do it.

In the living room I have the television on and it is showing MTV with the volume turned down low; it is the only source of light in the room except for the office lamp fixed to the window frame. I still haven't managed to add to the dining table and the two chairs. That is fine, I comment to myself. The smell of baked fish spreads through the flat. I stand leaning against the wall by the window smoking a cigarette and looking down from the three floors to the street. Frank's car drives up, he gets out with Jøns and they walk to the main entrance. My entry phone rings. I can see Frank step back into the road and gaze up at my window. Perhaps he can see the flickering light from the TV, perhaps I am in the toilet having a shit or down in the yard with the refuse. The phone rings again. Perhaps I just couldn't give a damn. I eat the fish. The telephone rings. I take a wedge of lemon and suck it while keeping an eye on the answering machine. After four rings it reacts. It is Frank: *"We have something to discuss, Allan. You can find us in Grøften any time over the weekend. Don't disappoint me."*

I consider whether Lene told Frank about our sex. I am sure he is using her . . . I did, too. Well, that is neither here nor there. I have to do what I have to do – then I will have to take the consequences as they come.

I open all the windows to create a through-draught, turn the volume right down on MTV and sit with my back against the radiator by the window – the fins cut into my back; it is a pleasurable sensation, I feel alive. Good. Drink coffee, read a paperback fitfully, but it is so fantastic listening to the birds singing outside. I have a pleasant pain in my stomach. Later I drag the box mattress into the living room again – I think it is because I feel less lonely like that; it is not nearly as outrageously unacceptable as a man lying alone in a bedroom. I turn off the TV and the lamp, leave the blinds open.

Lying on the mattress in the dark, I can see the cones of light from cars' headlamps starting in one corner of the ceiling by the window, advancing slowly at first, and then accelerating across the middle before slowing down again in the other corner of the ceiling by the window. It is comforting listening to the cars and the birds. I take a leak and go to the kitchen for a glass of milk before I sleep. There is a couple making love in front of an open window in one of the flats; the open area between the blocks of flats creates a resonance and amplifies the sounds the woman makes. He doesn't make much noise until the end. When cars come from both ends of the street at the same time the lights intersect on the ceiling and as they accelerate past each other, for one short moment, one patch of the ceiling is completely lit up.

All day at work on Friday I wonder whether I should go to town in case she might be there. Knowing all the time that it is a bad idea – a futile thought. Of course I shouldn't go. What can I achieve by going? By being pathetic? It is more important that I go down to see Carl. He has had the boat in the water for some time, but I haven't been down and I know he is unhappy about that.

Sitting in the car, after work, I can't resist and I drive onto the bridge. I convince myself that I don't realize that I am doing it and then suddenly I wake up: there I am on the bridge. Fool. I know that I can't knock on her door; I am too wretched inside. Still I somehow permit myself to drive past the parking lot in front of her place – to torment myself – before driving northeast onto the highway. Suddenly, right in the middle of the road, I am simply so bloody angry. There is not much traffic and as soon as there is enough room I slam on the brakes and swing the wheel round. I pull on the handbrake, release it, put my foot down on the accelerator again and smash the car into gear with my right hand, slipping the clutch and making the wheels spin. I drive in the direction I came from. I walk up to her place, knock on the door.

"Come in," she yells – perhaps she is expecting someone. I open the door; can't see her at first and lean against the door frame.

"Hi Maja," I say quietly, almost tonelessly. "I'd like to talk." She emerges from the kitchen niche – looking angry, it seems to me, but also surprised.

"No." She takes a swift stride towards the door, then changes her mind and stands still. Stares at me.

"I'd like you to tell me what the problem is," I say. She doesn't answer, she just glowers at me.

"Have I done anything wrong?" I ask and it is clear that she is considering this. Thinks twice before speaking:

"No – you haven't done anything wrong."

"What is it then?" She doesn't answer. "Shall I go?"

"It's what you *haven't* done."

"Tell me what the problem is."

"You haven't told me the truth. You lied to me."

"Yes." I lower my gaze to the floor and I shiver.

"Why?" she says.

"It was . . . ." I glance up at her. "Sorry."

"No," she says. "Why?"

"I was . . . ," I begin, and then I realize that I don't know if she is referring to the accident or my past as a speed freak when she says I lied. It is impossible to know. "I was frightened how you would react."

"So you should be. I *hate* junkies," she says. Junkie – quite a harsh term, I think, but this is not the time to pick up on that.

"It's a long time ago. I mean, you have to understand – I've been at sea for the last three years. Mostly oil tankers. I have . . . ." She interrupts me.

"I know," she says. Okay.

"I have nothing to do with these people any more . . . Frank and the others. It was pure chance that I ran into him. I have . . . finished – completely finished with that life."

She continues to stare at me. I begin to delude myself into thinking that her eyes say 'maybe'.

"I think you should go now," she says.

"No," I say. That is not good enough. "I have to . . . *know* if there's a chance that I'll see you again.

"I'll . . . think about it," she says, raising her index finger and adding: "But don't count on anything."

I open my arms wide, step back out of the doorway and as I grasp the door handle, say, "That's fine, Maja." The door is closed and I go down to the car. Throat feels dry as I drive north east again until I hit the highway which I stay on and return through the tunnel. Briefly I wonder who she has been talking to, though actually it doesn't matter.

On Saturday I wake up early. It is only a little before nine o'clock after I have showered and had breakfast. I consider going down to the harbour – to see if Carl is there. But there are lots of utensils I need for the kitchen and for some reason it is a matter of urgency that I buy them today.

Shop workers are slowly beginning to put their signs and goods out onto the pavement as I drive into Nytorv. I park by the harbour in front of the Limfjord terminal and nip down to where the tugs are. They look like prisons. It is half past nine. I walk up to Nytorv and go into Inspiration where I find a good frying pan and a large blue dish. Afterwards I turn a variety of whisks between my fingers – impossible to choose between them.

There is a woman who approaches me from alongside the stack of shelves where I am standing.

"Hi Allan" she says. Janne. I study her. She is well-dressed, she bares her teeth – it is a smile, but the toughness is apparent under the make-up.

"Janne," I say and nod.

"You're back," she confirms, her eyes fixed on my face.

"Yes."

"What are you doing?"

"Working. Yourself?" I ask. She looks away, the muscles tightening in her neck. Then she turns back her head.

"I still owe you for half of the furniture."

"Doesn't matter, Janne. Forget it," I say.

"Yes, but you should have the money, anyway."

"Janne, it's water under the bridge. I'm not interested in the money."

"No, I suppose you aren't," she says, thin-lipped now.

"Don't, Janne. It was bound to happen sooner or later – we'd lost it."

"Perhaps you think you got off lightly, letting me keep the furniture?" She spits the words out. She is ugly. Repulsive.

"It was you who wanted it and, yes, now you mention it, I got off lightly." She is so angry that tears form in her eyes as she moves to go. "Very lightly," I say to her back.

Bring my attention back to the whisks in my hands. Throw one of them back on the shelf, take two of the others to the cash desk. I have earned so much damn money since the furniture and I don't even know what to do with it. Buy a house? What is the point? I put the goods in front of the shop assistant.

"Going to do a bit of whisking, are you," he says.

"What?"

"You must have something . . . ." The words come hesitantly. ". . . Something that needs . . . whisking."

"Give it a rest, will you," I say.

"Right." He concentrates on packing the goods.

Carl is down by the boat when I arrive. She is a lot more attractive in the water. I help him to repair the sail for a couple of hours – he finds it difficult to sew because of the rheumatism in his fingers. We work in silence, except for Carl's instructions, which I follow.

"You don't look happy Allan."

"Girl problems."

"Remember to let them decide all the minor things so they don't feel they haven't got a say," he says. "Then stand firm when there are bigger decisions to make."

"Yes, that's what you always say." I keep sewing while wondering what the small things are. What are the big decisions? What are the big things in a relationship? One big thing is deciding where to live because the price of the property means you will have to slog your guts out for the rest of your life. But no-one can decide on their own. Having a child is an even bigger decision. This is no solo performance. Carl's shit words of wisdom. And above all this is hypothetical speculation when there is no fucking relationship in the first place.

When we have finished Carl wants to go out on a little trip. His face beams. I automatically make the excuse that I have a date with a girl. Why did I say that? I like sailing. Carl tries to hide his disappointment, but it only makes it more obvious. I spend the rest of the day chewing it over. Am I really so frightened of the water?

In the evening I go to an Italian restaurant and eat a pizza that tastes equally as good as those you have in Italy. When I received my first real wage I took Janne to a wonderful Italian restaurant and we ate gigantic pizzas and drank wine. On reflection, she was already beginning to lose it then. She was no longer the girl who clung onto me on the back of the moped and who panted in my ear in the parking lot outside the youth club. I didn't notice, but she had begun to spruce up her life and she tried to spruce up mine. After eating I go to the cinema to see some action film or other, but I can't concentrate on the plot so I leave. It had been the right decision to go to sea when I did. It wasn't good being here. Life at sea was boring. It isn't good being here now.

To torture myself, I walk over and stare up at her window. There is a light on behind the curtains. I can't go up there again. I see her silhouette outlined against the material – at least I think I can. I return home. There are no messages on the answer phone. Set the alarm clock for four o'clock in the morning.

Sunday morning five o'clock. Frank's car is parked right outside the entrance to his house and, on top of that, there is a light on in the windows.

As soon as he opens the door, I know how the land lies with him. Total exhaustion and uptight. Brain grilled. Welder's eyes – the eyeballs are bloodshot.

"Allan. About time, too," he says. "Come in." The bedroom door is ajar. Through the slit I can see Lene sleeping in his bed. "I'm watching Lethal Weapon 2," he says and gives me a sweaty grin. "I can't sleep, man." He walks into the living room talking over his shoulder: "Well, did you have any joy?"

Joy? I think. Oh, right, the girl. He asked me that before.

"Yes," I answer.

"Great dick sucker," Frank says, sitting in a chair. He gives me a look which I can only characterize as supremely gracious. "Bit too much of a screamer for my taste though," he adds.

Yes, Frank, you don't like her, do you. I seat myself in the armchair facing him and pour myself a cup of lukewarm coffee from the flask.

"Well," says Frank, looking business-like. "Now, just listen to what . . . ." I break in.

"Frank, I don't owe you anything and I don't want anything to do with you." I sit back – continuing to speak calmly. "I ought to knock the living daylights out of you for what you did to Maja and Susan, but for old times' sake I'll let it pass. We're quits."

He is astonished. He hadn't expected that. "Have you come here – to my own house – to *threaten* me?" he asks, puffing himself up, doped out, smashed. He cuts a ridiculous figure.

"Frank," I say. "If you get in my way . . . you know what will happen." I have beaten him up before, once when he made a pass at Janne.

"Hey, man," he says with a cold smile. "You don't know who I am now." And it is right, I don't know who he knows, what he can set in motion. I don't care. Stare at him, waiting. "What the fuck do you want with that little hippy whore?" he says. I stand up, slowly shaking my head.

"Well, I don't think that she was up to much in the sack," he says. Fortunately, I can't be drawn that easily. I move towards the hallway. Can hear Frank pushing his chair back, getting up and following me. "You shouldn't turn your back on me," he says. When I have opened the front door, I turn round; as I move I catch a glimpse of Lene in bed – her eyes wide open in surprise. I grab Frank round the neck with one hand, shove him up against the wall and press until I can feel his Adam's apple cut into the palm of my hand. With my other hand I force Frank's right arm against the wall. His left arm hits me feebly in the stomach. He can't get any air. I turn my head and glance at Lene. She is lying completely still with her head covered with the duvet.

"Keep away from me, Frank."

He is choking when I let him go. He holds his neck, panting. I manage to get all the way down the stairs and into the street, where I unlock the car, before he has enough air. His voice croaks down from the window:

"Allan, you're finished, man. You're fucking dead."

The week passes unbearably slowly. I am in for a beating – that much is certain. A beating. What can you do? Swallow it, don't let yourself be drawn.

A beating is something that comes out of the blue – it can be very painful afterwards, but it can do much more harm before if you sit and wait for it. That is my thinking. A kind of clearly defined logic.

The feeling is well documented; I am at my most vulnerable now. Ready, steady, crumble. The first thing I do when I get home is check for messages on the answering machine. There aren't any. The desire for amphetamines is indescribable. Cut loose, whoop it up, boogie through. Just the once. Why not . . . ? I imagine the rush: wonderful. Afterwards, though, I will just feel even more sickened by myself, and then it will be seriously difficult to fight the need. Perhaps I won't be able to stop; I will be swimming in the shit until I sink. I can see it in front of me – my humiliation of myself. Drink a cup of coffee.

Put on shoes and jacket and take a walk to Viggo Madsen's book shop, buy myself a pile of English novels and general dictionaries to supplement the technical ones I already have. All the words I don't know I force myself to check in the dictionary to improve my English. I have bought tea bags in case she should drop by.

After pulling down the new roller blinds I could just as easily be on board a ship; all I need are the vibrations and the right sounds. I toy with the idea of looking for work abroad, either in one of the oil-producing countries or on an oil rig off the Norwegian coast. But the whole thought process strikes me as ridiculous – like old ground. I consider blowing all my savings to travel somewhere, but I am conscious that it would only be an attempt to escape from my own problems and I don't want to make a fool of myself with my own money.

On Wednesday Iphone Vejgaard Soccer Club from work and find out that the Old Boys' team trains on Thursday evenings and on Tuesdays for those who can be bothered. There is a match on Sundays. I try to stop thinking about Maja. I think about her all the time; have an ongoing discussion with myself about what the right thing to do is. I dig out my old soccer boots from a cardboard box. Wait or act? Rub grease in until the uppers are soft again. How long can anyone wait? New laces. In the novel I am reading there is a woman who touches on it. She says it is the worst thing that can befall a man: to love a woman who is not interested in him. For a couple of hours I reckon I can come up with something worse, I just can't put my finger on what.

On Thursday evening I drive over and train. It is strange to meet so many men of my age. They all shake hands and say their names. Adrian is there. "Great you came," he says. The quips fly around about someone's gooseberry legs, another's belly, someone else's pregnant girlfriend. They ask me where I usually play. At the back. I apologize for my form in advance. No problem, they say, we all smoke too many cigarettes. It is as tough as hell and wonderful. We finish by playing a match across half of the pitch. I give everything I have until I almost throw up. I stand bent over with my hands on my knees trying to catch my breath. I realize that I haven't thought about girls, drugs, family, work, dubious friendships, the past, the future or anything at all for thirty whole minutes. I have just been here, now. Fantastic. Adrian asks if I want to play in the home match on Sunday – as a reserve at least. I say yes. Feel reborn.

On Friday morning my legs are so sore that I have a job walking down the stairs. As soon as I step out of the main entrance I see Jøns coming towards me. I am lucky or else he is simply slow – he was probably up all night. I stop and wait for him. When he is close he throws a right to my head. I jerk my head to the left, feel only the whoosh of air as his fist whistles by. My right hand is quickly up and grabs the right sleeve of his jacket. I have a handful of material in my fist, step almost completely behind him and thrust his arm down. My left hand grabs his left shoulder from the back so that I can pull him towards me while forcing his right arm up behind his back. He screams as I shove him against the house wall and flatten his cheek against the cement joint between the bricks. I can see the steroid pimples on his neck. He stinks of hash, beer and stale sweat. I push his right arm up his back one last time before I let go, walk over to the car, lock myself in, start up and drive – all without so much as a look in his direction. My arms begin to shake. I have to pull in to the side, leave the car and smoke a cigarette before I can drive to work.

I am not out of the woods. Perhaps I should have just let him work me over. It will certainly be a lot worse now.

After work I drive down to see Carl at the harbour. He invites me in for a meal. We eat. I suggest playing cards. It is quite late. I ask him if I can use his sofa – otherwise I am not sure I will be able to get up the following day to go sailing. It is all lies, though. There is no problem getting up. The problem is something else. I am afraid.

I stand on the landing stage, looking down at her. Carl goes on board. *Ella* she is called – after the jazz singer. Take it easy, Allan. We are talking about the Limfjord here. You can swim to the shore without even exerting yourself. I took a five kilometre badge in Haraldslund Swimming Pool when I was twelve years old and finally my grandmother let me take off the inflatable jacket, unless we were in open sea. I go on board and put on a life jacket before I slip the moorings. The surprise on Carl's face is obvious, but he quickly collects himself – doesn't say a word, behaves as if it were completely natural.

The sailing trip is a success. I forget my problems. Until we return. There are a few things Carl has to do before the evening as he has invited my mother, Mette, Peter and me down to the harbour for a barbecue.

I drive home for an afternoon nap. On the way in the car I force the fear out of my head. There is a message on my answer phone, but it is only Mette. She would like me to pick her up because she has asked Peter to stay at home. After a sleep I drive out there and when we arrive at the harbour, our mother is already there.

Carl has lit the barbecue by a table/bench set near his boat.

"It's like being on a camping site," my mother says, laying out paper plates, plastic cutlery and large plastic beakers on the tablecloth my grandfather brought from home.

"Well, we didn't come here to wash up, did we," he says, taking a swig of his beer and keeping an eye on the meat grilling on the barbecue. Mette brought bread and potato salad with her – bought in a shop, thankfully.

"You feel like a prole drinking red wine out of a plastic beaker," my mother says.

"Make sure you don't get too drunk now," Mette says to her.

"I'm not drunk," my mother says. "I'm just in a good mood."

We eat while Mette talks to my mother about clothes, make-up and all that. I talk to Carl about the boat. The skin on my face tightens and I sit rubbing it – that usually helps.

My mother looks at me with doggy eyes: "Oh, Allan," she says. "If you hadn't gone to sea, you wouldn't look like you do now." My grandfather looks as if he has just been slapped across the face; he stares at the table. My mother sits there with her shiny eyes and very erect back. I feel like telling my mother that if she had not put the beaker to her mouth two hundred times in the course of the evening she wouldn't be drunk. There is no point though.

"I'm just afraid that it will be difficult for you to meet a girl . . . looking the way you do," mother says. I am afraid that my problems are of a very different nature. "Have you bought some furniture?" she asks. Carl must have told her that I don't have any furniture.

"No," I say.

"Allan, that can't help . . . ," she starts to say.

"Stop it, mother," says Mette.

"What? What did I say?" She smokes her cigarette. For a second I am sure that she will burst into tears – and she can, too. "I'm just trying to help," she says, casting her eyes away from the table. The stink of burning plastic reaches my nostrils. My grandfather is staring vacantly ahead of him. Mette is sitting with her head lowered, though she glances furtively across at my mother. I follow Mette's gaze. The burning end of my mother's cigarette is resting against the plastic beaker, a couple of centimetres under the rim, and the breeze is carrying the stinking smoke over to me. The cigarette is burning a hole just above the wine, but mother doesn't notice anything. She grasps the beaker and takes it to her lips; very carefully, to hide how pissed she is. As she tips the beaker a look of wonder spreads across her face – no wine is coming into her mouth; it is pouring through the hole and over her silk skirt, so the pastel blue colour changes to something more substantial – bull's blood. Uncomprehending, watery eyes. Mette stares at her directly with compressed lips. Carl glances over at Mette, then at me and turns his gaze out into the darkness. He seems shaken.

"No," my mother says with a tearful voice, feverishly trying to wipe her bosom with one hand. Carl raises himself with difficulty and walks away, taking his hand to his face; to his eyes, I think. I look at my mother; see the shame spread across her face, penetrate and strike home. Fascinating, I muse, and the hairs on my neck stand on end. Would I sit like this if she were here – Maja? . . . No. Blood rises into my cheeks. What kind of person am I? Am I mean-spirited? Is this what I want? And then I expect another person . . . to feel tenderness for me? I gulp – the saliva in my mouth tastes of rottenness and iron. Feel shabby as I stand up and walk across to my mother, help her to her feet.

"Come on, let's go down to the boat and find some dry clothes for you." She sways and stumbles after the first couple of steps, so I have to put my arm round her shoulders and hold her up. I can hear Mette making a move behind us and when I turn my head I can see her spitting on the ground.

"I'll get it," she says, dashing past us to the boat, jumping on board and disappearing below the deck. My mother is crying now. I hold her tight and gently stroke her hair. "There, there," I say. "Mette's coming with a dry sweater for you now." Mette re-appears with one of my grandfather's large sweaters in one hand.

"That's nice of you to help your old mother," my mother says. For Christ's sake.

"Go behind there and take your blouse off." I point to a dark shed.

"Yes," my mother says, walking uncertainly in that direction. Mette walks behind her, to one side. Come on. Then Mette goes up to her and puts her arm round her.

I go back to the table. My grandfather is standing in the dark, slightly removed, but I can see from the glow of his cheroot that he is slowly shaking his head.

"Sit yourself down," I say.

"You children," he says without moving.

"Sit down." He does. I don't know what to say to him. He was at sea from the age of fifteen until he was 67. His relationship with my grandmother was an endless series of honeymoons. He has no idea what my mother is about – he doesn't know her. Mette comes back to the table with my mother and sits her down. Mother sits with her arms crossed around herself.

I am just about to ask her if she wants more wine, but I stop myself. My grandfather opens a bottle of beer and puts it in front of her.

"I want to go home," she says into her chest. She somehow gives the impression of being very innocent and beautiful in the large seaman's sweater.

"Oh, stay for a while longer, Dorthe," Carl says.

"Okay," she says, her eyes still lowered.

"Tell us about the time you came home after the war," Mette says.

"Okay, I can do that," Carl says and starts telling us about how he was sailing on one of the East Asia Company's cargo ships, returning home from

Singapore with a crate of Coca-Cola and a whole pile of American jazz LPs under his arm and became Aalborg's most sought after bachelor. That was when he met my grandmother. I sneak a glance at my mother. She reaches out warily for the bottle of beer and takes a swig. Then another swig, puts it back on the table and looks at Carl with an affectionate smile.

The entry phone rings on Sunday morning. Should I answer it? It could be heaven or hell. Luckily I am up and dressed – making coffee, hangover well under control.

"Yes?" I say into the receiver, without inflection.

"Allan," a voice says.

"Who's speaking?"

"Adrian, for fuck's sake."

"Okay," I say – taken aback.

"Open up, man. I've got fresh rolls with me," he says. I press the button. Adrian. I wonder what he wants. He must have found my address through directory enquiry. But it is great that he is dropping in. I glance round the living room to see if there is anything embarrassing I should clear away, but there isn't. There is nothing embarrassing in my life unless it is embarrassing to be lonely. I can hear him coming up the stairs so I open the door. He is in soccer gear, with a paper bag from the bakery in one hand and a litre of juice in the other. It had completely slipped my mind that it was match day.

"I hope your hangover isn't too bad," he says, passing me on his way to the kitchen. "We're playing Hjørring. They're no joke."

"I'm ready," I say as he takes the buttered rolls, slices of cheese and small plastic containers of jam out of the bag and puts it all on the biggest chopping board I have. I find plates and coffee mugs from the cupboards and pour coffee into the coffee flask.

"Yes, well, I didn't know if you would have any grub," he says nodding towards the chopping board before carrying it into the living room.

"That's great," I say, following him.

"What did you do yesterday?" he asks. "You look a bit the worse for wear."

"Family get-together."

"A walk through the minefield."

"Exactly."

"Your sister – isn't she alright?"

"Absolutely. But Mummy is an alcoholic."

"Not so good."

"Well, what the hell," I say, shrugging my shoulders and sinking my teeth into a roll. "What about you?" I ask with food in my mouth.

"Hey, my mother's cool."

"I was thinking more about what you did last night."

"Oh right. I was humping the wonderful Ulla."

"Okay. Ulla, she's your girlfriend?"

"Yes and no. I'm not really sure. In fact, I think she's in love with my pusher . . . but we have it off, that's the main thing, and we're good at it."

"In love with your pusher?"

"Yes, well, I'm not in love with her, so I guess it's fair."

"But why do you think she's in love with your pusher?"

"Every Sunday she goes to his place, does the cleaning, washes his clothes – that sort of thing. I've just dropped her off."

"You don't mind?"

"He pays her. He's my pusher. He's a nice guy," Adrian says, shrugging his shoulders. "Well, what the fuck. Once I went with a girl who liked me because I looked like her late boyfriend – that was a kind of living necrophilia."

"Did you know? . . . that was why?"

"No, not at first, but I found out," Adrian says.

"And then you cleared off?"

"No, no – she was . . . well, she *is* a terrific woman."

"And you didn't mind . . . being used?"

Adrian bursts into laughter. Then he goes quiet, gazing vacantly into empty space. "Fuck, yes," he says. "It wasn't great. And I moved out." He stares at me for a while, saying nothing.

"Would you like to have stayed?" I ask.

"You know, love – when you feel it . . . ," he starts saying in a voice that suddenly acquires a heavy edge to it, ". . . you'll do anything. However outrageous it is. You'll do everything to achieve it or keep it. And if you can't have it you'll do everything to destroy it." He leans back in his chair and concentrates on lighting a cigarette. I reach out for the coffee flask, noiselessly lean forwards and pour coffee for him. The only sounds to be heard are the splash of the coffee in the mug and the whistle from Adrian's cigarette as he sucks hard, keeping the cigarette between his lips while inhaling. He sucks again and blows the thick columns of smoke out from his nostrils. It feels like a defining moment, fragile. He looks out into the street.

"It was love at first sight, as they say." Adrian shakes his head; his eyes seem like voids as he begins to tell the story.

He had gone to the squatters' house in Kjellerupsgade; that was right back in 1985. He wanted to buy a cymbal from Sigurt – the drummer in a band called BÜLD.

There is a bonfire in the yard. People are sitting round drinking. Pusher Lars is there and Axel, the mushroom expert, as well as a slightly hysterical girl in yellow and Steso, whom Adrian had run into earlier.

I don't know any of the people except perhaps Steso, but I don't want to interrupt Adrian's flow.

Adrian goes to Sigurt's flat on the first floor, but the door is locked. Then he hears a noise coming from one of the other flats; the door is ajar so he pushes it open and goes in. The flat is dark and unfurnished, but he can hear sounds from the next room so he creeps up on tiptoes. There is a beautiful long-limbed girl on the mattress on the floor and on top of her a small, stocky guy wearing soccer boots with his shorts round his ankles – his muscular white buttocks contracting with every thrust inside her.

Adrian sneaks out again and sits round the bonfire in the yard. A little later the girl from the house comes out and strolls over to the fire with a faraway look in her eyes and a little smile playing round the corners of her mouth. She gives Adrian a grin as she rolls up her skirt and straddles the fire's glowing embers – then she unleashes a broad stream of pee. She has no underpants on.

She tries to focus on Adrian, talk to him – in the dark she thinks he is someone else.

At that moment Sigurt comes in from the street, his eyes shining, staring directly at Steso, and in unison they recite the same snatch of lyrics from Joy Division: "*Heart and soul – one will burn.*" Adrian calls Sigurt, but he does not react – he just continues on into the house.

Shortly afterwards, a car in the street hoots and the girl who peed on the fire disappears with Steso and the girl in yellow clothes.

Later Adrian rolls up at a BÜLD concert at 1000Fryd and the people from the bonfire in Kjellerupsgade were there. It was absolutely impossible to make contact with them – mushrooms, joints and alcohol.

Adrian stops speaking. I look at him in silence. He gives a brief, appraising look, takes a mouthful of coffee and gazes out the window before continuing.

"Five years later I answer an ad in *Rockshoppen*, someone looking for a drummer," Adrian says. He has to go for an audition in the practice room at Huset in Hasserisgade. He recognizes the girl who peed on the fire in Kjellerupsgade even though five years have passed. Lisbeth – all dressed in black – keyboards and vocals.

Apart from Lisbeth, the band consists of Korzeniowski, a Polish guitarist who works summers in Norway as a craftsman building log cabins. In the winter he hangs out in Skørping with a chubby, good-humoured nurse – a single mother with two children. And he plays a jangling melodic electric guitar. Their band is called *the expendables* – the initials are written in small letters, too; they are so unpretentious they are arrogant.

Lisbeth doesn't say anything – she just gives Adrian weird looks as he thrashes away on the tubs. Afterwards he has to go home with her to listen to some records so he can know where they are going, musically speaking. He and Lisbeth drink wine until they are both drunk. She wants to show Adrian some scars on her legs from a traffic accident. She strips off her trousers. Adrian asks about the accident. She says the driver died, that he was a childhood friend. Adrian asks further questions, but she is evasive and her eyes take on a faraway look. She takes off her sweater. Adrian drops the subject. She is very attractive. Then she takes him – cold. The guy with the white ass and the soccer boots is out of the picture, it seems.

"No," she says when Adrian suggests doing this or that. They won't do anything except practise as a band – and Adrian should be available when the spirit takes her. And he is wild about her. He thinks she is a wonderful human being behind the hard-boiled exterior. So long as he can penetrate the facade, everything will be fine.

They travel to Czechoslovakia as part of a campaign to promote Danish culture. Vodka-wrecked on the third day. Only the most elemental parts of their personalities left. Lisbeth and Adrian end up in a gay bar. The day after Lisbeth tells Korzeniowski about the night's excesses. She is criticized by the fat guy organizing the tour. He complains loudly about how she didn't help when they were packing the bus the evening before and tells her off for wandering away and making him worry.

"I'm responsible for you," he says self-importantly.

"Listen here sweetheart," Lisbeth says to him. "I was offered more cunt last night than you will *ever* get in your whole life."

They fly high on rock and alcohol and sex in the hotel rooms. Lisbeth's voice is a dream: heavy, wet silk pulled over smooth skin.

One night they have totally hopeless sex when they are pissed out of their heads, or to be more precise: they try to have sex, but they can't. Adrian pumps away, but simply can't get in. 'Shit,' they both shout and then mutter a few curses and pass out. They never fall asleep on the tour – they lose consciousness. The next morning Lisbeth comes out of the bathroom with a big smile on her face; in her hand she is holding a piece of string and on the end of it there is a completely flattened tampon. She is magnificent – but as soon as they arrive home the shadow settles over her again. Adrian begins to have his doubts. Is there anything behind the exterior? Is she just insecure? . . . empty?

Afterwards he meets her friends. Pusher Lars, yellow Tilly, Steso, Svend. He likes Svend. But although he moves in with Lisbeth and they are together for a long time, her friends continue to be slightly odd with him – especially Svend and Tilly.

It is a great band, though. Thunderous interpretations of obscure tracks, the drums like "Christian Death" at half tempo.

Gradually Adrian becomes good friends with Pusher Lars and Adrian tells him that he has serious difficulty getting through to Lisbeth. Pusher Lars answers evasively. A short time afterwards he seems to be carrying a burden whenever Adrian passes. He won't come out with what it is that is bothering him, he only sighs deeply.

"I want to show you some pictures," Pusher Lars says, pulling out a shoebox. There is a little pile of pictures on top which he takes, then pushes the shoebox away. He places each picture in front of Adrian and explains in a toneless voice who the people are. That is Steso, Svend, Tilly and . . . Lisbeth sitting beside Adrian. But it isn't Adrian. The similarity is absurd. The guy in the photo sparkles with brutality and energy.

"Little Lars," says Pusher Lars. "Lisbeth's boyfriend until he died in the car accident in which Lisbeth had her leg crushed."

Adrian is stunned. He goes home to Lisbeth and tells her that he loves her, that his name is Adrian and that Little Lars is dead. She says nothing. He sits in the kitchen and drinks a cup of coffee. Smokes cigarettes. Waits for a response. He can hear Lisbeth sniffling, moving around in the flat. Adrian turns round as she comes into the hallway. She puts two bags on the floor and looks at him with shiny eyes – the moisture is gathering into tears. "Sorry," she says with a throaty voice, swivels round and goes into the living room, closing the door to the hall.

The bags contain Adrian's things. He has to go now. I am silent as Adrian finishes speaking. He stands up as he lights another cigarette and opens the palm of his hand. "That was it," he says. "The love of my life down the drain."

6

It is my first soccer match for six years; I play right back. 5-2 to Hjørring. All the way through the second half my lungs are screaming – the only thing I can do is pull the emergency cord if I ever get near the man; the ball is completely out of my reach. And I am happy, I forget myself. It works.

Afterwards there are a few of us who go to a bar. We discuss the match over a beer. Then the others go – they have to go home to their partners.

"You have to get out and do some running," Adrian comments. I go up to the bar and fetch another two beers. I might as well ask him straight out, I think, as I take a seat.

"What's Frank doing at the moment?"

Adrian leans back in his chair, studying me carefully. "Isn't he your mate?" he asks.

"No."

"You haven't seen him?"

"Yes, I have."

"So you know what he's doing."

"I can hazard some guesses."

"What are the guesses?" Adrian asks.

"That he's dealing. Probably under some form of biker control."

"Good guesses – let me put it like that." Adrian nods in acknowledgement. "I'd keep away from that mob if I were you," he adds.

"Can you tell me any more?" I ask.

"No."

I hold his gaze; he doesn't elaborate. "This is important for me, Adrian. It's about someone I think a lot of."

"Someone involved with Frank and co?"

"Was – um . . . I don't know."

"Finish the relationship."

"Who with?" I ask with a desperate laugh.

"Just – you know, keep your distance."

"Hmm," I say. Somehow I had worked that one out.

"Keep me out of it," he says.

"Right," I say.

Adrian starts drumming on the table with his two forefingers. "Let's roll."

"I can walk home if it's out of your way."

"I've got to go your way anyway – I have to pick up the wonderful Ulla from my pusher."

We are sitting in the car, approaching my place.

"What – um – would it be bad style to go with you to your pusher?" I ask.

"Are you going to buy anything?"

"Yes, I could easily manage a little Sunday spliff."

"Of course. You're very welcome."

We drive for a while in silence.

"Is he . . . a biker-pusher?" I ask because I have the impression that the bikers are sitting tight on the hash scene in Aalborg, unlike when I used to live here – things were more fluid when Bullshit was disintegrating.

"No," Adrian says," but his older brother is a biker so he has a kind of . . . free pass, you could say." I sit wondering whether the big brother controls Asger, Frank – their activities, but it makes no difference. "He's an old-fashioned pusher, only hash – no hard drugs. A handful of Stesolid tabs if you insist."

We stop outside a grill bar and eat a couple of hamburgers for lunch before driving to Dannebrogsgade where we pull up outside a ground floor flat with an entrance onto the street – ex-shop premises.

"He lives in there," Adrian says, pointing. "Lars, his name is."

Practical from the point of view of neighbours' complaints, I think, as we get out of the car. A girl with an enormous bunch of flowers comes walking down the pavement – her eyes shining, silver blue.

Adrian says 'hi'. Maria. Standing in front of the door and knocking, I notice that she is pregnant – fifth month probably.

A tall bony guy opens the door. He looks like a scarecrow; there is almost no meat on him, and when he opens his mouth to invite us in I can see that his teeth are badly discoloured with greenish-black stains on them – signs of rotting.

"Are those for me?" Lars asks, surprised at the size of the bunch.

"No," Maria says, smiling. "They're for Ulla."

"She's just gone to hospital," he says.

"Has something happened?" Maria asks.

"No, no. She's visiting Steso. She'll be back soon."

"Mm. She's not usually that keen on Steso," Maria says.

"She's doing me a favour. Delivering a little Get-Well-Soon present."

Maria shakes her head. "Lars," she says reprovingly. He shrugs his shoulders.

"He's a customer. He's my friend."

Adrian introduces me and we go inside. It is obvious that some cleaning has just been done. Even the dining table is tidy. There is a big pusher's stash box, a little metal dish, a beautifully clean glass bong – ready with water at the bottom, a Trangia spirit stove and a huge ashtray. Serious stuff.

"Sit down," Lars says, going into the kitchen and returning with mugs of coffee. He eyeballs me. "Do you know him? Steso?"

"Perhaps. Isn't he a small, thin guy who took a load of tabs once?" I say.

"He still takes them," Adrian says.

"Yes, a little junkie asshole with demented eyes," Lars says.

"I've met him, "I say. "I was in hospital once after I went into a coma after taking laughing gas. He was there, too – Steso."

Lars pours the coffee. "I can remember hearing something about that. So it was you?"

"Yes," I say.

"What happened?" Adrian asks.

"Well, we broke into a dental clinic and I wanted to keep up with Steso, so I was sucking away like mad and then I went out like a light. Something about there being too much oxygen in the mixture – then it can be fatal."

Lars opens his stash box and takes out a very thin, square piece of foam rubber from a packet. He starts rolling up the foam rubber into a sausage, which he puts down a glass pipe in the bong. It is made with a kind of flask, the type you use in physics experiments.

"Was Steso out cold, too?" Adrian asks.

"No, he must have known that you have to make sure that the level of oxygen is kept high. But he didn't tell any one else."

"That's exactly his style," Lars says. He notices that I am sitting watching his handiwork. "It's a kind of filter – so I'm spared most of the impurities. A cleaner lung," he says. I remember the expression well.

"Isn't that what you use to wipe babies' bottoms?" Maria says, pointing to the packet of foam rubber strips.

"Right," Lars says.

"But is it fun – laughing gas?" Adrian asks.

"That's one of the reasons it's called laughing gas – and you have great hallucinations," I say.

"Coma," Lars says, looking pensive. "How long for?"

"Seventeen hours," I answer. "But why is he in hospital – Steso?"

"Coma. He went into a coma right here, in the bedroom." Lars points to a door.

"Just like that?"

"Yes, well, he came in – totally wasted. Adrian was here with Ulla, and we were sitting drinking wine and we'd also had a smoke." Lars has taken three Prince cigarettes, torn them in half and spread the tobacco over a piece of silver paper. He has lit the spirit stove; now he is toasting the tobacco.

"We were well gone," Adrian says. "It was black mixed with hash oil."

"Yeah, you really were," Lars says. "Then in creeps Steso, totally out of it and asks if he can lie down, for a rest. But we have to nip into town, so I go in to wake the man and there he is on the bed, his face a purplish blue. No breathing and there are large beads of sweat on his skin. None of us knows any first aid, so Adrianphones for an ambulance and I stand there hitting him hard on the chest. Well, for Christ's sake, I saw it in some film or other. I don't know if you have to give him artificial resuscitation first. But miracle of miracles – the man wakes up, breathes and is taken to hospital where he stays and is just as fucking irritating as he always is."

"But is he trying to kill himself – Steso?" I ask.

"Hm, I don't know. He doesn't have as much control over it as he used to have. Well, it's a hard life doing drugs."

"Yes, but he'll have a little rest now in hospital," Adrian says.

"I think he'll be very busy now in that hospital," Lars says, pouring the roasted tobacco into the little metal dish. He laughs, so I can see the greenish-black stains on his teeth. "In fact, this is a lifelong dream come true for him, legitimately being in a hospital full of medicine."

Lars takes scissors and a big lump of hash from the stash box and starts cutting small flakes off the lump into the tobacco in the dish. He mixes it and pours it back onto the silver paper where he briefly heats it over the spirit stove. Finally he pours it back into the metal dish. It is a huge mixture – there must be about three to four grams of hash in it and the smell suggests it is the finest quality.

"Where did you get the flowers from?" I ask Maria.

"From work. I'm a flower arranger. There were some left over from a conference I did the decorations for in Scheelsminde."

"Okay. Have you got your own shop?" I ask.

"No, no, I'm a wage slave," she says.

"Me . . . um I'm an engineer," I say in a rather odd way, I suppose, since she hasn't asked.

"I know," she says. "I've read about you in the paper."

"Maria's partner is Hossein. Iranian. Do you know him?" Lars asks.

"I think I know who he is. Tall guy?"

"Yes – and good-looking," Maria says with a smile.

"A year ago when I had some time off from sailing, my sister told me about a rumour that an Iranian had shot two Rottweilers," I say.

"Yes, that's a pretty stubborn rumour," Lars says.

"But is it true?" I ask, facing Maria.

"Perhaps," she says, smiling.

"How's it going with his apprenticeship?" Adrian asks.

"Oh, it's going well. He likes it. He is always going round saying: You want light? Hossein, he will make it," Maria says with a perfect imitation of a dago accent. She looks across at me and adds: "He's doing an adult apprenticeship course for electricians."

"Has he bought the Mercedes he keeps going on about?" Adrian asks.

"No, not yet, but he will," Maria says.

"What does he want with the car?" Lars asks. Maria shrugs her shoulders.

"It's something cultural – very important for him," she says nodding.

"Is he still pissed off that the Americans won't help the Kurds?" Lars asks.

"Yes, and how. But he has a plan for fixing all the extremists in the Muslim world," Maria says.

"Yes?" Lars says.

"He says that you can't kill the fundamentalist Imams because like that they become martyrs and go to Allah's heaven," Maria says. "You can't put them in prison either because then thousands of westerners will be kidnapped or blown up in the Middle East. But you can kidnap the worst of them, give them a sex change operation and send them back so they can have a taste of their own medicine."

"That's a good idea," says Lars.

"He's also considering an attack on *Kaa'ba sharif,*" Maria says.

"What's that?" Adrian asks.

"A sort of black building in Mecca which Muslims maintain is Allah's house. They have to visit it at least once in their lives – the pilgrimage," Maria explains.

"Does he want to bomb it?" I ask.

"He wants to use planes to spray estrogen over the whole area so that all the men lose their long beards and start sprouting tits," she says.

"That'll shake them," Lars says.

"Then they'll come to their senses," I say.

"Will women get bigger breasts then? Have you thought about that?" Adrian asks.

"Yes, " Maria says. "But believe me – Hossein doesn't mind."

"But . . . why is he so pissed off with the Americans?" I ask.

Maria starts talking again in her dago accent: "*West not tidy up properly in Iraq. And USA bend over for Zionist, and at same time they accept everything from Saudi fundamentalist because of oil and they in love with Attatürk – and that why they not care about Turkish abuse of Kurds. And so USA cannot understand why Middle East hate them. The politics don't make sense.*" She beams at us.

"Hossein should have been an international statesman," Lars says. He has taken the bong head out of the bong – that is the little pipe head made of porcelain. He holds it between his fingers with the funnel-shaped opening facing down and fills it from the dish. Then he picks up the bong head with some of the mix in and presses it into place with his thumb.

A large striped cat comes into the living room and lithely jumps onto the dining table where it lies down. The cat has scabs on its nose and its shoulders, and part of one ear is missing.

"What happened to it?" I ask.

"Been in a scrap," Lars says.

"Getting his end away," Adrian says.

"Yeah, he really fights for his lineage," Lars says, placing the bong head in the downpipe into the water and picking up the bong so the plastic tube is in front of his mouth.

"Pees in the gene pool," Adrian says.

"Does he often do that?" I ask.

Lars holds the lighter ready near the bong head and takes a couple of deep breaths before firing up. Of course it lights with the gas on full; a huge flame of almost ten centimetres. Then he sucks as hard as he can. I can see that the temperature increases explosively – the pipe mix glows white – and then the ash disappears down the little hole at the bottom of the bong head and lands in the water.

The cat has begun to purr with a deep growl. Lars puts his hand out and strokes it. He holds the smoke in for a while before speaking – slightly nasally as the smoke billows out of mouth.

"Yes. In fact, he disappears for days at a time and returns home torn to pieces. He stands outside the door and when I let him in he goes and lies down by the radiator until he has healed. He only moves to eat . . . yes, and to have a smoke, like now.

"He smokes?" I say.

"Yes."

"Is he addicted?"

"No, he's just like me. He has what I would call acceptable consumption. He uses it as a recreational stimulant."

"Mr. Leary goes in for the curative power of hemp," Adrian says.

"Mr. . . . what?" I say.

"Leary, after Timothy Leary," Lars says.

"The name rings a bell, but . . . ."

"Okay, well, it doesn't matter. Leary – the number one LSD guru in the world. But Mr. Leary over there," nodding towards the cat, "is mostly addicted to the ladies. That's how it is." Lars passes the bong over to me. "Help yourself," he says.

"No thanks," I say. "I don't play in this league but if I could roll myself a little joint from the mix? I would pay, of course."

"Please do," he says, passing me the dish with the mix in and a packet of Rizla papers – the large format. "It's on the house," he says. I sit fumbling with the papers. Adrian is preparing a bong head for himself while Maria watches my efforts with strong disapproval.

"Why don't you let me do it?" she asks, taking the things out of my hands. "I'm an old pusherfrau. She pronounces the last word in German: "*pusherfrau*." She rolls a joint in no time at all with a cardboard filter and everything.

Adrian sucks at his bong head while Lars strokes Mr. Leary.

"Thanks," I say when Maria passes me the joint. "Don't you want to light it?"

"Sorry," she says.

I gesture with my hand to my stomach: "Right, because of . . . ?"

"That's not why – I just don't need it any longer."

"Have you stopped for ever?" Adrian asks as I light the joint.

"No, I still smoke once in a while for pleasure, but only on special occasions," Maria says.

"Yes, I should cut down, too," Lars says.

"Do you think it's too much?" Adrian asks.

"Yes, absolutely. And your lungs have difficulty coping."

"How much do you smoke?" I ask, blowing the smoke out – it is really good hash.

"Eight grams a day over the last few years. Well, I have tried ingesting it, but is simply too slow."

"Ugh," I say – not because of his eight grams, but because the joint is going to my head.

Lars laughs at me. "Yes, – that's the odd thing about grass: the more you smoke, the more you can take and the less you smoke the less you need to have an effect."

"I don't know . . . ," I say doubtfully. "Could I buy a couple of grams?"

"Yes, of course," Lars says. "But, umm, where do you usually buy?"

"I've been at sea. I only recently . . . ."

Lars breaks in. "Yes, I know that."

"Okay, but in the old days I used to hang out with Frank . . . ?"

"Yes," Lars says, apparently well aware who he is.

"We were at school together and did our apprenticeships at the shipyards. But . . . we aren't . . . how shall I put it? He and I don't get on . . . ."

"That's fine. You don't need to explain," Lars says.

I buy two grams off him. "And I'd like to give you a little thing," he says, digging out a tobacco tin from his stash box. "Have you ever tried mushrooms?"

"No," I say.

"Okay. I'll roll you a hash joint mixed with oil. But take care when you smoke it – for the uninitiated it's like being on mushrooms."

"Oil?" I say.

"Comes from cannabis oil, the oils in the hemp plant," Adrian says. When the tops of the shoots have been harvested, you dry the rest of the leaves – even if they are too weak to smoke – and extract oil from them."

"Extract?" I say.

"You crumble the leaves and pour Isopropanol or ether over them so the ethereal oils are drawn out into the alcohol, then you sieve off the greenery and let the alcohol evaporate. What's left is hash oil, which you can mix with tobacco" Lars explains. He checks to see if I have understood.

"Yes, of course," I say – flying high now. Sitting there with an overwhelming desire to ask them if they know Maja – if they know anything about Frank, Asger, Nina, Lene, Susan, Leif, the dead scaffolder; the whole business. I don't want to offend Adrian, though. He has only just introduced me and it takes time until you have some standing with a pusher, even with one as likeable as Lars. I don't want to abuse his hospitality. Money changes hands – I receive my purchases.

"I'd like to thank you for – the coffee, smoke, good treatment," I say, shaking Lars's hand.

"You're always welcome," he says.

"Thank you very much." Adrian offers to drive me home, but I refuse – I want to walk. I say goodbye to Maria, wish her all the best with her pregnancy, stroll homewards; the world is oddly diffuse.

Once at home I start washing up. Perhaps I should drive over to Nørresundby and view some houses – that is what I have been thinking. I have got plenty of money. I don't even need to work for a while – I only do it to keep myself busy . . . to be near people. I could buy a house that needs a bit of loving care and do it up. A redbrick house with a steep pitch roof, which is structurally alright: a solid base, good masonry, good floors, preferably a good roof – at least the rafters, new tiles are not a big problem. I take out the old, leaking windows and put in new ones with bars, knock the plaster off the indoor walls, scrub them down with water and whitewash them. Plane the floors. Then install a new kitchen. The basic structure is in position and I construct it so that there are deep drawers by the floor instead of a plinth to use the space better. There is dust everywhere and my clothes are filthy – I am filthy and I am sweating as I cut the hole for the sink in the worktop with a jig-saw and then she comes in the door. I stop the jig-saw and hug her. "Phew, I'm tired," she says, wiping her brow with the back of her hand. She stands with a slight curve to her back and her stomach sticking out. A couple of strands of hair are stuck to her cheek and I gently curl them behind her ear, dusty as my fingers are. There is an old dining chair where I sit with my sandwiches. "Come here," I say, leading her to it. I sit down and draw her to me so she can sit on one thigh and I let the palm of my hand run over her taut stomach as I support the small of her back with my other hand and tell her how beautiful she is. The tea towel glides across the rounded far side of the large dish; I look down at it, I am in my kitchen. The dish is blue.

I don't wake until the evening from a dreamless sleep. I am lying on my bed fully clothed, and I know that I must live for a long time yet and that I am dying inside.

Heat the remains of a meat sauce, boil pasta and eat before going to the marina. The boat is empty. Carl has gone home early – or hasn't he been here at all?

I sit on the bow and dangle my feet in the water. Feel . . . defeated. What if she could see me now? If she was following my actions. I pull myself together – try to . . . appear strong. Or what if she could see I was depressed? Would she take pity?

What are you doing? She isn't here. She can't see you. You are all on your fucking own. The hash oil joint is burning a hole in my pocket. What the fuck. Light up. Take off into the sky – the laws of physics are suspended. I am submerged and the light spreads across the waves as if I were flying over the flames, taking in water – cool against the blood vessels of my lungs. The smell. Red. Hot. Moist. The dry cotton cloth. What was I thinking about? Glance to the side. Chris smiles wryly. He isn't there, but he is there anyway and I chat with him. I tell him that he isn't there.

"What are you talking about, man?" he says, taking the joint from me and inhaling deeply; "My oh my oh my," he says.

"Where are you at the moment?" I ask.

He makes a vague movement with his hand.

"What are you doing?" I ask.

"Hanging out."

"You're not here" I say.

He passes me the joint and says: "Allan, you're also what you don't possess."

"What?" I say.

"What's behind you; what you've lost – that's you, too," he says.

"Chris – you're dead."

"So what?" he asks. "It doesn't make me less meaningful."

I don't know what to say to him. "How is your father actually?" I ask.

"The guy who throws coins in the urinal so that little boys will put their fingers in his urine." Chris shrugs his shoulders and starts laughing. "You think it hurts inside you," he says.

"It *does* hurt."

"Just think that you also have to live with the things you don't do."

"I don't think I understand what you're talking about, Chris. Well, you aren't here."

"No, but you are." I turn my head to catch a glimpse of him, but he has gone. Only the lapping of the waves is there – the foaming sea. I push myself away from the railing, from the water, try to stand up. Everything becomes dark – my sight gone. Sweat breaks out all over my body. I carefully sink down onto one knee so I can feel the deck with the palms of my hands. The grain in the wooden boards tells me which direction I have to go. The bow is behind me – that much I know; I am almost sure of that. The hull is beneath me, resting in the water. I am on the deck. The boat is moored to the landing stage. The landing stage leads to land. I have to keep a mental grip on all the elements – or else they are null and void. I crawl down the deck on all fours. The railing is already disintegrating. I hope I can keep the rest of the world together long enough. Things dissolve and vanish. I pull at the mooring ropes with unfeeling hands until I feel a bump as the stern hits the landing stage. Dark, hazy structures begin to dance in front of my eyes. They vanish again if I try to stand up. Slowly I manoeuvre myself backwards over the stern until my foot touches the landing stage. Then both feet. Let myself down gently – my back towards the landing stage, the planks. Hear the water coming up through the cracks. The stars appear above me. Infinitely slowly I raise myself, staring intensely at the land, retaining a little of my sight. Move uncertainly along the landing stage. Reach terra firma; my clothes soaked with sweat.

At night I sleep badly. Monday is one protracted hell. When I come home, the flat feels like a small room, a cell – nowhere to go. I can't bear to see the sea charts in the living room so I drag the TV into the bedroom. Eat rye bread sandwiches, try to drink an export beer, but I don't like the taste; watch appalling shows on TV, turn it off; try reading, but my concentration fails me. I have a headache. Go to the bathroom and brush my teeth, brush my tongue until it feels raw. Back in the bedroom. A muffled click; for a second it is pitch black, then the light suddenly floods back – inspect the light bulb hanging from the ceiling – is it about to explode? It happens again – I haul myself up on the tips of my toes and give it a tap, make it swing spastically on the end of the cable. Nothing. The bulb still works. It happens again. Darkness. Light. I stare at the lamp. Blink. Again. The world is blacked out every time I blink. Hits me in the pit of the stomach. I am afraid to die. Numb with fear, I stand rooted to my footprints. My face feels like an open sore covered with icy water. Lie down. Stare up at the ceiling, feel a void inside, restless. Very tired, but nowhere near sleeping. Sometimes it can help to satisfy yourself to fall asleep. Show me a man who doesn't masturbate and I will show you a lying shmuck. Lying and thinking that there are four kinds of sex. Hand job, bought sex, sex with someone you don't love and sex with someone you do. Then there are, of course, the hybrid forms. Someone you love and buy sex from – not so rare. I laugh, but it sounds like a convulsion. I can't think about her – it is wrong – and I don't feel like thinking about anyone else while I do it. My porn magazines are at the bottom of the sea in Chris's cabin. That is not amusing. My brain is like a pot of spaghetti, the same as if I had taken too much speed – my thoughts are entangled and there is an unending number of loose ends. In the end I realize that I am close to tears, but then, luckily, I fall asleep.

Why I thrust open my eyes I don't immediately know, but I can hear that the rhythm of the engine has changed. I am already out of my bunk and pulling on my boiler suit when I am hurled against the wall and I hear the bang. Collision. A moment later the general alarm. I can feel that the way she is lying in the water is slightly different and as I shove my feet into my protective shoes I draw the curtain in front of the porthole – it is not dark as it should be. I can see a diffuse, flickering light – flames casting light through the mist. The fire must be on the opposite side of the ship. I fling myself onto my bed, tear the drawer out and pull at the folded sea chart; and then I sprint out of the door with my life jacket in one hand while stuffing the sea chart down against my stomach with the other. I see the chief engineer is out of his cabin and the engine guy is on his way down the corridor towards the ladder.

"Hurry, Allan," he shouts over his shoulder.

"What's up?" I shout back even though the answer is obvious – I can already smell the smoke; thick ochre-red crude oil is alight.

"We're going to jump overboard. She could explode at any moment." I think it is the chief engineer shouting as I step onto the deck – with my life jacket already on; my hands do it automatically. Almost the whole crew is on deck on the port side in front of the living quarters – faces lit up and pale – and I turn towards the sharp yellow light on the starboard side where the flames are now ten metres

above the railing and have seized hold of the living quarters, from where they will spread to the engine room. Black smoke is billowing skywards. It is not difficult to work out that there must be a hole in the hull on the starboard side and that the oil is escaping and burning on the sea. Lifeboats. The flames suddenly double in height. No time to put boats in the water. The fire makes almost no sound – liquid fire. The captain has appeared on deck.

"JUMP NOW," he yells. Three of the crew wearing life-jackets clamber up onto the railing.

"NO," I shout as I run over to them. Something isn't right, but they have already jumped and then I feel it: the movement – the ship is turning on itself so the clear water on the port side will soon be replaced by thick, burning oil. The men will be swallowed up if they can't put enough distance between them and the ship in time.

"We'll have to go the bow, otherwise . . . ." I shout, but no-one takes any notice of me; I see panic-stricken eyes, the heat is unbearable.

The ship's movement on its own axis accelerates. Several jump from the port side. The rest . . . I haven't seen Chris. Now she is shifting faster. The burning oil is gaining on the men in the water. I stand in the middle of the deck, paralyzed. I see the orange lifebelts in the water being swallowed up by the inferno; the heat is now so great that I can smell my hair being singed. The sea is almost completely calm. The mist is burnt off by the heat. Two more orange dots are caught up by the flames which are spreading slowly, hypnotically, across the sea, completely surrounding the ship now. I run up the deck and cross to the starboard side of the bow; perhaps there is still some clear water unless she has already completed the circle. As I run, I tear off my life jacket.

"TAKE OFF YOUR LIFE JACKET," I scream at the captain as I throw mine away. I remember thinking he is not in full possession of his senses – his eyes are like glass. My brain tells me that he is dead – that I am going to die. The column of fire grows. I reach the bow. The flames are racing across the sea – there is nowhere to jump. Kick my shoes off, clamber up the railing, see the fire darting across the water, bend my knees and push off to jump clear of the drifting hull. The fire reaches out towards me for a brief moment before I close my eyes to the flames and I feel an unbelievable heat, like when you put your hand over a lit gas ring, only it is all-enveloping and much briefer; it is replaced by the freezing cold water and my heart freezes in my chest as I open my eyes and I am sucked down into a darkness; the cold is intense. Straighten the downward movement of my body from my dive, swim under the water. Already sense that I am rising too quickly from the cold. I make out

light above me, stronger light behind me as I continue swimming, order myself to stretch with every stroke, to complete it quickly and to follow one completed stroke with the onset of the next with no interval.

The light above me grows in power and I can see it extend a long way ahead. I try to swim even faster, but the wet boiler suit is weighing me down and my body has become stiff. I remember thinking in a cold, detached way that I have lost my way, that I am swimming in the wrong direction and that now I am going to die. Everything I have read about drowning surges through my mind: that it is a physical reflex action to hold your breath under water. And that it is a physical reflex action to take a breath when the body is short of oxygen and that you can control this reflex action – be without oxygen for much longer than you think. But there are limits to this control. After a few minutes you inhale water into the lungs and the heart stops. The brain works for a brief moment longer. It can think. Pictures from a documentary about crab fisherman in the Barents Sea flash through my brain. When they are caught by the line and are dragged down to the bottom of the sea with the crab cage. What do they think? At that moment the cramps set in and I open my mouth and let all the air out. In slow motion I observe the bubbles drifting away from me and then they race to the surface of the illuminated water – towards the fire. I see a dark blotch on the surface of the water a little further ahead. Something inside me springs into action; I take a stroke. My body does it, through the cramps. Saw blades cut into my legs; part of my brain soberly confirms it, from the sideline as it were, after which it stares in wonderment as the body takes another stroke – upwards – but my body is depleted of oxygen. I slowly float up in a small dark tongue of water set in the burning sea of oil. The lungs suck in air. I cough. The stench, the heat.

The sea is moving, the oil racing closer, the flames devouring the oxygen around me. I want to take another deep gulp of air before diving down, but only feel the stinking heat in my throat – oxy-acetylene torches on my cold skin. Fight my way under the surface where my body automatically performs swimming strokes. I want it. Intestines feel vacuum-packed, muscles wooden. I reach the fringe of the light, press the water down under me to rise, my lips firmly pressed together to counter the urge to open them. The water above me is still there . . . still there. And then I am on the surface again – guzzle the air above the dark water. The air is wonderful. My lungs are enormous – I adore the air. The weakest flames are maybe two metres away. I gasp for a second. Behind me the intensity of light increases and illuminates the sea in front of me. I turn round, treading water. The ship. A burning figure appears and topples over the railing – falls into the sea of flames. The ship is then surrounded by a ball of fire that stretches far up into the air. Not far from the sea of flames is a cargo ship with a crumpled bow. The fire has caused the mist to disperse over a radius of several hundred metres from the tanker. No lifeboats. My eyes are working, I think. That is good. My face feels like an open sore. Legs and arms are numb where they are attached to the torso. "The body has natural buoyancy." I repeat the sentence to myself. Close my eyes to the light, which is blinding me. Sink down in a velvet bed. You can lie like this for hours, I tell myself, but I know very well that the water is too cold. The sound of rotor blades pulsates faintly through the air. Establish that I have at most three minutes left to live, until my body temperature falls below the minimum.

Vomit is pushing up into my throat when I awake. The sheet is crumpled and wet beneath me. I stagger to the toilet with my hands in front of my mouth; try to hold back the vomit. Some spills out between my fingers and splashes on the hall floor before I can get to the toilet bowl, kneel in front of it and empty my stomach. My head throbs. I wipe the pools of sick on the floor with a cloth, which I throw in the waste bin. Take a mouthful of water, put toothpaste on the brush and go into the shower. Dizzy. What happened there? After a couple of badly buttered slices of white bread and half a litre of skimmed milk I am well enough to drink a cup of coffee and smoke a cigarette. I am better. I have to go to work.

It comes as no surprise: when I step out of the house I see my car has four flat tires. The side mirrors, the windscreen wipers and the radio aerial have been snapped off, the windscreen is smashed and the paintwork has been scratched; to be honest, it all seems somewhat superfluous. I hop on a bus going to Nytorv and walk the rest of the way to work. Wonder whether that is supposed to have any impact on me. I doubt it. Quarter of an hour late for work. I don't have access to a workshop, so Iphone a car mechanic who I know has a good reputation and tell him what the problem is. We agree that he will pop round to my flat when I have finished work – he needs the car key.

"Anything else I should have a look at while I'm at it?" he asks after we have changed the rear tires and put the front wheels on the lifting unit he has at the back of his four-wheel drive. He hangs around – runs his hand across the scratched paintwork on the hood.

"Can you do re-spray jobs?" I ask. He grins and jumps into the front of his car to bring out a book of colour samples.

"Beige, gloss," I say.

"And the chrome?"

"Yes, why not," I answer, resigned; the chrome parts are pitted from flying stones and the car has to look good anyway if I want to sell it. I have no interest in being the owner any longer if she won't come in it with me.

On Wednesday nothing happens. I take stock: what does my future have in store for me? Work, check the answer phone, soccer training on Tuesdays and Thursdays, a growing friendship with Adrian, occasionally getting drunk with Mette and Peter on Fridays, going sailing with Carl on Saturdays and a match on Sundays. Sometimes I go for a run in the evening, do arm presses and abdominal curls. In the paper I read ads for jobs, houses, lonely hearts, the deaths column, marriages and invitations to receptions. I almost do it as a habit; it is not because I am looking for something, it just seems a lot more real than the articles themselves.

On Friday I get my beating. They attack early in the morning. As the first guy comes towards me I remember thinking that it is extremely odd that I am going to be clobbered now.

He throws a punch, I parry. The other one comes up behind me, grabs me round the neck. I manage to elbow him in the stomach before the first guy punches me in the same place. The one behind me has released his grip, but the one in front catches me on the mouth as I swing my fist at him and miss. I turn to regain my bearings and I am punched by both of them and half fall over in front of a car parked by the pavement. I catch a glimpse of one of them; he is familiar – perhaps he is the bouncer in Jomfru Ane Gade? I can vaguely hear a man's voice shouting from a house, saying he is phoning for the police as the blows rain down on me. My only thought is that I don't want to fall – I don't want to be kicked. Then they stop. Through swollen eyelids I can see them briskly walking down the pavement and disappearing round a corner. A dark drop quivers on my eyelash. I wipe it away, my face is sore to the touch. When I lower my hand, my fingers are covered in blood – my eyebrows are split open. I spit – it's red. My lips are intensely painful. Gingerly, I put my fingers in my mouth; the right front tooth is missing – I think I swallowed it.

"For Christ's sake, Allan. Just look at yourself." Peter is standing beside the dentist's chair and gesticulating. The X-ray showed that the root of the front tooth had gone, too. So there is nothing he can use to fasten on to, but then again there is nothing to drill out, either. He has to make an implant. I have to have a titanium screw in my jaw and it will be there for three months before I can have a gold crown put in – something about the screw growing into the tissue. Apart from that, the teeth to the right of the front tooth are chipped – the canine and one on the side – but the nerve cells have not been exposed so I am spared root canal treatment. Just need some gold putting on.

I have rarely seen Peter so agitated.

"What?" I ask.

"Burns on your face, split lip and eyebrow, covered in tattoos," he points to me as he speaks. "And then you want a *gold tooth*. People will think you're a thug." He pulls on his rubber gloves and thwacks them against his wrists.

"Now you'll have to develop a sense of . . . ," I search for the right word, ". . . aesthetics – won't you. There should be . . . some kind of unity in my appearance." He sighs loudly.

"The only people who have gold teeth nowadays are people from the Middle East," he says.

"You said yourself that gold is the best because it wears at the same rate as your teeth," I say. Peter shrugs his shoulders and starts stuffing things in my mouth. It is bloody painful. The glove-clad fingers taste like condoms smell. In reality I have somewhere between three and five rubber-coated penises in my mouth. Horror and anger mix inside me – I have to restrain myself from taking a good bite.

"What about some laughing gas?" I ask with a half strangulated voice.

"Oh no," he says with a deep sigh. "You've been opening bottles of beer with your teeth. You've got two cracked fillings." I shrug my shoulders.

Gold is attractive, but that is not the reason. I want to be reminded of the beating when I see myself in the mirror – to remind myself that I chose to have it. That seems important to me.

"HNNNGGG," I exclaim involuntarily.

"Sorry," Peter says with a concerned glance at my mouth. He takes a paper serviette and wipes round my chin. It changes colour – my lips are bleeding again.

7

My lips heal well enough, so long as I don't smile too broadly – and there is no reason to do that. Home from work: the answering machine is blinking furiously; in other words, there are several messages. I hold my breath and tell myself that they could be from anyone. The first one starts with a deep growl. I breathe out – it is Carl: "*Hmmm . . . er, it's me . . . Carl . . . Bloody hell, I HATE these machines . . . .*" There is a long pause and then he says: "*Sailing . . . we have to go sailing, Allan. Well, okay, bye then.*" The man has an old black phone with a dial. He refuses to change it.

Nobody says anything on the next message. The phone is put down immediately. All I can hear is some slight noise in the background – an electric machine with an extremely high gear ratio.

The third message, same noise in the background: "*Hi Allan, Maja here. I'll try and phone again later . . . tomorrow. I'd . . . I'd like to see you . . . Bye.*" Such a cheery way she says: "*Bye.*" I rewind the tape. "*. . . well, okay, bye then,*" says Carl's voice, then a series of beeps, the silent message and then: "*Hi Allan . . . .*"

"YEEEEES," I shout out loud. I beam. My lips start bleeding again. It is wonderful. Go into the kitchen, put some water on for coffee, take a shower, put on clean clothes, have a shave. I know it is stupid, but I stand there in reverence and rewind the tape several times to hear her voice again while drinking coffee and carefully smoking a cigarette between split lips. It is a sewing machine I can hear in the background. Her voice is beautiful.

The next day Iphone from work. Bingo: the third furniture upholsterer I talk to says he can renovate the rustic painting on the soot-damaged chest of drawers I pretend to own. The firm's address is in Nørresundby.

To be allowed time off I have to confess to the boss that this is a matter of "love and eros." Then he goes trumpeting all round the workshop that 'our punch ball' has got a date while I go to the changing room, take a shower, clean my nails and have a fresh shave. I cover my blue, black and yellow bruises with clothes. Am I being over-hasty? "Am I hell," I say aloud. I have been open about my intentions. They are bloody genuine enough.

I find a place to park and I am on the point of lighting another cigarette, to smoke it before I make my entrance, but then I tell myself a couple of home truths and wriggle the unsmoked cigarette back into the packet. In the shop window I see a newly upholstered sofa and two dining chairs. A little bell tinkles as I open the door to the shop which is devoid of people but full of beautifully upholstered and freshly painted rustic furniture, very clean – the furniture Danish customers want is apparently not fake antiques. Behind the counter there is a door leading to a back room and out of it steps Maja, breathing out, and I can see thin wisps of smoke on her breath.

"Can't even have a smoke in peace," I say and before I have even finished the sentence I curse myself for being so fucking cheerful, so I add a "Hi" and nod, mostly because I can't smile properly on account of my lips.

"Oh no," she says, both surprised and frightened. I begin feeling uneasy.

"What happened?" she asks. Okay, it is just my face.

"My past caught up with me," I say. She comes out from behind the counter and over to me, staring at the gap in the top row of my teeth, examining my face, gently touching the skin – it is hugely pleasurable.

"Who did it?"

"I didn't know them."

"But why?"

"Rent-a-mob."

"But *why?*"

"I turned down a job offer."

"What do you *mean*?" Maja has steeled herself for the answer – I will have to be honest.

"Frank," I say. "Frank wanted me to do something for him. In fact, I don't know exactly what it was, but I turned it down. Maybe there was something else involved, too . . . It's very hard for me to work out, but at any rate this . . . ," I motion with my hand towards my face, "was kind of the result – a settling of accounts."

"Can I . . . ," Maja starts. At that moment I notice a middle-aged man come out of the back room. He stops.

"Um, sorry," he says, turning round and going back.

"Just a moment," Maja says to me and goes out. I can hear the sound of muffled voices, then she returns with her jacket.

"Let's go," she says.

"What were you about to say?" I ask when we are outside.

"It doesn't matter," she says and seems to shake herself. "We'll go back to my place." I wait for her to take my arm, but she doesn't. We smoke and walk. She asks me about my face, I tell her about the gold tooth I am going to have put in. It is clear that we are going to talk about generalities until we arrive.

"Do you want something to drink?" she asks when we are in her room. "I've only got squash . . . ."

"Yes, that's fine." I sit down on one of the two dining chairs – it is just like my place, the furnishing is a disgrace. She returns with a jug and two glasses.

"I just have to . . . ," she says, pointing to the toilet door.

"Of course." While she is in there, I fill our glasses – it is a blended fruit squash. There is something in my glass. I lean forwards to have a closer look – a little white flower of mould is floating round on the surface of the squash. I check her glass and the jug. There aren't any more. When I hear the toilet flushing, I quickly take a used match from the ashtray, put the unburnt end under the mould and lift it up so that it clings to the match, which I put back in the ashtray. If you look closely you can see there is a foreign body on the match, but I don't think she will notice.

Maja comes back and sits on the bed with her legs tucked under her. She takes a deep breath.

"Allan," she says. "You have to be honest with me. I have to know what happened . . . ." She lets it hang in the air for a while, then adds: "With Frank and so on . . . ."

I tell her about it – after all, there is nothing reprehensible about our common pasts: eighteen years old, too much speed, a bit of selling, too much booze, a couple of burglaries, one sentence – general stupidity; final piece of work for the apprenticeship that only just scrapes through. School of marine engineering, sharing a house with Janne, world's most boring life;

back on speed. Carl, who pulled strings so that initially I could get a job on a coaster. When it was over with Janne, I switched to oil tankers. In all, three years at sea plus an accident.

"That's the long and short of it," I say.

"And what now?"

"Mm, I don't really know what's going to happen, but . . . ." She interrupts me.

"With Frank and all that?"

I laugh and have to put my hand to my lips because of the pain.

"Well . . . I don't have anything to do with Frank. I assume that now he feels," I point to my face, "that he has humiliated me. And because I haven't taken my revenge on him I have lost his respect, but I will be left in peace. I imagine that's how his mind works and that suits me fine."

"Hmm," she says, nodding. I would like to move on – away from this topic: the past.

"Carl – my grandfather – he says that I should take you out sailing."

"Your grandfather?"

"Yes, Carl – ex-first officer on the world's oceans."

"Sailing?"

"He has a sailing boat – an old wooden yacht."

"Yes, but what does he know about me?"

"I told him . . . I happened to tell him that there was a girl I was, you know . . . interested in. And he said that all girls fall for the sea and spray and the wind in their hair and . . . I think it's worth a try." Maja gives me an old-fashioned look.

"I don't know if I can trust you," she says – bluntly.

"I . . . ," begin but I am lost for words. I point to her and then to myself and then I make a questioning gesture in the air with my hand. I really don't know what the hell to say. She seems to be on the verge of giggling, but checks herself.

"Allan, there's something I have to do now," she says, getting up. Okay, I know this move. A simple demonstration of power – you always have to be put through this one.

"Okay," I say, getting up and walking to the door.

"What now then?" I ask anyway, but you can hear from my voice that I haven't fallen for her bluff.

"You'll have to wait a bit," she answers and now she is smiling, like the time I met her outside the cinema. She is teasing me. Playing with me. I have to stay cool.

"I hope we'll see each other again," I say with a grin. She is laughing now. She can't help herself. Her laughter is wonderful.

"Bye," she says, and I close the door behind me.

The days are abnormally long, but pleasant, except for one unpleasant afternoon in Peter's clinic when he performs an extensive piece of construction work in my mouth.

Something good will happen, I know – I just don't know when. On Friday I am on tenterhooks, but nothing happens. I resort to self-abuse. On Saturday I get up early and run until my lungs hurt. I have to meet Carl at eleven at the latest. We are going to have lunch on the fjord. I buy rolls and a paper at the bakery on the corner. I turn on TV1, the test picture is being shown with radio 3 in the background and I listen to the weather forecast. After doing some stretching exercises I have a shower and I am sitting eating my rolls when there is a ring on the entry phone.

"Hi," she says. I mumble something or other until I notice that I am rambling.

"Come in," I say finally and press the button. I hurriedly scan the kitchen and living room to see if there is any mess. There is nothing. I storm into the bedroom, manage to grab hold of the duvet to make the bed, but I can already hear her steps on the stairs. Oh, fuck it. I open the front door and there she is. Her face, body, clothes – she is so damn good-looking.

"Hi," I say.

"Hi."

"Come on in." I hold the door for her. She walks by, stands in the hallway and lets her army knapsack slide to the floor while glancing into the rooms.

"Would you like a cup of tea?" I ask.

"Yes, please," she says.

"Yes, it is a bit Spartan." The situation is a little awkward. Maja walks into the living room, unconcerned. I go to the kitchen and put some more water on, wondering what she will think of it: a dining table, two chairs, a TV on the floor and a row of books leaning against it.

"Nice maps," she says as she passes my field of vision on her way from the living room to the bedroom.

"Thanks," I say over my shoulder. The bedroom: a box mattress on the floor, a wooden box beside the bed with clock radio and novel on, a fitted wardrobe, the naked bulb in the ceiling. I suppose I could have made more of it, I think, while pouring boiling water on the tea bag.

"What do all the lines and dates on the map mean?" she asks from the hall, on her way into the living room again.

"That's the trips I've been on with my grandfather and six months as apprentice engineer on a coaster. And the big one over the TV is where I have been in the last two and half years as second engineer."

She is back in the living room and casts her eye over the charts before returning to the kitchen and leaning against the door frame. "You've been around."

"Yep."

"But you haven't exactly accumulated a lot of possessions." There is a question in this statement of fact, in her eyes.

"I lived together with a girl for a couple of years, before I went to sea," I say, later realising that this was not really an explanation. "You see, I chucked out all my own furniture when I moved in with her and then I left her and the furniture we bought together when I started as second engineer." She just nods slowly. She is wearing shorts; her skin is so smooth that it seems unreal. Her body is . . . captivating. "So a little while ago I started from scratch again."

"Why did you leave the girl?"

"She wanted us to buy a house," I answer before giving myself time to think, develop some kind of strategy.

"Nothing wrong with that, is there?"

"No, it was just . . . I dunno."

"What do you mean?"

". . . too much."

"How do you mean, too much?" Maja asks.

"You know . . . she'd started buying me clothes that I refused to wear, and she couldn't stand my friends."

"But they were speed freaks, too, weren't they," Maja says, and there is no question in that statement of fact.

"Yes," I say, "but that's where we were coming from . . . . It's true enough that they were a bunch of assholes, but from there to not saying 'hello' to them, that's a big jump." After saying that I realize that I have ended up in exactly that same situation now – I wouldn't say 'hello' to them, either.

"And so you packed your bags and went to sea?" She is not happy with the explanation.

"I've missed you so much that . . . ." I say, turning to face her. She lowers her gaze, looks up again and gazes into my eyes. My arms are hanging down by my side.

"I wanted to see you, too," she says, still keeping her arms hanging in front of her, her hands intertwined.

"I'm sorry I lied. I hope you can . . . ," I say, but I am interrupted by Maja who holds my gaze and says:

"So you just hopped it?"

"Well, there's just and just . . . ," I say, breathing in. "She took our bankbook and went off to OBS! while I was at sea – working, that is – and bought a living room suite with our combined savings, for over twenty thousand kroner. You know: L-shaped sofa, marble-topped coffee table, two armchairs, shelving and a TV unit."

"Without you knowing?" Maja can't keep the astonishment out of her voice.

"Yes. We'd talked about it and I'd said no – I didn't want to spend so much money on that."

"What did you want to do . . . with the money?"

"I didn't have a clue – but I definitely didn't want to sit on it." Finally she laughs, her moist tongue peeping out between glistening teeth. I laugh with her – it is funny now, but it wasn't at the time. There I was, home after two months on a coaster, and then I see all that shit in the living room – Janne has had it all set up. She has bought steaks and red wine – everything ready for a celebration. She has an attractive dress on, and I am in no doubt about what she is wearing underneath: something tarty. At first she started crying and then she became hysterical and called me "a bloody stupid speed freak," which I was not at that time, and said how angry she was with herself that she had wasted her youth on someone like me and that I was a . . . .

"What did you do?" Maja asks as I pass her a mug of tea. I don't answer – I light a cigarette for each of us instead. Why is it that many important conversations take place in kitchens? I put one of the cigarettes between her lips, just far enough in, and I can see from her reaction that she likes that.

"I stood there thinking . . . It all fell into place while I was standing there: we had nothing in common any more. We wanted two completely . . . *completely* different things." Maja doesn't say anything. "I realized that I didn't like her any more and it was a long time since we had . . . loved each other."

"How long had you known her?"

"We were childhood sweethearts."

"And so you buggered off just like that?"

I think: No. I hit her – the first and only time in my life I have laid a finger on a girl . . . apart from my mother, but she was no girl when I hit her. And then Janne, right there in the living room, surrounded by the furniture. Once – with the flat of my hand. Not because it was the right thing to do – it was the only thing to do.

"I yelled a bit at first, and so did she," I answer.

"And then it was over?"

"Yeah, well, we must have yelled at each other for about three weeks."

"And the furniture?"

"Stayed where it was."

"You didn't take it back?" Maja asks. I laugh at the question.

"I said it should go back, that it was me or the furniture. She had the receipt, but nothing happened. She chose the furniture."

"You let her keep the furniture?"

"Yes."

"Furniture costing over twenty thousand kroner?"

"Yes."

"You thought you'd got off lightly?" Maja asks, and I don't know if I can explain it to someone younger than myself, let alone a girl.

"No, that wasn't why I let her keep it. I'm not proud to admit this, but I hoped she would choke on the furniture. That she would have to look at it every day and she would eventually realize how wrong she'd been."

"Do you think that happened?" Maja asks.

"I don't think so," I smile.

"Why not . . . have you talked to her?"

"No, but my sister told me that she'd married a salesman and they've had a child, and I wouldn't mind betting she has changed the furniture and her friends at least once since I last saw her." That is how I answer and I omit to tell her that I have just received a cheque through the post for 11,300 kroner. Not because I can imagine that Janne has ever felt any distaste for the furniture – she would have thought she deserved it as compensation for staying with me throughout my escapades. But I am afraid that Maja might misunderstand, as if Janne was trying to make up for what happened or . . .

"And now you've completely stopped buying furniture," Maja says, smiling.

"Yes. It doesn't amount to much, does it."

We go into the living room. Maja sits opposite me with her legs tucked under her on the dining chair, eating a roll with jam on. I stand up and tell her that I am just going to phone Carl and cancel our sailing trip.

"Had you arranged to go sailing now?" she asks.

"Yes, we'd arranged it for eleven o'clock, but I can easily cancel it."

"No," she says. "I want to come along."

"Okay!" I say.

"In fact, I was hoping it would be today you were going sailing," she says.

"That's bloody great by me," I answer, sitting down again. Then she gets up and comes round the table and my heart begins to beat faster. She sits on my lap.

"Can I kiss you?" she whispers. "If I'm careful?" I nod. She does – she slowly moves her tongue into my mouth – her touch is salve to my lips.

"Show me your teeth," she whispers. I do. Then she kisses me again.

The car is still at the garage so we cycle to the harbour on Maja's old bike – her on the back, me thrashing away on the pedals. She puts her hands on my hips.

"Do you often go sailing?" she asks.

I tell her that I go sailing with Carl every Saturday if I can because he has rheumatism and can't sail on his own even when the weather is only vaguely rough. "But you mustn't talk about it – the rheumatism – he is very sensitive."

"Is he like you?" she asks.

"Shit, yes. Or rather, I'm like him. So you can see what I'll look like when I'm a tattooed old git."

"In *personality*, Allan," she shouts. "That's what I mean."

"Judge for yourself," I say briefly because I can sense that a car has slowed down and is driving right behind us.

"Just a mo," I say over my shoulder to Maja and pull into the side. The car – a white Ford Mondeo – pulls up in front of us.

"What's up?" Maja asks.

"It's the police," I answer.

"Shall I get off?" she asks and I start laughing.

"No," I say.

"Right, okay," Maja says and moves to get off.

"Stay where you are," I say. "I meant it. Just . . . let it wash over you." She sits down again. A middle-aged man gets out of the car.

"Allan," he says, closing the car door behind him, and strolls over towards us.

"Martinsen," I say with a little nod.

"Long time, no see," he says.

"May I introduce you to Maja." I point my outstretched arm in Maja's direction; she is sitting behind me with her hands on my hips. She removes one and reaches forward.

"Maja, this is Police Officer Martinsen," I say.

"Hello," Maja says, shaking his hand – she is cool. Martinsen takes a few steps back so he can have a good look at me.

"Where've you been hiding yourself, Allan?" he asks.

"At sea – oil tankers," I answer, even though I am sure he already knows.

"And now you're back," he says.

"Yes, I am."

"The old hunting grounds?"

"New hunting grounds." I shoot a cheeky glance back at Maja.

"Same old chums?" he asks. I serve him up my earnest look.

"New chums."

"Someone has given you a going over."

"I fell, of course."

"That goes without saying." He stands there studying me, the bike, glances at Maja, looks up at the sky and says:

"And what are we doing on such a wonderful day, then?"

"We are going sailing with my grandfather on the fjord unless you delay us any further. He shoves off at eleven," I say.

"I'm happy to hear that. I hope we don't have any further business together, Allan." Then, so help me, he winks at Maja and says, "Miss Maja," swivels on his heels and strolls back to his car. "Cycle carefully," he says before opening his door, scrambling in and driving off.

"Who was he?" Maja asks, astonished. I twist my head to face her.

"Martinsen, the narco cop, a bit fatter nowadays but still as courteous as ever."

"But what was it all about?"

"He . . . ," I begin. How should I answer? "It meant, I think, that he's keeping an eye on Frank, who you saw me with. And he just wants to check because we were doing a lot of shit together a few years back."

"How did he know you were here?"

"It might just be chance or perhaps I popped up on his screen when I registered a change of address at the town hall." I think it is much more likely that they are keeping an eye on Asger's flat, but this is not the moment to tell her that I know who Asger is – that I have met him; this is a topic I would like to avoid altogether.

"Why didn't he just ask if you were doing anything illegal?" Maja asks.

"That would be impolite," I say.

"What . . . now, then?"

"Nothing – he was just leaving his calling card with an built-in warning. Let's get going." I start pedalling.

"Do you think . . . he believed you?" Maja asks.

"Yes."

"Why?"

"It's just the whole . . . impression, kind of thing. Cycling along on a Saturday morning to go sailing. And with you on the back – he liked you." She gives me a dig in the hips.

"Do you think so?" she asks.

"The way he winked at you; I've never seen anything like it. I reckon he thinks you're a nice bit of fluff." She slaps my back.

"I am not *fluff*," she says.

"*Miss Maja,*" I say in a deep, courteous voice, like Martinsen's. Maja laughs and hits me again, but then she is quiet for a few seconds.

"What about . . . Frank?" she says.

"What about Frank?"

"Well . . . are you going to say anything to him?"

"About what?"

"About . . . them keeping an eye on him?"

"Are you crazy? No." I say.

"Why not?"

I stop the bike again, turn round, and put my hands on the saddle. "Frank can get stuffed. To hell with him. He's on his own."

"Because of . . . ?" She points to my face.

"No," I say, shaking my head. "I don't care if he gets done. All that shit . . . stopping you in the street when you're cycling . . . it's too much. I don't need it. It's embarrassing – in front of you, too. I mean what impression does it give you of me? If Frank's doing something illegal, bang him up, chuck away the key, let him rot." I get heated – what crap. Maja rests her hands on mine.

"Good," she says, giving my hands a squeeze. "Let's get going."

"Yes," I say. "Good." We cycle on. Maja asks about Martinsen. I try to explain to her what it is like, I mean, with a decent policeman like Martinsen who doesn't feel *forced* to behave like an asshole. How you sort of establish a relationship – a certain kind of topsy-turvy respect. You can say 'hello' in the street, off duty, so to speak. And otherwise you play your role as well as you can.

"It's like cops and robbers: he knows I'm going to do something and keeps me under surveillance. But he has other business to take care of, so I do my thing when he's not paying attention. When I've done it he can work out that it was probably me. His job is to prove it and my job is to stay cool. In a way I'm the employer – without me there is no him. That's what makes it so topsy-turvy."

"Weird," Maja says. "Did you stay cool?" she asks then.

"Not cool enough – he nabbed me."

"*Tut, tut,*" I hear behind me.

We are close to the harbour now.

"Does he tell old sailor's stories, then? Your grandfather?" she asks.

"If you put the charm on."

"How do you do that?"

"Smile, put your hand on his arm, that sort of thing – he's very fond of girls."

We sail astern, in the direction of Hals. I put on a life jacket to show solidarity with Maja – at least that is what I tell myself as I tighten the straps.

"What about you, Carl? Are you going to put a life jacket on?" Maja asks. He just snorts.

"He's counting on me rescuing him if he falls in the water," I say. Carl gives Maja a look.

"It's different when you know your way around a boat." He points towards the DLG grain silos. Alongside the quay there is a little tanker – probably carrying about 25,000 tons by my reckoning. "It was one like her Allan was on, only a lot bigger."

"It must have been quite different when you were sailing," Maja says. I go up to the bow to make sure everything is okay.

"I'm still sailing, you know, my girl. But not in those floating high-rise jobs – ugh, not likely."

"I mean . . . ."

"Yes, I know, it was quite different. I can't tell you how sorry I am that I filled the lad's head with all those tall stories when he was small. It just hasn't been the same experience for him – not at all." Their voices are carried to me on the wind.

"When did you first go to sea?" Maja asks.

"In the 1930s, as a deck hand. Fifteen years old I was."

"Why so young?"

"I was up to no good, so my father found me a place on a boat to see the world and become a man." Carl laughs his gravelly old man's laughter.

"What do you mean . . . up to no good?"

"Pinching stuff," he answers. I go below deck to make coffee and tea. I have brought some tea bags along in my pocket. Inwardly, I praise myself for being an attentive, courteous gentleman, then remind myself not to be too cocky.

Maja has got Carl talking. He tells her about the time he signed on a ship sailing to the Far East. He was jumpy – this was his first long voyage. When he had been shown to his bunk, breakfast was served. The whole crew was very attentive so he knew something was in the air. Carl took a piece of white bread and one of the men passed him the jam. He spread it on lightly, trying to be well-mannered. "You're not at home with mummy now; you don't need to skimp," the first officer said. "Spread it on thick." So Carl slapped it on and as soon as he had taken his first mouthful, it burned like fire, but he just looked round at the others while chewing away and then took another bite. And with food in his mouth he said, "Mmm, lovely jam," and nodded to the first officer. He ate the rest of the bread and jam with the sweat running into his eyes while the others watched him. When he had finished, they all laughed and slapped him on the back. "Well, we've got a real man in the making here," they said to each other and welcomed him on board. Later he found out that it was extra strong mango chutney from India. Carl could also have told her a few naughtier stories, but he doesn't do that with people he has just met – let alone girls.

"Drinks up," I announce on my way up to the deck and pass them each a mug before taking a seat. We are skimming along nicely. Carl leans over to me.

"Nice legs," he says loud enough for Maja to hear.

"You keep your hands to yourself, old boy."

"I can't promise anything," he says. My grandmother was also a bit on the short side – we share the same taste for small, robust girls. With long-legged girls there is something you can't quite get your head round – they don't seem to hang together properly. Maja is smiling.

"Chauvinists," she says.

"We-ell," I say. Carl shrugs his shoulders and adjusts the course. We are sailing towards a small bay where we can lie leeward and eat lunch. If you have guests on board you can't ask them to eat in rough seas and you have to let their stomachs settle before you continue if you want to avoid any mess on the deck. I reef the sails and Carl casts anchor. As we do so Maja disappears below deck with her army knapsack. We ride at anchor. A moment later she climbs up – wearing a dark blue bikini. She smiles at me. I am breathless. She asks how you get back on board. Carl produces a little aluminium ladder which he hangs over the stern. Maja comes over and stands next to me.

"Are you coming?" she asks, angling her head to the water.

"I think I ought to help Carl make lunch," I say quietly.

"Okay," she says, going up to the bow and diving into the water. Shocking; I am madly in love with her. I go down to help Carl.

"I'll sort it out," he says firmly. "Go for a swim with your girl." I find the swimming costume I keep on board in a cubby hole on board and as I change clothes the fear comes sneaking up on me, wringing my chest. I have goose pimples when I go up on deck. Maja is swimming a fair distance away from the boat. She waves when she sees me.

"Come on in – the water's great," she shouts. I can't get my breath down into my lungs. Stand at the bow. The water pitch black before my eyes, legs shaking, sweat breaking out – cold and stinking. Swallow a mouthful of air and push off, my knees giving way beneath me; I topple over the edge. The water swallows me up. Cold. Endless darkness beneath me – above me the light. Swim feverishly forwards, sob under the water, air slips out of my mouth, bubbles race towards the flames. The cramp sets in as I gaze up into the infinite light . . . it is only the sun – there is air up there. I see a lighter patch on the surface a little further ahead. Something clicks into place; I start a new stroke – upwards. Her shining skin. Still there is water above me. My arms outstretched. Still above me. My lungs about to burst. The tips of my fingers touch Maja – I break the surface of the water with a hand on her hip. She squeals. She has air. She shines.

From the harbour we cycle to a Chinese take-out and buy food plus a bottle of wine. We are given plastic cutlery, but they don't have any plastic beakers. Instead they give us two glass tumblers that are so scratched from being in the dishwasher that it is as if they have been sandblasted. We cycle to Kildepark and find a snug spot.

We don't have a corkscrew.

"Just a sec," I say and tear the plastic seal off the top of the bottle, fold my jacket and walk towards a tree. I hold the jacket up against the tree trunk. "Don't try this at home," I say aloud and carefully start banging the bottom of the bottle against the jacket and the tree. I know that Maja is following my actions closely, but I don't look at her, just concentrate on getting the cork further and further out of the neck of the bottle. I know this is a party trick, but I am a man – I love impressing girls. I walk back and sit opposite her on the grass and pull the cork out the rest of the way with my hand. Maja claps.

"Wow – I've never seen anyone do that before," she says. I shrug my shoulders.

"Perhaps a sign that I've had too much practice," I say, basking in her gaze like some bloody reptile. We eat. Then we lie on the grass and . . . sort of kiss a little – and then we fall asleep, like animals. It must be the sea air. We both sleep for more than an hour and only wake up because it is getting chilly. Maja needs a pee so we walk to the station. I nip into the gents and throw water over my face and then I stand waiting for her. Iphone Adrian and tell him that I can't make it to the match the following day. He asks why. I tell him the truth: I might be making it with the loveliest girl in the world. He wishes me luck.

Maja still hasn't turned up. Time drags. I peer through the glass partitions to see if she has come out. She hasn't. Has she left? She can't just have left. I scan the station hall and cast my eye round the station kiosk.

"Shall we have a cup of cocoa?" asks a voice behind me. I twirl round. Here she comes – smiling – out from the toilets. What the hell was I thinking about?

"Yes, let's." We buy a cocoa for her and a coffee for me and sit in John. F. Kennedy Plads. She asks about the accident. Whether I was close to anyone in the crew? I tell her about Chris. There isn't a lot I can say.

"You must have talked about something."

"Yes, too damn right we did," I say. We talked about engines and cooking and life and . . . girls."

"Do men talk a lot about girls?"

"It happens," I say.

"Are we that interesting?"

"You can't imagine."

Maja holds up her fist with the tip of her thumb sticking out between her first and second fingers. "Is it . . . ?"

"No, no. Not only . . . . It's more that we haven't a clue. We simply don't understand you girls."

"You don't think men understand girls?"

"I'm willing to bet that you agree."

"Yes," she laughs, nodding her head furiously. She adds, "We're not so different, though." I chew on that for a moment.

"It's not . . . you we don't understand; it's what you do to us."

"What do we do to you?" she teases.

"You bring us to our knees. Make us worship you."

"Can't say I have noticed."

"No, we try to hide it."

"What is it about us you worship?"

"That's what we don't understand. It's tiny things."

"Come on then." She digs me in the side with her elbow. "Out with it."

"Yes, well . . . just like when I . . . when we . . . were in bed together. The morning after when you came out of the bathroom you did something with your hair."

"And?"

"Umm, you sort of . . . ."

"Brushed it?"

"No, it wasn't so much that, it was more . . . ." I bend forward a little and make an awkward attempt at tossing my head back. "You did something like that with your head and all your hair flopped onto the other side and then you sort of glanced up at me and went on brushing and you were giving me that . . . *look* all the time."

"You were naked."

"Yes, but that was . . . ."

She tugs at my arm and laughs, staring at me in surprise as if I had totally freaked out. "Sort of *how*?"

"It was just the way you did it, the way you looked at me. It made me feel very . . . very intense about you."

"Do you mean that?" she says, pulling a brush out of her bag, brushing her hair and tossing it onto the other side of her face, glancing up at me and brushing it again.

"Yeeaah, like that," I say. She roars with laughter. Puts the brush away.

"Men," she says.

We go into Mallorca Bar and drink more wine. I feel strange drinking wine in a pub, but it is okay when Maja is with me. She wants to stay for a while and then see if she can spot Susan – her girlfriend whom I have not met yet.

"I'll have to tell her that you're alright."

"I would appreciate that."

We leave the bike and walk to Jomfru Ane Gade. Maja wants to go to Rock Nielsen to search for Susan. It might have been the bouncer from there who knocked my tooth out. I am not sure that I can stand facing him without losing my head. I tell Maja.

"Okay," she says, "I'll just pop up and do a quick lap." I lean against the fence surrounding an outdoor terrace café. It is almost eleven o'clock and Jomfru Ane Gade is beginning to fill up. I want to leave. Then I spot Asger coming down the street towards me. Hell. At that moment Maja comes down the stairs from Rock Nielsen and I hear Asger calling her, see him waving to her. She stops next to me and stands still.

"Hi Maja, how goes it?" Asger says, leaning forwards as a sign of intimacy. "Is Susan here?" he asks.

"No," she says and there seems to be a tinge of scornful pleasure in her voice.

"Do you know where she is?"

"No, I haven't seen her for a while."

"Fuck it," Asger says. "I've been looking for her. You know, I wanted to . . . ." Asger looks somewhat harassed. Maja says nothing. Asger's glance takes me in, but indicates no sign of recognition. He seems doped up.

"When you see her," Asger says," tell her I'd like a word with her. She's got my number." He pats his mobile, which is in a case on his belt.

"I'll see what I can do," Maja says.

"Good. You know . . . I . . . I'd like very much like . . . to see her," Asger says, patting Maja gauchely on the shoulder and going up the steps to Rock Nielsen.

"I'm not bloody saying 'hi' to Susan from that fool," Maja says through gritted teeth as she puts her arm round my waist.

"Why not?"

"He's an idiot."

"Where does he know Susan from?"

"That doesn't matter," she says, taking my arm and putting it round her shoulder – we start walking. "Let's go back to my place," she says, pressing herself up to me.

"Maja . . . ," I begin. Pause to think it over. "It does . . . matter. I'd like . . . ." I come to a halt. We have reached the end of Jomfru Ane Gade, facing the Limfjordshotel. The taxis are dropping off a steady stream of people.

"Hang on," Maja says; she presses my arm to indicate that we have to cross the street. We stroll past Maxim and Valhal and pass through the little arcade-like overhang by the Chinese restaurant at the corner of Borgergade and Vesterbro and then we are on our way towards the bridge.

Maja takes a deep breath, exhales, walks for a while in silence. "I need a cigarette," she says eventually. I give one to her.

"That guy . . . ," she says. "Asger's his name. Him and the guy I saw you with – Frank – they sell . . . dope. I think they do it through the bouncers, but I'm not sure. Anyway, it doesn't matter. They're always running around here the whole weekend." She doesn't say any more.

"And Susan . . . ?"

"Susan was his girlfriend at one point."

"Did he treat her badly?"

"Not while they were going out . . . ," Maja hesitates. "But then he threw her out because he'd met some nasty bitch who had somehow . . . twisted him round her little finger."

"That doesn't sound too good," I say and add: "Pushers – they're not always particularly appealing." Apparently she doesn't want to tell me what happened. That is fine by me.

"No, and they think they're something special," Maja says.

"How so?"

"Have you seen that film called *Light Sleeper* with William Dafoe?" she asks. I saw it at sea; State Seamen's Welfare Service releases the latest films on board ships at the same time as they are premiered in Denmark. The film is about a pusher who admits the error of his ways and when he attempts to rectify it everything goes wrong.

"No," I answer.

"Well, Dafoe is a kind of pusher going round selling dope to people . . . . He delivers it to their door; people phone in their orders and then he acts as their junkie courier. It's all very dignified; private chauffeurs, wealthy clients and so on. Of course, the goods are delivered for security reasons – and as a service. And then all sorts of horrible things happen to a girl." Maja stops and takes a last drag of her cigarette. We are standing outside the tower which controls the moving parts of the bridge. "Limfjord Bridge – Office" it says on the door. Maja throws the cigarette down and meticulously stubs it out with the toe of her boot.

"What has that got to do with Asger?" I ask as we walk over the bridge.

"The guy you were with the other night when I got . . . angry, Frank," she enunciates his name with a sneer. "People contact him on his mobile phone, then he collects the . . . stuff from Asger and drives around delivering it to his customers."

"And that's because they saw the film?"

"Yes. Susan says so, anyway. And then there's something about having to buy at least ten grams of hash because they . . . ." her voice changes to a hiss, *"don't deal with any of those raggedy assed smokers."*

"That sounds bloody ridiculous," I say.

"Yes, doesn't it?" she says, relaxing and smiling. "You could kill yourself laughing if it weren't so sad."

"Sad? Why's it sad?" I ask and add: "I mean, of course it's sad, we can agree on that, but why do you get worked up about it?"

"Because Susan still thinks she's in love with Asger."

"Not so good."

"No, it's not, is it."

"But she keeps away from him?"

"Yes, she knows it's stupid," Maja says.

"It's complicated."

"What?"

"Life."

"Oh, it's not that complicated," she says, groping my ass lustfully.

"It's getting easier and easier," I say, pulling her into me. We kiss passionately. My dick is pushing against my trousers, towards her. We laugh.

"Let's go home," Maja says, pulling at me. We are almost on the Nørresundby side of the fjord and we walk briskly hand in hand to her flat, hurry up the stairs and turn into the dark corridor. Maja finds the switch, puts on the light and then we see Susan curled up in front of her door, asleep.

"There she is," Maja says enthusiastically, running up to her, squatting down and gently waking her.

"Susan, Susan, you have to go to bed," she says.

"I was so tired," mumbles Susan and, catching sight of me, she opens her eyes wide and wakes up.

"He's okay," Maja says, producing her keys. "I've found out that he's alright." Thanks, I think. Susan stands up, leans against the wall, eyes me suspiciously and tries to smile – she's not very successful.

"Why are you so tired?" Maja asks when we are inside. Susan answers that she has been working all day. She kicks off her shoes and flops down onto the bed. There is not much bloody room in that bed for three people. I am in the way, just inside the door.

"She works for the post office," Maja tells me.

"Post slave," Susan mumbles from the bed as I curse the thought that I might be sleeping on my own tonight. Maja comes over and looks up at me apologetically.

"She'll have to sleep here – she lives in Vadum."

"Dear, oh dear." I let out a deep sigh and flash a meaningful smile.

"Yes, it's almost too much to bear," she whispers.

"We could go to my place?"

"It's a long way and my bike's at the station."

"We can take a taxi."

"Yes, can we?"

"Yes, we bloody can," I say softly.

"I'll just write a note," Maja says and asks me to repeat my phone number for her so that Susan can phone if there is anything she needs. Shortly afterwards we are sitting in the back seat of a taxi. I tell the driver to go to the end of Vesterbro, turn down Prinsensgade and then along Jyllandsgade to East Aalborg. "And you can put your foot down," I say finally.

"Why's that?" Maja asks. I tell her to lean her head back so she can see up through the rear window and say she should stay like that until we arrive. We are off, the driver goes for it. When we have passed the bridge, the buildings begin to whistle by on both sides like massive walls speckled with lights; the dark sky hangs in the middle.

"This is absolutely great," Maja says, fumbling for my hand on the seat between us. She squeezes it.

My head and shoulders feel like one big wound – the rest of my body just aches. I am lying in a single ward in crisp, clean bedding. Touch my head and find there is a drip in my arm. The hair on my skull has been shaved off – only stubble left. My face hurts; it feels uneven and covered with small, hard edges. The skin must be ravaged. The pain is worst just above my eyebrows which have disappeared. I sniff cautiously to see if I can smell my own open flesh; there is only a faint aroma of hospital. I am very tired. My chest is constantly trembling. They must all have died. Chris.

A nurse appears at the side of my bed. She speaks to me gently, straightens my pillows, holds the urine bottle for me, feeds me with a spoon. Nods energetically and sympathetically to me, says: "You will be alright," in what must be a Dutch accent. They can do what they want with me.

Soon after a doctor comes in through the door. In better English he explains to me that my condition is as good as can be expected. Mostly I have contact burns – superficial second degree burns which are not too deep. The scars will not be unsightly.

The treatment is called "exposure" – the wounds are exposed. You let them heal themselves for two weeks – just wash the edges of the wounds. I have a ward to myself to avoid bacteria.

The doctor says that if I had surfaced in the oil I would have caught fire and been disfigured for life – not even plastic surgery would have helped. "But you have been very lucky."

Luck . . . I almost weep when he says the word – don't know why. Have to clench my teeth. I wish I could punch him. That is what I feel like doing.

"Maybe later we move some skin," he says, but I don't completely understand – somehow I feel his voice is very distant. He talks about cooling down and shock. Shock? Why isn't there anyone here I know?

I doze, keep waking with a start, because I am shaking. A thin young man in an ugly grey suit is standing by my bed. He says that Mette is on her way. Mette? I realize he is speaking Danish.

"Who?" I ask.

"Mette," he answers, looking frightened. "Your sister?"

"You?" I ask. He looks even more frightened. An idiot.

"Who . . . are . . . you?" I ask. He is one of those fools from the Danish embassy. He says something about identifying the dead victims. About "terrible burns" and "no relatives" and more.

"Yes" I nod. He says something else, looks relieved, goes on his way. Good. A nurse fetches me in a wheelchair. Wraps me in a blanket. We walk down hospital corridors, take a lift, then another long corridor and into a sort of ante-room with TV, a sofa, two chairs and a small table – nothing on the walls. The doctor I met before is standing arguing with a sweaty man in work clothes. Something about TV. The TV cameras don't work. It's a long time before I realize what that means. I can't see the corpses on the TV screen. The doctor apologizes.

"It's okay," I say. I am wheeled out again. A medical room with large metal cabinets. It is like a film – white tiles, stainless steel. It is cold here. It seems very

remote. Burnt bodies. There is a faint smell of pork . . . roast joint. I am wheeled in, I shake my head – then the next. The bodies resemble each other, their heads too awful to describe. Focus on a pair of feet. There is no string round one toe with a note on. They don't use it. There is a plastic bracelet round the wrist, covered in numbers. Next. Another man's body, difficult, no distinguishing features; I can't make out who it is.

"Next," I say. We move on. Drawer out. I recognize him immediately. It is him . . . slim, long legs . . . something about the shape of the face. They aren't white any longer – his fingers. Thin, mangled.

"Chris," I say. Then I break down.

My limbs are stiff when I wake up and through a tremendous headache I can feel a damp sheet creased up under my back. My stomach aches. There is the splashing sound of a shower nearby. I stretch and survey my hairy chest.

"Hi." It is Maja with a towel wrapped round her body. Her skin looks fresh. "You had a bad night."

"Yes, it's strange. I've got a headache, too," I say. Wonder if I have been dreaming again.

"Come on, little puss puss," Maja says. I glance up at her. She is pursing her mouth.

"Perhaps I was just afraid that it was something I'd dreamt?"

"What?"

"That you slept here last night." She sits down on the edge of the bed and lays the top of her body over mine. The damp towel against my skin, her firm body immediately underneath. I remember what she looked like between her legs; small slivers of gravadlax – soft and smooth. I am not content merely to think about it. My headache lifts. We take our time.

Then we lie on our backs and hold each other's hand, breathing hard. I caress her hand with my fingers. I feel good now.

"Was it good for you, beautiful? "I ask, continuing to scrutinize the ceiling and touch her fingers.

"Oh, it wasn't too bad, I suppose," she says, hard-nosed. There is silence for three seconds, then she laughs and rolls over to me, stretching one leg across my body.

"Scandalous," I say. "Dreadful – a farce."

"I'm a girl of honour," she says. "You can have your revenge any time you like."

We fool around a little more until she says: "Have you no idea what he did before he went to sea?" I had told her about Chris the night before. It eased the pain.

"No, it was out of context – a chance encounter. It was . . . great in one way because we only knew each other there – on board the boat. I mean, there was no mention of our former lives.

"Like us," she says.

"Yes, until you found out I was lying to you."

"That doesn't matter now," Maja says.

"Yes, it does," I say. She lowers her voice:

"I haven't told you very much about me, either."

"No, but that's okay – I like it like that."

She looks at me questioningly. I don't want to scare her off. I would like to know everything. But if she doesn't want me to know the things I know, that is absolutely fine by me.

"You mustn't be offended," I begin. "It's . . . . For me you only begin to exist when . . . no, that's not true. It's as if . . . all the things that happened in the past, they could be upsetting, I mean, right now when we're . . . ."

"I understand exactly what you mean," Maja says.

"So, save it for later, okay?"

"What?" she says, sitting up abruptly – and straddling me. "Later?" she laughs.

"Well, I hope we can be . . . like – you know?"

"No, I don't know what you mean. Tell me."

"Together," I say. "You and me. I'm like . . . ." I can't finish the sentence. She sinks down on me so her hair falls like a curtain around our faces.

"I'm happy about that," she whispers.

"Do you mean that?"

"Yes."

"I . . . ." I start off, then come to a halt. We drown in each others' eyes until Maja breaks the silence.

"Allan?"

"Yes?"

"I think I could manage an omelette – or just an egg."

"Yes?"

"Yes."

"I'd like to make one for you."

"An omelette?"

"Yes."

"Do you know how?"

"You bet."

FUNERAL

I

The man has picked her up from work, and in the car on their way to the shops they have been discussing the preparations for their daughter's wedding.

The smell of burnt lasagne hits them as they unlock the door to their terraced house in Thulebakken in Hasseris.

"Do you think it's . . . ?" the woman begins, looking up at the man with a frightened – but also an angry – look on her face.

"Don't know who the hell else it could be," he says, lifting the Storkøb carrier bags into the hall. "Thomas?" he calls out. Their grown-up son doesn't have a key, but he might have found the one the man keeps on top of the beam at the back of the carport.

Walk through the kitchen and the thick, foul-smelling smoke from the oven; the man's lively eyes begin to flash. He is in his fifties – a little on the heavy side – his shoulders roll with every stride he takes.

Opening the door to the living room, he sees that the TV is tuned to Discovery Channel, but with the volume turned down. In the background he can hear the stylus of the record player scratching away at the end of an LP. In the kitchen, the woman switches on the cooker hood and opens a window.

"Thomas, for Christ's sake!" the man angrily exclaims as he enters the living room. On the Persian carpet in front of the stereo their 29-year-old son is sitting in the lotus position, his sunken body naked from the waist up, his chin slumped against his chest. Jumper, T-shirt and socks have been slung over an armchair. The woman comes in and stands behind the man. She gives a snort of anger. A needle hangs from the skin of the son's forearm; above it a slackened piece of extension cable.

"Get him out of here," the woman hisses through gritted teeth, turning and going back to the kitchen. The man moves towards his son. He stops in his tracks. Stands motionless, then slowly raises his hand to take off his driving glasses. It is dark in the living room. His muscles go limp; the man hangs there – detached from his own body – as he crouches down and lays a hand on the boy's shoulder. Cold. Completely cold. He carefully lifts his son's arm. It feels heavy – the stiffness is beginning to set in. The man remembers a first-aid course for construction workers he once attended. It begins after three hours.

From the kitchen the woman says: "He's not going to Rikke's wedding after this."

The incontrovertible signs of death: rigor mortis, death spots, decomposition.

The man's heart is beating hard in his chest, his ears are buzzing. He wants to feel the boy's pulse, but he knows it is pointless – his skin has already taken on a bluish purple hue. The man's breathing comes in short, sharp bursts; his eyes and lips tightly compressed. Even though the boy's body is emaciated, the faces of father and son resemble one another . . . the narrow lips. The man reels as he half gets to his feet and frantically reaches out for the remote control to put an end to the silent tumult on the screen. The weight of the disposable syringe forces the skin up where the needle enters. He pulls it out; the scratching sound of the stylus fills the air. Before he can call her, tell her, he has to stop the noise. He lifts the lid of the record player. It is *The Ventures in Space*. An LP the man was given by his younger brother in 1965. How often have the man and the son listened to that record when the woman was not at home and the boy was visiting. He goes back to the boy and squats down. He has to do it now. She has been expecting this for twelve years. He calls his wife – his voice sounds like soaked cardboard.

A moment later he hears the stifled "Oh, no!" from the kitchen. He looks in her direction. She appears in the doorway, swaying, clutches the door frame, her knees give way. She sinks to the floor. The man observes her frail body – so similar to the son's here by his side.

"Oh, no," she says again, "I . . . ."

Her body trembles and she collapses into a heap; she hides her sobbing face in her arms on the parquet floor. Her shoulders heave.

The man gets up, takes a step towards her – but no. He goes down on his haunches again, behind the boy. He removes the cable before carefully lowering his son's torso onto the thick pile of the Persian carpet. The boy's upturned palms from the Lotus position splay outwards from the body at an angle of almost 45 degrees. The man unfolds the boy's legs; with one hand on each bare ankle he straightens them out. They feel hard under his palms and he can feel the scar tissue on the boy's feet.

He rises with difficulty and goes over to his wife, squats down beside her. He puts his hands on her shoulder. She shakes her head, sobs. He caresses her back. The consoling words come out as an incoherent mumble. He gropes for the telephone. He calls. His voice is hoarse, he stammers into the receiver, provides the details and hangs up.

"They'll be here soon," he says. She slowly stands up. He walks over, puts his arms around her, kisses her forehead and smoothes her hair. Resting her hand on the man's chest, she looks down at the young man on the floor, her son. Her breathing is spasmodic.

"Put one of your shirts on him," she says – her voice is frail, croaky.

"Yes, alright," the man says, but dithers until she looks up into his face and nods. Then he trudges out of the living room – along the hallway.

"The dark blue one," she calls after him.

What is he thinking as he takes his best shirt out of the wardrobe? What can he think? He flops down onto the edge of the bed; his fingers numb, he undoes the top two buttons of the shirt, so he can take it off the hanger. He will give her time. The feeling surges through him – a deep loathing for his own warm flesh; the blood which pulsates blindly through his veins; the heart's spasms; the eyes' ability to see.

On rare occasions, when she is out of the house, he will listen to his Ventures LP. He won't tell her even though he knows that she would understand. One thing he is sure of: she will always blame herself – and no doubt everybody else, too – she just won't be able to help herself. No words will ever be able to soothe her pain.

Slowly he walks back along the hallway with the material of the freshly ironed shirt billowing from his awkwardly outstretched hand. He only hopes she has moved – that is the only thing he hopes for. At the door he pauses.

She is sitting on her knees, bent over her son. She combs back his straggly, dirty-blond hair with her fingers and exposes his pallid forehead. Her hands hover over his face, lightly touching it. She wishes his eyes were open so that she could close them. So that she could gaze into them one last time. Her face it is – out of her womb – the quick eyes, the lively movements. She can't hold back the tears – they fall on her son's cold skin, where they linger with the same quivering surface tension as drops of water on wax. The man steps up behind her, looks towards the street even though none of the windows face in that direction. She gets to her feet. Unable to meet the man's eyes, she gently touches his arm before making her way to the kitchen.

He has already completely unbuttoned the shirt without realising. He sees that the boy is wearing socks; she must have put them on him while he was away. Good.

He guides one of the boy's arms into the shirt sleeve – his skin is already colder than before and the scar tissue feels like wrinkled parchment. Then he positions himself behind the boy and lifts the top part of his body up off the carpet. But the man can't both hold up the body and manoeuvre the shirt at the same time. The head suddenly flops down – forwards at first. It looks so menacing. The man feverishly tries to pull the shirt down over the boy's back. But the head has kinetic energy – it flips round towards him. He looks down at his son from above . . . on the bike, on the way to the kindergarten, the boy sitting on the child's seat fitted to the crossbar. The boy leans his head back and shouts: "Faster, Dad." And he does go faster, his legs moving like drum sticks, the sweat bursting from his forehead, the hedges whizzing past. "Yippeeee!" the boy shouts.

The man's stomach contracts – he takes a deep gulp; quickly lowers his son – gently, though, so that the head does not bang against the carpet. The shirt lies crumpled beneath the boy's back. The man rushes to the guest toilet and empties the contents of his stomach into the toilet bowl. Flushes, rinses his mouth, returns to the living room. He finishes the job, puts the shirt on, buttons it up and smoothes out the material. Against his hand he feels the sharp contours of the ribs.

The aroma of coffee beans drifts in from the kitchen.

She has made coffee.

What can you do?

He goes into the kitchen. She has poured him out a mug of coffee – he can hear her bustling about in the bathroom. Mug in hand, he goes back and contemplates the boy. The upturned palms give the impression of . . .

openness. The boy seems stately in the navy blue shirt, which is far too big for him, and the worn jeans. Cheeky as hell.

The man sits down on the sofa, or rather on the edge of the sofa. He pushes the coffee table aside so that he can spread his legs. The boy's Bali Shagcigarette tobacco is in its pouch on the table by the side of a scarred Ronson lighter. In the ashtray there is a ready-rolled cigarette – no ash, no butts – just the cigarette; completely white, slightly conical in shape.

He picks up the cigarette between his thumb and forefinger. The coffee is steaming and smells good. He has not smoked for four years. He looks over at the boy, raises his eyebrows questioningly. The boy looks completely composed. Then the man quickly glances up – maybe a little embarrassed – to see whether the woman has returned. She hasn't. He winks at the boy and passes the cigarette under his nose, sniffing at it. The smell of tobacco. He turns towards the boy, gives a little upward jerk of his chin and arches his eyebrows.

"Okay, then, is it?" he says with a wry twitch of his mouth. Out of habit he shields the flame as he flips the boy's lighter. The man takes a drag and automatically slips the Ronson into his shirt pocket. The smoke feels familiar in his lungs. He exhales and studies the glowing tip. The nicotine makes him feel dizzy.

He takes out the lighter again and lights the two candles on the coffee table – it seems the right thing to do. He nods to his son, then takes a mouthful of the coffee to get rid of the taste of vomit in his throat; the heat in his stomach is almost painful. The upward thrust of air from the flames causes the cigarette smoke to ripple idly in the air.

Now she reappears from the bathroom.

"Come over here next to me," he says. And she does. She sits beside him, very close, takes one of his hands in both of hers and rests her head on his shoulder.

"Our little boy," she says.

"Yes," he says, "our boy."

For a time they say nothing. He smokes the cigarette – careful not to inhale too much – flicks off the ash, drinks from the coffee mug, which he holds in the same hand. His nose is blocked, and the smoke glides down his throat like weightless satin. He would like to say something, but he can't.

Finally, he forces himself: "We have to phone Rikke."

"Soon," she says. "Just now we have to sit a while with Thomas."

"Yes," he says.

A moment passes.

"I'll call Tilly's mother, as well," she says.

"Mmm," he says, somehow relieved that she is going to call Rikke. Not because he wants to get out of doing it himself, but more because . . . she feels she is capable of doing it.

And Tilly – poor girl. Lisbeth, too. And what were the others called? Lars. Svend. There were so many of them. Then. Wonder what has become of them? He will soon know – he is going to find out where they are. It is important.

He is about to take the last puff of the cigarette when the doorbell rings. With meticulous care he stubs out the cigarette in the ashtray. As he does so, the woman gives his other hand a squeeze before letting it go. He stands up, wiping the tears away from his cheeks with the back of his hand, and walks towards the door. He would rather be dead than subjected to this.

11

Only a few cars are to be seen as Svend turns into the Sønderholm Church parking lot. He can see a handful of people standing in front of the porch. Looks instinctively out over the churchyard towards Little Lars's grave. Lisbeth is standing there – of course. Just seeing her . . . now he won't be able to think about anything else for three weeks.

Svend checks his face in the rear-view mirror: short dark hair, shirt for the occasion, clean-shaven – he removed the stubble at the youth hostel. Swings his legs out of the car, finds a cloth under the front seat and dabs at the dirt on his boots. His trousers are clean, at least. He is in good time. Ambles down to the far end of the parking lot and up though the front garden of the vicarage, from where a gate in the rustic stone wall leads into the churchyard. This way he avoids the crowd assembled outside the porch.

Lisbeth is standing gazing at the gravestone: Lars Bjergholt; 3.5.1966–12.8.1985. Rest in Peace. Little Lars who, two weeks after starting the second year of his exam course, had stolen a car and driven it into the main doorway of Hasseris High School to demonstrate what he thought of the education system. Almost nine years ago. Lisbeth came off best – crushed bones in one leg. She looks great, a shade heavier than before, but undeniably a tall, good-looking girl. When she hears Svend's steps on the gravel, she turns and limps towards him. Every time he sees a girl with eyes like hers, slightly hooded . . . he falls in love on the spot – it's like an acid flashback.

"Hi, Lisbeth," he says.

"Svend." They embrace. "Good you came," she says, fortunately without elaborating. She lets go of him, but takes his arm, and slowly they make their way towards the church. Svend feels he should say something as they lost contact when he moved away two years ago.

"Sad occasion," he ventures. She is leaning slightly towards him as they walk along.

"Yes," she says, simply.

"Tilly . . . how's she taking it?"

"Surprisingly well," Lisbeth answers. "I don't think she'd expected anything else from him."

"No," he says, trying to pick out Tilly in the crowd in front of the church porch. "Isn't she here?" he asks. It was Tilly who had rung and told him about the bereavement.

"No," Lisbeth says, smiling. "She can sense that he's already back."

"Reincarnated?"

"Yes. She thinks he's in South America, but she's not certain."

"I can imagine a couple of things he could while away the time with in South America," Svend says with a smile.

"Yes. But she might come over for coffee with his parents in Hasseris," Lisbeth adds.

"Oh yes? She doesn't want to miss out on the wake, then?"

"Maybe. She wanted time to consider whether the function in the community centre had any connection with *the phoney ceremony in the church*, as she phrased it."

"Bonkers?" Svend asks.

"Do bears suck dick, does the Pope walk on all fours – who knows?" Lisbeth replies with a slightly embarrassed laugh – because of her language, he supposes. In fact she has stopped using that kind of language, as far as he knows. It must just be the present circumstances weighing down on our minds, he thinks. "No, it's not that bad," she adds. "Tilly has a latent tendency to madness, but she gets by."

"But is she okay?" he asks.

"Yes, in fact she's got to know a bunch of those young . . . I don't know what you call them . . . hip-hoppers, is that the word? – they've all got skateboards. They reckon she's terrific fun."

"She's become a bit of a turn for them, has she?" he asks.

"No, they treat her well. They like her," Lisbeth answers.

"That sounds . . . really . . . well, good – actually," he says.

"Probably the best thing that could have happened to her," Lisbeth says, glancing up at him from the corner of her eye: "How about you? How are you doing?"

"Bad time to ask," he replies.

"Spit it out," she says.

"Some other time, Lisbeth – okay?"

"If you say so."

"I do. What about you?" he asks, even though he knows perfectly well how things are with her – Tilly has told him.

"Things are fine. I've got a part-time job as a music teacher at Hasseris High School while I finish my degree in Danish," she answers.

"Yes, so I heard. The irony of fate. But are you getting on okay *otherwise*?"

"I need a man," Lisbeth says, squeezing his arm. "So if you're interested you'd better get your act together." Then she laughs, but it doesn't sound very convincing.

"I don't think I'm a good bet at the moment," Svend says casually and can feel the skin tightening around his eyes.

"Then you're not, if that's the way you feel." Lisbeth continues to speak candidly as they approach the church. People are beginning to go in.

"The vicious circle," he adds in a feeble attempt to explain himself. Kicks himself inwardly.

"I don't want to hear about it," she answers. He seizes his opportunity.

"Tell me something I don't already know," he says – a line they used to use years ago, to which there was only one reply:

"I can't," Lisbeth says, true to convention. She smiles and lets go of his arm as they pass through the porch.

Svend stops, while Lisbeth carries on and says 'hi' to Michael and his girlfriend – an alternative type called Louise. Michael is straight-backed with a healthy, athletic body; as a social worker he works with young delinquents. Svend can hear him talking to them: *Yes, I've been there, done that. Nothing good ever comes out of it.*

Oh yes, Svend thinks, so why was it that you swallowed all that shit and sat in your room *perceiving the wall* for days on end? Why was it you felt a need to do that? Who's talking out of your mouth today?

Svend runs his eye across the rows of pews. Where is Pusher Lars? He is not so easy to spot any more. The man has lost at least twenty kilos of muscular tissue since he finished his apprenticeship as a bricklayer in '85. Last time Svend saw him he looked like a scrawny, plucked goose – bags under his eyes, ashen skin, rotten teeth. Smoking eight grams a day. Svend can't see him, but hopes he is coming – otherwise it is going to be a tough day. Fortunately Bertrand isn't there – fortunately for him.

Svend takes a seat towards the back of the church so that he will be able to see when he has to stand. Concentrates on the ceremony, which at best is indifferent. Jesus is hanging on his cross – a little flabby and unafflicted compared with the man in the coffin. Steso-Thomas. It is difficult not to think of his body. The restless, almost fanatical eyes, now motionless in his skull. The wide mouth with the narrow lips, the small, sharp nose, the thin cranefly-like limbs. Now pale and cold, but then again that is nothing new; that is how he was most of the time. Svend is jolted out of his reverie by the sound of a chesty cough at the very back of the church.

It was the winter after Lars had died, Little Lars, that is. The others kept trying to get Lisbeth to go out with them so she wouldn't just sit staring at the wall over in Nørresundby.

They go to a concert at Café 1000Fryd to see BÜLD – the melodic, local post-punk heroes whose concerts they always go to. The atmosphere is really intense. Lisbeth has been eating mushrooms with Svend and has had a drink or two.

Steso is on pills; he strips to the waist and dances the pogo so wildly in front of the band that people start to get angry. But he soon tires and drifts from the stage.

When the concert is over Lisbeth can't find him, but his jacket and jumper are still there, so she asks Svend to help her to look for him; he searches outside while she scours the building.

Lisbeth finds him lying pale and cold on a mattress in a room upstairs. At first she thinks he is asleep, but she can't wake him even though she slaps him. She becomes frightened. It is almost as if he is in . . . a coma. Their heads are fuzzy. Phoning for an ambulance – that thought doesn't even occur to her. She finds Svend who eyes up Steso for about two seconds and says:

"We'll have to warm him up." They lie on either side of Steso and rub the upper part of his body – his skin is like wax. Their hands meet on top of his chest as if they are lying together with their child between them, trying to save him.

"Talk to him," Svend says.

"But what should I say?" Lisbeth asks.

"Think of something," he answers. So Lisbeth tells Steso that she loves him and that he must wake up; but Svend interrupts her:

"No, no," he says, "tell him that you've got some coke and amphetamines and some other shit, and that if he doesn't wake up soon he won't get any." That makes Lisbeth laugh, so Svend whispers into Steso's ear that William S. Burroughs has rung and left a message in the bar to say that he has cleaned out a main pharmaceutical warehouse in Mexico, and he hopes Steso will soon come over to visit him so they can do important business together.

Steso begins to get some colour in his face, so they lie right up against him, on either side, open their jackets and wrap them around his body. Svend's hand touches Lisbeth's – he doesn't move it; she thinks it is . . . strange to be lying so close to him. She tries to keep her hand still; she can feel the roughness and weight of Svend's hand against her own, her palm grows moist with sweat. Svend grasps her hand, gives it a squeeze. "Everything will be fine," he says, without letting go of her hand. What is he referring to? She would just like to stay there.

"What are you two doing?" Steso says out of the blue, very suspicious. She withdraws her hand – away from Svend's, and the moment has passed.

"Thomas," Lisbeth says. "Hi."

"We're just exploiting your body," Svend answers.

"Oh yes?" Steso says indifferently. "What about me? What am I *doing?" he asks – he gradually realizes that their hands are on his chest.*

"You fainted," Lisbeth tells him.

"Oh, all right," he answers, as if it doesn't matter. "What was that about Burroughs?" he asks.

"Burroughs?" Svend says. "You must have been dreaming."

"Hmmm," Steso says. "He called me – it was about something VERY important." Steso always turns up the volume on particular words.

"You'd better give him a call," Svend suggests. Steso nods:

"Yes," he says and adds, with a serious, almost offended, expression on his face: "Svend, is it true that you've got some coke?"

Hossein has driven down to Randers to scrape in some money he is owed; he left early in the morning to catch the man napping. Maria has to wait for him as her mother can't look after David today; and Hossein is taking a bit longer than they had expected. She calls Ulla in a last ditch attempt to persuade her to come to the funeral, but Ulla doesn't want to. She has never been very keen on Steso-Thomas.

"Lars has gone out," she says. Pusher Lars, her new boyfriend.

Hossein wasn't remotely interested in going. *"If you dead, then you dead. It don't help if you sit in the church,"* he said to Maria. It has got something to do with the war, so she doesn't want to press him.

Finally Hossein comes in through the door and takes charge of the little one. Maria jumps into their big Mercedes and speeds over to where she works – the flower shop in Kirkegårdsgade – to pick up the enormous laurel wreath she has made.

When she arrives at Sønderholm Church the doors are closed, the service has begun, and she can't bring herself to go in. She lifts the laurel wreath over her head and lets it rest on her shoulder so that it hangs diagonally across the upper part of her body. The air is cool and fresh – it smells of damp earth. On one of the churchyard pathways there are two trestles, and beyond them she can see the open grave; the edges covered with freshly cut spruce branches. She is standing there smoking a cigarette when a shiny beige Ford Mustang pulls up in front of the church; the chrome sparkles, vying with the sun's rays which skip over the paintwork – the colour so deep that the eye is drawn into it.

Pusher Lars jumps out dressed in the brand new suit Ulla bought for him yesterday. He looks flashy, but in a laid-back, stylish sort of way. He is followed by Adrian, who waves to Maria before squeezing himself back into the car and occupying the vacant seat next to the driver.

The car roars off as Lars trudges up towards the church.

"Maria, what's going on?" he says. Maria feels there is something not quite right about the way he looks. The teeth . . . they are white. So he got the dentures. She smiles at him, taps a fingernail on her own teeth and points at him.

"They look great," she says. He gives her a broad smile, the whiteness gleaming between his lips. "Isn't Adrian coming to the funeral?" Maria asks.

Lars turns his head in the direction of the rumbling sound from the car which is fading away in the distance. "No, he's playing in a soccer match in Nibe."

"But I thought . . . ," Maria begins, as she thought Adrian and Steso had been pretty good friends.

"Yes," Lars says with a gesture towards the church, "but some of the others and Adrian . . . it's not so good." She is about to ask who, why, but Lars looks distressed.

"Whose car was that?" she asks.

"Allan's," he says. Maria looks puzzled. "The guy with the burns, my dentist's brother-in-law," Lars adds.

"Oh, right," she says.

"Why are you standing here?" he asks.

"I've just arrived, but they'd already started."

"Aw, bloody hell," Lars says, looking at his watch and shaking his long, lanky body. He fishes out a cigarette, lights up, looks at her. "I shouldn't have had that joint," he says, gingerly rubbing one of his cheeks.

"That's the way it goes," she says, while thinking that the stumps of his own teeth must have been pulled yesterday. "What about . . . Tilly? Is she here?" Maria asks. She hasn't been able to get in touch with Tilly since Thomas died.

"No," Lars says, sceptically scrutinizing the treetops around the churchyard.

"But . . . ," Maria begins. Lars is silent. "Do you think . . . ," she begins again, but he cuts her off.

"Maria," he says. All of a sudden he seems tired. "Just over there," he points to the far side of the churchyard. "That's where Little Lars was laid to rest; he was very good friends with Tilly and Steso, and Lisbeth's boyfriend." Maria doesn't know who Little Lars is. Lars sighs: "Tilly had predicted his death, but no-one believed her."

"What did he die of?" Maria asks.

"A disturbance in the cosmic order," Lars says.

Maria stares at him in disbelief.

"Wasn't it a traffic accident?" she asks, as she has heard something about the driver being killed at the time Lisbeth had her leg crushed; maybe it was him.

"That was the effect. The cause was different," Lars says.

"What?"

"Forget about it, Maria."

"The cosmic order – do you believe in that sort of thing?" she asks.

"No, but Tilly does."

"What's that got to do with Steso's funeral?"

Lars shrugs his shoulders. "Tilly logic," he says. Maybe he can't talk about it without betraying a confidence, Maria thinks. She knows him quite well, but he always keeps her at an arm's length when it comes to the most intimate matters in his life.

"You know how she is," Lars says. "If God exists, then she curses him. At any rate she refuses to set her foot in His house, as it symbolises the subjugation of mankind."

"Seriously?" Maria asks.

"Tilly's words," Lars says. "I'm just the messenger." He gives a resigned laugh, then asks: "What about Hossein?" – clearly trying to change the subject.

"He's looking after David," she answers.

Lars walks up to her, smoke in mouth, bends his knees slightly and, cocking his head to one side, adjusts the position of the laurel wreath against the top part of her body. He takes a step backwards.

"You look like a speedway rider on the victory podium."

She smiles at him. Once he told her about how his dad used to take him to watch speedway when he was a boy.

"Go into the bends fast and ride faster still along the straights," Lars says, taking a couple of deep drags on his cigarette and then letting it fall onto the cobblestones in front of the church, where he grinds it out with the toe of his shoe, before saying: "Well, I'm bloody glad I'm not on my own. Let's go in and say goodbye to that little junkie asshole." He walks over towards the church door.

"We can't just traipse in when they've already started," Maria says.

"It's Steso we're burying, right?"

"Well, yes."

"He'll forgive us," Lars says, pushing open the door. They find themselves in a small anteroom where the congregation can leave their coats. The roar of the organ from inside the church can be heard clearly. Lars goes up and puts his hand on the door handle, ready to open the door into the interior of the church. She considers whether it is blasphemous to be late. She takes her place by his side.

"Just walk straight up to the coffin and place the wreath on the floor in front of it so that it leans up against the pedestal," he says. "I'll be right by your side." Lars opens the door, and now they can also hear the singing from the few people who are sitting grouped together in the pews at the front of the church. Maria notices Svend and Michael – she has had both of them. Lars leads her up the aisle, lightly pressing the lower part of her back with his hand. Her heart is pounding, the organ is roaring, heads turn, the priest stares, motionless. Lars begins to cough. You can hear the viscous mucus moving in his throat. They reach the coffin and she lifts the laurel wreath off her shoulder and leans it up against the pedestal the coffin is placed on – crouches down and adjusts the broad red silk ribbons with the message printed in gold letters: *Have a good trip, Steso. All our love, Maria, Hossein and David.*

Steso, she thinks, I'm going to miss you; you were arrogant, but at the same time you were honest in a way, too, and you were always good fun.

Maria rises to her feet. At that very same moment everyone else stands up. What is happening? She looks around, can feel her cheeks flushing. She walks over and stands next to Svend who gives her a solemn nod. It is a couple of years since she has seen him. He seems to have aged – the lines in his face are more pronounced.

The boys wanted to go to Østre Anlæg Park to play soccer – the girls went with them. They walked along Østerbro so that Tilly could see the tall Nordkraft chimney again; it hadn't been painted over. BÜLD it said, up at the top in large, white capital letters. She was so proud of Thomas. Together with Sigurt – the drummer in BÜLD – he had climbed over the fence and up the chimney with a bucket of paint, a stick, a paintbrush, and a roll of duct tape. They had taped the brush to the stick and taken it in turns to lean out over the edge. But Aalborg Stiftstidende *had not written a word about it even though Lisbeth had tipped them off anonymously.*

After the soccer game they go over to their squat in Kjellerupsgade and the boys light a bonfire in the yard. Pusher Lars is there and Axel, the one who is good at collecting mushrooms. Lisbeth and Little Lars have gone into one of the empty flats for a kiss and cuddle. Thomas has brought his rat along, and has managed to lay his hands on a bottle of Red Aalborg akvavit. He is in the middle of explaining about Martinus, the peasant's son from the Vendsyssel area who had a divine revelation: "There are the PLEASANT blessings and the UNPLEASANT blessings. The unpleasant ones are ALSO blessings because we can LEARN from them. And EVERYTHING is VERY GOOD."

At first Tilly thinks it is Little Lars walking into the yard, but . . . it is his doppelgänger. All of a sudden she turns cold, shivers, breaks out in a sweat. She quickly looks about her to see whether Little Lars is nearby. Because it is really dangerous if you happen to meet your doppelgänger; it can cause disturbances in the cosmos. But Little Lars is inside the house.

"Have you seen the paper today?" the Little Lars look-alike asks, pulling the Stiftstidende *out of his back pocket. Thomas snatches it out of his hands. There is nothing on the front page. Thomas quickly thumbs through the other pages. A paragraph relegated to page eighteen, alongside details of the Sunday for the Elderly event in Nørresundby, the water temperature in Aalborg Open-Air Swimming Pool and the boy scouts' waste paper collection. There is a small picture of the tip of the Nordkraft tower and the following article:*

DAREDEVIL PRANKSTERS

Graffiti vandals with a good head for heights have expressed their frank opinion about Nordkraft. They painted "Yuk" across the top of the tall chimney, 150 metres above the ground. On the opposite side they daubed another word, one which is alien to the Danish language: "Büld." Unless it is a misspelling. This has been the subject of a great deal of conjecture, as indeed has been the identity of the intrepid culprits. Their names are not known to the management of the power company either, as no note or

> any other form of visiting card was left . . . . One thing is clear, though: the pranksters were extremely single-minded since access to the top of the chimney can only be gained by means of a vertical steel ladder between the inner smoke duct and the outer concrete wall. There are at least 600 steps or a 20-minute climb up to the platform at the very top. And that means a 150 metre drop when you stretch out to wield the spray can. As a rule the door to the chimney is kept locked, but there has been an opening a little higher up in the tower during the ongoing construction work. The electricity station has taken steps to prevent a recurrence of this kind of caper, but does not wish to reveal the nature of these measures.

"That's Aalborg to a TEE," Thomas shouts. "Even the idiots working for the local rag don't know that the town's most VISIONARY band is called BÜLD." There are posters all over the town announcing their next concert at 1000Fryd. "Tilly," he says, "we just HAVE to go down and listen to them."

The doppelgänger asks where Sigurt is.

"He's up in his flat," Axel says, "on mushrooms." The doppelgänger disappears through one of the entrances to the flats, and Tilly is afraid that it is the same entrance Lisbeth and Little Lars used. He may bump into them. She tugs at Thomas' arm.

"You've got to do something," she says. That was Little Lars's doppelgänger." Thomas takes her hand and gives it a squeeze.

"That's just superstition, Tilly."

"No, it's not," she says. A little later the guy emerges from the entrance to the flats again and sits down by the fire.

"We'll have to get away from here," Tilly says to Thomas. But he says they should wait, and at that moment Lisbeth comes out into the yard – she is drunk, and smiling. Tilly looks at the doppelgänger. It is dangerous for Lisbeth, too. Then Tilly notices Little Lars standing in the darkness some distance away from the fire, staring at the guy as if transfixed. She makes eye contact with Little Lars, and waves her hand to warn him to leave. He nods – using a kind of sign language, he explains that he is going to fetch a car. He disappears.

"We should try to . . . put out the fire somehow before we . . . go," Tilly says. The situation is completely out of control. Lisbeth grins at the doppelgänger as she

hitches up her skirt and straddles the glowing embers – then she unleashes a broad stream of piss. She isn't wearing any underpants.

"Lisbeth," Tilly says, trying to keep her eyes off the Little Lars look-alike. "You pee like a horse."

Lisbeth tries to focus on the guy standing in the gloom.

"Lars?" she says.

"No, my name's Adrian."

"Are you sure?" Lisbeth asks.

"You can call me Lars if you like, beautiful," he says.

Pusher Lars looks up: "What's up?" he asks.

"Where's Lars gone?" Lisbeth says.

"Little . . . ?"

"Yes, my Lars." Lisbeth is confused.

Axel says: "He's gone to look for a car so you lot can get home." Axel must have seen him leave.

"Watch out your pussy doesn't catch fire," the doppelgänger says to Lisbeth. She laughs.

"My pussy already IS on fire," she says.

Luckily just at that moment a car out in the street hoots its horn. It is Little Lars who is ready to drive them home to Sønderholm, and Tilly hurriedly gathers the others together before disaster strikes.

The week after, they go to the BÜLD concert at 1000Fryd. Tilly and Thomas talk to Sigurt, the drummer. He tells them that he was close to being thrown out of the band because the bass player went paranoid – he was afraid that the Stiftstidende *hadn't written anything about the band in the article because of an agreement the paper had with the police not to mention them, and then the police would storm in during the concert and arrest the lot of them up on the stage.*

The concert begins. Tilly is standing next to Little Lars. "Bloody hell," he says, staring over towards the bar, a scared look in his eyes. It's the doppelgänger.

"Get out of here quick," Tilly says, and he pushes people aside, runs out of the door – he knows how dangerous it is.

They talk about it the following day, Tilly and Little Lars.

"It's a bad omen," he says. He has seen his doppelgänger twice now. Where will the misfortune strike? They are both agreed that he should keep away from

Kjellerupsgade, keep away from 1000Fryd. Stay at home as much as possible until they can come up with a solution.

But it didn't help. Two months later Little Lars smashed up his car, with Lisbeth in the passenger seat.

Everyone is looking at Steso's single room lodging. Pusher Lars nods to people as if he knows what he is doing, even though he has no idea what is going to happen next. It is a pity the coffin is closed, he thinks. Steso is without a doubt a fine-looking corpse – he was embalmed internally even before he died.

Pusher Lars catches sight of Svend. Maria has gone over to stand by his side. Svend gives him a smile, but looks defiant. Lars hopes things will work out smoothly today. It is important.

Then a couple of people advance towards the coffin. Okay, now it is time to do the carrying. Steso's father, Arne, moves towards one of the handles at the front; Lars has met him a number of times. Opposite him – on the other side of the coffin – is Steso's little sister, Rikke, and behind them comes a man Lars takes to be Arne's brother and two others who must be Steso's mother's brother and sister. Apparently none of Steso's cousins are present at the funeral. There is still an unclaimed handle at the back of the coffin. The organ starts up again. Steso's father looks across at the congregation; Lisbeth is ruled out because of her leg, and the others are embarrassed and look down at the ground. They don't seem to be aware of the problem, so Lars gives Steso's father a nod and makes his way towards the handle. He would be only too happy to help bear Steso's corpse to its final resting place; the soul has slipped off – he's sure of that. In a way he believes that it lives on inside himself and the others, whether they like it or not – Steso was too much of a little turd to let go just like that.

The six pallbearers look at one another.

"Are we ready?" Steso's father murmurs. They nod to him in response. "Right . . . lift," he says, and they all heave together. A verger opens the doors to the outside. Their progress is like a Santa Lucia procession through treacle. Lars wonders whether he is at the head end or by the feet – he doesn't know which way round they place these coffins in the church. They leave the smell of whitewash, the swell of the organ behind them. The sun shines down on them, birds sing, the fragrance of earth and vegetation washes in over them, even though the trees are still leafless; the gravel crunches under their feet.

Lars glances behind him when he hears Svend's voice. Svend is talking a little too loudly:

"They ought to have cremated him, really," he says to Michael – together with Louise they bring up the rear of the cortege of mourners following behind the coffin.

"Why?" Michael asks under his breath. Svend makes a sweeping arm movement to encompass the churchyard, and says:

"If archaeologists do some excavating here in a hundred years' time . . . what are they going to think?"

Steso starts to become surprisingly heavy. When he was alive he was no more than a skeleton, skin and bone; now he weighs a lot more than a living person. A dead weight.

The priest comes to a halt. The bearers lift the coffin over the two trestles which have been placed in the middle of the pathway, and lower it. It must have happened that someone dropped a coffin and the body rolled out, Lars thinks – otherwise they wouldn't have introduced this arrangement. Nobody says anything, and they feel a little awkward when they change sides – like when the music has stopped during a chaotic game of musical chairs. There was no prior instruction for this event, of course, or maybe it was just that Lars missed out on it. He passes Lisbeth and Steso's mother, Bodil, as he walks round the rear of the coffin. Lisbeth looks him straight in the eyes. He looks at her – looks at Svend. He knows they love each other. They know it, too – Lars is sure of that. Resumes the walk in the direction of the hole – everyone is completely silent. The grave has been dug. There is no frost in the ground – wonder what they do when there is? Do they light fires on the ground – use gas burners to thaw it out? Hack their way through the crust? Freshly cut spruce along the edges and over the pile of excavated soil. Probably so you don't see the old bones. They lower the coffin onto the two boards that have been placed diagonally across the pit. Coils of good, stout rope at the ready. Lars is absolutely desperate for a joint. On an ordinary day he wouldn't even have got up yet.

In his inner eye he sees Steso impatiently hopping up and down next to the priest: "*What are we WAITING for, you fisher of souls*?" Steso complains as he points down into the pit; "*I have to be on my WAY.*"

Calm down, Steso, we'll soon have you six feet under. You know that crazy grandmother of mine, the one I told you about? She feeds my granddad. *I've just been out to the cemetery,* she says when I call her; *He says to say hello.* She goes out there with another crazy woman. *I had some dry bread,* she says. They bury the bread 30 centimetres down in the ground; *Just a little piece – so they can reach it from down below.* And on Sundays, Steso, they put salami on it: *Our menfolk need to be spoiled once in a while, too,* she says. I'll call by and bring you a little something one day.

Lars eyes the others. Maria winks at him. Being a mother has turned her into an incredibly good-looking woman.

Each of the bearers takes a coil of rope which they thread through their handle so that they will be able to lower the coffin down into the hole. Steso's father goes over and adjusts Rikke's rope while quietly explaining to her how it should be done; if you haven't allowed yourself enough rope to reach the bottom, you can come a cropper at the edge of the grave, you can fall in – yes, you can.

Rikke nods, Lars sees her lustrous, glazed eyes, the red marks on her pallid neck.

Inside his head he is talking to Steso: I'm pleased to be here, he says. And I have to say hello from Adrian; he'll drop by later on, but, you know . . . all that stuff with Lisbeth and Little Lars, yes, and Svend, too. Adrian didn't want to roll up and complicate the situation further; he feels like a necrophilia victim every time he sees her.

Using the ropes, they raise the coffin slightly, and the sexton removes the two boards it rested on. Then they begin to lower it. Keep hold of one end of the rope with the left hand, and release with the right – it is difficult.

Michael, Louise and Svend concentrate on their footing during the lowering. Lisbeth has her arms around Bodil. They are crying. Steso is laid to rest by the side of his grandparents – Arne's parents. *1994* is the highest figure on the new stone; it occurs to Lars that really it ought to have been have been about . . . 2040. Then the priest says something. Earth is sprinkled on the coffin. Earth to earth.

Afterwards Arne comes up to Steso's old friends as they are walking over to the parking lot.

"You're coming over for coffee, folks, aren't you," he asks, without directing his question to anyone in particular. Svend is standing with his back to him, lights a cigarette and . . . rubs his eyes. Lars feels awkward about talking to Arne, who is well aware that Lars is a pusher.

"We'll be there," Lars answers.

Arne nods. "Good," is all he says in reply. Lars looks at him and is filled with awe. The day after his son's death he managed to trace them – Steso's old friends. In the midst of his grief he rang round, all the while being unable to keep the thought out of his mind that it might have been *his* fault. Even so he has seen to it that his son has been given a dignified funeral, surrounded by people who were fond of him – and knew he was a good guy.

Lisbeth takes her leave of Bodil and Rikke. She stops and looks back at the grave. Steso is dead. Little Lars died many years ago. Now only Lisbeth and Tilly are left of the crowd from Sønderholm.

Lars's thoughts turn to the time when Little Lars took him with him on a joyride in a stolen Morris Mini. He overtook cars on the inside using the cycle paths – his robust frame bent over the steering wheel. Adrian's build is the same – there is even a certain likeness in the face.

Svend has stopped. He looks at Lisbeth, a lump of cartilage working in his jaw. Then Lisbeth walks away from the grave.

"the expendables" *were signed up for a small tour of Germany as the warm-up act for an English punk band. Steso-Thomas went over to see Lisbeth in Nørresundby and asked whether it wouldn't be possible for them to take Loser along as their driver. "And you have to call him Valentin – that's his name now."*

"Isn't he a bit too pathetic to have in tow?" Adrian asks. But he agrees to it because in this way he gets out of having to do the driving with a crashing hangover every day. And Loser has changed. Off drugs. Weird.

"I'll put on a stage show if it's okay with you," he says on the first day.

"Yes, sure," says Korzeniowski, the guitarist. And that afternoon Loser – or Valentin – disappears for a couple of hours.

When the concert starts he is sitting stock-still on a chair behind a small table he has placed on the stage; one of his arms is resting on the tabletop. After a while he picks up a crowbar from the floor and begins pummelling his arm until some red fluid squirts through the torn material. His face is completely expressionless as sections of the audience start screaming and others are stunned. It is an artificial limb which he had bought at a second-hand shop and taped plastic bags filled with ketchup to under the sleeve.

A few days later Steso-Thomas arrives via a pensioners' bus tour to Flensburg where he deserted and jumped on a train to meet up with the band in Hamburg. Thomas and Valentin are extremely secretive – the members of the band are completely in the dark. When the concert begins, Valentin is lying stretched out on a table on the stage, and at one point during the concert Thomas comes up and stands next to Valentin. He draws a flick-knife out of his pocket, flicks out the blade and slits open Valentin's belly through his T-shirt – from his abdomen to his solar plexus. Strings of pale butchers' sausages covered in ketchup come pouring out; they have packed them into a plastic bag on Valentin's stomach together with lots of small pieces of white bread to make a thick, porridge-like mush. The band is so stupefied that they stop playing. The rattle from Valentin's throat is clearly audible as Thomas, using both hands, begins to dig ketchup-smeared sausages out of Valentin's belly and stuffs them into his own mouth while grinning like a maniac at the audience who are horror-struck. An ashen-faced Nazi punk just stands there, rooted to the spot. After a while Thomas throws the lifeless Valentin over his shoulder and staggers out of the hall, shaking under the weight, a string of the ketchup-besmattered sausages trailing along after them. In the dressing room Lisbeth sees Valentin happily smiling for the first time . . . ever, in fact. Thomas has already dashed off into town to check out the local drugs scene. After Thomas has returned to Denmark, Valentin commits harakiri on stage; two kilos of raw herrings spew out of him. He kneels down and picks up the herrings one by one, takes a handful of mayonnaise out of one of the plastic bags he has ready in his trouser pocket, slaps mayonnaise on each fish carcass and hurls it out into the audience.

"It's pure therapy," he says, after Adrian has saved him from being beaten up and they are sitting getting drunk in the dressing room.

Lisbeth gets on well with Adrian . . . while they are on tour; but when they get back to Aalborg everything begins to go wrong again. Adrian calls her a ghost. He demands some answers, and she has a mental block; she is afraid. Adrian has become good friends with Pusher Lars, who asks her to sort out the problem.

"Tell him and see what happens," Lars says.

"No," Lisbeth says.

"Go on, do it. Or else I will."

She begs him not to. Pusher Lars is adamant. Lisbeth is helpless. It is impossible for her to tell Adrian anything. She just waits, until one day he comes in through the door, grey in the face, walks up to her, holds out his hand and says:

"Hello, my name's Adrian, I love you. Little Lars is dead." Lisbeth doesn't know what to say – there is nothing she can say. She is numb. He stands looking at her.

For a long time. Slowly shakes his head. "All this reminds me of a bad Nick Cave song," he says, turns on his heel and goes into the kitchen.

She goes into the bedroom and packs Adrian's things into two bags. Turns the washing basket upside down and picks out his clothes – puts them into a separate plastic bag so they don't soil the rest of his clothes. The snot pours out of her nose. All her movements are as if in a fever. She carries the bags out into the hallway. Adrian is sitting at the small table in the kitchen. He turns his head. Lisbeth sees him, her vision blurred by the water gathering in her eyes . . . Little Lars . . . his doppelgänger, Adrian. "Sorry," she says. To both of them.

"Okay – I'll go, then," Tilly says to herself in her parents' living room and gets up from the armchair. Because she reckons that they have . . . that they have FINISHED by now.

"What was that you said, dear?" her mother shouts from the kitchen. Tilly goes in to talk to her.

"Bye, Mum," she says, giving her mother a hug, and kissing her on the cheek.

"Now don't you be . . . ," her mother says, looking worried: "Don't you be getting too upset about it, will you now, Tilly?"

"No, no, Mum – I'll be all right," she promises.

It is not because . . . She walks towards the church. She just doesn't want to SEE it. In the coffin, all pale and cold, and he is no fun any more. He can't do what he used to do then . . . can't do anything at all now. Back then when they became friends – I mean, it was a secret, wasn't it? In the old trucks round at the back of the haulage contractor's, when they were in the fifth grade, then she didn't mind him looking at hers, and he didn't mind her having a look at his, as long as they didn't tell anyone. Just looking. And maybe a bit of kissing, but not with the tongue. Or only a little bit. Now he is just ROTTING. And Tilly is looking forward to seeing Svend. It is a long time since she has seen Svend – he is a good guy, too. Hopefully Bertrand will stay well away today, she thinks. It is a drag when Bertrand is there, and it puts Svend in a bad mood, too.

There is the church; they haven't finished yet. Tilly leans against Svend's car. It is the same one he had when he visited her last autumn. They drove up to Rubjerg Knude, north of Løkken, where they jumped down off the dunes and slid to the bottom. That was fun. They got sand in their pants, and it itched. They went for a swim, too, even though the water was freezing cold.

The coffin is already in the ground. So they'll soon be finished. Tilly can see Rikke. It is such a shame for her because Thomas was going to go to her wedding in two weeks' time; Tilly is going, too. Rikke cried so much yesterday when Tilly was over visiting the family, and so did she. And the guy who is Rikke's husband-to-be couldn't come to the funeral as he travels round repairing photocopiers for rich companies in the Persian Gulf. And Bodil – it is quite impossible for Tilly to say hello to her today because . . . it . . . she is completely crushed inside.

Now Maria comes walking down towards the parking lot. She is walking quickly, jingling the keys to the great big car that guy called Hossein bought for them. She spots Tilly and changes direction. She comes up and gives Tilly a big hug, kissing her on both cheeks.

"We're going to miss him," Maria says. She holds Tilly close.

"Yes," Tilly says.

"I have to go home and look after David now, but I'll see you soon," Maria says.

"Yes."

Maria kisses her once again, lets go and walks over to the large car. It is a Mercedes Benz, just like in the song.

Now Lisbeth comes along. She is crying, and Louise is walking by her side. Tilly rushes up to Lisbeth. That starts Tilly off crying, too, but then Svend and Pusher Lars come by, and Michael, who goes over to Louise. Svend and Lars come over and put their arms around Tillly and Lisbeth. Tilly cries a bit more, and it is as if everybody is looking at each other in a slightly strange way; and that is not how she wants it to be today. Pusher Lars smiles to her and shrugs his shoulders. He has such fine-looking teeth now, and he puts on a pair of big old reflective sunglasses with the word HONDA written across each lens. Then they all have a cigarette. Tilly can see that Michael is about to spit on the ground. Then he remembers that Thomas is lying down there – that is something you always have to bear in mind now. Louise is standing next to Svend.

"What are you up to these days, Svend?" she asks. Tilly feels that it is sort of strange for her to ask him that. Really, she doesn't know him all that well. He tells her that he has been fired from the job he had at the market gardener's. Tilly already knows that, as he sometimes gives her a call. The girl he was living with has thrown him out, too. She must be out of her mind, but then she was a bit weird, Tilly thought; that time she met her, it was as if she felt she was better than everyone else, even though Tilly could see straightaway that she wasn't a very nice person. And it was Tilly who knew where Svend was when they needed to tell him that . . . well, that Thomas . . . had died.

"They almost went bust after that truck blockade at the border. They lost close on a million on withered plants," Svend explains to Louise, in simple terms so that she can follow what he is talking about. "You know how it works: last in – first out," he adds.

"Aren't there any other jobs going?" Louise asks. Tilly suspects that Svend thinks it is a funny question to ask since he kicks the ground before replying: "Christmas trees. Only Christmas trees. For the Germans. Tending little Christmas trees until they're ready for planting out . . . I just wasn't prepared to do that."

Tilly goes over, holds him and says: "Svend, you're a little Christmas elf." She starts giggling.

Pusher Lars comes up. "Let's get going," he says.

Tilly wants to be with Lisbeth in her car because Lisbeth is just such good fun when she is behind the wheel. Louise can come with them and all the boys can be together in Svend's car. Tilly would like to go with Svend, too, but perhaps there is something he has to say to those boys. Just so that everything is alright.

"Can I have a drag on that joint?" says a voice, and Maria lifts her eyes from the flagstones on John F. Kennedy Plads. There he stands – the maniacal eyes hidden by a pair of Ray-Bans. That man can smell a joint a mile away. Maria holds it out to him. He spits on the flagstones then raises the joint to his lips.

"Hi, Steso," she murmurs. Half an hour has passed since she slung her belongings into a hold-all and a garbage bag and fled from her pusher boyfriend, Asger, before he got home. It is a really shitty day; in fact it is the shittiest day in all her hopeless life. Here she is sitting on the steps in front of the railway station, smoking herself silly on pot and having to choose between moving in with her overprotective mother, travelling out to her alcoholic father's or going down on her knees to a dishy but shady Iranian war refugee who carries a gun and wants her.

"Have you walked out on that idiot?" Steso asks, blowing out smoke and spitting again.

"Yep."

"Wise move." Steso takes another drag and hands the joint back to Maria. She wonders what the last thing was he had had between his lips. They are very close to the bus station and she knows he works as a rent boy to buy drugs. In her mind's eye she can see Steso now, down on his knees, working, while his fingers pick their way through the trousers hanging round the man's knees until he is able to pull the wallet out of the victim's back pocket and extract the prize.

"Where do you live, Steso?"

"Round about," he answers.

Maria is in no doubt that she will have to go and stay with her father, but she also knows that she will go spare out there with him. I mean, what is there to do in Store Ajstrup and district? She has got hardly any money and assumes that her social benefit will have been stopped because she has skived so much from the adult education college she has to attend.

"I don't suppose you know anyone who's got a room to rent?" she asks.

"Tilly," he answers. Maria looks up at him to see whether he is pulling her leg.

"Yellow Tilly?" she asks.

"That's her."

"Has she got a room to rent?"

"Flat – to rent out," he elaborates before answering the question on her face: "She's going on a course at a folk high school.

"What . . . does she want to do that for?" Maria asks. The joint – the whole day in fact – has made her paranoid.

"The social security people don't know what else to do with her," Steso says. "She is completely beyond the boundaries of their experience." Maria has never met Tilly. She just knows that Tilly is good friends with Svend and Pusher Lars.

"Where . . . did you get to know her?" she asks.

"Primary school. We love each other, Tilly and I do."

"You've certainly got a funny way of showing it," Maria says. Steso gives her a look of indifference.

"I'm a freebooter – like the great majority of men; only I don't try to hide it."

"And what are we girls, then?"

"Bounty hunters, but you do everything you can to hide the fact."

"Then why do you want to help me now?"

Steso clicks his tongue: "Tut, tut. A bounty hunter is one of the most PATHETIC things on the planet – should be shot down like mangy curs."

"Shot . . . ? Why do you say that? Curs?" Maria asks nervously. This afternoon she saw two Rottweilers being shot because their owner – Asger, now her ex-boyfriend – didn't want to keep dogs that were addicted to THC. Junkie dogs. He was the one who had decided to call them Twister and Tripper. There was no logic to it.

"Believe me, I'm only helping you because there is something in it for me, too," Steso continues.

"But why aren't you going to live there when she's away?" Maria asks.

"Tilly is sweet, good-natured, innocent, confused, cosmic, occasionally phobic, prone to anxiety, neurotic; but she isn't stupid enough to let me stay in her flat," Steso says.

"Where does she live?"

"Dalgasgade."

"Can we . . . give her a call?"

"She's at home – in any case she will need to see you to be able to decide about you," Steso says. Maria gets to her feet and lifts the bag up onto her shoulder. "Got another joint?" Steso asks. She gives him one, which he lights with a smart Ronson lighter and sticks between his narrow lips – then he plunges his hands in his trouser pockets and sets off walking.

"Steso," she says. He turns round, a quizzical look on his face. Maria nods down towards her crammed full garbage bag. He gives her a wry smile.

"Maria, I'm not your lackey," he says, and saunters off.

They take a taxi at Maria's expense. And she is adopted on the spot. Tilly serves them a meal of vegetable soup, boiled spring cabbage, whole meal bread and beetroot salad. For dessert they have coconut-topped chocolate snowballs and herbal tea. Afterwards Maria does Tilly's hair, and Tilly gives Steso a haircut and two hundred kroner before kicking him out. "Otherwise he'll be stealing things." Then she lets Maria sleep on the sofa, and the following day Maria starts to look for a job.

Michael's girlfriend, Louise, was in hospital with galloping anorexia, so Svend and Steso went to pay him a visit. They took him with them to the chalk quarry in Hasseris, where the excavators had once hit a pocket of groundwater with the result that the whole crater was filled with fresh water. That was before the algae arrived; all the punks and hippies still went out there in the summer to swim even though the local council was not in favour and refused to lay out a decent beach. The well-to-do inhabitants of Hasseris complained about the human scum that was invading their area, lighting bonfires, smoking joints, getting drunk. They were afraid that their offspring would see the light.

Svend has an axe and a hand saw with him and they walk some way through the bushes on the eastern side of the quarry before Svend sets to work clearing a piece of ground right down by the waterside. He wants to create a spot where he can lie down and enjoy the afternoon sun. Michael and Steso have swum out to the raft and are now lying on it. The sweat runs off Svend's body as he chops through the roots of the bushes with his hand axe.

"Hi, man." It is Lisbeth. She is standing behind him – a bit higher up the slope; it is impossible to know how long she has been watching him. A piece of cloth wrapped round her hips, an open blouse over her swimming costume.

"Lisbeth," he says, looking behind her to see whether Adrian is with her. She is alone. She comes down and runs two fingers down Svend's upper arm, then shakes her hand to flick the sweat off her fingertips.

"I think you need a good cooling off, Svend."

"You can say that again," he thinks as she loosens the cloth around her hips and hangs it on a branch. She walks out into the water, her long legs glistening, and lazily swims out towards the raft. Svend puts down the axe and follows her into the water. She is just in front of him. He could sink his teeth into her as she heaves herself up onto the raft, and he catches sight of the delicate blonde down on her buttocks.

They throw Steso in the water, dive in head first, race each other. Svend is longing to ask where Adrian is. Is he off the scene? But he doesn't want to break the magic spell.

"It's about time we had a joint," Steso says and they swim in to the little beach that Svend has cleared. The sun beats down. Lisbeth swims around close to the shore while Michael sits there silently, wearing sunglasses and swathed in his towel. The situation isn't easy for him

Svend sets about rolling the joint.

"Thomas, you'd better put your shirt on," Lisbeth says – she and Tilly always call him by his official name. Steso is as pale as a corpse.

"What for?" he asks, adopting a bodybuilder pose and tensing his sinews – his muscles are non-existent. "How do you LIKE my GORGEOUS body?" he asks, admiring his protruding veins with a self-satisfied air.

Getting out of the water, Lisbeth smiles at him in a motherly fashion. "You're going to get burned, Thomas," she says.

"Oh, alright," he says and starts to pull his shirt on.

Lisbeth is standing at the water's edge, running her palms down over her arms and legs to remove the drops of water so that her skin will dry faster. Svend has to force himself to look away.

"How's it going?" she asks Michael. He is sitting quite motionless – seems absent-minded, probably because the sunglasses are shielding his eyes.

"39 kilos," he answers.

"But you're hanging on?" Lisbeth asks.

"Yes, I love her," he replies without any emotion in his voice. Steso looks over at Michael and says:

"Even though there's not much to hang on to."

"Thomas!" Lisbeth raps, adding: "I think you're doing really well, Michael. How . . . is she?"

"She is in a black hole," Michael answers.

"Yes, women shouldn't get too thin – their good humour is lodged in their fatty tissue," Steso says.

"That's not inconceivable," Michael says dryly. "She's certainly lost hers, that's for certain."

"Body fascism," Steso says. Nobody speaks. The tobacco rustles in the roll-up paper. Insects buzz.

"But if we just forget about the fact that overdoing it can be fatal . . . is it so . . . attractive? When a girl's very thin?" Lisbeth asks.

"Actually she was a bit on the fat side when I first met her, and then she began to look better and better until she started burning up her muscle tissue," Michael says.

"And now she's just as thin as I am," Steso says. "A control freak who is going to snuff it as a result of an OVERDOSE of slimming."

Michael jumps to his feet. Svend gets up and holds out an arm to stop him. Lisbeth moves a step closer behind Steso, who is standing at the waterside with a smirk on his face. She pushes him over so that he lands on his backside in the water. He sits up, spluttering but still smirking, until his jaw drops and his eyes widen. "HEY," he shouts, frantically rummaging in his drenched shirt pocket. "My pills are all wet."

Michael smiles sardonically. Lisbeth sits down next to Svend.

"Got a ciggy?" she asks.

"Course," he answers, passing her one and lighting it for her. He hands the joint to Michael. They smoke in silence. Steso is picking out saturated fragments of the pills from his shirt pocket, all the while cursing under his breath and licking his fingers, a look of pure disgust on his face. The sun shines down on them. Svend is sitting at Lisbeth's side. That is the way he wants it. Then they hear a splashing sound from the opposite side of the chalk quarry. They all look over to where it comes from. A figure is swimming front crawl at high speed directly towards them. Svend swallows, suddenly feels cold inside.

"Oh, that must be him," Lisbeth says, squinting into the sunlight. She gets up and shields her eyes with her hand. The figure veers off and swims over to the raft. The powerful, V-shaped torso as he hoists his stumpy body out of the water. Silhouetted against the light, he is a spitting image of Little Lars.

"Aren't you coming over?" Adrian cries. Lisbeth glances round at the others. Maybe it is just something Svend imagines, but he thinks she seems embarrassed.

"I'm going to join him," she murmurs, setting off. Adrian pushes off from the raft, does a forward flip, and hits the water like a bombshell. Svend takes the joint out of Steso's hand, inhales deeply twice, hands it back, bends down to pick up his tools and begins to make his way up the slope.

"Svend?" Michael calls after him.

"Aw, sod it!" Steso says.

Svend has had enough.

"Music," Pusher Lars shouts from the back seat as soon as Svend has started the engine. He turns on the cassette player: *Candy, Candy, Candy – I can't let you go . . .* Iggy Pop.

"Rock freak," Michael comments, his face turned towards Svend.

"Always will be." Svend nods.

The back seat is great, thinks Lars. Then he isn't drawn into their sparring match. This is what always happens, and this time Svend has been away for . . . well, quite some time. So it is unavoidable, even though Lars knows that they are good friends. They know, too, but all the same the shindig begins as soon as they have turned into Nibevej and Svend is heading in the direction of Aalborg.

"How's it going with you?" Michael begins. Svend heaves a sigh which Lars hears over the music.

"Don't ask," Svend replies.

"So things aren't going so well, then?"

"No," Svend answers without elaborating. He doesn't want to go into it.

"Why's that?" Michael refuses to let the matter drop. Meanwhile Lars is sitting in the back seat humming to Iggy. Michael has heard from Tilly that Svend has lost his job, has broken up with his girlfriend and is now crashing on an ex-workmate's sofa in Ballerup; he can understand all too well that Svend doesn't want to talk about it. Svend answers without taking his eyes off the road:

"That's the reason why you should never admit that things are going badly." He looks over at Michael: "People react by being slightly concerned and then they always ask why."

"Of course," Michael affirms. "Why?" he asks again.

"Things are just not working out. Life is . . . – Svend searches for the right word – rotten." In the back seat Lars nods quietly – there is no more to be said.

"But what about Copenhagen, that's a great place to be, isn't it?" Michael continues.

"I'm moving," Svend says.

"Where to?" Michael asks. Lars pricks up his ears; he would like to know that, too . . . .

"Back here."

Lars raises his eyebrows.

"How come? I thought you liked it there," Michael says.

"Copenhagen or Aalborg . . . ," Svend begins. "Yes, alright, Copenhagen isn't Aalborg, it's a different place. That's the only positive thing you can say about Copenhagen. Otherwise there's not a lot in it."

"Really? I thought you'd made lots of friends over there," Michael says.

"I have, but we're not . . . friends any more. We're . . . spectators. Spectators viewing each other's lives. That's the way it is," Svend says. Lars can hear that Svend has been giving it some thought. This is not how he usually talks. Lars feels sure that Svend often thinks like that, but usually he doesn't come out with it.

"I don't follow. Spectators? What's that supposed to mean?" Michael asks.

"Basically it means that we've all become acquaintances instead of being friends."

You hit the nail on the head there, Lars thinks. That is what has happened. Steso was once your friend, but today you have buried an acquaintance. You held out for a long time, Svend, but in the end you came unstuck, too. Michael continues:

"But how . . . sort of . . . I mean . . . Is it because you don't see each other any more?" Michael looks at Svend, who keeps his eyes on the road though there is only light traffic.

"Oh, yes, we see each other often enough – idiomatically speaking, as it were – but we don't *see* each other."

This is not very inspiring, Lars thinks. He lights a cigarette and leans his head right back so that he can look up at the sky through the rear window. Bluish-grey with static, dirty clouds. The sun has vanished. Strange to see fields again. He can also see something gleaming over to the left. Must be the fjord. He lets his tongue run over his dentures – strange that the others didn't notice. Oh well, that is for them to figure out. It suits Lars fine that his teeth were white at Steso's burial – it marks a kind of . . . change, transition. He hopes.

"Isn't it because you fucked up? Don't you think that's the reason?" Michael asks.

"Fucked what up?" Svend retorts.

"Your life?" Michael suggests. Lars leans forward from the back and blows smoke rings in between them. The rings are so tightly formed that they don't disperse until they meet the dashboard.

"No," Svend replies in a calmer tone – the questions are not as specific as he had feared. Michael is not in a position to ask him that kind of question; neither is Lars.

"You don't think you did, or you didn't?" Michael asks.

"What?" A slight element of irritation is working its way into Svend's voice.

"Because you fucked up your life or because it is fucked up?" Michael says.

"All amounts to the same thing, doesn't it?" Svend asks.

"Not by my reckoning," Michael says, shaking his head.

"To me it does," Svend insists, his voice back to normal. "All the rest is splitting hairs."

"So you're sure what you say is right. You haven't fucked it up."

"Yes. That's what I think – it's the same thing. I know, I'm sure," Svend says.

"But . . . ," Michael gets no further.

"Just shut it," Svend cuts in, a tired smile on his face. "Course I've fucked up my life, who the hell else could have done it? But does it really matter, now that it's happened? Come on now, does it?"

Svend drives fast, he drives well. They are already in Skalborg, and he turns into Letvadvej by Skalborglund old people's home. Now there is no getting out of it; they are going to drop by.

"So you regret some of the things you've done?" Michael asks and adds a "Sorry" because he can hear how pathetic he sounds.

"I regret . . . everything," Svend replies, surprised at his own words.

"You aren't in one of your better moods at the moment, are you? You almost sound as if you're a bit . . ." Michael says.

"Well, maybe not everything, but it's like there are . . . patterns. Tramping around in a fucking maze – what's the point?" Svend asks.

"You'll peg it at some point," Lars pipes up from the back seat. Svend turns his head and smiles at him.

"Yes, Lars, that's what I console myself with.

"Maybe you'd like to go the same way as that junkie did we planted today?" Michael asks, suddenly adopting a hostile tone.

"Don't speak ill of the dead," Svend says.

"Look – he was your friend. You're the one who loved him." Michael sounds like a pedagogue, and as if he is leading on points.

"Yes, as a person," Svend says, "but he had nothing going for him."

They drive along Skelagervej and turn left at the traffic lights into Hasserisvej. Lars is gazing at the field on the right but still turns his head to look at Hasseris High School. Little Lars, you damned fool, why did you have to fill yourself with all that shit? To be like your charismatic friend? Now both of you are six feet under."

"Are you trying to say that it's good that Steso is dead because he didn't have anything going for him anyway?" Michael asks.

"That's the inner logic – the consequence," Svend replies.

"Have you considered topping yourself?" Michael won't let this absurd conversation rest.

"Yes," Svend answers.

"Why don't you then?"

"I'd miss all this."

"Funerals?" Michael asks.

"Hmm, yeah, course . . . . No, all this – bullshit."

"You don't mean that." Michael is beginning to take offence – that is how it always ends up; he is well-meaning but far too emotionally involved to take part in a discussion with Svend.

"Yes I do, but I'm banking on there being something on the other side."

"You think you'll be in a better mood in the future?" Michael asks.

"Yes." Svend nods.

"Are we talking about a time in the foreseeable future?"

"What's foreseeable for you?" Svend asks.

"So it's not going to happen today?" Michael asks, at which point Lars decides to break in. He is on the verge of becoming severely depressed.

"Can't you two philosophers just stuff it for a while?" he asks. Peeved, they mutter something in reply.

"Junkie romanticism," Michael says in disgust.

"Don't take the last hope from a broken man," Svend says with a grin.

"That wasn't what I meant," Michael says.

"Oh yes you did. You're playing the respectable citizen," Svend says.

"Thank you." Michael is approaching the point now where he inevitably throws in the towel. Lars keeps a close watch on their faces in the rear view mirror.

"Look, I'm not sitting here trying to fuck about with your brain, if that's what you think. We're having a conversation," Michael says angrily

"Fine, but you see . . . ," Svend goes on – in a more serious tone now. "Or – I don't think you do see. I've sort of . . . lost . . . ."

"Lost what?" Michael asks.

"Faith."

"The will, you mean," Michael counters.

"There you go again," Svend complains.

"What?"

"You really would like to get your hands round my throat, wouldn't you."

"You're just using your failure like a baby's bottle." Michael says in disgust, but there is an element of triumph, too – he knows he is right.

"I have to use whatever I've got," Svend says quietly and calmly.

"You're a nitwit," Michael says, and Svend grabs his chance:

"Tell me something I don't already know," he says.

"I can't," Michael answers, a slight smile creeping across his face. "You're a clever nitwit."

"Yes, and they're the worst kind, aren't they," Svend says, rhetorically.

"No doubt about that," Michael agrees as they turn into Thulebakken and keep an eye open for the community centre.

It wasn't much fun for Tilly when Thomas moved out of Kjellerupsgade and she was left all on her own. But she still saw him. She got her own flat in West Aalborg – a decent flat – and Thomas occasionally dropped by. They weren't a couple any more, though – the pills had taken their toll on him and Tilly couldn't trust him any longer. Then Tilly had begun to go to bed with Bertrand, but theirs wasn't a steady relationship either – except in bed.

One evening Tilly was at 1000Fryd with Bertrand. They were sitting on a sofa in a dark corner making themselves cosy. Bertrand put his hand on her thigh. He went to the bar to get some wine for both of them.

Then Thomas comes barging in through the door, his eyes aflame. He laughs. He heads straight for Tilly. He sits down. He is pale and sweating a little, but Tilly can see that he is in good spirits.

"Mmmm . . . ," he says, giving her a surreptitious smile. She giggles. Now the evening is going to be fun. She points at her glass of white wine with one finger in such a way that Bertrand doesn't notice. Thomas grabs it and empties it in one gulp.

"Tilly, you cosmic pearl, are you hobnobbing with the BOURGEOISIE?" he asks. Because Bertrand is certainly . . . good in bed, and he is loaded. But he is also a bloody snob who is afraid to be seen together with Tilly.

"Weeell . . . a little bit," she says, sending Bertrand a little smile while edging away from him on the sofa because she wants to sit next to Thomas. She would like to hear what he has been getting up to since they last met and she has promised his mother, Bodil, that they will drop by.

"I'm not the bourgeoisie, Steso. I'm a poor student," Bertrand says. But that is a lie, of course. It is also unwise of Bertrand to call him Steso. Bertrand looks annoyed. Because of the wine. Tilly would much rather have beer.

"No, you aren't," Thomas tells him. "You are a son of the exploiting classes. They've always been the WORST." Thomas laughs, then becomes serious again. He fixes Bertrand with a gaze. "Isn't it time for more wine?" he asks, giving Tilly a smile. She looks to Bertrand questioningly; he is the one with the money. He stands up to go for some more wine.

Thomas picks a cigarette out of Bertrand's packet. He gallantly offers Tilly one. Lights it for her with Bertrand's Ronson. Then Thomas buries his nose into her hair. He likes her lemon fragrance.

"We've got important things to do," he whispers to her.

"Such as?" she whispers back.

"First we've got to go outside and have a smoke," he continues in a whisper.

Bertrand comes back to the table with three glasses of wine.

"Why aren't you over in Jomfru Ane Gade with your bourgeois friends planning the continued exploitation of the proletariat?" Thomas asks, then adds, "But perhaps you're already plucking a little FRUIT?"

Bertrand looks nervous. He is completely out of his depth with Thomas.

"Skol," Bertrand says.

"Skol," Thomas says, emptying his glass. Tilly sits looking at him, waiting to see what he will come up with next.

"You see, it's always been a tradition for the sons of the ruling classes to rub shoulders with the proletariat whilst they are young; sort of . . . becoming acquainted with the enemy, as it were, right?" Thomas elaborates: "We see it with the Saudi Arabian princes who abuse their Filipino housemaids, the sons of the Afrikaaners with their fieldworkers' black daughters and the plantation owners in the Southern states with their army of imported slaves. The only difference here being that it won't be apparent from the COLOUR OF THE SKIN if your vile, amoral enterprise succeeds."

"You're crazy, Steso, "Bertrand says. He shouldn't say things like that, Tilly thinks. Because it is not true.

"Your counterargument has always been that we are crazy, stupid, underfed, and thieves, too. AND IT'S TRUE – we are . . . ."

Bertrand lights a cigarette. Tilly can already see that he is a beaten man. Thomas has not finished yet:

". . . but whose fault is it? IT'S YOURS." Then Thomas smiles and shrugs his shoulders. "But let's not talk about that this evening," he says, wrapping his arm around Tilly's shoulder. "This evening we're going to drink wine; but first I have to go outside and have a smoke. Anyone want to join me? "

"I'll come," Tilly says. Bertrand doesn't smoke so often, but occasionally he buys some hash from Pusher Lars. Because he likes it when Tilly smokes. Even though she prefers to drink beer. Bertrand remains seated.

Tilly and Thomas go outside.

"Well, I don't want to smoke," Tilly says. But she would like to keep him company.

"I know that, Tilly. We just have to get away – Svend is waiting for us." Thomas is searching around for a bike that is not locked. "I only came to fetch you," he says. That makes Tilly happy.

"What are we going to do?" she asks.

"It's a surprise. Svend's got a surprise for you. We'd better get a move on."

"My bike's over there," Tilly says. She doesn't want to say anything to Bertrand since Svend is tired of having him hanging round.

Tilly unlocks her bike. Thomas sits on the back. Because she has more strength in her legs. They cycle up to the North Jutland Museum of Art. They have to walk the last part of the way but Thomas won't say what they are going to do. They climb the steps up through the woods to the Aalborg Tower. It is exciting. The restaurant called Skydepavillionen at the side of the tower is in total darkness. There is no-one about.

"Come on," Thomas says, dragging her over to one of the tower's three legs. A picnic bench has been up-ended against the leg.

"AHOY," someone shouts from above. Tilly is startled. It is Svend. Thomas laughs.

"IT'S ME," Tilly shouts back.

"UP HERE IN HEAVEN WE'VE GOT SOME GOODIES FOR YOU," Svend yells.

"What's up there?" she asks Thomas.

"Something nice," he says, crawling onto the picnic bench so that he can reach the bottom of the steel ladder which runs up inside one of the legs of the tower. Tilly crawls up after him. The glimmering town lies spread out below them. The higher they climb, the windier it becomes. Tilly can just make out Svend on a little platform up at the very top, just under the observation deck. She makes it to the top.

"Hello, beautiful," he says, handing her a beer. There is a full crate of Tuborg on the floor. "There are more where they came from." He has broken in through the trapdoor at the bottom of the tower. There are also some chips and candy and cigarettes. Thomas lights their cigarettes with the Ronson. He has also brought Bertrand's Ray-Bans along. Tilly puts them on and looks down over the darkened lights of the

town while holding Thomas's hand, as she feels a little giddy. That is our town, she thinks. People just don't realize.

They arrive in good time at the community centre in Thulebakken, the road where Steso's parents now live. Lars is rolling a joint on the car hood. The girls have not turned up yet. Michael stares at Svend.

"You probably think it's hypocritical what I'm doing now," Michael says. Svend wonders whether people run others down in order to put themselves in a better light. He doesn't think he has anything for Michael to be envious of.

"Am I so easy to see through?" Svend asks.

"I simply assume you think the worst of me, and I turn out to be right."

"So kind," Svend says.

"My pleasure," Michael replies.

Svend is quiet. Walks restlessly around the parking lot. Then the girls arrive.

"What's wrong?" Tilly asks straight away – she is like a barometer.

"These two boys have embarked upon a classical philosophical debate," Lars says, smoking his joint.

"What are they arguing about?" Louise asks. Lars answers solemnly:

"The subject is: Which of them is the greatest idiot?"

"Who's winning?" Lisbeth asks. Lars winks at her:

"It all depends on whose side you are on. But in my opinion both of them," he adds with a sly smile.

"Why do you two always have to be like that?" Lisbeth asks, looking from Svend to Michael and back again.

"Us two? Aren't you one of us?" Svend says.

"Look, I've given up all that . . . crap," Lisbeth says.

"Well I think it's a very appropriate day to do that on," Svend says. "We're here to honour Steso's memory."

"Yes, he never gave anything up," Michael says.

"No, he didn't. He didn't give up," Svend says.

"What do you mean: *didn't give up*?" Michael asks. Louise has come over and is standing just behind him.

"He kept on searching," Svend explains and adds: "Even though I've a sneaking feeling that he'd forgotten what he was searching for."

"Were we searching for something?" Tilly asks, baffled.

"I might be rationalising after the event here," Svend says, "but I think I can recall that we were looking for some answers."

"Answers to what?" Michael sneers. Louise has put her arm around his waist and with a nervous glance at Svend gives him a little squeeze.

"To the bigger questions of life. Why? What are we here for?" Svend says. Michael says no more. Looks away in disgust.

"Svend," Lars says, "it should have been you holding the sermon in the church." He laughs.

Svend's face contorts: "You can take your irony and shove it up your ass, you shit," he snarls.

"Whoa big boy, walk all over the weak and defenceless, won't you." Lars averts his eyes. They used to call him Big Lars, but in the course of time he has become a lot smaller than Svend. Around town he is known as Pusher Lars – a seedy, small-time trader.

"Svend. What did you have to say that for?" Lisbeth asks.

"Oh, fuck it," Svend says.

"Go on, then, tell us why you stopped searching," Louise says. Now she's interfering, too; probably imagines she's supporting her man – how pathetic, Svend thinks.

"A tourist who became homesick?" he suggests. Louise is silent.

"What do you mean?" Lisbeth asks.

"There wasn't anything there," Svend replies. "I mean . . . we had some intense experiences – at least I did, but it didn't change our lives in any real way. That's sort of . . . how it is."

"What does that say about you then?" Michael asks.

"Do you really *have* to be such a dickhead, Michael?" Lisbeth says.

"No, alright. But how do you see it?" he asks.

"See what?" Svend asks.

". . . the whole thing," Michael says.

"Big questions you're asking today."

"Okay. Sorry. You know what I mean," Michael offers.

"Yes, Michael – I know what you mean."

"Can you explain how you see . . . everything, Svend?" Lisbeth gives him a questioning look.

"Yes, but what's the point?" he says.

"Come on now, we're at a funeral," Michael says. "So we're already depressed to start with. Enlighten us with your insight and wisdom."

"Sarcastic bastard," Svend mutters. Tilly is standing some distance behind him, fidgeting with her hands.

"Come on, then, let's hear it," Lisbeth says to him.

"I'm not going to stand here and be made a bloody fool of," Svend says; his jaws are working.

"Svend . . . ." Tilly has joined him and it looks as if the tears are about to flow.

"Hello, Tilly, you beautiful creature," he says.

"Try not to be so negative today," she says in a soft, throaty voice.

"Alright, alright . . . Just give me a minute."

"No, tell us what you know now," Tilly says, pulling at his jacket sleeve like a little child.

"Well okay, then." He gives in; talks hurriedly as if he were reeling off the items on a list: "Everything became transparent, all the books were open. Good and evil only exist inside yourself. On earth there are only events. It makes no difference whether these are chance occurrences or not. The question of pre-determination is irrelevant. Everything is meaningless. Completely useless knowledge . . . ." Svend shakes his head, looks depressed.

"No," Michael says. "What *you* got out of it may be useless. That's not for me to say. By and large that was how I experienced the world, too."

"But you've turned your back on it, just like a bloody politician," Svend sneers.

"No. I've turned things around – it's me who decides what has any value, and then I do something about it," Michael says.

Does he deserve a response?

"That's precisely what scares me," Svend says.

"Good old C.E. ," Lars says from the sidelines.

"Who?" Michael asks. Lisbeth sighs.

"Cause and Effect," she says, shaking her head, and Tilly titters.

"*The road of excess leads to the palace of wisdom*," Lars says, his worn out body dancing a little jig in the parking lot.

"Don't be so puerile," says Svend.

"Don't be so conformist," says Lars, already out of breath.

"Give up," Lisbeth says.

"Yes, mummy," Svend and Lars say in unison, making everyone laugh apart from Louise and Michael.

"Tilly," he says, "have you heard Svend's moving back?" Tilly slowly turns her gaze from Michael to Svend in disbelief.

"*Is it true*?" she cries, skipping over to Svend and throwing her arms around him. He tries to laugh, but it comes out strained. "Is that right, Svend?" she asks, her voice trembling.

"Yes." He smiles down at her.

"Why didn't you tell *me*?" Tilly asks. Svend ruffles her hair with one of his hands.

"I've only just decided," he answers.

"How come?' Lisbeth asks in amazement. Lars is slowly nodding, a satisfied expression on his face.

"Seems as if I can't do without you guys," Svend answers without emotion.

"You *miss* us," Tilly says, pressing her body tightly against him.

"*Yes*, damn it." He takes a step backwards and looks away. He doesn't want to talk about it.

"You'd never know to look at him," Michael says drily. Svend laughs, then lunges at him, hitting him hard on the shoulder. Just like in the old days when they were always scrapping, just for fun.

"No," he says, "I hide it well."

Tilly popped in to see Pusher Lars. She wanted him to visit Svend with her. Sometimes she was on bar duty at 1000Fryd when Svend was there, too. He wasn't an activist; he just sat on the other side of the bar drinking. He had begun to do that more and more often recently. He didn't look happy.

"You'll just have to have a talk with him," Tilly said nervously. Lars knew that it wouldn't have any effect – Svend was down in a black hole, cursing – but for Tilly's sake he was willing to make an attempt.

They walk towards the large flat that Svend and his girlfriend, Line, share with Sigurt, the drummer, who was a member of BÜLD until the band broke up.

"Line's expecting," Lars tells her.

"But . . . that's great," Tilly says, without any conviction. Lars suspects she knows how things are with Svend.

"Svend doesn't think so," he says. Tilly is silent for a moment.

"But . . . doesn't he love her?" she asks.

"No," he answers, "Svend doesn't even love himself."

"You mustn't say things like that, Lars."

"But it's true."

Tilly looks down at the ground. "Yes," she murmurs. Lars tells her about Svend. Besides Line, there is another girl Svend has spent one single night with. She is pregnant as well and claims Svend is the father.

"But . . . Line, does she know?" Tilly asks. Neither she nor Lars actually knows Line even though Svend has been living with her for quite some time. He is not interested in them getting to know her.

"No, she doesn't know anything about it," Lars answers.

They ring the doorbell. Svend opens up and waves them in with a tired sweep of his arm. His face is covered with thick stubble, his clothes are grubby, the air in the hall is stuffy and stale, permeated with the stench of hash. In the living room the shelving unit is on its side; LPs and books are scattered all over the floor, along with a smashed potted plant and a wrecked stereo set.

"Has Steso been here?" Lars says in a futile attempt to lighten the atmosphere. Steso has been known to go berserk in other people's homes. Tilly doesn't say a word. Svend doesn't even say hello to her.

"The lady lost her temper," Svend says, sitting down at the dining table with a sigh. He pours himself another tumbler of red wine and takes a long swig. "Help yourselves," he says, pointing to the two other bottles of wine standing unopened on the dining table. Tilly goes into the kitchen to fetch some glasses.

"What made her so angry?" Lars asks.

"She was at her prete-natal classes and then of course she met that cunt who maintains I put her in the club."

"NO," Lars says.

"Yes."

"Oh no, bloody hell. But . . . what are you going to do?"

"I don't know, man. I . . . I'm going to deny it. Well, not to Line. I can't sort of explain away the fact that I was with that cunt while I was living here, and that's why . . . ," Svend points to the mess on the floor, ". . . Line was upset. But I'm not going to accept responsibility for the other kid. It's not mine. She'll have to drag me into court. Then I can reel off the names of the seven other guys she was screwing at the time."

Lars is miserable. Tilly comes into the living room again, deathly pale. "Are you sure about that?" she asks.

"That's what I've heard," Svend says.

"Have you told her?" Lars asks. Svend throws his head back and howls with laughter.

"Ooooh," he says, drying his eyes. "I've told her bloody parents."

"How come?" Lars asks.

"Well, you see, I wanted to talk some sense into her. You know, tell her that even if it was my kid, we were only together for one night – pissed as newts – and that I didn't want to have anything to do with her. I made that quite plain to her. She only has to say that she doesn't know who the father is and social security will pay the child maintenance. She'd have to pay a 500 kroner fine, but I can sort that out. But she fucking refuses. She wants my name on the dotted line. Father: Svend the Idiot, who is trying to fill the great void in his soul with girls so that he can tell himself there's nothing wrong with him."

Lars can tell by the look on Tilly's face that she is furious. She knows what it is all about. You have to piece all the broken fragments of your life together and make them mean something.

It takes Lars a moment to know what to say: "But why you?" he asks.

"Of all the guys she's screwed, I'm the least pathetic," Svend explains. "Frightening, isn't it."

"But why did you go and talk to her parents?" Lars asks.

"She went AWOL. So I tried her parents. And that's where she was."

"How did it go?"

"Fantastic," Svend says. "I made a really bad impression on them. Told them their daughter was a slut and spelled it out for them what the paternity suit would involve: eight men who would all have to give a blood sample. Made it clear that I'd never have anything to do with their daughter's effing offspring . . . that's what I said."

"And?" Lars says.

"Well, then I cleared off."

Lars doesn't ask any more questions. Tilly looks as if she is cold – her eyes are glossy. A shiver runs down Lars's spine. He has never seen Svend as unfeeling as he is at this moment.

"And what happens now?" Tilly asks in a squeaky voice. Svend looks across and throws his hands in the air.

"Well, I'm hoping that her parents will talk some sense into her."

"And what about your girlfriend?" Tilly asks. "What about Line?"

"Girlfriend?" Svend says. "It seems to me that people are somewhat careless about the way they use that term nowadays." He empties his glass.

Lars is thinking about Lisbeth – about how she will react to all this. But she is too preoccupied with herself to see that Svend is in the process of burying himself alive.

"But what will happen now?" Lars asks. Svend stares at him in incomprehension. "What do you plan to do now?" he adds.

"These worn floors are telling me to move on," Svend says with a wide sweep of his arm, taking in the whole of the flat. In a flash Lars sees the animal trails before him; Svend's eternal wandering between the water hole, the feeding grounds, the sleeping quarters, the living room and the bathroom. He knows the feeling. Life is unbearable; that is the reason he smokes hash – to lower the bell jar down over himself, blunt the sharp edges, assuage the fear. But Svend has no need for that. He can fight. Trouble is he just pisses on others – completely indifferent.

"You can't just check out," Tilly says. "That's . . . inhuman."

"Tilly," Svend says, "The acid I took that time burnt away a lot of my feelings." Lars feels like telling him that is the most callous thing he has ever heard, but he knows it is impossible to get through to him. Svend has barricaded himself in. Lars just wants to get out of the door and go home. Smoke some grass. Tilly begins to cry. Svend turns away, so as not to see.

"Svend. That's callous," Lars says.

"Yes, Lars, I am. It's about time these . . . women . . . told their men when they were going to stop taking the pill. It would have been nice to know so I could have put a raincoat on. What this is, is a con."

"Svend," Tilly sobs, but she doesn't continue until she has his full attention. "Svend . . . I don't like you when you're like this."

His gaze is unbending. She sniffles but holds his gaze until he turns his head away.

"No," he says, "I don't, either."

All of them have lighted cigarettes in their hands and down one glass of wine after the other. Anything to ease the pain. Svend moves his head slowly from side to side, looking in wonder at the things about him.

"Svend?" Lars says.

"The acid's beginning to work."

"Are you on mushrooms?"

"LSD."

"You're insane," Lars says.

"Not yet, but maybe I soon will be."

Lars gets up and hands Tilly her jacket. "Let's go," he says.

"Yes," she says.

"You can't run away," Svend says. "You can't run away from yourself."

They leave. From the staircase they hear Svend shouting from inside the flat: "How long are we relevant to ourselves, Lars?"

Tilly cries all the way to Lars's place. She cries herself to sleep on his sofa. He can remember that night. He sat watching her, thinking that it was all over now. Everything they had shared together had been cast to the winds. Steso, Lisbeth and Svend were all in the shit. Little Lars was dead. They weren't so young any more and they hadn't shaped up very well. The sanest of them were a pothead and a fruit-cake. The pusher and the yellow girl. Lars and Tilly.

A large, shiny metal ball begins to spin inside Svend's head; it colours everything as it increases in size, growing larger than the circumference of his skull and continuing to rotate around his head until it becomes a gigantic globe-shaped tinted lens.

Svend walks through sparkling pink champagne along the long corridor towards Sigurt's room. Sigurt is in the bathroom brushing his teeth; the thick toothpaste foam runs down his chin. Svend can hear the sounds of cicadas, helicopters, hysterical Vietnamese, bursts of machine-gun fire coming from Sigurt's room. He walks on – into the room. Steso is lolling in an armchair. On the TV screen: a gigantic Negro from Tuscaloosa, Alabama – wearing camouflage gear, his voice rich and deep:

"We are stationed up in Da Nãng, trying to kill the yellow man for the beast, 'n' this honky motherfucker thrown us into the bush – we just sittin' there on our sorry black asses waitin'. Charlie he can smell your Luckies, your Marlboro 'n' shit two miles down wind – you dig? You be smokin' you gonna be fuckin' dyin'. Charlie he come runnin' like a motherfucker, shoot your nigger ass into oblivion."

Steso turns round to face him in the armchair. "Svend," he says slyly, "you look like a foreign worker."

"Foreign?" Svend looks down at himself.

"On the inside, man. Whose slave are you?"

Svend racks his brain for a suitable answer, but he can't think of one.

Sigurt returns from the bathroom, toothpaste in the corner of his mouth. He strikes his new crash cymbal, which is on a stand in the middle of the floor. "I'm going down to Huset to practise," he mumbles, then takes a couple of steps backwards, pulls up his T-shirt, stares with wide-open eyes at the quivering cymbal and then down at his stomach. "I can listen with my skin," he says to no one in particular before turning to address Svend: "That's because I've abolished the laws of gravity."

Svend swallows – is uncertain whether it is always like this or whether occasionally it is different. The TV screeches – the jungle is deep green.

"Afterward we's lookin' to get our funky asses into some R & R action. Ridin' down into poontang garden to regroup, retrack and just get recomposed completely. Sittin' in a cathouse in Nha Trang watching the floorshow – amazing Charlie lady, she out of sight."

"I have to brush my teeth," Sigurt says and goes out again. Steso lays a hand on Svend's shoulder.

"Potchai," Steso says, nodding, "I'll fix something up for us."

Am I in the jungle? Svend wonders. The soldier is as black as the ace of spades, relaxed – he laughs and spits:

"The bitches won't go with us – turns out this confederate beast been tellin' them that the brothers too big. At midnight the brothers grow tails 'n' shit. This man has been a beast all his life. The way he acts – his very nature is beastly. This shit has grown in him from constantly fucking over people – he's got it down to a fine art. Burns me up, man."

Steso leads Svend along the hallway, the sounds of Sigurt brushing his teeth in the background. Scouring. Svend washes up on the sofa . . . it is a beach. Looks out over the horizon. The smell of seaweed. Sailing ships in the distance. The sun bakes down. The waves lap against the shore. Save for the window in the middle of the horizon. Through this he can see cars driving past in the street. And the door to the hall is throbbing like a heart. Time has ceased to exist. Svend hallucinates: observes his parents' car driving past the window on the beach. Steso is clattering about in the kitchen. Svend's mother is down in Aarhus visiting his sister. His mother walks past the window. Svend goes into the kitchen to help Steso. Suddenly there is a ringing sound.

"That's the door," Steso says. Yes, it is throbbing. Steso goes over to stop it.

"Your mother's out there," he says. Aarhus? Svend's pupils are enormous. His mother is in the living room.

"Hello, Svend. We were wondering whether . . . ." She promptly melts into a blob on the floor and Svend keeps trying to lower his gaze from her head to the tips of

her shoes in order to make eye contact. She doesn't say a word. That makes it extremely difficult to communicate with her.

"Come and have dinner tomorrow." What? She's gone. Her feelings are in Svend's mouth. They are yeast and flour. He tries to restrain his saliva. Swelling up.

Steso has . . . vanished? Svend is lying in bed. A girl arrives. She sits on the edge of the bed.

"No." Did he say that?

"It's me . . . Line?"

"No. You aren't . . . ." Her hand is holding Svend's – she places it on her belly.

"Can you feel it – our child?" she says.

"No," he whispers. A sobbing wells up in his throat – uncontrollable tears. She's not . . . real. Foul-smelling mercury flows from her palm into his body and makes a slopping sound; nausea, seasickness. Pushes himself away from her – up into the corner.

For the first few days he was incapable of doing anything. Then he slowly began to perform everyday actions such as eating, going to the toilet, doing the shopping. But for a couple of months it was difficult for him to be with other people as he didn't know whose company they were in when they were with him. He had to reconstruct his soul out of the materials that were available – bits and pieces lying about, something he saw on TV, elements he invented; begged, borrowed or stole.

A large, lavish table has been set in the community centre. Bertrand arrives, and Lisbeth notices that Svend gives him a dirty look. She is well aware that they don't like each other; it just seems strange on a day like this. Come to think of it, it is odd that Bertrand has turned up at all. Pusher Lars served his apprenticeship in the contracting company that Bertrand's father owns. Bertrand himself was taken on as an apprentice in the bookkeeping department. But it is a long time since Bertrand hung out with them – must have been towards the end of the eighties. She is sure that he didn't really like Thomas.

Adrian ought to be here, as he and Thomas were very close, and the reason Adrian is staying away is obviously because of Lisbeth, and she is both pleased and sad about that and . . . she doesn't want to think about it.

When they have taken their places at the table and have been given a piece of cake, Arne rises to his feet. He looks like Thomas as he clears his throat several times before beginning to speak:

"We are gathered here today to say goodbye to Thomas. It is of course a sad day for all of us, not least . . . ." He lays his hand on his wife's shoulder and, looking down at her, gives it a little squeeze. Bodil's face is as if carved out of wood – she stares stiffly out into space. Rikke is sitting at her side, the tears rolling down her cheeks, her arm around her mother. Only a few of the relatives have come. In fact, it is Steso's friends Arne is addressing. The whole of this gathering in the community centre is for them, so that they can take their leave of him in a fitting manner – Arne has seen to that.

"I would like us to remember him with fondness. Although Thomas was in many ways a . . . disappointment to us, I know that he relished life. He chose to do what he liked doing best, and even though that was very much against my wishes I am nonetheless happy that my boy enjoyed himself." Arne pauses for a moment, trying to collect himself. Then he proceeds, his voice heavy with emotion:

"Even though Thomas would never really acknowledge the pleasures of alcohol, no matter how hard I tried to tempt him . . . ," they smile respectfully and nod, knowing full well that he did acknowledge alcohol, too – he was not finicky when it came to the pleasures of the palate, ". . . I hope you will light up your cigars . . . ." Arne makes a gesture, people catch on to the fact that the time has come and they all do their best to light the unaccustomed cigars which have been passed around.

Tilly weeps as she tries to get her cigar alight. It looks completely surreal, and Lisbeth is afraid that she is going to break down altogether. Lisbeth is trying to swallow the huge lump in her throat, as she has promised Tilly's mother to look after Tilly today; so Lisbeth has to be strong. But then Svend passes his lighted cigar to Tilly and explains to her how to smoke it; that she shouldn't inhale so much of the cigar smoke because it is too strong. Tilly nods solemnly as she concentrates on puffing at the cigar while he lights her cigar for himself.

The tears trickle down Bodil's cheeks. Her face is expressionless. As soon as the clouds of smoke drift up into the air above the table, Arne continues:

"Please join me in a toast to Thomas. Many unpleasant things can be said about him – but he was never boring." That's right, Lisbeth thinks.

Arne's son was the best entertainment imaginable. Thomas *always* caused trouble, but in a charming way – the malicious side didn't appear until later on when he needed money.

Everyone rises. The family don't say a word. Svend and Lars say: "No, he bloody wasn't; he was never boring." The small glasses are raised and emptied. Everyone sits down again. A short lull ensues in which a few of the guests talk to each other in subdued voices.

"He was certainly an entertaining little fellow," Svend says.

"What did he do?" Louise asks – she never really got to know him. Thomas was already in the process of drifting away from them when she was beginning to recover from her illness, or maybe they were all drifting away from each other.

"Everything imaginable," Svend says. "He has pissed on me, vomited all over me – quite literally. Tried to kill me with a chair. Sold my stereo when he was spending the night at my place and I'd gone out to the shops to buy him some grub.

"Wasn't that infuriating?" Louise asks.

"What?" Svend says.

"Knowing somebody like that, someone you can't trust – having him inside your home?" Louise asks.

"You're bloody telling me – but at the same time he was as unpredictable as hell . . . I mean he was always interesting and it was *never* boring."

It happened at Huset in Hasserisgade where Svend was taking job training at one point.

Steso came in and was acting strangely, but then there was nothing unusual about that. He went up to the toilet on the first floor, but moments later came rushing down the stairs.

"SPIDERS, SPIDERS. Aaahhh . . . There are spiders EVERYWHERE," he shouts. Jumps up and down, shakes, sweats, eyes like saucers. Svend asks him where the spiders are.

"They're pouring out of the CAN. I need a SHIT," Steso screams. Since this is not a frequent event, it requires immediate attention when it finally does occur. Svend goes to the toilets with him and steps into one of the cubicles. Steso won't go in with him. Stands outside the door, screaming and pointing:

"UGH, SVEND, they're crawling about EVERYWHERE," he shouts, brushing invisible spiders off his clothes and stamping on the floor by the doorway:

"DIE, DIE, DON'T YOU FUCKING COME OUT HERE. DIE." And then: I NEED A SHIT, SVEND." Svend goes downstairs and mixes a bucket of soapy water, takes it up to the toilet and starts washing down the walls with a floor cloth.

"See how the soapy water kills them, Steso?" he asks.

"YES, YES. KILL THEM," Steso shouts, hopping wildly up and down.

"Look how they're being washed down onto the floor," Svend says, continuing his work and taking care to cover all the wall. Meanwhile Steso stares at the spiders with a fiendish, happy smile as they slither down the wall to their piteous deaths on the floor.

"The ones on the ceiling, too, Svend. They have to die, TOO," he says, pointing at the ceiling. So Svend has to stand up on the toilet seat and wash the ceiling. Finally he wipes the floor and the toilet itself with the cloth, then throws it into the bucket.

"Look," he says, pointing down into the bucket. "They can't swim."

"YEEEAAAH," Steso yells. "Those FILTHY VERMIN. Let them DIE. Let them DROWN."

"You can go in now," Svend says. "It's okay now."

"Yes," Steso says, shaking his hand. "Thanks a lot, Svend – I'm TERRIFIED of those creepy-crawlies." Then he goes in and has a shit. Sits there shouting:

"Ha, they're DEAD now. HA. Svend has KILLED them." Svend went downstairs to empty the bucket. Never boring.

Bertrand has . . . well, Tilly saw him coming in through the door just as they were going to have coffee, but now they have finished the coffee, and he is still here. People can sort of circulate now and she doesn't want him to come over and talk to her. That is what he always does, so Tilly quickly goes over to Svend, who is busy talking to Lisbeth and Pusher Lars; Bertrand joins them all the same. He reeks of perfume – like some tart.

"That was when we were invulnerable," he says. What does he know about being invulnerable? Nothing at all. He looks stupid with that cigar hanging out of his mouth.

"That's what we used to think," Lars says.

"Were you there that time we swam out to Egholm?" Bertrand directs his question to Svend.

"Yes," Svend replies. Tilly can see that Svend is already fuming.

"And Lars stole a great big plastic canister from the quay and took it with him so he wouldn't drown," Bertrand says. He is already lying.

"Did I?" asks Pusher Lars.

"*I* gave it to you," Tilly tells him, because she did.

"You've always been such a sweetheart," Lars says, smiling. She beams back at him.

"Yes, you didn't want to risk it," Bertrand tells him.

"No flies on me," Lars says. His smile broadens. His teeth look really good.

"Don't you remember that swim?" Bertrand asks.

". . . can't remember a thing," Lars replies, shaking his head. He doesn't want a a scene – Tilly is sure he can remember. Lars wants to avoid trouble. But Svend can't stop himself.

"There's one little detail you've forgotten," Svend says. Tilly knows what he is referring to. She tugs at his sleeve and quickly puts her mouth to his ear:

"Forget about it, Svend," she whispers. She doesn't like this. It would be a shame for Thomas's mother, too, if there were any fuss. And that would make Tilly sad.

"No," Svend tells her, looking daggers at Bertrand.

"What's the problem?" Bertrand asks.

"You weren't with us," Svend says. There is no stopping them now. Tilly just watches, trying to hold back the tears. She doesn't want to be crying all the time.

"What the hell are you talking about, man?" Bertrand says. "Course I was with you. First we went . . . ." Svend cuts in:

". . . to the Kliché concert and then down to the fjord, yes – but you did not *cross* the fjord with us."

"Aah, you don't remember a fuck, either," Bertrand says. Tilly goes to stand next to Lisbeth, who takes Tilly's hand and holds it in hers. Their fingers intertwine. Let the boys have it out if they want – it doesn't matter to Tilly and Lisbeth.

"Leave him alone, Svend," Lars says.

"Not bloody likely – I'm not having him feeding off my memories."

"What is this shit?" Bertrand says.

"Where did we find that boat we rowed back in?" Svend asks.

"How the hell should I be able to remember that? Down by the shore, I suppose," Bertrand says. He probably shouldn't have said that, Tilly thinks.

"Nope," Svend says, slowly shaking his head.

"You and Lars were so out of your skulls that time, it's a wonder you can even remember you existed," Bertrand says. Lars raises his eyebrows and looks at Bertrand. Lisbeth gives Tilly's hand a squeeze. Svend continues to shake his head.

"When I talk about the past, I stick to things that actually happened – you should, too," he says.

"If you think I'm going to stand here listening to any more of this shit, then you're wrong," Bertrand says as he turns to leave.

"What's all this about?" Lisbeth asks.

"*You are and you always will be a lying coward*," Svend shouts after him.

"This isn't the time to settle old scores, Svend," Lisbeth says.

"Quite the contrary in my opinion," he replies. Lars has a faraway look in his eyes.

"Hell of a job it was," he says, bringing a smile to Tilly's face.

"What?" Lisbeth asks.

"The boat . . . All the boats were moored to the jetty, so we went and found one round the back by the café. Hell of a job.

"So you do remember, then?" Lisbeth says.

"Course I remember. Steso . . . Thomas, I mean, almost drowned – he was hanging on to that plastic canister Tilly had given me and yapping on about not wanting to die in water. He thought that *lacked style*." Tilly giggles. When they got back, Thomas had to borrow her light-blue tights and yellow quilted waistcoat. His whole body was shaking. He kept banging on about going to emerg to have some adrenaline injections. Because he was about to have "COLD SHOCK." But Bertrand didn't cross the fjord with them – he spent the whole time on the quay, dry as a bone, trying to make it with Tilly.

Svend shakes his head. "Why the hell didn't you tell him he was full of shit?" he says to Lars, jerking his head over towards where Bertrand made his exit. Svend is furious at Bertrand – he has been for ages. Ever since that time . . . .

"It's a hell of a long time ago, Svend," Lars answers.

"What are you trying to say?" Lisbeth asks. "Wasn't he with you?"

"No, he bloody wasn't," Svend says. "He's always been a liar – a parasite."

"There's no need to bear grudges," Lars says.

"If you're prepared to turn a blind eye, then okay – that's up to you. But I can't," Svend says.

"For God's sake, Svend, he probably really believes that he *was* with us," Lars says.

"I think it is quite unacceptable to stand around with your hands in your pockets while he distorts the historical facts," Svend says.

"The other stuff, that was over and done with years ago," Lars says.

Tilly frowns. No, Lars, you mustn't talk about that, not when Lisbeth's here. Lisbeth doesn't know anything about the time Bertrand . . . used Tilly. Tilly hasn't told her anything about that. Because Lisbeth had enough of her own problems to cope with, and Tilly knows it is awful. When she always feels . . . like that.

"I can't help thinking about it every time I see his ugly mug," Svend says quietly. Tilly goes over to Lars. Because Lars has decided he is not going to say any more about it. He is the one who knows Bertrand. But they aren't friends any more. That is definite.

"Svend," Lars says, "I could mention a couple of dodgy things you've been involved in, too."

Lisbeth has a puzzled, serious look on her face.

"What are you two on about?" she asks because she thinks they are acting pretty weirdly, and she knows that . . . that it is a difficult day. Svend . . . she is not sure what is up with Svend. And Tilly is so edgy. Sometimes she can be irritating, Tilly can; but she can't help it.

"Forget it," Svend says. Pusher Lars goes over to a small table and starts fiddling with his rolling tobacco.

"You guys . . . ," Lisbeth says. "Every time you're together all sorts of old grudges start flying around."

"Hmmm," Svend says. Then Pusher Lars comes over with a great-looking joint in a really smart ivory joint filter. He taught them how to roll joints like this many years ago. He asks Lisbeth if she wants to light up.

"I don't smoke that stuff any more," she says, smiling at him.

"Just for old time's sake," Lars says.

"No, no, no, no, no – you're not allowed to smoke in here either, Lars," Lisbeth reproves.

"No," Lars says, "it's not a joint. I mean . . . it is a joint, but there's only tobacco in it." Lisbeth shakes her head.

"That's a lie – you always smoke Queen's."

"I swear on my mother's grave," Lars says.

"Good job she can't hear you saying that," Svend says.

"True," Lars admits.

"Want me to light it?" Lisbeth says.

"It's just because . . . I liked it so much when you smoked. You looked so beautiful when you lit up a joint."

"Do you mean that?" Lisbeth asks – she glows inside.

"Yes, do it, do it for me." Lars is serious. Lisbeth winks at him and takes the joint, and Lars watches her contentedly, and she remembers how it used to be; her head bent slightly back and with half-closed eyes – she pulls on it greedily, inhales, and then you wait for the smoke to do its trick in the bloodstream; but luckily this is only ordinary smoking tobacco.

"Yeah, that's so beautiful," Pusher Lars says. "That's a perfect image of the meeting of man and euphorica. That's the way I feel about it, anyhow," he concludes, nodding to Svend – Svend shrugs his shoulders. Lisbeth suspects that Svend's attitude has something to do with Thomas. She misses Thomas. And Lars . . . Little Lars. God, how she misses him – not because he was her boyfriend but as a living being, someone who trod the earth. Lisbeth was completely unprepared back then . . . unprepared in human terms, not mature enough, to deal with anybody dying, least of all someone who was so close to her. It completely knocked her out of kilter . . . for several years. She still is. Now she will never know how it could have been.

It was only an argument. Lisbeth made some empty threats. That he took it the way he did, that she will never be able to understand. But there were so many inner forces raging in him, so much aggression. And she knew that he would never lay a finger on her. It was too much for him to handle – his anger always surfaced. For God's sake, Lars, we were nineteen years old – what were you thinking of? For nine years she has tried to tell herself that it wasn't her fault. And she knows she is innocent, but she doesn't believe it. It is as if his death has changed her whole personality. Permanent damage . . . well, not damage maybe, but a permanent change. It has made her see the world in a radically different light. And it is no brighter.

Lisbeth blows out a thick cloud of smoke and coughs. She can taste something else apart from nicotine – just a trace.

"There's something else in this," she says.

"Oh, that's just a bit of fluff that was in the tobacco," Pusher Lars says.

"You rogue," she says. Lars is talking to Svend who has just taken the joint from Lisbeth's hand and is smoking.

"All that crap you came out with before, Svend – to Michael; it doesn't mean a bloody thing to me." Svend shrugs his shoulders again, puffs out some smoke. Lisbeth thinks he misses Thomas, too. And her Lars. Little Lars. She knows that Svend was really fond of Little Lars. It wasn't until after he died that Svend really turned his attentions to her. But she just couldn't . . . she felt it would be disloyal to her Lars. And Svend couldn't either . . . all that business with Adrian. What a fucking mess I have made of my life, she thinks. In the last few years she has become clearer in her mind about it: she can't love anyone else until she has stopped loving Lars. And she can't stop loving Lars until she loves somebody else. And Lars isn't here, so it is impossible for her to stop loving him. And he will love her forever – she can sense that. And every time she imagines that she has finished with the past, she discovers it has not finished with her. It keeps projecting its shadows.

Lisbeth looks up at Pusher Lars: "Maybe I'll invite you over to my place some day to smoke some of your weed with me," she says, because she realizes that she misses him, too. He is at ease with himself. That is beautiful . . . rare. He smiles.

"Thank you, I'm truly honoured," he says with a slight bow, which sets Tilly off giggling; it is good that she is happy again.

". . . and to listen to Birthday Party and L'Amourder," Lisbeth continues.

"I'm ready and willing," Pusher Lars says.

It crosses Lisbeth's mind that the other guests might be thinking they are smoking a joint. She glances at Bodil, but she is sitting there as if in a trance – not registering anything at all.

Arne joins them and stands next to Svend.

"It's almost time . . . for you people to . . . be moving along. The wife, you know . . . ," he mumbles sheepishly, clasping his hands in front of his body and bending slightly forward.

"Of course, Arne. We'll just say goodbye and then we'll be off," Svend replies, putting his arm around Arne's shoulder.

"It's umm . . . it's probably best if you lads just leave and . . . ," Arne says, looking apologetic. "Just let Tilly and Lisbeth go over and . . . you know . . . ." Quickly looking from one to the other, he lets the sentence hang in the air.

"We understand," Lars says.

"It's not that I . . . ," Arne begins.

"Arne, we quite understand," Lars repeats.

"She . . . Only those she knows. The girls," Arne says with a sigh. Louise looks perplexed – she is a girl, too, but she doesn't know Thomas's mother.

"Aren't you going to come out to see us off, Arne?" Svend asks. Arne nods.

"You'll wait for us, won't you?" Tilly asks anxiously.

"Of course we will," Lars says. Michael wraps his arm around Louise's shoulder and she goes out with them.

Bodil is . . . inconsolable. She won't let go of Tilly. Lisbeth is looking out of the window. Bertrand has turned up again; he is standing to one side of the community centre as Arne shakes each one of them by the hand before he swivels and goes back in. He goes over to his wife and gently separates her from Tilly.

"Please do drop by some time," he says to Tilly and Lisbeth. They promise to do so even though Lisbeth knows that . . . yes, they will – because they have to.

Lisbeth has her arm around Tilly as they leave.

"How sad she was," Tilly says, quietly crying. Lisbeth takes her in her arms. They join up with the others, then they all walk down towards the parking lot. Tilly has her head on Lisbeth's shoulder and is walking at her side with her eyes shut.

"What was that all about?" Lisbeth asks.

"What?" Lars says.

"Arne not wanting you to say goodbye to Bodil?" she says. Lars shakes himself like a dog.

"She blames us for leading Thomas astray," Svend answers.

"Wasn't it more like the other way round?" Lisbeth says.

"You know . . . for selling stuff to him." Lars says.

"Did you?" she asks.

"I'm a pusher, Lisbeth. It's sort of . . . my job," Lars answers.

"Yes, I know that, but not . . . heroin?" Lisbeth is alarmed.

"No, no, but to her it's all the same," Lars says.

"That's fair enough," Svend says, "It's the same difference."

"You mean she thinks he could have been saved if you lot hadn't been around?" Lisbeth asks.

"Yes, that's precisely it," Svend says. Michael and Louise say nothing. Bertrand brings up the rear. They make an odd-looking crowd as they walk between the rows of two-storey terraced houses. Lisbeth sees Louise slip her hand up under the back of Michael's top, caressing his skin as they march in step towards the parking lot. Spare me, she thinks.

"It's not like him to make such a serious misjudgement with the dose," Svend says.

"He was in a bit of a bad way towards the end," Lars says.

"But . . . wasn't it suicide?" Louise asks, surprised. Lisbeth glares at Michael – that must be something he has put into her head. Tilly opens her eyes.

"No, no, no," Svend and Lars say in unison.

"He'd never do anything like that," Tilly says in a reproving tone. Shaking his head, Lars looks at Michael.

"How can you know?" Michael asks.

"He was in the middle of cooking," Lisbeth says firmly.

"Yes," Tilly says, "and he'd stolen some Neapolitan ice cream from the grocer's." She presses her lips together, forming a thin line. In the frost box his parents had found a block of Neapolitan ice cream which they were 100 percent sure Thomas had put there.

"Who the hell did he buy it off?" Svend asks.

"I'll try to find out," Lars says.

"And when you've found out . . . ?" Svend says.

"Depends on who it is," Lars answers. Svend raises his eyebrows, looking at Lars while pointing his finger at himself. "Sure," Lars says. "You'll be the first to know."

They walk on in silence.

They talked Bertrand into driving them into the country. Walked to a stretch of meadowland. The conditions were perfect: the right amount of rain had fallen; the cows had delivered appropriate quantities of shit. The beginning of October – the first light night frosts had set in. Psilocybin mushrooms. They ate the first ones they found – psilos are best when they are freshly picked, and it also makes it easier to concentrate on the job of collecting them.

When they are well underway a farmer comes strolling along over the field in his rubber boots and a flat cap. He asks them what they are picking. Pusher Lars shows him his little plastic bag. We're out mushrooming," he says.

"You'll need a lot if you're only picking those little ones there," the farmer says.

"Yes, that's right, but they're very tasty," Lars answers, adding: "You know, on top of some warm pâté with a bit of bacon."

"I didn't know those ones were edible," the farmer says sceptically.

"Oh, they're really delicious," Lars says.

"You'll need a lot of them," the farmer repeats.

"Yes, but we've brought packed lunches with us – we're going to make a day of it," Lars explains. A little further ahead Steso turns round and shouts:

"They're SHINING, they're SHINING," with crazed, restless eyes. He sweeps his arm over the field: "Just like a town at night . . . just like . . . SMURFVILLE. Yeah, man."

The farmer looks bewildered.

"He's not well," Lars says in a confidential tone, and points at Tilly, who is walking at Steso's side: "That's his social worker."

The farmer looks at Tilly in her yellow knitted sweater, dark blue tights, pink wellies and Indian scarf tied around her tousled blonde locks. Not a shadow of doubt. Social worker. Lars offers him a Queen's, lights it for him.

"Thanks a lot," the man says, puffing away: "Strong tobacco this."

"Yes, but they taste of something," Lars says.

The farmer nods: "Very true. The full flavour of tobacco is only brought out when it doesn't have to pass through a filter."

"Like life," Lars says.

"Well, there may well be something in that," the farmer says.

Lisbeth joins them and stands at Lars's side as if she were his girlfriend. The farmer gives her a once over as if she were a beef cow – Lars suspects he considers her to be too lean.

"I'm sorry we didn't ask permission first," Lars says to him.

"What do you mean?" he asks.

"You know, we just wandered into your field."

"That's alright," he says.

"Are you sure?" Lars asks.

"Yes, you couldn't know whose field it was, and my cattle aren't out, either."

Lars asks him a few questions about his work:

Had the harvest been satisfactory?

I should just about manage to break even.

Had the milk quotas been up to scratch?

No.

What about the effect of the environmental action plan on the industry's profitability?

A disaster.

Finally the farmer points into the distance and says: "It'd be well worth you trying over there at the edge of the wood by the trough. There are usually masses of chanterelles round there and you can make a very nice white sauce with them."

"Cuckoo's Nest No. 2," Svend says when the man has gone.

When they get back to town they have over a thousand mushrooms, even after eating twenty-five each. Bertrand doesn't want to try any; they are too weird for him. Tilly doesn't eat any, either – she is allergic to them.

Bertrand parks the car in C.'.Obels Plads. Lisbeth, Svend and Steso start walking towards the pedestrian area when Lars hears Bertrand say to Tilly:

"What about just going back to your place?" he asks very softly, but because Lars is on mushrooms he can hear everything.

"No," Tilly says, and sets off walking. "The boys have arranged to spend part of their trip in the Jomfru Ane Gade. " Good," Lars thinks. Tilly is cool. She goes to bed with Bertrand – that much he has figured out, but she is not going to let Bertrand boss her about. Hell, they aren't a real couple; he's just not up to it. He was born with a silver spoon in his mouth. His father owns a big contracting company which Bertrand is set to take over some day. His mother would have a heart attack if he rolled up at their swanky house with Tilly at his side. Lars did his apprenticeship in the company at the same time as Bertrand was an apprentice in the offices, and Bertrand is now one of his customers – pleasant enough in his way, but too small-minded to be honest with himself. Bertrand lives in permanent fear of his fine friends finding out that he smokes pot and hangs out with riff-raff.

They turn into Bispensgade. Their objective is Jomfru Ane Gade and to walk around in their tripped-out state among people who are having an ordinary night out in town – just to see what it is like.

"We should be totally spaced out by the time we get there," Lisbeth says.

"Yes," Svend says. "It could be a really spacey experience."

"I want some MORE mushrooms," Steso shouts, first to Svend and then to Lars.

"I'm really in eighth heaven," Lars says.

"You'll have to wait," Svend says to Steso.

"But they're NOT WORKING. I want to TRIP out," Steso shouts.

They turn into Jomfru Ane Gade. Lars notices that Bertrand looks feverishly about to see whether there is anyone there he knows.

They go into Café Rendezvous. Svend and Lisbeth stand next to each other, analyzing the struggle for status – the methods people use to find their places in relation to one another.

"Do you know why mankind is the dominant race?" Svend asks.

"There wasn't any competition," Lisbeth says. Tilly giggles. Bertrand has disappeared. They leave again, walk further down the street. Lars turns round to see where Steso has got to. He is on his knees on the terrace café in front of Rendezvous *– one of those raised decking floors with tables and chairs on. Steso is bent face down on the floorboards; he is like a Muslim praying. Bertrand emerges from the café just as Lars comes up to Steso.*

"Hey, Steso, what's going on?" Lars asks.

"Lars," he whimpers. "My STESOLID tablets, man; my Stesolids have fallen between the cracks."

"You don't need to worry about that. You can have some more mushrooms," Lars says. Steso immediately gets very excited, so Lars adds: "But Tilly's got them, of course, so you'll have to wait."

"But where is Tilly?" Bertrand asks.

"TIIIIILLY . . . ?" Steso shouts. Lars laughs.

"She's gone to Paragraph 43," he says – that is their nickname for Tilly's enormous flat. The social security office pays the rent.

"We've got to go there NOW," Steso says.

"Why's she gone there?" Bertrand asks.

"She's gone to buy some food and then we're going to meet at her place," Lars answers absent-mindedly – the street has turned into one gigantic pulsating womb. "Wow . . . ," he says, "this is totally weird."

"Why did she go without me?" Bertrand asks. Lars is standing staring at the womb. Blood and alcohol are glistening on the paving stones and in people's mouths.

Steso grabs hold of Bertrand's upper arm, digging his fingers hard into his muscles. Steso shouts at the top of his voice:

"You interrupted your SURVEILLANCE *to evacuate your* BOWELS *and Tilly took advantage of that* WONDERFUL *opportunity to* ESCAPE *from your* SLIMY CLUTCHES.*"*

People are looking at them. Bertrand's head recoils to avoid the purplish waves of breath and beads of spit emanating from Steso's mouth. Bertrand tries to tear his arm free, but Steso's fingers are locked around his biceps.

*"Stop playing with her, Bertrand. Or I'll kill you," Steso says; and then he is already off down the street shouting, "*SVEND, LISBETH, WHERE ARE YOU? WE'VE GOT TO GO NOW. TILLY'S GOT THE FOOD READY.*" People stare at Bertrand as he hurriedly makes off down the street. Lars ambles after them, cautiously picking his way along the street so as not to slip on the blood-spattered paving stones.*

Later they are all over at Tilly's and Steso has another twenty-five mushrooms.

"It's close to the limit," Lars says, "but I think he's hardened enough to take it." Steso is still not satisfied.

"They're not having any effect AT ALL,*" he says again and again. Svend puts the plastic box containing the mushrooms on top of the wardrobe in Tilly's bedroom. Steso can't reach it there – he is only small. They are all sitting in the living room eating and watching the video of* Dr. Strangelove.

"Where's Steso?" Lisbeth asks after a while. Lars and Svend jump up and rush into the bedroom. Steso is standing there chewing with a broad, manic grin on his face and mushroom stalks sticking out of his mouth. He had sneaked into the kitchen, found a stool, carried it into the bedroom and crawled up on it so that he could get at the plastic box. And then he just stuffed himself. He has eaten about half of the thousand mushrooms when they manage to stop him. Svend holds him down on the floor with one knee and forces his jaws open with his hands, while Lars tries to extract some of the mushrooms from Steso's mouth. But he has swallowed most of them. And all he does is chortle: "Hee, hee, hee." They can do whatever the hell they like with him. He is happy – he has what he came for.

"We'll have to tickle him," Tilly says.

"Right," Lisbeth says. The girls throw themselves over him while Svend and Lars hold him down. Bertrand is standing in the doorway, looking sullen. Steso writhes like a spirit possessed, screaming with laughter.

"I'm going to PUKE,*" he shouts.*

"Oh no, better stop then," Svend says, and the girls stop.

"Yes, there's no need to stop him enjoying them," Lars says.

But the absurd thing was that Steso was on Stesolid – he had taken some of the pills before he dropped the others. What they didn't know at the time was: If you are having a bad trip and take a Stesolid pill, the trip will be over fifteen minutes to half an hour later. Steso just couldn't get a trip because he was on Stesolid to begin with. He had eaten 500 psilocybin mushrooms without them having the slightest effect. All that happened was that it was bloody painful when his kidneys were flushing out the toxins.

"Where are we going?" Bertrand asks, taking his car keys out of his pocket. They are all standing in the parking lot. Nobody answers him. Lisbeth has had a bit too much to drink to be able to drive, but she is very reluctant to leave her car parked here – that would mean her having to walk all the way out to pick it up tomorrow.

"Are any of you fit to drive?" she asks.

"What, a teacher's Fiat?" Pusher Lars asks, as if the very idea were obscene.

"Yes, *I* am," Svend says, but he is in his own car so that isn't much help.

"Come on, where are we going?" Bertrand asks again, impatiently.

"No, he can't bloody drive," Michael says, looking at Svend. "He's too drunk."

Tilly goes over to Svend, places her hands against the small of his back and pushes him forward, away from the parking lot.

"No, you mustn't, you naughty little boozer," she chides in her little girl's voice.

"If *you* say so, sweetheart, then I won't," he says, turning round to wrestle with her; but she offers no resistance, just laughs. Svend bends down and uses a wrestler's grip on Tilly, lifting her up in the air and holding her lengthwise across his shoulders. Then he carries her down towards Hasserisvej.

Michael and Louise follow Svend and Tilly. Bertrand is standing next to his car, looking annoyed. Pusher Lars shrugs his shoulders and follows after the others. Lisbeth casts a glance at Bertrand. Someone really ought to tell him where they are going, but she doesn't know, and she suddenly realizes that she doesn't give a damn about Bertrand. She doesn't feel he belongs with them and she sees no reason to be polite. She turns and hobbles over to Lars who has stopped to wait for her so they can fall into step and walk side by side.

Further ahead Svend says to Tilly: "Well, then, my lovely, shall we get drunk tonight?" She is still lying across his shoulders. Lisbeth can hear Bertrand's car starting up and angrily reversing out of the parking lot.

"Yes, why not," Tilly says, then laughs as Svend seems to be tickling her stomach with one of his hands as he walks along the road. Lisbeth can't help feeling envious of her because she just . . . shows him that she likes him and Lisbeth knows that Tilly takes everything that goes on around her far too much to heart, but . . . .

Bertrand trundles slowly past in his smart car, the side window wound down.

"Are you going to 1000Fryd?" he asks.

"You'll see us somewhere around," Svend shouts. To Lisbeth his voice sounds cold.

"Someone really ought to tell him where we're going," Louise says to Michael. Michael says nothing.

"Are there so many places to choose from?" asks Lars, who is walking next to Lisbeth. Bertrand is still crawling along at the side of the pavement.

"Do you want a lift, Tilly?" he asks through the side window.

"No, I'd rather walk," she answers, sniggering from the top of Svend's shoulders. Bertrand revs up and his red tail-lights soon disappear around a corner.

"Hey, mind your driving, man," Lars mutters as Svend lowers Tilly to the ground. They stride off, Svend and Tilly at the front, Michael with his arm around Louise's shoulder, Lars at Lisbeth's side. She is glad they didn't call for a taxi – this suits her better, even though her leg is beginning to ache. They are approaching the town centre now, past the jail, the florists, the cemetery.

"Let's go to V.B. ," Svend says.

"But isn't Bertrand on his way over to 1000Fryd?" Louise asks.

"Good," Svend says. Lisbeth doesn't understand what it is all about.

"What's V.B. ?" Louise asks.

"Vesterbro Bodega," Lisbeth replies.

Tilly and Thomas moved into the squat in Kjellerupsgade while Little Lars and Lisbeth moved into an apartment in Nørresundby. Two months later Little Lars was dead and Lisbeth was in hospital with screws in her leg. Tilly found her an apartment in Kjellerupsgade but she didn't want to live there; she wanted to stay in Nørresundby. Tilly suspects that Lisbeth didn't want to see them every day because that would just make her think of Little Lars and then she would be unhappy all over again. But she kept thinking about him all the same.

As for Svend, he lived in Kjellerupsgade, too – well, not really; he was just staying with a girl called Line. Having it off with her. So he could borrow her thick towelling dressing gown and shuffle over to the Job Centre to get his card stamped – that was the time when it had to be stamped every two weeks. Always early in the morning.

Svend goes round to where Tilly and Thomas live, wakes Tilly up and puts her coat over her nightdress. Because Tilly and Svend have to have their cards stamped on the same day. They go over together. The lady behind the counter is really grumpy every time they roll up and stand there with their dishevelled hair and sleep in their eyes. Thomas always says that Svend is nouveau riche when he goes to the Job Centre looking like that. Afterwards they go back to Thomas with fresh rolls and pastries. He is always there rolling a morning joint for them while talking to the zebra fish in the aquarium.

"Shall we get them stoned?"

"How – through the pump?" Svend asks.

"No, poor things," Tilly says.

"Blow smoke in under the glass cover, then the spirit of the hemp will hover over the waters and some of it will be drawn down because of the CIRCULATION," Thomas says.

"Do the fish get stoned then?" Svend asks.

"They get calmer," Thomas answers.

"But poor things – they don't understand what's going on. Just like that time you gave him that maggot," Tilly says.

"What?" Svend says.

Thomas points at himself: "Josef MENGELE."

"What did you do?" Svend asks.

"Axel gave me some psilos, and there was a little MAGGOT on one of them. I tossed it into the aquarium and the male fish ate it all – in terms of size that's equivalent to one of us eating a whole SALAMI," Thomas says, lighting the joint.

"Which is the male?" Svend says. Thomas points at the biggest of the zebra fish. "But, what happened to him?" Svend asks.

"First he completely lost his sense of direction and swam around more or less on his side for three days."

"Mm, that was so weird," Tilly says.

"Yes," Thomas says, "he could only use one of his fins and kept swimming into the glass."

"What happened then?" Svend says.

"Then he began to keep to himself, as he's doing now. Normally zebra fish swim about in schools, but he keeps to himself – always over by that big stone." Thomas points to a large stone at one end of the aquarium.

"Doesn't he like the others any more?" Svend asks.

"Well, it's not because he's turned hostile – it's more like he's become THOUGHTFUL."

"He's achieved a higher awareness," Svend says.

"Yes, I think so, too. It's hard to mix with others when you've had an experience like that."

"What, when you've had mushrooms?" Tilly asks – anxiously. Because Thomas eats mushrooms all the time and she doesn't like . . . well, if that means that he won't be able to mix with other people . . . her.

"No," Thomas says, "achieved a higher AWARENESS, Tilly."

"There may be something in that," Svend says.

Their neighbours in Kjellerupsgade were pushers, a couple of punks and a bunch of weirdos whom they didn't talk to, of course. Because the weirdos went around in suede shoes and mauve clothes; well, so does Tilly – only hers are yellow – but that's different. Because she is Tilly. And Thomas said that the weirdos were just PSEUDO-HOLISTS. But then, when they moved out, Tilly and Svend discovered that they had weakened the whole roof by sawing lots of sections out of the load-bearing timbers. To use in their wood-burning stoves. That earned them a lot of respect with Tilly and Svend. That was cool.

Thomas always had to take care when he went out. Because the Bullshit bikers sold hash just round the corner at the Yo-Yo bar in Brettevillesgade. If the bikers saw anyone with punk hair they chased after them and beat them up. It was worst for Svend as he used to go around in the same type of leather jacket as they did, but he had painted a circle on the back with a large red A for Anarchist in the middle – that was just too much for them.

But Bullshit weren't quite so dangerous any more because the Hells Angels had shot their president, the Mackerel, in 1984. The strange thing was that if anyone was accompanied by Pusher Lars or Axel they were always treated well. Because the bikers were crazy about buying mushrooms and it was too much hassle for them to traipse out to the fields to collect them themselves.

In fact, Kjellerupsgade wasn't a squat at all. Aalborg Town Council owned it. There were no development plans for it and then it was taken over by squatters in 1983 because it was empty. Tilly and Thomas moved in in 1985 when Tilly was eighteen. So both of them could draw social security benefit. And the Council was crafty enough to foresee that they could avert a possible conflict with the squatters by making a deal with the residents in the building. To "LEGITIMIZE the situation" as Thomas put it. "They're trying to fend off the confrontation; think they can buy us off with FALSE promises."

The agreement was that the residents should pay a symbolic rent and that the building should be vacated by August 1986. Afterwards it was to be demolished. Thomas refused to pay, but that didn't matter. Tilly simply paid the stupid 10 kroner and 40 øre a month for their two-room apartment. And it was a nice place even though it only had electricity and cold water. They heated the place with electric bar fires they bought in second-hand shops – those old-fashioned ones with glowing filaments just like in toasters. The social security office paid the electricity bill: 3,500 kroner a quarter.

Tilly had laryngitis three times in the winter of 1985–86. After Little Lars died Thomas kept disappearing. For weeks at a time. Finally Tilly was so fed up with it that she went home to her parents for three days. When she came back the apartment was freezing cold and the light switches didn't work. She entered the living room and almost slipped over – the floor was covered with a glass-like layer of ice, and there lay the male – the zebra fish – frozen solid to her rag rug. The aquarium had shattered because the water had begun to freeze. All the fish were dead. Tilly ran over and fetched Svend from that girl's. He came back with her.

"The fuse has blown," he said.

1000Fryd, where they usually hung out, was dropped in favour of V.B. – that suits Lars fine. He feels he is too old for 1000Fryd – hasn't been there for a couple of years now. Wake beer should be drunk by mature people at a mature place – there appears to be an unspoken consensus about that.

They seat themselves in a booth. Dark panels on the walls, rustic oak tables, yellowing pictures. The décor is very apt as they are all wearing their Sunday best; that isn't saying much in Svend's case but it has turned Tilly, on the other hand, into an almost psychedelic blaze of colour.

Lars hopes for Bertrand's sake that he won't find them – the funeral has put Svend's nerves on edge, as it were. He is quite calm and pleasant on the surface but Lars can see . . . there is something about the way he moves – he can turn violent. What the hell is Bertrand hanging around here for anyway? The party is over for him, Lars thinks.

Tilly calls some of her skateboard friends – Lars's new customers – to ask them to join them. Svend and Michael are at the bar, getting the beer. Then Tilly goes over to take hold of a surprised Louise and drag her to the pinball machine. Tilly can't turn a blind eye if she sees that someone feels left out – everyone should be happy. Except for Bertrand. She has learned that Bertrand doesn't deserve to be as happy as he wants to be.

The pinball machine is an old Kiss model, a classic. They each have a flipper button and Lars can see that they aren't doing too well, but they are enjoying themselves. Everyone at the table follows the game in silence.

"Valentin says 'hello'," Lars says.

"Thanks," Lisbeth mumbles.

"Valentin?" Svend says.

"The guy they used to called Loser, who knocked about with Steso until a few years back," Lars explains.

"Yes, okay – now I'm with you. How's it going with Loser?"

"Valentin," Lars says. "He's not a loser any more."

"Okay," says Svend, who didn't really know Valentin. "What's he up to now, then?"

"He's doing a foundation course and wants to study Marine Biology at university," Lars says.

"Time to make a fresh start," Svend says.

"Exactly," Lars says, turning his head to see what is wrong with Lisbeth. She is sitting next to him, up against the wall, biting her lower lip. Then she turns her head, presses her face into Lars's shoulder and begins to cry. He puts his arm around her while glancing over his shoulder to see whether Tilly is still at the pinball machine. She is. And of course that is why Lisbeth only lets her emotions flow now – so Tilly doesn't see her, because that could take Tilly over the edge. Lisbeth's sobs shake her whole body – fortunately the music is loud enough to prevent Tilly from hearing. Lisbeth weeps uncontrollably. Lars smoothes her hair.

"There, there," he says – can't think of anything else to say – thinks: Christ, how unfair it is. First her childhood sweetheart dies and she is completely devastated . . . for years. And now, when she seems to be getting on top of things again, Steso goes and drugs himself to death. Not that she saw a lot of him, but Lisbeth has always tried to keep a watchful eye on Tilly, and it may be much harder now. Steso was still Tilly's best friend even though he let her down time and time again. But at least it has brought Svend back to town. Maybe it was Steso's last stage production, bringing Svend back home to Lisbeth and Tilly. And to Lars. Svend is Lars's friend. Lars misses him.

Lisbeth's weeping slowly subsides.

"That fucking little idiot," she mutters into Lars's shoulder. "Idiot, idiot, idiot." Then she sniffles and wipes her eyes. Svend gets up and goes to the toilet. "Why do all my friends have to die?" Lisbeth asks, her face swollen. Svend comes back with some toilet paper and hands it to Lars to give to Lisbeth. She blows her nose. "Ohhh," she says, eyeing them all. She makes eye contact with each one of them in turn: "Don't you dare die," she says, wagging her forefinger. "Or you'll have me to reckon with."

When Tilly and Louise have finished playing on the pinball machine they go back to the table with their cheeks flushed. They all raise their bottles to Steso.

"I miss him . . . and Little Lars," Lisbeth says, composed again.

"Yes, my namesake, too," Lars says.

"Here's to Little Lars and Steso-Thomas. May they rest in peace totally stoned," Svend says, and they all click their bottles across the table.

"He was such fun," Tilly says with a giggle.

"Incredibly thin limbs," Lisbeth says.

"And that scar he seemed almost proud of," Svend says.

"Oh, yes," Tilly says.

The reason was that they were at a . . . sort of party at the allotment cottage Pusher Lars had at that time. Just one of those winter evenings with a keg of beer Svend has stolen from the back of Jomfru Ane Gade and Lisbeth has been home to her parents to pick up an old Soda Stream machine so that they can put some gas in, and Svend says she is a "brilliant woman." Tilly reckons Svend is fond of Lisbeth.

Actually, it is not really just one of those evenings. Because Pusher Lars has come up with something different this time. As he is concerned about Lisbeth. She has started university but spends most of the time in her flat with dark rings under her eyes. She doesn't want to go out with them. She is always in the dumps. Tilly is unhappy, too. Because she can't talk to Lisbeth about it. Not about . . . about the Bertrand business, either. Talking to Lisbeth might well help Tilly sort things out in her mind. Anyway, they are not going to drag Lisbeth around the town with them if she doesn't feel like it. So it was the allotment cottage. Without Bertrand.

Michael doesn't want to join them as he is busy with his new girlfriend, Louise. He is probably anxious about how things will turn out when she meets them. Whether she can cope. At any rate, Tilly definitely thinks that Michael is hiding Louise from them.

Tilly and Svend have gone for pizzas in Svend's car. They have eaten them. Now the boys are busy melting snow in a zinc bucket on the wood burner because they are going to smoke a bucket.

They have put the keg of draught beer out in the snow to cool it, and that is also where . . . when they need a pee they have to go out there. And with all that beer – they have to pee all the time. Tilly is out there with Pusher Lars. He is standing making patterns in the snow. Tilly is squatting. Then she falls over backwards and ends on her bum in a pile of snow. She gets snow in her underpants. Lars laughs when he sees the imprint of her buttocks in the snow.

"You've got a heart-shaped ass, Tilly," he says. She likes him saying that – it is true, too. They go inside again and he throws some more wood on the stove, which is already . . . it is sort of aglow. Svend has cut the bottom off a large plastic bottle and pushes it down into the water in the bucket, which is now on the floor. He has placed his chillum in the neck of the bottle and sealed it with some damp paper towel.

"You first, Lisbeth," Svend says. Lisbeth comes over and kneels down in front of the bucket. Svend puts his lighter to the mixture in the chillum and very slowly draws the bottle out of the water. Air is sucked down through the burning mixture in the chillum. Smoke begins to fill the bottle.

"Dinner is served," Svend says, pulling the chillum out of the neck of the bottle. Lisbeth puts her mouth over the bottleneck and then slowly pushes the bottle back down into the water so all the smoke is forced into her lungs. When she has taken the whole hit, she promptly gets to her feet.

"Uuuwaaa," she says, rolling her eyes and swaying slightly. Pusher Lars gently takes her by the shoulders and leads her over to an armchair where she can sit down.

Then it is Thomas's turn, Pusher Lars comes next, and finally Svend. Tilly does not want to smoke a bucket. Svend has already rolled a little schoolgirl joint for her.

Shortly afterwards Lisbeth falls asleep in the chair. Svend tucks her up in a sleeping bag. The rest of them get even more drunk and stoned. Then Svend and Thomas go outside to pee in the snow. Lars puts a tape by a group called The Jesus and Mary Chain into the ghetto blaster and then they sit on the sofa listening to PSYCHOCANDY. Lars is showing Tilly how to stick several Rizla papers together to make a bomber – a really big joint. Thomas comes in muttering something or other. Lars asks Tilly whether she has noticed that Thomas's eyes look like the pee holes in the snow outside. She thinks that is a bit hard on him, but funny, too. Because what he says is right. Thomas leans up against the wall and slides very slowly downwards until he is sitting on the floor. He is completely bombed out.

Tilly is watching Lars roll the Rizla papers so that they fit tightly around the joint filter. Then she looks over at Thomas. As soon as he is flat on the floor he topples over to one side. Neither Lars or Tilly have time to do anything about it.

They hear a SSSZZZ as his cheek bangs against the stove and is scorched. Tilly struggles to her feet and scatters the stuff Lars has been mixing all over the floor. As she does so, Thomas flops forward – he is lying absolutely motionless on the floor. He is still muttering. Svend comes in through the door and says:

"Wow! . . . Grilled junkie." That really upsets Tilly, really and truly, because he . . . says that about Thomas. Tilly goes over to him, but he has already fallen asleep. At that time she thought he was dead, so she became . . . hysterical because . . . she thought they should do something, call an ambulance, but Svend said he was still breathing so they should just cool the burn down.

"We can put him outside in the snow," Lars suggests.

"Don't you think he'll freeze out there?" Svend asks. But now Tilly has already started crying again. Lisbeth wakes up. She is hardly able to get up off the chair. She yells at Svend. She tells him to go outside for some ice and put it in a plastic bag and crush it with something or other and then wrap the bag in a tea towel. He does that and Tilly sits with Thomas until the morning, holding the ice bag against his cheek. The others mostly sleep.

Lisbeth wakes up in the morning and she is in a really bad mood because . . . Tilly thinks it is because of what happened and they were, like, at a loss as to know what to do. Lisbeth goes out and finds a taxi. They wake Thomas and go with him to emerg. *One of the doctors there gives them a talking to. Tilly bursts into tears. Lisbeth says something to the effect that he should mind his own business and not be so "bloody high and mighty." Thomas is given a morphine injection and so he is in a good mood as he sits on a couch going on about how many medicine cabinets there are in a place like this. And every time someone in a white coat walks by he says: "Hey, it's hurting MORE now. I think I need MORE injections to, like, FIX it."*

Lisbeth feels drained inside after all her crying, but she doesn't want to go home yet. It is good to be with Pusher Lars and Svend today – she thinks they should just have a few drinks, think about Thomas and have a nice time. She can feel that Svend has his eye on her as he pushes the conversation along.

"He always had burn marks between his fingers, too," Svend says.

"Yes," Lars says, "that was a permanent injury." Lisbeth looks at Lars's fingers. There aren't any burn marks on them, they are just yellow.

"Where did he get them from?" Louise asks.

"He forgot about the cigarettes in his hand," Svend explains.

"What do you mean . . . forgot?" Louise asks. She is not the brightest of lights, Michael's weirdo girlfriend; Lisbeth assumes that that is how he likes it.

"You know, he lit a cigarette and then he fell asleep or something and then it burned right down between his fingers," Svend explains with a broad smile; he looks at Lars's hands.

"I haven't got any," Lars says.

"No," Svend says. "But what's that on your right thumb?" he asks with a laugh. Lars hides his right hand with his left, but then he laughs, too, and holds up his thumb. The top joint, including the nail, is completely brown.

"That's my permanent mixing injury," Lars says.

Louise questions Michael, who, with a resigned look on his face, begins to explain until Louise says: "No, you're kidding, aren't you?"

Lars shrugs his shoulders. "It's the truth," he says. Lisbeth wonders whether you could get stoned just by sucking his thumb.

"Can I suck your thumb?" Svend asks Lars with a leer.

"Yes, course," Lars says, smiling at him. Svend turns to look at Lisbeth. She wants to go and sit next to him – he seems to be okay now – not the way he was before he moved to Copenhagen. She hopes he will be moving back, but doubts whether he will. She cautiously stretches out her legs under the table and wraps them around Svend's legs. He is sitting looking at Lars when she closes her legs; she can feel Svend's calf muscles between hers. Svend's shoulder twitches and then he beams, slowly closes his eyes and leans back.

Michael is weighing Svend up – he has been doing that for some time. They are not as similar as they once were, Lisbeth thinks. Michael has become much . . . smoother. She respects him for his endurance throughout Louise's anorexia but . . . now he is making a way for himself whilst Svend with all his jagged edges is only slashing at air. All the same, Svend seems to her to have much more life in him.

"Svend," Michael says, to catch his attention.

"Yes?" Svend says, opening his eyes and looking straight into Lisbeth's.

"What about when you move back, what's going to happen then?" Michael is met with a blank look from Svend:

"A job, an apartment, new brakes on the car," he answers tonelessly.

"But . . . ," Michael begins, breaks off, shakes his head.

"But what?" Svend asks.

"You always used to say that anything might happen . . . ?" Michael says.

"Yes," Svend says, "but that doesn't seem to be so. I was naive." Then he laughs; and he isn't laughing out of desperation or because he thinks it is sad. He is laughing at Michael.

There is still a chance that . . . things will happen, Lisbeth thinks, and laughs along with Svend. It is just ironic that Michael sees himself as a success and a better functioning individual while always hoping that Svend will do something wildly off the wall, something that can provide Michael with some entertainment. Svend winks.

"Look, I'm a fucking gardener. I make things grow," he says with a smile and a shrug of his shoulders. Michael looks embarrassed.

Louise says nothing. She looks from one to the other.

"But . . . didn't he have any aims in life?" she asks.

"Who?" Lars asks.

"You know, Steso . . . Thomas?" Louise says.

The door bursts open and Steso comes rushing into 1000Fryd in his hectic fashion, moves to the middle of the room and stares at the people on the stools at the bar with their backs to him, draught beer in their hands, Thursday afternoon.

"Who's got a TYPEWRITER?" he shouts aggressively – it is quite evident that he is high on pills. "I NEED a typewriter, NOW." People swivel round on their bar-stools, all of them thinking: Oh, it's Steso. Wonder how strung out he is today?

"Come on then, for CHRIST'S SAKE," he says, "I'm applying for a place at the School of Journalism and I need a typewriter – I've got to PRACTISE." Svend goes over to him, puts a hand on his shoulder and asks him what he is up to.

"From the inside," he answers. "I can see it now . . . I've got to change it from THE INSIDE."

"What have you got to change?" Svend asks, realizing as he speaks what Steso means.

"The fucking SYSTEM, of course." Steso stares up at Svend, condescendingly, with pinpoint dots of blood in his eyes.

In the end he borrows an electric typewriter from a girl who thinks he is just so interesting, and then he goes home to practise.

It seems a frightening thought – Steso as a journalist, but it could be entertaining to watch how he makes out. And Svend is in need of some entertainment – his relationship with his girlfriend is on the rocks and his job stinks.

Svend goes home and applies to take the entrance exam for the School of Journalists. His application is accepted.

The evening before the exam he takes Steso and the borrowed typewriter back to his flat with him. Steso is totally stoned and Svend doesn't actually reckon he will be fit for anything the following day.

Next morning Svend packs a limp Steso into the car and they set off for Aarhus. They stop at apull-over area for Steso to take a leak. Soon afterwards he comes to life.

They are lucky enough to be allocated places in the same examination room; Svend up at the front, Steso a little further back. Svend has brought his old Remington along.

In the first test they have to write a summary of a videoed discussion program. As soon as the video has finished Steso immediately begins to thump away at the keys like a madman, quietly mumbling to himself, as is his wont. Svend turns round – Steso has a knowing smirk on his face. All this makes the other examinees nervous – they can't concentrate. This is almost certainly part of Steso's strategy. Svend can't collect his thoughts, either – writing has never been his strong point.

In the break before the second test Steso is exultant: "In that program I managed to get to grips with the REAL discussion that was going on beneath the surface," he says.

"And what was that?" Svend asks.

"You'd really like to know that, wouldn't you?" Steso says with a malicious laugh. He continues: "We just need to have a little smoke. The next test is one of those commentary things. We'll have to be SHARPER than the others at finding associations to stay AHEAD," he says, after which they smoke a little pot and then go in to take the second test.

A quarter of an hour or so later Svend can hear Steso cursing behind him. Svend turns round. Steso has opened the lid of the typewriter and is fiddling about with something inside it. The lady invigilating at the desk at the front glares down at him. Then he begins to pull the ribbon out.

"What the devil IS all this?" he mutters, continuing to pull metre after metre of the ribbon out over the table and onto the floor. Everyone else has stopped writing – they just gawp at him in disbelief. Steso gives up trying to solve the problem with the ribbon and begins to pound the typewriter with his fists – now he is going to force it to behave itself.

"Stop, stop," the lady says, jumping up and making her way towards him. Steso looks up, waiting to see what will happen.

"Didn't you bring an extra ribbon with you?" she whispers.

"A WHAT?" Steso asks.

"That's a disposable ribbon," she says, pointing at the tangle of ribbon.

"Disposable . . . ?" Steso seems baffled. The lady explains that there might be an old typewriter outside in the corridor he can use. Steso darts out and comes back lugging an antiquated portable model; then he gets going again. Svend watches him. 30 seconds later Steso looks up at the lady.

"There's no bloody ink in this ribbon," he says indignantly. She shushes him and, pushing back her chair, looks completely flummoxed; that is the effect he has on most people, but she isn't aware of that, of course. As she passes Svend on her way down, he stops her:

"You can give him my machine," he says, ripping the paper out of it.

"But . . . ," the lady begins. Steso, who is sitting further back, says:

"I knew they'd try to stop me. It's a fucking CONSPIRACY."

"Go on," Svend says to the lady as he gets to his feet. Gives Steso the thumbs up and leaves the room.

Steso is in high spirits when he comes out for the break. He speaks quickly:

"I managed it. That was very generous of you, Svend. You SACRIFICED yourself for me – I'll never ever forget that. Those imperialistic BASTARDS will have to deal with me."

The third test consists of general knowledge questions. Steso has an arch expression on his face when he comes out.

"You know what, Svend, they were strange questions, man. But that was because most of them were TRICK questions – I could see that right away," he says with an air of superiority.

Then they drive home. Stop at the first roadside cafeteria to grab some fish and chips and a cup of coffee.

"You were surprisingly fresh today, Steso," Svend says to him.

"I was well-prepared," he says, slyly looking up at Svend. Steso obviously feels that Svend has underestimated him.

"How come?" Svend asks.

"Pills," Steso replies. "I've found a BRILLIANT cocktail. It's like . . . STEEL. I take them and within half an hour the world is made of STEEL . . . STAINLESS STEEL."

A couple of months later Svend asked him about the result of the exam.

"It was just as I expected," Steso said through clenched teeth. He hadn't been accepted. The system had "stigmatized" him as he put it, and then he rabbited on about how the eminences grises after due jaundiced deliberation had sidelined him: ". . . stigmatization of the few CLEAR-SIGHTED individuals . . . who have SEEN THROUGH the ploys of the upper echelons . . . imposing a MENTAL QUARANTINE . . . silent NETWORK of closed doors . . . MARGINALIZATION . . . institutionalized intellectual EXILE . . . manipulation of the masses by means of a SEQUESTRATION of the truth . . . ."

One of Tilly's hip-hop friends comes in through the door. He has a skateboard under his arm. They hug and talk in whispers. Tilly smiles at him.

"I'm going to the kiosk," she tells the others.

"Are you going for some marshmallows?" Lisbeth asks.

Tilly nods. "Yes, of course," she says and asks whether any of the others want anything. Svend gives her some money to buy some cigarettes and she scurries off with her friend.

"The world just won't go away," Pusher Lars says out of the blue.

"Damn," Svend says, grinning at him. Years ago they would often talk about that. The world won't go away, so you have to try and hide away from it – or at least forget it.

"Grow up, will you," Michael says.

"It's hard to be grown up when the price you have to pay is endless compromises," Svend says.

"True," Lisbeth says, smiling at him.

"Steso called it *the banal phase,*" Lars says. Michael looks puzzled.

"Just like in psychology," Lars explains. "There's the oral and the anal phase, and then finally there's the banal phase."

"O-kay," Michael says, apparently not having heard Steso's exposition. "What are the characteristic features of the banal phase, then?"

"Let me see if I can remember," Lars says. "The bottom line at any rate is that you lose your naive illusions. You start out believing that you're something very *special.* A *special* person: more profound and more discerning than everyone else. You've passed through the banal phase when you realize that you're merely expendable and that you're going to die like everyone else and be eaten by worms and forgotten by posterity. Then you're grown up."

"*the expendables,*" Svend says – that was the name of the band Lisbeth once played in . . . with Adrian.

"Exactly," Lisbeth says with a slightly embarrassed laugh. "A sort of inverted megalomania, as it were."

"Yes, that's what you had – and it was brilliant," Lars says.

"Life is banal," Svend says.

"Homespun Stesolid philosophy," Lars says.

"But what about . . . Steso?" Louise asks.

"Easy, now," Lars says. "It was us he was talking about. He was above such trivialities. He was engaged in a constant process of self-realisation.

"How do you mean?" Louise asks.

"He experimented with drugs – chemistry – in his body. New combinations all the time. He was a sort of researcher – that was his goal in life, and he loved it," Lars says.

"He was a great guy," Svend says.

"He was bloody evil, too. He was always . . . so nasty to people," Michael says with a defiant glare at Svend.

Lars nods: "Yes, he was *almost* always malicious.

"Give me one example, then, of when he wasn't a nasty piece of work," Michael says.

"Valentin," Lars says without hesitation. "The time Steso helped Loser transform himself into Valentin – shortly before he joined us on the expendables' tour of Germany."

Lars glides over the floorboards, tingling, he flows outwards, changes, stretches. The sounds colour the air. The walls are moving. He sees atoms – coherence. Uncontrollable laughter. Everything is insanely distinct – can move things with his eyes, stretch them out of shape, pull them through the horizon, twist them. Knock them down he can, if he wants. The room is twenty times longer than normal. Loser is hovering over the sofa, Steso changes face and body. Lars caricatures himself in a dream, looks down at himself: his legs stretching down 120 metres to the ground – feeling giddy. When he breathes in, the suction from his lungs pulls at the clouds. A cup moves on the table and he can hear every single microscopic unevenness in the paint; and suddenly he holds the whole world inside himself. It is everywhere – all values are absolute. The apple he holds in his hand, big and alive, throbbing with fluid and energy. Looks out through the walls – at the sky. Divides it up; it becomes squares on a chessboard, Lars moves them about, the edges sparkle with neon birds. Consistency has gone. Explores the universe. The humidity in the clouds, the water, as in his blood, he gathers it for rain.

"The night just keeps on coming," Loser says after Steso has wandered off into town.

Lars finds his sleeping bag, gets Loser to bed down on the sofa. Lars is becoming nervous. He can see by the expression on his face that Loser is entirely empty inside, and naturally he is afraid of that emptiness – that is obvious.

Emptiness, Lars thinks. Emptiness is on the increase everywhere. Svend went off to Copenhagen more than a year ago now and Lars has heard nothing from him. Lisbeth is buried in her studies. Michael has finished his training and taken a job working with young people – his girlfriend is apparently studying to be a social worker, too. Bertrand still drops by once in a while to buy a couple of grams, but that is not a friendship. Tilly is the only one Lars sees regularly, and she is dependable. And then she keeps in contact with Svend, though it doesn't sound as if Svend's life is as stable as Lars would wish for him.

Finally there is Steso. Lars still sees him and greatly enjoys his company even though Steso is high maintenance. He reappears when Loser has been cocooned on the sofa for several hours. Steso casts a fleeting glance at him.

"Bad experience?" Steso asks.

"Yes," Loser says.

"Tell me how it feels," Steso says.

"No,"

"Why not?"

"I know what you'll say." Loser cries noiselessly – the tears roll down his cheeks. "Everything has gone," he says.

Steso makes a sweeping gesture around the room. "Everything's still here, Loser – NOTHING has changed."

"Everything inside me has . . . gone."

"And . . . ?" Steso says.

"You can see right inside me."

"There's nothing there, you say?"

"I have to get it back." Loser's voice sounds hollow.

"Why?" Steso asks.

"Because . . . it's me."

"Yeah – maybe." Steso doesn't sound convinced.

"Maybe?" Loser says.

"Maybe it was just something you'd acquired. Manners. Window-dressing."

"What do you think we should do?" Lars asks.

"Loser should just EXPERIENCE this. It's a unique OPPORTUNITY for him," Steso says.

"No," Loser sobs, "it's . . . awful."

"That's just because you're AFRAID – there's no NEED to be."

"Steso," Lars says firmly. "How can we help Loser?"

"Have you got any more mushrooms?" Steso asks.

"Look, this is serious," Lars says.

"I AM serious." Steso points at Loser: "He needs another trip so he can come back."

Lars watches as Loser opens his eyes wide and recoils against the sofa, staring all the while at Steso.

"Sounds like a bad idea," Lars says.

"I admit it's a hippie method, but on the other hand, how much WORSE can it be?" he says, looking over at Loser, who whispers:

"And what if it goes wrong?"

"That'll only happen if you put the brakes on."

Loser buries his face in the sleeping bag, shouting: "I DAREN'T." He sobs out loud. Lars is becoming genuinely afraid, as he has never experienced anything like this before. He has heard that Michael once had a bad experience with mushrooms; and Svend, too, totally blacked out once. Line, his then girlfriend – and the mother of Svend's daughter – held his hand to comfort him. Afterwards Svend explained how he wasn't able to hold anybody's hand any more because he had a greater perception of her when she took his hand than he had of himself. But . . . if this meant that Lars had to accompany Loser to the psychiatric ward, then yes of course, he would. But what a fiasco that would be. Steso is standing in the middle of the room. Lars looks at him. Steso starts to rock up and down on the balls of his feet.

"Hmmm," he says, shaking his shoulders and reaching out his hand. "Cigarette," he says. Lars lights one and hands it to him. Then Steso drags a chair over to the sofa and sits down on it directly in front of Loser; then reaches out and takes one of his hands which are clasped around his bent-up legs.

"Loser – you were NOTHING before," Steso says, massaging Loser's hand and forearm. "Now you have the chance to make a new start. You have been REBORN – this has never happened before in the history of mankind – you are your own MESSIAH – you are luckier than JESUS."

"Completely empty," Loser mumbles, shaking his head, his face still buried in the sleeping bag.

"Can you remember who you are?" Steso asks in a business-like manner. Loser raises his tear-ridden, swollen face:

"Well, I can remember people, places – everything. There's just no . . . no feelings connected with what I can remember." Steso sticks his cigarette between Loser's lips.

"That's PERFECT," he says, looking across at Lars. "PERFECT," he repeats. "Got a joint?" Lars takes a ready-rolled joint out of his pusher box, lights it and then hands it to Steso who takes a drag before offering it to Loser.

"Want a smoke?" Steso asks.

Loser looks confused, removes the cigarette from his mouth. "I don't know. Do I?"

"No, it's never really been quite your style, has it," Steso says, taking another drag and shrugging his shoulders.

"Why not?" Loser asks.

"The hypophysis, maybe," Steso says philosophically. "Your righteous soul probably can't stomach it." Steso holds the joint up in the air in front of Loser and

the smoke wreathes out of his mouth as he speaks. "That's what turned you into Loser – now you can be . . . what was your name, now?"

"Valentin," Loser says.

"Welcome, Valentin." Steso puts out his hand again and energetically shakes Loser's hand up and down with a very solemn expression on his face. "Let's go to the zoo, Valentin."

"What for?"

"You're a vegetarian, you like animals – you remember that, don't you?"

"Yes," Loser says.

"That's not a bad starting point, Valentin," Steso says. Loser looks as if he is beginning to pull himself together.

"Yes, dolphins, sea lions, penguins – things that can swim. But it's the wrong time of the year – the middle of the night – they're closed."

"Yes, I know," Steso says, "but you also like to crawl over fences – you're not afraid of anything."

"Aren't I?"

"No. You can do ANYTHING." Steso stands up purposefully and prepares for their departure. Loser slowly disentangles himself from the sleeping bag and walks with uncertain steps out to the toilet.

"Are we still going to the concert tonight?" Lars asks as that is what he has arranged with Steso – Union Carbide Productions are playing at 1000Fryd in eighteen hours.

Steso points towards the toilet door. They can hear Valentin snorting and splashing water about.

"He's an unstable soul – an empty vessel," Steso says. "Almost like a teenage girl. We'll have to be careful what we put in him."

Bertrand comes in through the door. "I thought you were going to bloody 1000Fryd," he says. Nobody answers him.

"Well, anyway . . . ," Michael murmurs, budging up a little to make room for Bertrand; but he squeezes himself in next to Tilly who has returned alone from the kiosk and is sitting munching marshmallows.

Bertrand calls the bartender over and orders a round of large draught beers and a Ballantine's whisky for everyone, even though they all have bottles of beer in their hands. Lisbeth notices that Svend glares at Bertrand when he puts his arm around Tilly and whispers: "What about us two driving out to the coast tonight?" Tilly looks awkward.

"I just have to go to the toilet," she says. Bertrand stands up to let her out, then sits down again. His eyes wander around the room as if he is searching for something. Then he gets to his feet and makes his way towards the toilets.

"Bertrand," Svend calls out after he has taken two steps. Bertrand turns round.

"What?" he says.

"Stop following her around, Bertrand," Svend tells him. Lisbeth is taken aback – doesn't understand what is going on.

"What are you on about?" Bertrand asks – annoyed, but nervous, too.

"Actually, I think it'd be best if you left now," Svend says. Lisbeth looks round at the others to see whether they understand what is going on. Michael looks confused; Lars is sitting with slumped shoulders, staring down at the table.

"Who the hell do you think you are?" Bertrand says, both afraid and angry.

"She doesn't need that," Svend answers. Even though he doesn't raise his voice he sounds . . . intimidating. Then Michael pipes up:

"What the hell are you playing at?" he says to Svend. "Just calm down a bit."

"Don't you interfere in something you know nothing about," Svend says with a dismissive sweep of his arm, but without taking his eyes off Bertrand.

"I'm not bloody trying to . . . ," Bertrand says, but stops because Svend jumps up and pushes the table right over towards Lisbeth and Lars so that he can easily get past Michael and Louise, who are sitting next to him on the bench. Svend's voice is level, cold:

"Let me put it another way: If you don't leave now, I'll shove a beer glass in your face."

"Michael leans over to Pusher Lars: "What the hell's going on, Lars?" he asks.

"See for yourself," Lars says, without raising his head.

Bertrand studies the glass of beer he has just bought for Svend and then looks round at the others. Lars is slowly shaking his head; Lisbeth is watching Svend, with her teeth clenched. Louise appears scared. Nobody says a word.

Lisbeth leans forward and puts a hand on Svend's arm – he shakes it off violently, remains standing.

"We're only . . . ," Bertrand starts off, then falters – his voice sounds strangely dry.

"Bertrand," Svend says – he articulates his name in two discrete syllables: *Ber-trand*. Svend continues: This is not a matter for discussion. I should have done it then, but God help me if I don't do it now . . . unless you clear off." Bertrand is rooted to the spot, his eyes are fixed on Svend, who stands there unflinching, coolly alert.

SMACK. Svend has taken a long stride out onto the floor, his hand has struck Bertrand's cheek and has already been withdrawn. Bertrand has tears in his eyes.

"*Svend!*" Michael shouts. Svend keeps his eyes fixed on Bertrand.

"Lars!" Lisbeth screams, shaken; but Lars just keeps staring down at the table top.

"Shut up," Svend snarls at no-one in particular – maybe it is addressed to all of them. Bertrand grabs his jacket from a hook on the coat rack. As he does so, Svend sits down again. Bertrand is standing some way from the end of the table – almost certainly so that Svend is out of his striking distance.

"Svend, you're a bloody psychopath," he says, in a quavering voice, then hurries off out of the door.

Svend sighs when the door has closed behind Bertrand. Lisbeth is dumbstruck. Lars shakes his head, looks up and across at Svend.

"Not a word out of you," Svend says, pointing at him.

"No," Lars says, "but couldn't you have been a bit more diplomatic? Couldn't you have just asked him to leave her alone?"

Michael straightens his back, takes a deep breath, stares hard at Svend and is on the verge of saying something. At that moment Tilly comes back and they all go quiet.

"Where's Bertrand?" she asks.

"There was something he had to sort out," Michael says, confused.

"Okay," she says, looking genuinely surprised and happy. Tilly squeezes in past Louise and Michael and sits down on the bench next to Svend. She starts chattering away about some plants he once found for her so that she could create a rain forest environment in her living room.

"There was just so much oxygen in the air," she says enthusiastically. Svend nods and says:

"That's right, Tilly. You can really notice it."

Then two of Tilly's hip-hop friends come in through the door. One of them was here earlier on, Lisbeth seems to remember. They are slightly older than her students at the high school. Tilly gets up and throws her arms around them and they greet everyone at the table – especially Pusher Lars, whom they appear to know. Then they take Tilly to the pinball table with them. One of them – with an immensely long baggy seat in his trousers – stands behind Tilly with his hands over hers, trying to teach her how to keep the ball in play using the flipper buttons. She is happy and laughing.

"What did you do that for, Svend?" Michael asks when Tilly is out of earshot. Svend is sitting with a tired look on his face. It takes him a few seconds to answer.

"You don't know, Michael, because you haven't been paying attention. And I am not in a position to tell you why." Lisbeth can see that Michael feels personally under attack. She feels the same way because she doesn't know what all that to-do with Bertrand was about. Michael is in no mind to let the matter rest.

"Here we have a man who lives in a shithouse and he slings shit around." He is alluding to Svend's child, Katja – there is no doubt in Lisbeth's mind about that. But Tilly has told her that Svend feels bad about all the things that happened. Svend doesn't respond.

"What have you got to say for yourself?" Michael asks. Svend is silent. "Lars?" Michael says. Svend lights a cigarette and slowly gets to his feet. Lars raises his face to look at Michael.

"Svend's right," he says – and no more.

"I'll get a round of shots in," Svend says and walks towards the bar. Lisbeth follows him.

"Will you tell me what it was all about, Svend?" she asks. She tries to hide it but her tone is still accusatory.

"You don't want to know, Lisbeth," he says.

"Yes, I do," she says.

"Don't say I didn't warn you, then."

That is right. She doesn't really want to know what Svend tells her. About the time Tilly was so mixed-up that she had to be admitted to be hospital.

About when Bertrand had been going to bed with her for months but had made it plain that she was not to tell anyone. It was *their secret*. They couldn't be seen together. Lisbeth knows that Tilly was crazy about him then; but she can't really believe that Bertrand . . . abused her like that. How could she have failed to notice?

"How do you know?" she asks.

"She told me so."

"Don't you think it was just something she made up?"

"I confronted him with it," Svend says.

"How?" she asks, feeling stupid – she can work that out easily enough.

"That's not important," Svend says, dismissing it with a wave of his hand. His face is grim. "He admitted it."

"Do you think that's why she . . . ," Lisbeth asks.

"How should I know," Svend says. "I only know that she was on home release from the funny farm and I went into Klostertorvet with her. We were only going to have a beer and she didn't want to go to 1000Fryd. And there was Bernard canoodling with one of his nice girls, and then she completely cracked up."

"And told you about it?"

"Later on," replies Svend. He grimaces as he checks the money in his hand and hands the bartender his due.

"Tell me about it, Svend. I'd like to know," Lisbeth says. Now she *has* to know. Tilly used to tell her everything. In fact, Lisbeth thought it was still like that. Svend sighs, as if bracing himself: "The week after I wanted to visit her at the psychiatric ward. The doctors wouldn't let me in, but they weren't able to explain what the problem was, either. I insisted . . . you know."

"Yes, I do know," Lisbeth says and can't help smiling even though the skin on her face feels as if it is about to split.

"It turned out that she'd been smearing herself with all sorts of things: and I mean *all* sorts. She said that she'd been burned."

"Couldn't they . . . do anything?" Lisbeth asks. Svend gives a tired laugh: "It was something that was sort of beyond their experience."

"And then . . . ?"

"Then they let me in to see her and after several visits I got it out of her . . . what had happened."

"How . . . was she?"

"She'd smeared toothpaste all over her face. Some evil man had *burned her*. Then she told me that I was a bit burnt, too . . . you know how it is. So I had some toothpaste plastered over my skull, and then it was as if we were on the same wavelength."

"And that was that?"

"Yes, well I promised her of course that the *evil man* wouldn't burn her again."

"And that's what this is all about now?"

"Lisbeth, for Christ's sake . . . ," he begins, then raises his eyes to the ceiling – the veins in his neck protrude, the sinews tauten. Then he looks at Lisbeth again; an expression of distaste painted all over his face.

"I don't know what the hell to do. The girl is off her nut – it might not be so bad at the moment, but beneath the surface . . . I've promised her. She's made new friends – it looks as though they treat her decently. Bertrand has always been a parasite – a creep." Svend begins to seethe again: "That time we were, like, all together . . . were here . . . When we met him in town with his well-dressed friends they weren't to know that he knew us. He told them we were some people he had *gone to primary school with*. I mean to say, what sort of shit is that?"

Lisbeth nods. It is true. Bertrand has never wanted to be identified with them. Svend takes the tray with the vodka shots.

"Forget it," he says and goes across to Tilly and her friends, gives them a vodka, stands chatting with them for a while before returning to the table.

Svend sets off from Aalborg in his car at dusk. Steso is with him because he is going to visit his little sister who is on a training course in Copenhagen. Even before they have left the town behind them Steso has passed out on the back seat and Svend is thinking about Little Lars – about the time he died seven years before.

Shortly before the accident they had been at Stedet in Maren Turis Gade. Lisbeth was cross with Lars for spending too much time with Steso, taking too much acid.

"Go home and see her," Svend said.

"She's out," Little Lars answered. They drank. Not much was said. At one point Little Lars got his finger stuck. They were sitting on stools with round metal seats which had holes punched in them. Little Lars had stuck a finger down through one of the holes and couldn't get it out again.

"Easy now, Lars," Svend said because on previous occasions when Lars was angry he had seen him hammer his fists against a wall until they bled. "I'll go and get some soap." Svend stood up and went to the toilet where he pumped some liquid soap into the palm of his hand. On his way back he saw that Little Lars had put one foot on the stool to give him some leverage and then he simply pulled his finger out. When Svend arrived Lars was sitting looking at his red-raw finger; the blood was streaming down his forearm. A couple of girls screamed. The doorman came rushing up.

"Don't worry," Little Lars said, "I'm going." And to Svend: "You stay here. See you." A couple of days later Pusher Lars told him how Lisbeth had come home late at night and when she lifted the duvet to climb into bed the whole bed and Little Lars was covered in blood. She was horrified. A few days after they took the bus to Sønderholm to visit their respective parents. Late that evening Little Lars picked Lisbeth up from her parents' place in a stolen car and they drove towards Aalborg. She never told anyone what had happened, but he ploughed the car into the front of Hasseris High School, hit a wall, was rammed in the midriff by the steering column and died. Lisbeth sustained multiple fractures to one of her legs.

Steso gives a grunt from the back seat and Svend feels ill at ease. The car tires sing on the tarmac. Aalborg slips further and further into the distance behind them; but the events . . . all the events weigh heavily on Svend's mind. He is due to start his new job on Monday morning – at a nursery in Amager – and has rented an apartment in Njalsgade. The future seems as meaningless and frightening as the past.

Night has now fallen and fog has settled in thick, white belts over the countryside. He pulls into a pull-over area. Switches off the engine, leaves the headlights on. Gets out to stretch his legs. Walks in front of the car. Profiled against the fog by the frosty glare of the lights. Smokes a cigarette. The air is mute as the fog greets the smoke and, even though it is unreal, he needs her as a husk to encase his blood. Lisbeth. Everything has gone belly up. How long has he been waiting to tell her? After Little Lars died – it was impossible, she was mentally paralyzed – for years. The first time he saw her . . . all the time he has thrown away, wasted, on hoping. Maybe she wasn't even aware. They had been friends for too long. And the girlfriends he had had, they didn't know what they were up against – they were fighting against a ghost, a castle in the air; they didn't stand a chance. Adrian fought against her ghost; he didn't even realize that she picked him because he looked like Little Lars. And Adrian lost. Svend knows all too well that she may no longer be someone who could be loved; maybe there is nothing left.

The car door opens.

"SVEND," Steso shouts, "You're too OLD for juvenile dementia."

"I was only having a smoke," Svend says, embarrassed. Steso is out of the car, walking towards him:

"You stand smoking in the clinical light of the automobile," Steso says. "The smoke mingles with the fog, the tarmac glistens with moisture. Anyone would think you had a UNIVERSITY DEGREE in Weltschmerz. Stop being so fucking banal." Steso spits before continuing: "It's unsavoury for a man to have Weltschmerz while AT THE SAME TIME multiplying upon the earth." Steso steps up to Svend: "Give me a smoke." Svend hands him one.

"I've just lost my access rights," he says. "I'm out of the picture now."

"You'll never be out of it, Svend. You have MULTIPLIED. Blood is thicker than water."

"But woman is as treacherous as water," Svend says in a tired voice – he read that somewhere and it has stuck in his mind.

"Which is thinner than wine," Steso says promptly – suddenly very alert: "Didn't you have a bottle of wine, Svend?" Svend tells Steso that he has a whole case full.

"SUPERB," Steso says, walking over to a bush. Svend studies his back – it is not like Steso to leave a conversation without firing off a Parthian shot. The splashing sound seems very loud in the silence. "She doesn't want you, Svend. She's not ready. You're not AT ALL ready. Perhaps you never will be."

"What are you talking about?" Svend says.

Steso shakes his head: "Stop insulting your own intelligence," he says.

Svend goes back to the car and selects a bottle of wine in the trunk, takes out his pocket knife, pulls out the cork. Takes a couple of extra bottles into the car with him. Steso sits in the passenger seat. Svend starts the car; reminds Steso that his job is to keep the driver from falling asleep.

"Okay," Steso says, "I'll tell you about the Muslim veil." This is his latest talking point. He has struck up a friendly relationship with Hossein – Iranian war refugee and loan shark – and Steso has begun to devour information about Islam and Muslims. According to Hossein, Muslims are to blame for everything and, as usual, Steso wants to debate the issues of the moment. The veil is of central importance.

"It says in the Koran that people should be dressed MODESTLY. And that women should not DISPLAY their beauty. Nothing else. Then some misogynistic imams over-interpreted the Hadith – the body of tradition related to the sayings of

Mohammed – to mean that modesty is synonymous with COVERING. In fact, Mohammed was only talking about MENSTRUATING women. He was visiting some people and then their teenage daughter came home – a right little Arabian bimbo. She was flying the red flag and was dressed a little too provocatively for Mohammed's taste, so he said that a menstruating woman should only display this . . . ," Steso lifts his hands to frame his face. "The hair and neck should also be concealed. But it was quite alright to expose the hands and feet." Svend doesn't comment. Steso rambles on: "And of course it's normal in many cultures to regard bleeding women as UNCLEAN, to be hidden away. Men are physically more powerful and we simply don't UNDERSTAND bleeding women."

"And women? What power do they have?" Svend asks.

Steso smiles at him: "The reason you're leaving Aalborg – they have PSYCHOLOGICAL supremacy."

Svend sighs: "And how the hell did they manage to get that?" he asks.

Steso puts a hand on his arm: "Drop it, Svend. It seems to me that it ensures the survival of the species," he says. "But in ACTUAL FACT the whole veil farce stems from a classic colonialist strategy which the Muslims employed when Islam was expanding. In the pre-Islamic kingdoms of Persia the ruling class kept their women in a harem, which means forbidden. When the women were outside the house they were required to cover their bodies and were forbidden to work. It conferred status if you could afford to do that; poor women who had to work didn't go round with all that clobber on of course – it would get in the way. Then, when the Muslims gained power, naturally they had to show that ALL Muslims were rich, and therefore ALL women had to wear the veil." Steso takes a long swig from the wine bottle, fiddles with the car radio, pulls out a couple of cigarettes from Svend's packet on the dashboard, lights one for each of them. "And in North-west Africa there's a tribe – the Tuaregs – where the women wear casual clothes and the MEN wear a veil – even on their wedding night. They don't even know why they do it. But it PROVES that the veil is a cultural phenomenon which has NOTHING to do with the Koran."

"Fuck all that political stuff," Svend says. "What about the Tuaregs – do they still exist?"

"Christ, yeah. They smuggle weapons and trade in slaves.

"Slaves?" Svend asks in surprise.

"You know how the world is," Steso says with a shrug. Then he begins to rummage in his bag looking for a book: A Thousand Miles through the Sahara *by*

Otto Zeltin. Steso shows it to Svend, eulogising it as he flicks through the pages. And he talks all the way down through the foggy Jutland night, interrupted only by regular swigs from the wine bottle:

About the Hoggar Tuaregs from the Ténéré, the Land of Fear, in the southern Sahara. About the man who keeps slaves who deceive him, but like the true aristocrat he is, he is only interested in playing the imzad *at the* ahâl *and singing songs in praise of his people's women, who let their hair hang loose in the wind. And his song oozes with his yen for battle and blood. He sallies forth across the wide expanses on his white mehari; he is a feared man with his broad, two-edged sword; an aristocratic figure completely enveloped in vivid indigo robes; his black veil – the* lithâm *– which only reveals his mysterious, flashing eyes; his pure white skin; the shape of his face and his voice, entirely European in nature; dignified, measured and reserved – every single movement bearing the mark of self-control and natural elegance. Where does he come from? Is he a Berber – a descendent of the Carthaginians and Numidians? Does the blood of Rome course through his veins? All this is beside the point. He plunders – a worthy occupation for men.*

And Steso talks about the Djinn, the demons of the desert; El-Goléa – the town with the spellbinding perfumed gardens; Tanezrouft – the Land of Thirst; well-divers; oases, sandstorms; scorpions. Steso is in his element – intoxicated and expounding on important matters. It is well into the night when Svend drops him off at Otto Mønsteds Kollegium in Copenhagen. On stepping out of the car Steso shouts to Svend:

"Allah akbâr; Allah akbâr! Allah akbâr! La illaha la il Allah, Mohammed rassúl Allah!"

The jerky gait along the pavement until the narrow body disappears round a corner.

Svend never saw him again.

Lars pulls a large fistful of crumpled-up banknotes out of his pocket and selects a few. He pays the bartender who has been called over to the table with a fresh round.

"The pusher puts his hand into his pocket," Lisbeth says. But it is not like that at all, Tilly thinks.

"You're so loaded you don't even know how much you've got," Svend says.

"2,350 kroner – that's what's left," Lars says, eyebrows raised and resolutely staring in front of him. He stuffs the rest of the money in his pocket. Lars is in total control.

Tilly looks across at Louise and Michael. They are smooching as they feed coins into the jukebox. Thomas will never be coming back to her again. Not even just for a haircut or some money, a bath, a bite to eat, a kiss.

A man in a postman's uniform comes in and sees them at the table; he stops, a surprised look on his face. "Lars?" he says. "I'm on my way over to your place. Is the fort unmanned?"

"The old lady's there," Lars says. He hates talking to customers when he is not working, so he turns to face Svend again.

"Okay," the postie says, then leaves.

"The old lady?" Svend asks.

"Ulla," Lars answers, "my girlfriend."

"Girlfriend?" Svend says. He doesn't know that Lars has a new girlfriend.

"Oh yes," Lars says.

Lisbeth says with a laugh: "I didn't know you were into, you know . . . sexual contact, Lars." And then she gives him a playful slap. He laughs as if he were embarrassed. But Tilly knows he is really fond of Ulla. He has told her so himself, and she can see it in his face, too.

"No, but well . . . I was actually beginning to think myself that I had forgotten how to do it," Lars says, "but . . . we screw all the time."

"Can you manage it when you're stoned?" Svend asks.

"Well, I couldn't before, but I've cut down on my consumption and now I've hardly got time for anything else. Can't you get it up?" Lars asks. He is really cheeky, Tilly thinks. But she feels a bit sorry for Svend, too. Because he hasn't got anybody. Tilly keeps a watchful eye on him.

"I can't say I've had a chance to find out recently," Svend says.

"What? Sex and drugs and rock'n roll on the mattress?" Lars asks.

"In any shape or form," Svend answers drily.

"But can Ulla take care of the business?" Lisbeth asks.

"Yes, she always does when I'm off," Lars says.

"You take time off?" Svend sounds surprised. Lars never used to take time off when Svend lived in Aalborg. But Tilly knows why he does now.

"I've begun to," Lars says.

"But, what do you do on your . . . days off?" Svend asks. Lars turns his head away and puts both his hands up to his mouth.

" *Lars, don't,* " Tilly shouts.

"Yuk!" Lisbeth screams when Lars faces them again. His cheeks are completely sunken. His lips have disappeared. All the lower part of his face is . . . deformed. He holds the two things with teeth in them out in his hand and opens his jaws wide, displaying some fragments of metal here and there in his gums. They gleam in the light. Michael and Louise have turned round to see what is happening. He puts a hand up in front of his mouth.

"Go to the dentist," Lars says from between his toothless jaws, and laughs maliciously. He looks like an old man.

"Ugh, that's bloody disgusting, Lars," Svend says as Lars puts the false teeth back in place.

"Sorry, Lars, I hadn't noticed. I'm really sorry about that," Lisbeth says.

"That's alright," Lars says.

"Do you keep them in a glass of water on the bedside table, then?" Svend asks.

"For the time being, I do," Lars says. "But these are only temporary dentures. I've had ten titanium screws screwed into my jawbones, you see – six at the top and four at the bottom – and when the tissue around the screws has healed I'll be getting some dentures that click into place on the clips at the end of the screws. Then they're fixed tight." Lars tells them that the false teeth are acrylic and that he has to take them out every day so that he can brush the implants – the screws, that is – so he doesn't have any muck accumulating. He also has to brush the dentures, especially on the inside, where they press against his gums.

"But . . . why?" Michael asks.

"Rotted away," Lars says. Tilly thinks it is strange that they haven't noticed anything. Because previously his teeth were black and green and brown and yellow. There were even a couple missing.

"Must have cost a bloody bomb," Svend asks.

"Under the counter," Lars says.

"How did you find anyone who would do it?" Lisbeth asks.

"The brother-in-law of one of my customers."

"How much?" Svend asks.

"68 grand."

"Wow," Lisbeth says.

"Good for you," Tilly says, as Lars has really worked hard at building up his business. To be able to afford them.

"The price of neglect," he tells them. ". . . And love."

"What do you mean . . . love?" Svend asks.

"Would you have given me a tongue sushi before?"

"Any time," Svend says. "You know that."

"Have you had a smoke today?" Michael asks.

"No," Lars says. Tilly can remember that he smoked a little stiffener in the parking lot before coffee, but there was no need to remind the others of that. If they can't remember. And he really has cut down – he doesn't smoke a bong at all any more. "I have to admit that reality is beginning to make its presence felt." Lars looks frantically from side to side as if he is paranoid. He is only joking.

"But you lit a morning bowl, didn't you?" Svend asks.

"I did – and it was a big one."

"Are you afraid of us," Tilly asks, giggling.

"Well, I'm shit scared of Svend, but I don't think that's got anything to do with the THC level," Lars answers.

Svend holds his hands up as if he is surrendering in a western. "Do accept my apologies," he says.

"You shouldn't say things like that," Tilly tells Lars. He puts his arm around her shoulders.

"Don't worry, Tilly. I'm not serious. I just love the big guy."

It was actually Pusher Lars who had brought them together. He was doing his apprenticeship as a bricklayer, and a bit of dealing on the side. That was when he met Thomas, who was tearing around Aalborg, his eyes wild, looking for dope.

"What are you after, Thomas?" he asked. That was before he found out that Thomas was crazy about Stesolid, and coined the nickname.

"Well, what've you GOT?" Thomas yelled. He wanted the lot. He became Lars's best customer and bought loads of bad weed, which he sold in and around Sønderholm – it was like having a satellite outlet. He also bought loads of good weed and swallowed loads of pills. Lars had no idea who the hell he was; he came, did business, went on about anarcho-syndicalism and heteronomy, and was off

again. He was a couple of years younger than Lars, around seventeen or eighteen, the same age as Svend and Michael. They bumped into him a couple of times when they were up at Lars's doing business or just visiting. Svend began questioning Lars about what sort of a guy Thomas was.

Then one day Lars asks: "Who are you, Thomas?"

Thomas gives him a fierce look. "Hey, Lars – I've got my own people, you know," he says emphatically. "I'm not alone – there are LOTS of us. . . ." He lets the words hang menacingly in the air, so Lars asks him if he would like to bring his friends along to a little party on the Saturday. He doesn't reply to that, just nods. Instead he says:

"Lars, I'm starting at the Kathedraleskole this August."

"So you want to study, eh?" Lars says.

"For Christ's sake, man . . . use your HEAD," Thomas shouts, pointing at his skull with a furious expression.

"What?" Lars asks. Thomas is already on his way out into the hallway.

"Extending my CUSTOMER BASE for fuck's sake," he says over his shoulder before slamming the door behind him. A couple of years later Steso did in fact start at the Kathedraleskole, but he was soon thrown out.

On the Saturday they – Svend, Michael and Lars – are sitting around as if they are waiting for Christmas.

At nine o'clock in the evening there is a knock at the door. Pusher Lars opens up, and there they are: brightly coloured Tilly, good-looking Lisbeth, energetic Lars, and Thomas.

"These are my people," he says, pointing at Lars, who strides into the flat unbidden. "My man, Lars . . . ," Thomas announces. He points to the girls: ". . . and my girls, Tilly and Lisbeth."

"Okay, let's see what we've got here," Pusher Lars's namesake says – a stocky little guy who, it transpired, used to steal cars. He nods briefly to Svend and Michael, who are sitting on the sofa, and then he gives the whole flat a systematic once-over. Then he looks at Thomas and says: "Fine," and grins – and then he grins for the rest of the time he is there.

Pusher Lars is standing by his side and looks down at him.

"My name's Lars," Pusher Lars says, offering his hand.

"It's ME that's called Lars. Who are YOU?" asks his namesake, and points up at him – fearless.

"Then we'll have to call you Little Lars," Pusher Lars says. Instead of answering, Little Lars throws his jacket to the floor and rips off both his sweater and T-shirt in one go. Pusher Lars has never seen anything like it. I mean, he was strong himself in those days, but Little Lars was like gnarled wood. Then Little Lars points at Svend and says:

"I bet I can beat your man at arm wrestling." Pusher Lars thinks: OK. After all, Svend did do an apprenticeship as a landscape gardener in his time; he carried flagstones around and poured concrete for flower containers all day long.

"What are the stakes?" Pusher Lars asks. Little Lars points at Lisbeth:

"My woman," he says.

Pusher Lars doesn't need a stake – Lars doesn't ask for one. He looks to Lisbeth to see how she reacts. She seems neither angry nor offended – just giggles and smiles dotingly at Little Lars.

Meanwhile Thomas is sitting at the dining table with Tilly. He nods to Svend on the sofa, smiles, and says: "Hmmm . . . Yes . . . ." Svend smiles, too. Neither of them speaks to the other, but the atmosphere is electric.

Little Lars kneels down and starts to cut up a candle with his pocket knife, after which he melts two of the pieces so they stick to the mosaic tiled table in front of the sofa. He lights them.

"Right," he says with a shrug. "I don't actually need a candle on my side, but just so it's all according to the book." He gives Svend a friendly smile. Then they get to grips. Little Lars forces Svend's hand directly over the flame – Pusher Lars can see that Svend is trying to pull his hand down to put out the candle, but he can't. Four seconds pass.

"That's enough, now," Thomas says, and Little Lars presses Svend's hand down onto the wick so the flame goes out. Svend groans as Little Lars stands up and offers his hand. Pusher Lars can see that Svend is working out the odds until he accepts the situation and grasps Lars's hand.

Little Lars is still smiling as he dons his sweater again, sits down at the dining table and starts kissing Lisbeth after winking at Svend and Michael. It looks totally strange – she is over a head taller than him. Michael is sitting open-mouthed; he is in a state of shock. Svend is waiting to see what will happen next. So is Pusher Lars.

"It's not really all that bad," Thomas says to Little Lars, who asks:

"What?"

"Being called Little Lars," Thomas says.

"No, it's okay by me," Little Lars replies, and turns his attentions to Lisbeth's mouth again.

Now everything seems to be sorted out, and Thomas and Tilly are rattling away like machine guns to everyone in the room, everyone drinking and smoking.

The evening ends with Thomas standing up on a chair and drinking home-made apple wine whilst delivering a sort of Sermon on the Mount to Svend about THE REALITIES OF LIFE *– there are lots of them – while everyone exchanges grins. Then Thomas draws a deep breath and throws up a long stream of vomit, which lands on the floor about one and a half metres away from him. When he has finished spewing, he faints and slowly sinks to the ground. Svend leaps over the tiled table and grabs him in the nick of time. Thomas is gently lowered down onto the sofa where Michael is sitting asleep; Tilly is immediately at his side wiping his mouth and checking his breathing.*

"Wow," Svend says, his eyes agape. "Now HE'S got style." Platonic love at first sight. Little Lars just sits there grinning until it is time to carry Thomas down to a stolen car, and then they all drive home to Sønderholm.

It was always like that when you were with them in those days. Like having a walk-on role on other people's acid trips. Shortly afterwards they moved into town.

It is late at V.B. They are getting drunk. Svend is standing at the bar with Lars, buying last round. They drink a whisky and soda while waiting for the beer.

"Christ, what a hangover I'm going to have tomorrow," Svend says.

Lars winks at him: "Help is at hand," he says, and fishes a couple of pills out of his inside pocket. Gives them to him. "Epilepsy medicine, One's enough – it draws fluid to the brain."

"And . . . ?" Svend says.

"It's the lack of fluid that gives you a hangover. That's why salt's good – it binds the fluid. All the doctors use them," Lars explains, pointing at the pills in Svend's hand.

"Where do you get them?"

"Buy them off an epileptic."

"What does he do then?"

"She. She goes to her doctor and tells him she dropped them when she was having a bout of the shakes.

"You're joking.

"Yes," Lars says with a grin. "I've no idea how she explains it."

They return to Lisbeth with the beer. She had been quiet for a while – there was something she had to digest, but now she is okay again. Svend sits next to her and they talk about what they hope the future will bring. But Svend isn't being honest – he hopes that she isn't, either.

Tilly has slipped off with her friends after a tearful parting. Michael and Louise have gone home with their love.

Svend needs a place to stay for the night. Well, he could take a taxi out to his folks, of course – it is not all that far to Gug. But he hasn't been out to see them yet, and it wouldn't be much fun having to play the part of the ill-mannered 29-year-old brat who knocks on their door in the middle of the night. Is there any reason to live up to *all* their prejudices?

"Can I spend the night over at your place?" he asks Lisbeth.

"On the sofa," she says sternly.

"Hey, did I say anything else?" he asks.

"Just so we've got that straight," Lisbeth says, looking away because she is starting to blush.

Just so we've got what straight? Svend thinks. He knows that she is in . . . well, that she likes him – simple as that. And he is . . . ready.

All three of them stand up and leave the pub. Svend and Lisbeth say goodbye to Lars down by the Bull statue; they arrange to meet again. Lisbeth hobbles slowly along at Svend's side as they make their way towards the Limfjord Bridge. Aalborg has changed since Svend was here last – it is beginning to resemble one of those well-groomed North German market towns. He puts his arm around Lisbeth and kisses her on the chin. She smiles.

"The sofa," he says. "That's really cool. As long as you don't kick me out without breakfast."

"Of course I won't," she says, removing Svend's hand from her shoulder and holding his wrist. "Are you able to hold hands, Svend?"

He didn't think she knew about that. "Where did you find out about that?" he asks.

"Um . . . Pusher Lars told me."

"Well, I never," Svend says impassively; it is not a period in his life he is especially proud of.

Lisbeth takes a deep breath. "I think he was trying to show me that I wasn't the only one with . . . complications.

"Yes, well . . . I think I can with you," Svend says.

"Oh, yes? Only with me?" Lisbeth says. "Shall we give it a try?"

"Yes," Svend replies, and she takes his hand in hers. And he can feel her, but it isn't unpleasant. It is difficult. And it is good – she feels sombre and good. He knows that it is something he is imagining, that the visions and feelings he senses emanating from her hand really come from himself – his own notion of her. But that makes them no less real.

"It's good," he says. She doesn't say anything. They walk hand in hand.

"Do you ever see your little girl?" she says – Svend and Line's daughter who is called Katja, or Kat as Svend is in the habit of calling her.

"No," he replies.

"Haven't you got access?"

"Not any longer," he says, and he can feel that she is waiting for the explanation. He would like explain it to her, too, even though he doesn't like to talk about it. He raises her hand as if he is a referee and she is the victorious boxer. "The hand was the deciding factor."

"For access?" she asks, bewildered.

"Yes."

"Did you *hit* her?" She releases Svend's hand, stops, turns to face him front on.

He steps back. "No, Lisbeth, no." He is shocked, holds his hands up, feels awkward. She mustn't think that.

She looks distressed.

He goes over and sits down on the knee-high, foot-wide parapet separating the pavement from the cycle path the length of the Limfjord Bridge. His hand feels lonely. He can't walk and talk at the same time. It is important for him to be able to see Lisbeth's eyes.

She is standing an arm's distance away from him, her arms crossed, waiting.

Svend tells her what happened: the court's decision went against him. He appealed to the Civil Law Directorate. They were sitting in a higher court in Viborg – his case looked promising. Then Line broached the matter of drugs. Svend had prepared his lawyer for this. Svend told the judge that all that was finished and offered to give a blood sample – his blood had saved him in a paternity case on an earlier occasion. Lisbeth looks attentively at Svend while he talks:

"Then Line says that she doesn't want her daughter to be with a father who is so debilitated by LSD that he can't even hold another person's hand. The judge says: *Is that true?* And I say to my lawyer: *Give me your hand,* and we grasp hands. *"Shall we proceed?"* I say to the judge, and Line points to me and my lawyer and says: *"If Svend can hold his hand for one minute, I'll drop all my objections."* My lawyer says: *"Is this a courtroom or a circus?"* But the judge thinks it is immensely interesting, and I sit there thinking that now it's now or never. I take my lawyer's hand and look demonstratively at my watch, also to divert my attention.

Svend pauses to spit. It is a good story, but telling it is not particularly pleasant when it is about yourself. He is also beginning to get a cold bum sitting on the parapet, but his legs feel weak. He has to finish telling the story before he stands up. "And then thirty fucking seconds have hardly passed before my whole body's shaking and dripping with sweat," he says. "Total acid flashback, and I can feel EVERYTHING inside my lawyer, and the man's a bastard."

"Christ," Lisbeth says, positioning herself between his legs.

"Yes, 1-0 to him," Svend says.

Lisbeth takes his head between her hands, presses it in against her stomach, runs her spread fingers through his hair. It is wonderful. He puts his hands on her hips. Then she takes one of his hands in both of hers.

"We'll have to be getting home," she says, pulling him up. They start walking – hand in hand again. "But . . . how is it that you can sense him? I mean, can you just feel how he is?" Lisbeth asks.

"No," Svend says. "It's as if . . . I disappear, become all empty inside, and then he flows into me, like a fluid that . . . simply fills me up. And then I'm him, with all that that entails, while at the same time I can observe . . . as myself I can make judgements about the person I've suddenly been transformed into."

Lisbeth asks whether he will ever be able to see Kat again? Svend tells her that he has to go through an assessment procedure:

"The worst thing about it is – and Line knew that, too . . . that it's no problem at all for me to hold Kat's hand. Sometimes I held her hand for hours when she was asleep because . . . she was so unspoiled inside."

"But why did she do that – Line?" Lisbeth asks.

"I didn't love her."

Lisbeth looks at him in silence.

"When she asked me point blank, I was stupid enough to give her an honest answer," Svend says.

"Didn't you even love her that time you . . . when you lived together?"

"Oh yes . . . at least I conned myself into thinking that I did. But it was all a lie."

Lisbeth squeezes his hand. "But now your hand works?" She intones it as if it is a question.

"With you," he says. They are approaching Nørresundby. Svend swallows, breathes in some fresh air. "You're very beautiful inside," he says, ". . . and outside."

"Stop it, Svend."

"I can't promise you that." He waits for her to say something. He doesn't want to force the pace.

"Are you moving back here because of Kat?" Lisbeth asks, without looking at him.

"No," he says. Lisbeth doesn't ask the next question, and he doesn't answer it. They walk on in silence.

"I'm moving up here," he says.

"I'll believe that when I see it," she says.

"Good." He can't ask for any more right now. They arrive at her place, and she makes up a bed for him in the living room. While she is in the bathroom, he takes off his clothes, turns off the light, and crawls under the duvet on the sofa. Okay, he thinks, that is the way things are; Steso is dead now – I can't do anything about that. Lights a cigarette. It is still upsetting. Steso . . . is missing.

Lisbeth comes into the living room. Svend looks around at her things in the dim light from the hallway. He tries to appear calm. It feels strange to be here again.

"What's the matter?" she asks.

"It's just funny to see how you live nowadays. It's nice; it's just different from how it was; but I recognize some of the things."

"Just make yourself at home, Svend," she says, walking over to the sofa. She removes the cigarette from his hand and takes a drag.

"Yes," he says, trying to be relaxed, friendly: "I'm lying here, and you're lying in the next room. And tomorrow I'll go down to get some rolls and a couple of newspapers – and then we can sit here and grumble about the world. Long breakfast with loads of coffee. I'm already looking forward to it."

She gazes at him in a slightly odd way, but it is dark in the room and he is too drunk to notice. She looks as if she would like to have a child. He can help her with that. He is ready . . . He *wants* to. Calm down, he says to himself.

"You don't have anything else on tomorrow, do you?" she asks.

"No, do you?" Svend asks. He can hear in his own voice that he isn't right; that he isn't able to hide it.

"No," she answers and hands back the cigarette. "Svend," she says. He feels a lump in his throat. It has something to do with the incisive way in which she says his name. "You mustn't . . . ," she begins, but breaks off. She takes a deep breath – he wishes that she would stop there. She continues: "There wasn't anything you could have done," she says in a firm voice. The pressure is building up inside his skull, under the skin on his face – everything feels hot and is trembling.

"Hmmm . . . ," he manages to say, nodding in the murky light of the room and puffing at his cigarette. That was why he moved away; not only Steso, but . . . the whole situation. Her words don't make him feel any better.

"That's what he wanted," she says quietly. Svend feels a sharp metallic taste in his gullet.

"It's hard . . . ," he says, not daring to continue. His face is burning.

"Goodnight, Svend," Lisbeth says. He can't speak. She goes into her bedroom. He lights another cigarette. Lies there blinking – concentrating on the glow, the ceiling.

When he has finished his cigarette he goes to the bathroom for a leak and to brush his teeth. Splashes ice-cold water on his face and mouth – that helps. He steps out into the hall again and quietly closes the bathroom door behind him. Under her bedroom door he can see that her light is still on. She hasn't gone to bed yet – or at least she hasn't put out the light. He stands there looking at the strip of light and listening, but he can't hear anything. The floorboards creak as he goes into the living room and lies down on the sofa. Some time later he falls asleep.

"If you steal my things, I'll report you to the police." That is what Lisbeth said to him when he knocked on her door one Friday evening because he had nowhere to go. She hadn't seen him for several months, and he hadn't visited her flat for over two years. He hadn't been allowed to.

He said: "That eventuality won't arise. I have what I need."

He had begun to take treatment for his addiction – methadone. Rikke was due to be married six weeks later, and his father had been to see him and told him that his mother wouldn't let him go to the wedding if he wasn't in good shape. He liked Rikke.

Lisbeth had known him since they were six years old. She let him in. "I could really do with a bite to eat," he said. Lisbeth made him some asparagus soup and garlic bread, and he ate everything. He seemed to have put on a bit of weight.

"I'm getting my appetite back," he explained. They sat on the sofa watching a video of Heaven's Gate *again. They drank red wine. He smoked four bong heads without it having any effect on his behaviour – Lisbeth felt that she was getting stoned just breathing in the air. It was the first time for many years that she had seen him so clear-headed – and calm; she had to ask why.*

"Thomas, why do you do that?" He misunderstood her.

"Smoke a bong?" he asked in surprise.

"No," she said. , "Take all those . . . drugs?"

"Boredom?" he suggested, shrugging his shoulders.

"Is my life so boring?" she asked. He thought for a moment.

"Yes," he answered, looking her squarely in the eyes.

"Is that why you began – boredom?" she asked.

"Maybe," he answered, gazing into space. Then he looked at her. "Do you remember that time, Lisbeth . . . when we were kids?" She nodded.

"Me and Tilly, we . . . ," he smiled. "We lay down in the cabin of one of the old trucks behind the haulage contractor's and undressed each other and kissed using our tongues and so on. I think it was when we were in the fifth grade – we were very mature."

"Yes, she came back and told me about it every time – right after," Lisbeth said, and smiled.

"Yes, I know," Thomas said, nodding. "But then later it was sex . . . me and Tilly. And sex was fine, it was fun, we had a good time. But it wasn't . . . ENOUGH fun. And it didn't keep on being . . . EXCITING."

"It was for the excitement? . . . the drugs?" she asked.

"Yes, to begin with. Later on it was the whole scene, the activity. The level of craziness. The entertainment value . . . I've had a great time, Lisbeth. I feel like the replicant in Blade Runner*; at the end when he says: I've seen starships burn on the shoulder of Orion. Do you understand?" he asked. Lisbeth shuddered.*

"Yes, it's been hard, too, though," she said, without being able to look him in the eyes.

"Suppose so." Thomas shrugged, took a swig of red wine.

"Yugh," he said, and shook his head as he pushed the glass away from him.

"Is there anything wrong?" she asked.

"No, but . . . I get drunk on that stuff . . . ." He pointed to the bottles. ". . . Vino," he said.

When it was time to go to bed, he asked her if he could sleep beside her in her room. She laughed.

"Maybe it's not just your appetite that's come back?" she asked.

"Don't worry," he answered. "I'm not capable of that." All the same when they were lying in bed he asked her if he could look at her breasts.

"I won't touch them," he said. "I would just love to SEE them." Lisbeth got up on to her knees and unbuttoned her pyjama top.

Then he lay by her side, his body lean and pale, scars on his arms and feet, and he looked at her breasts for thirty seconds or so before his head fell back on the pillow.

"You should have children," he said. She said nothing. She asked him what his plans were.

"Are you thinking of carrying on with the methadone?" She tried to sound forthright.

"I don't know," he replied, and told her that the junkies queued up at their G.P.'s at nine o'clock every morning to get their "drink," as he called it.

"Then when I come out of the doctor's I run along the street. It's so crazy," he said, and smiled. She had no idea what he was talking about.

"Why do you do that, Thomas?" she asked. ". . . Run?"

"Oh that . . . ," he said – he suddenly became aware of her limited mental powers. "To disperse it through the body," he explained. "We all run to get it to . . . work." He laughed. She saw it all before her and grinned.

"I know, I know," he said. "Foolish – emaciated junkies running along the pavement." Then he lit a cigarette and stared into space. Lisbeth lay there watching him, thinking about all the things he could have been. When they were children he

constructed these massive things in the garden with water channels lined with plastic and mountains and bridges and roads and futuristic towns out of cardboard and coloured cellophane with Christmas tree lights for the street lighting. Lisbeth's mother has pictures of Tilly, Little Lars, Lisbeth and Thomas. "You can see the madness in his eyes – even then;" *that is what her mother says every time Lisbeth takes out the pictures.*

"Lisbeth," Thomas suddenly said, in a very insistent voice. "Where's Svend?"

"I don't know," she replied, trying not to sound despondent.

"Svend has abandoned me." His voice was quite calm.

"Yes," she said. That was right: Svend had abandoned him.

"I miss Svend," he said.

"I do, too," she said.

"Hmmm . . . . Yes . . . . ," Thomas said. Four weeks later he was dead.